LOST WITH YOU

LOST *with* YOU

Part one of the *Lost and Found* series

ANNA LENORE

The characters and events portrayed in this book are fictitious. Any similarity to real persons, living or dead, is coincidental and not intended by the author.

ISBN: 9798472206211
Imprint: Independently published

Cover design by Anna Lenore
Cover photography by Shifaaz Shamoon

www.annalenore.com

For my husband, who never stopped believing in me.

ONE

I wasn't ready to die.

Not yet.

Death was for people who'd lived full, abundant lives—not for people like me. I'd hardly begun to explore the countless dreams I had for myself. Yet, here I was, trapped inside an enslaving aircraft cabin, falling from the sky, 30,000 feet above the salty Pacific.

I gripped my armrests like a vice, turning my knuckles white and taut with fear. The whirring of the failing engines grew higher and higher in pitch until, without warning, they both gurgled their last valiant effort.

And then…silence. Not perfect silence, we were still traveling at high speeds through the air, but there was a strange quiet when the engines finally ceased to function.

I leaned forward, bracing my head and arms on the seat in front of me, staring wide-eyed at the murky gray carpet at my feet. A bag slid between them, headed for the front of the plane.

And then we were nosediving.

My throat burned with an urge to scream, but I clamped my mouth shut and took a long, trembling breath. A single tear escaped down my cheek. Would it hurt? Would I know I was dying? Or worse, would I be fatally injured and then have to float around the ocean in a fiery wreckage until I finally *did* die?

Was a water crash better or worse than a land crash? Did it even matter?

"Brace for impact!" The pilot was yelling.

My ears strained against the pressure, popping as we descended quickly. I squeezed my eyes shut as my heart thrummed loudly in my chest. I wanted to yell out to someone, *anyone* who could make this all go away. But I couldn't utter a sound.

The whirring continued—a chilling warning of our impending fate—and just when I questioned how much further we had to go, everything went black.

24 Hours Earlier

The tray of turkey sandwiches almost slipped from my hands as I stumbled across the threshold of the bustling Stage 16. It was an exceptionally warm October day in Southern California, and my "Dale's Catering" embroidered blouse was sticking irritatingly to my skin as I shuffled past crew members running in all directions on the studio lot.

Dale was my father, and *Dale's Catering* was his *baby;* his moderately-performing dream business that, according to him, 'just needed to get its foot in the door,' and then it would 'take off.' He'd been trying to get his foot in for over twenty years now. He'd put me behind the stove when I was just fifteen, claiming I could make the 'best dang grilled cheese this side of the San Andreas fault.' And at that age, I'd jumped at the opportunity to make a little extra cash, learning the ropes and my way around the kitchen with ease until I could find my path to bigger and better things. Now, a twenty-eight-year-old head chef—well, the *only* chef—at my father's struggling business, I still put my apron on every single morning, and I still stood in front of the same sweltering stove, albeit a slightly upgraded version.

Dale's Catering managed to keep its head above water, but the competition was fierce in Burbank. There was always a need for catering services among the film industry, but our small-scale operation was usually left serving dental offices and law firms for their employee anniversary luncheons, or making cartoon-shaped sugar cookies for a local birthday party. We were respected among those who knew us, but we were a gamble to those who typically hired the high-volume, corporate-owned staples of the area.

Today, however, was an exception to the rule. At eight in the morning, we'd received a frantic call from a representative for a production at the nearby Universal Studios lot whose usual caterer had bailed on them at the last minute, and they were scrambling to find a replacement. Even though we already had a lunch client lined up for the day, we'd accepted their request and asked what they'd like us to deliver. They'd replied in a hurried panic that *anything* was fine, as long as their cast and crew were fed.

My father had dashed to the freezers and the storeroom, trying to figure out what we had enough of to feed thirty-eight hungry Universal employees and actors, *and* make a good first impression.

"What about those roasted turkey sandwiches you make, Cora?" he'd called to me from beside the packages of fresh meat. "Those ones with the herbed cranberry goat cheese and baby spinach? They're easy to eat on the go, and everyone raves about them."

Thinking on my toes, I'd agreed and suggested a side of heirloom tomato salad and baked sweet-potato chips I'd made too much of last night.

Our team of five had sprung into action, pulling together the recipes, plating them, and packing them up to be delivered. But when eleven o'clock had rolled around and my father had already sent out two of his other employees to deliver our smaller client's order, he'd turned to me with a hopeful glint in his eye.

"Cora, we're understaffed today. You and Tess are gonna have to make this delivery. I need to stay here at the kitchen for a meeting with a potential client from Glendale."

I hadn't run a delivery in years, and certainly never to a place like Universal. I'd pleaded with him once, asking if I could conduct the meeting instead. But he'd insisted I wasn't trained for that responsibility yet, and now, here I was scrambling through unfamiliar territory to serve my mediocre turkey sandwiches to a crowd who'd hired us as a last-ditch option.

Tess, my best friend since the sixth grade, was my less begrudging partner in the adventure. She was also my roommate, and she'd become my finest helper in the kitchen since she'd joined the team two years ago. It was her second job because it didn't pay as well as my head chef title did, but when she was there, she was *on it.*

"Cora, where do you want the salad?" she asked as she weaved between Universal employees, carrying two giant bowls toward the catering table.

"Uh, how about there, next to the napkins?" I set my plate of sandwiches down and tore my eyes away from the impossibly high ceilings and the intricately designed sets that were built around us. Even though I'd lived in Burbank my entire life, I'd never even been on a studio set. It was a world I didn't dare venture into.

"Do you know what they're filming?" Tess whispered to me, tucking a strand of her curly, fiery-red hair behind her ear.

"I have no idea. *You* should know, though." I replied, placing plastic tongs into the salad bowls.

Tess followed Hollywood with a magnifying glass, but I kept my distance as best I could while practically living on top of it. The fake personalities and obsession with fame didn't sit well with me. If it were up to me, I'd have moved to Colorado, away from the hustle and bustle, and opened my own quaint, small-town restaurant by now.

Well, it *was* up to me. I was twenty-eight, after all.

But I couldn't bear to disappoint my father; not when his venture meant so much to him. I was his only child, and his aspiration was to pass the family business to me. Plus, every time I'd brought up the idea of opening my own restaurant, he'd shut down my dream quickly with a list of reasons why most brand-new restaurateurs failed miserably.

I glanced at Tess. With her crystal-clear blue eyes, her perfect complexion, and that unique ginger appeal, she looked like she could be right at home with the actors that probably frequented these stages. I, on the other hand, had a head of bleach-blonde kinky waves that went up in frizz every time I stepped outside. My mother liked to tell me my hair was 'kissed by the sun,' but to me, it just looked like some sort of messy blonde mop. My complexion was as fair as my hair, and the angles of my face were plain and lacked much character, but my eyes were actually something I took pride in. They were a rare blue-green, the color I imagined the calm waves on an exotic beach would be. They were vivid and distinct; the one feature that made me feel unique.

I wiped my hands on my apron, studying the table alongside Tess. "I need to unwrap the sandwiches and talk to the client about payment. Can you grab the rest from the van and bring it in?"

She winked and gave me a salute. "Yes, ma'am."

I rolled my eyes at her grinning retreat, and then I went back to my work, pulling the cellophane from the plate of sandwiches and stacking them neatly on their tray. As I set the wrapping to the side and turned to figure out who was supposed to pay, my hand came down hard on the set of tongs that were perched on the salad bowl, sending them flying high into the air and over my shoulder, spewing lettuce and dressing as they went.

"Shoot," I hissed, spinning around to search for them on the floor. But as soon as I turned, I slammed into the broad chest of someone who had been standing too close behind me. I stumbled backward as the stranger clasped his large, steady hands onto my shoulders.

I regained my bearings and straightened my apron, saved

from falling flat on my face. The man bent down to pick up the tongs, which were still covered in shreds of lettuce, and then held them out to me with a smirk.

"I do fancy a tossed salad occasionally, but I think you've outdone yourself here." He winked.

Barely catching sight of his face, I quickly took the tongs from him and placed them to the side on the table. "I'm so sorry, I'll get a fresh pair for..." I finally took a moment to look at him. "...the salad." The last few words fell slowly from my mouth as I realized who the stranger was.

Standing in front of me, grinning from ear to ear, was People Magazine's heartthrob of the year, *'Modern Cinema's Number One Leading Man, on the Screen, and on the Dance Floor,'* Liam Montgomery.

Now, while Hollywood may have nauseated me, I had one guilty pleasure I couldn't shake. I'd ogled Liam from my sofa for at least the last six months, replaying his latest film, *Until Dawn,* enough times to thoroughly embarrass myself. His character, an experienced dancer, slowly fell in love with his beautiful but reluctant partner as they competed in modern-day Paris. I'd re-watched it until Tess had threatened to take the DVD away from me, claiming she'd lose her mind if she had to listen to the soundtrack one more time.

Liam had started his career as a professional dancer before slowly inching his way onto the big screen. And now, he was known more for his acting chops than his skilled feet. He was tall and handsome, with wild, dark curls, and a smile bright enough to touch the corners of his eyes.

Plus, he was British, *of course.*

He was the one exception to my Hollywood rule. When it

came to Liam, all bets were off, and while I knew that underneath his charming exterior, he was probably like all the rest of the greedy, fame-seeking celebrities out there, I allowed myself to slip into the fantasy of being swept off my feet by him, just like his leading ladies had been.

And now, he was staring right at me.

"That's just fine, darlin'." He stepped around me and picked up a sandwich. "I'm just glad lunch is finally here. I'm starving."

I gaped at him in awe. He was gorgeous. His shoulders were broad and toned, and he was so much taller in person, towering over me by quite a few inches.

With his back turned, he took a bite of his sandwich, but then stopped mid-chew and rotated to face me again. "Did you make these?" he asked through a full mouth.

I nodded with a gulp, trying not to stare directly into his perfect hazel eyes.

He continued to chew as he studied the sandwich in his hand. "These are fantastic. Is it your recipe?" He looked at me again.

I nodded once more. My cheeks grew warmer, and my mouth had gone so dry I wasn't sure I could form a response if I tried.

"Liam!" someone called from set. "We're going to need to kick it into high-gear to wrap this scene today."

He held the last bite between his fingers and raised it to his lips, grinning down at me. "Thanks for this. Cheers." And then he turned and disappeared into the crowd, just as fast as he'd come.

"You're welcome," I squeaked once he was out of earshot.

Even when he'd vanished from view, I continued to stare

at the last place I'd seen him, trying to memorize each and every line of his face and the way his eyes had smiled when he'd looked at me.

"Ok, that's everything. What else can I do?" Tess said from behind me just seconds later. "...Cora?"

I blinked back to reality, turning slowly to her with wide eyes. "I just met Liam Montgomery..."

She reeled back in shock, scanning the room quickly. "Wait, really?"

For the last six months, I'd fantasized about what I'd say to him if we'd ever meet, planning to wow him with a clever compliment, yet here I was, gazing blankly at the pile of sandwiches, having spoken almost zero words. "He ate my turkey sandwich... He said he liked it."

Tess smirked and raised an eyebrow in my direction. "Oh dear, he liked your sandwich? Well, that sounds like love at first *bite*."

I turned back to the table, nudging her out of my way. "I didn't even know he was in L.A."

"He's probably here a lot." She paused. "You know, visiting his *girlfriend*. She lives here, doesn't she?"

Tossing the dirtied plastic tongs into the trash, I carefully laid a new pair into the salad bowl. "Yeah, I think so."

Liam's girlfriend of almost a year, Kate Taylor, was a tall, gorgeous brunette, who like him, was also a dancer. She practiced competitively on a few reality shows, and also occasionally dipped her toes into modeling opportunities. They were the picture-perfect couple, and Hollywood ate them up quicker than the media could pump out photos and stories about them.

They probably loved it.

Tess straightened the napkin-wrapped utensils and smiled at me. "Well, I know you probably want to stick around on set for the rest of the day to catch another glimpse of your beloved, but your dad said we can head home as soon as we drop off the van, and I know we both still have a lot of packing to do before tomorrow."

I nodded and scanned the room one more time. Liam was still out of sight, probably preparing for his next scene, and I had no business hanging around to spy on him, so I followed Tess to collect our payment and head back to Burbank.

Tomorrow, we would be making the long trek to visit Tess's aunt in New Zealand. The woman who acted like she was maybe twenty years her own junior was less of a parental figure to Tess and more of a friend. She had the same gene for 'spunk' that her niece was granted, and a fashion sense much better than mine. Plus, she was *rich*. Like, *so* rich that she not only flew Tess across the Pacific to visit her at least once a year, but she'd also paid for *my* airfare, *twice.*

In exchange for your lovely company. That's what she told me the first time I visited two years ago, and she'd used the same phrase again this year when we'd booked our tickets.

I'd been counting down the days, packing, planning, and scheduling my time off work. But now, knowing that Liam was in town, I briefly questioned if staying in the city and camping out at the Universal Studios lot entrance for a zero-to-none chance to see him again was a better option.

To embark on a free trip to a foreign country, or to stick around and stalk a celebrity who loved my turkey sandwiches?

The irrational side of me was already mentally preparing a new sandwich recipe that would surely knock him off his feet next time. But the rational side of me knew there wouldn't be a next time. Tomorrow, I'd head to New Zealand with Tess, and I'd never see Liam again. And that was just going to have to be ok.

TWO

Los Angeles was a mess on Saturday morning as we took a taxi through stop-and-go traffic to the airport. Every time I ventured out of my little local nook in Burbank, I was reminded why the city was not my scene.

Once we were dropped off and had made it inside, everyone moved quickly—a sharp contrast to the traffic outdoors. Donned in flip-flop sandals, tank tops, and board shorts, the couples and families with their strollers and rogue rolling bags pushed past each other urgently. But I breathed a sigh of relief, knowing I'd be spending a week in a much more tranquil, less populated atmosphere. I needed a break from the frenzied pace of L.A. and the seemingly endless demands from my father and his business. I was ready to chase my dream. Not his. One day I'd work up the guts to move away to the mountains and start over on my own terms.

Shuffling through the hordes of people, we finally reached

our gate to see bright red letters reading "AUCKLAND" on the digital display above the desk. When we found two empty seats and sat down together, I pulled out my phone and flipped to the Instagram app. My feed was filled mainly with updates from my personal friends and a few photos of Liam peppered throughout from the fan accounts I followed. There was one that had been posted just a few hours ago. A paparazzi had snatched a photo of him holding hands with Kate. They strolled down Sunset Boulevard. She smiled at the camera, but he looked down at his feet. I squinted and leaned in, trying to read his expression. Closed off, distant. It was a far cry from his happy disposition yesterday.

The gate attendant had finished calling first class just before we sat down. Tess's aunt was rich, but not rich enough to afford us that luxury. We'd fly comfortably enough in business class.

"NOW BOARDING, GROUP 3 AT GATE D5." The intercom sounded loudly into our section of the airport.

We stood up and I pulled up my digital boarding pass. The rest of our group three companions began to line up and we followed the slow queue to the jet bridge. Tess was ahead of me, and when she scanned her phone over the reader, she was met by a long beep. The gate attendant frowned and turned to her computer.

"Tess Adams?" she confirmed.

Tess nodded, pulling back her phone quickly like she'd gotten in trouble.

The attendant squinted at her screen. "We have a full flight today. It looks like we've had to move you to an alternate flight."

Tess frowned. "But, I bought this ticket months ago…"

The attendant plastered a fake smile on her face. "I'm sorry

Ms. Adams, but we've had to make some adjustments to accommodate our guests. We'll be happy to seat you on the next flight in first class, at no extra charge. That flight departs in two hours."

Tess glanced at me and then back at the attendant. "But, I'm flying with my friend. I'd prefer we weren't separated."

I stepped forward and flashed my boarding pass at the woman. "Can you move me to the next flight too, then? My name is Cora Parker."

She smiled again and shook her head. "I'm sorry, that flight is full too. I apologize for the inconvenience, but you'll both arrive in Auckland within a few hours of each other. Ms. Parker, I'll take your pass now and I'll direct Ms. Adams to her new gate."

Tess took a deep breath and rolled her eyes as she looked at me and stepped back. "Well, I guess I'll see you in like fifteen hours, then."

I frowned and slumped my shoulders. "Ugh, I'm sorry."

"Ladies, we have a line waiting behind you." The attendant reminded us.

I shot her a glare before I nodded at Tess. "It'll be ok though. We'll both probably sleep most of the trip anyway."

I grasped her hand and squeezed it. She exhaled a frustrated huff of air before squeezing back and letting go. "Have a safe flight."

I smiled. "You too. I'll find your gate when I land."

I reluctantly turned away and pulled my suitcase down the jet bridge. A flight attendant greeted me happily as I stepped inside, and I turned right to pass through the first-class cabin, briefly envying the oversized, cushioned seats until I remembered how much extra they'd paid for those while I was getting my trip for free. At least Tess would get to enjoy the upgrade on her flight.

Most everyone in first class were businessmen in black and grey suits and elderly couples who had the funds for such extravagance. They were already situated with their fancy glasses of wine and complimentary lap blankets. I smiled lightly as I passed them, trying not to linger too long. But three rows back, my eyes caught a glimpse of someone who didn't fit the rest of the crowd. He was younger, maybe in his thirties, broad-shouldered, dressed in jeans and a black leather jacket, and he was sitting, hunched over in his seat, deeply engrossed in his phone. I couldn't see his face, but his deep brown curls looked just like Liam's.

Wow, get a grip, Cora.

I blinked and stared closer at the top of his head, but the person behind me crowded my space and pushed me further down the aisle. I craned my neck, trying to get another look, but the mystery man kept his head down and I wasn't able to catch a glimpse of his face.

When I found my seat, I looked up the aisle, trying to see back into first class, but the flight attendant blocked my view and shut the curtains.

Dang it.

I sat back and stared blankly at the ads that looped on the screen in front of my face. I did remember hearing the crew member on set yesterday mention that Liam was wrapping his scene. I supposed it was possible he could be flying out today, but to *New Zealand?* The odds of that seemed a bit of a stretch. But I smirked to myself. If Tess couldn't be here on this flight, it would be nice to know that Liam was at least tagging along.

I laughed out loud at my absurd train of thought just as an elderly couple stopped at my aisle and asked to slide past me into their seats.

"Yes, sorry," I cleared my throat, standing up and letting them through.

"What a beautiful smiling face you have, dear." The woman beamed at me as she sat down.

I blushed as I took my seat again. "Thank you."

"Are you traveling alone?" she asked.

"I'll be meeting a friend in Auckland, actually," I returned.

"Oh, that is lovely. You'll have a wonderful time. We've lived in New Zealand for almost twenty years now." She gestured to her husband. "It's a beautiful country."

I nodded with a smile. "It sure is. This will be my second visit."

"That's lovely, dear." She politely let me be then, and I buckled myself in, preparing for the long flight.

I took out my book and turned to my earmarked page, disappearing from the world around me as I knew so well how to do. Soon we taxied to the runway and began to pick up speed before lifting smoothly from the ground and into the air. I looked past my fellow row-mates to watch the softly lit coast of California, dotted with sparkling lights, disappear from view as the pilot banked toward the ocean. The entire flight would travel above the vast, desolate waters of the Pacific, so I wasn't too heartbroken that I didn't have a window seat.

I read for almost an hour, pausing to peek up the aisle at first-class every time the curtain opened for the flight attendant to pass through, but I was never able to catch a glimpse of the

Liam Montgomery doppelganger. When I'd given up on my ridiculous fantasy, I sighed and settled back into my reading while sipping a soda from the snack cart. In my novel, the heroine was being swept off her feet by a man who fell for her despite his betrothal to another woman. It was a heartbreaking tale of yearning, of sacrifice, and of pure love. Those were my favorite kinds of stories; the ones that reached the furthest depths of the heart.

But as engrossed as I was, I eventually felt my eyelids grow heavy, so I tucked the book into the pocket in front of me and reclined my seat. I tried to drown out the noises of the plane as I settled against the headrest and closed my eyes, thinking about the man in first-class with the deep brown curls.

***

Without warning, I was jerked awake by a sudden bout of violent turbulence. I sat straight up in my seat, wide-eyed and searching the flight attendant for an explanation. She was nowhere in sight, so I held onto my armrests and looked out the window. The sun was now high in the sky, which meant I must have been asleep for hours. I rubbed my eyes and tried to dissolve my grogginess as the turbulence reduced just slightly. I glanced around at my fellow passengers, hoping I was alone in my shock, but they held expressions that mirrored mine. I tried to sit back calmly into my seat, but the vibration was still more noticeable than it should be. I glanced out the window again, furrowing my brow.

The 'fasten seat belts' light blinked on and a voice came over the intercom. "Ladies and gentlemen, the seatbelt light is now on. Please remain seated."

A flight attendant came whooshing past me from the back of the plane. Her speed was unsettling. My eyes darted from face-to-face. Everyone was watching her.

The captain spoke again. "Ladies and gentlemen, my apologies, but we've appeared to have encountered a minor engine issue and will need to change our flight path to land at the nearest airport, Faa'a International Airport in Tahiti."

A whispering of voices surrounded me. They were mostly murmurs and groans of disappointment.

The intercom clicked on a third time. "In theory, with the current engine status, we could make it to our final destination of Auckland, but for best safety practices, we'll be stopping in Tahiti to change planes." The captain continued. "Please remain seated, and should we experience any change in pressure in the cabin, the oxygen masks will drop from the compartments above you. Please refer to your in-flight manual for instructions on correct use. Again, my apologies for this delay."

I sighed and rubbed my forehead. I knew safety was the top priority, but I hated that this change of plans would cut into my vacation time. Tess would definitely beat me to Auckland now. I hoped she wouldn't fret when she found out I still hadn't arrived.

The abnormal vibration continued, and everyone was craning their necks to look out the left side of the plane. I followed their gazes, noticing that the windows were a shade of grey instead of a bright blue like they should have been. It didn't make any sense until someone gasped.

"The engine's on fire!"

My heart stopped. The commotion began immediately.

Everyone was shifting in their seats, trying to get a better view.

The captain came back on the intercom again and cleared his throat. "Ahem, ladies and gentlemen. As some of you may have noticed, our left engine has encountered a malfunction. Again, we plan to make a safe emergency landing shortly. However, in the unlikely case that we need to make a water landing, the cushions on your seats can be used as flotation devices, and lifeboats will inflate at the emergency exits. Please familiarize yourselves with the emergency procedures in your pamphlet. Please continue to stay seated. Thank you."

The chatter inside the plane continued to grow as everyone fingered through their pamphlets and gawked at the windows in fear.

I stared, unblinking down the aisle toward the front of the plane. Was this a precaution, or an emergency? The answers weren't clear, but airlines always seemed to be too cautious about these things. I knew planes could fly with one engine. Landing at the nearest airport made sense, even if the plane was designed to operate as-is.

I turned to my row-mates; the elderly couple who'd been so friendly when we'd first sat down. They were looking out the window too, and when I gazed down at the armrest between them, their hands were clasped together tightly.

I looked down at my own hands, knuckles white as I clenched them firmly into fists. I had no one to hold onto, and I suddenly felt very alone. I'd grown accustomed to the feeling lately, but it was largely inflated in this moment.

Seconds later, I was pulled from my thoughts as a large flash of light burst outside the right side of the plane this time, and the cabin shook again, more violently than the last.

I was hurtled forward into the seat in front of me, just barely catching myself with my hands as countless screams erupted around me. The plane rattled and rocked, sending under-seat bags scooting across the floor and triggering all sorts of alarms and buzzers inside the cabin. The compartments above our heads burst open and yellow oxygen masks tumbled out to dangle in front of us.

Everyone was scrambling. My heart was skipping beats and thrumming erratically as I grabbed my mask and placed it over my nose and mouth, pulling the elastic around my head. I turned to the couple next to me as they fumbled with their masks in confusion. As I reached toward them to assist, I caught sight of the window beyond them. The right engine was now engulfed in bright orange flames and black smoke, spiraling past our view and into the atmosphere.

"Oh my God…" I breathed, fastening the woman's mask across her face.

Both engines had exploded into flames in mere minutes. There was no third engine. We were out of options. The chaos grew around me as a painful knot formed in the back of my throat.

The flight attendant appeared in the aisle again and began helping passengers apply their masks. She looked absolutely *terrified.* Her hands shook as she held onto the seats, trying to steady herself. I'd always been told, when feeling strange bumps or sounds on an airplane, to look at a flight attendant, and if they remained calm, then everything was fine.

This time, everything was not fine.

The pilot spoke through the intercom again, a new strain in his voice. "Attention passengers and crew. We will be making an emergency water landing. Flight attendants take your seats." There was a garbled mumbling between the pilot and his co-pilot before he spoke again. "Please prepare for a significant amount of turbulence."

What? What do we do? A water landing? In the middle of the ocean? The fear-induced nausea hit me like a tidal wave. People were beginning to cry. I looked from wide-eyed expression to wide-eyed expression. No one was prepared, but we were all strapped into our seats, equally helpless.

The intercom clicked on again. This time it was a different voice. The copilot, probably. He began to describe the brace position and the locations of the lifeboats and our life jackets. We all placed our hands on our heads and leaned forward into the back of the seat in front of us.

The buzzers continued to sound, but the typical rumbling of the engines was erratic and strained. We were now soaring through the air with nothing but the wings to guide us.

I shook my head and squeezed my eyes shut. What if this water landing wasn't so much a landing, but more of a crash? I thought of Tess, arriving in New Zealand, only to find out I would never get to join her. I thought of my parents, and how they would react to the news. A tear escaped my eye and dropped down onto the floor beneath me, heavy and wet.

My forehead began to sweat, and I was starting to feel faint. If I had any chance of surviving this, I'd have to stay conscious. I tried to breathe the flow of oxygen more steadily, but I struggled to slow my frenzied breaths.

The intercom clicked on one last time. "Brace for impact!"

THREE

I was on fire.

At least, that's what it felt like. There was intense, burning heat all around me, scorching my skin without relent. I had collapsed forward, head wedged against the seat in front of me. The rough fabric of my jeans pressed against my right cheek. The jeans felt wet. My forehead felt wet. My body felt numb. My ears were ringing. I could hear *nothing*. I tasted salt and iron. My mouth was dry. I felt like I was floating. Up and down. Up and down.

A small pressure touched the side of my neck, just under my jaw. It was warm, but not burning. It retreated.

I tried to lift my head, but my muscles didn't respond. I opened my eyes slowly. There was only blur. Black and blue, orange and yellow. It was calm...yet chaotic.

The orange and yellow were shadowed by a moving figure. I couldn't make it out. I tried to reach toward it, but my arm felt like it was strapped down.

Then there was the same warm touch on my back and under my legs, lifting me from my seat. I tried to speak, tried to get words to form on my lips, but before I had a chance, I drifted from reality again, sinking back into the dark blue depths of my consciousness.

***

Breeze.

I felt a breeze.

The inside of my eyelids glowed red.

Daylight.

I tried to move my fingers and toes.

Still numb.

I slowly opened my eyes.

Bright blue. The sky.

I experienced the same floating sensation again. But I wasn't in my seat anymore. I was in a boat. It was soft and forgiving. A lifeboat.

I tried to turn my head. It obliged, but it sent a searing pain through my neck. I saw the same blurry dark figure next to me, but the agony was too much. Bright white pain seared through me, and the blackness returned.

***

My eyelids were red again. But this time, they flickered in

time with the breeze.

I breathed deeply. A dull ache radiated through my chest.

I opened my eyes to see the sun, shimmering and sparkling behind what looked like palm fronds twisting and turning over my head. My vision had cleared, and I could make out the edges of each leaf—fresh, vibrant, and green.

I touched my fingers to the ground beneath me. They found sand—smooth, soft, and cool. There were birds calling in the distance. I braced my hands in the sand and tried to sit up. But as soon as I did, a tremendous pounding in my head made itself known. I closed my eyes again and pressed my palm to my forehead with a groan.

"Whoa, hang on. Don't sit up just yet," a deep voice spoke from nearby.

I felt the ground beneath me echo slightly, and then sensed the increased proximity of someone moving closer. With my eyes still squeezed shut, I lowered my head back to the earth.

"That's right. Just don't move too much yet," the voice spoke again. It was unfamiliar, yet it sparked a memory. The accent wasn't American. But I couldn't place it in my half-conscious state.

I tentatively squinted into the daylight again. Someone was sitting next to me, staring down at my face.

It was a man. I could tell that much. His expression held a strange mix of worry and relief as he assessed me. I tried to understand why, but my comprehension was cloudy and disjointed.

"How are you feeling?" the man asked.

I peered at him, studying his features. Dark hair and eyes the color of honey. They were handsome eyes, but he had a deep gash on the side of his face that had just barely missed one of them.

"My head hurts," I replied. My mouth was drier than I had anticipated, and my words came out scratchy and coarse.

"Yes, you hit it quite hard." His voice was kind. I liked it.

I furrowed my brow and winced again. *Where was I?* I tried to remember the last place I'd been, but I came up blank. The sand, the leaves, the sun—they all confused me. Nothing made sense, so I closed my eyes tightly, trying to clear away the mirage, but when I opened them again, they landed on a dark brown curl dangling across the man's forehead. The startling recognition overcame me, and I squinted at him as the pieces began to fall into place.

Before I had a chance to consider them, the words flew out of my mouth. "You're Liam Montgomery."

He paused, blinking down at me, and then he held out a bottle of water. "Yes, I am. Here, you should drink something."

"But…" I blinked up at him, peering at his face and trying to figure out why I was hallucinating so strongly. My heart leapt into my throat as shock was quickly added to my long list of symptoms. "But, you're…Liam Montgomery."

He continued to push the bottle toward me. "Well at least one of us is acquainted. Here, let me help you take a drink. You're dehydrated."

I stared at him with wide eyes now. He placed his hand under my head and lifted it gently while he held the bottle of water to my lips. I kept my gaze on him as I took a sip. The liquid ran into my mouth, coating my tongue and cheeks, and immediately, I realized how thirsty I was. My eyes began to drift shut as I took larger gulps until the bottle had run dry.

When he pulled it away, I tried to sit up again, ignoring the searing pain in my leg.

"Hang on, let me help you." He grasped my arm and guided me up, assisting me to scoot back and lean against the trunk of the palm tree that shaded us.

I still stared at him, unbelieving. Had I died? Was this some disjointed version of Heaven? His curly hair was wild and unkempt, dark stubble framed his jawline, and his warm eyes looked cautiously into mine.

"What's your name?" he asked.

My head continued to pulse with pain, and I winced again. *Definitely not Heaven.*

I tore my eyes from his and looked around to take in our surroundings. We were on a beach dotted with tall palm trees, and the turquoise blue ocean waves lapped at the shore a few dozen yards away. Why was I on a beach with Liam Montgomery? If this was a dream, it was wildly realistic.

"I'm Cora," I replied quietly, looking at him again.

"It's a pleasure to meet you, Cora." Liam extended his hand. His voice was laced with a thick British accent that I finally recognized.

When I tentatively took his large hand, it encapsulated mine easily with its warmth. "Why are you…? What…happened? Where am I?"

Liam sat back and rested his elbow on his knee. "Well…" He sighed. "Do you remember the plane going down?"

The plane? Oh, right, *the plane*… It suddenly dawned on me. I *had* seen him in first class. My extravagant imagination had been accurate after all.

"You were on the plane?" I asked breathlessly.

"Yes, do you remember what happened?" He looked concerned, probably because I was focused so intently on him rather than the fact that we were obviously in peril.

"Where is everyone?" I looked around the empty beach, trying to draw my attention away from him.

Liam took a deep breath and furrowed his brow. "Were you traveling with anyone, or were you alone?"

Cautiously, I replied, "Alone."

His face turned serious. "I think we were the only survivors."

My breathing halted and I brought my hand to my mouth. "Are you sure?"

He stared out at the water, void of expression. "I checked everyone I could reach. You were the only one with a pulse. I wasn't even sure you'd ever wake up."

I gulped. *No one?* I could still see the faces of my fellow passengers as our plane had fallen from the sky. I'd seen the horror and fear there. In the last moments, I don't think any of us thought we'd survive.

And as it turned out, most of us did not.

I looked down at my lap and gulped. Liam scooted toward me. "It was really bad. You probably have a concussion. I honestly don't know how either of us survived."

I looked at him closely again, studying every detail of his face. It *really was* Liam Montgomery. He'd survived too. Just the two of us. He was so familiar, yet so new as he sat next to me. Those eyes I'd met just yesterday on set were looking into mine again.

I felt a blush try to touch my cheeks. Shyness mingled with my terror and grief. I looked down at my hands again, wondering if he remembered me. "How…?"

"Pure luck, I think," he replied.

I turned my gaze to the waves. "How did we get here?"

"The lifeboat." He pointed toward a yellow inflatable raft a few yards away.

"I don't think I remember the boat."

"You were unconscious when I put you in it."

Oh.

My mind flashed back to my half-unconscious memories. I remembered being lifted from my seat in the plane. That meant he had carried me himself to the lifeboat.

He'd saved me.

"…Thank you," I whispered, feeling like the wind had been knocked out of me again.

"Thank *you* for surviving and not leaving me out here all alone." He gestured to the desolate landscape around us. "I'm not sure what's to be done, but I'd lose my mind without you."

Without me? In what world did Liam need me?

This world, apparently.

"We were on the boat for a few hours before the current dragged us here," he continued.

"How long ago was that?" I asked.

"You've been out for almost twenty-four hours. It's midday Sunday." He looked at the sun directly overhead. "And I have no idea where we are…somewhere in the South Pacific…"

I peered across the trees and out at the horizon. "Surely there must be someone living here."

Liam shook his head. "This island…well, I actually think it's an atoll…is less than two kilometers across. I've been around it twice already. We're alone." He sat back on his hands. "But they'll find us soon. I'm sure they'll search all the islands in the area."

"An *atoll?* What's that?" I squinted at him.

"It's an island in the shape of a ring, with shallow water at the center. It forms when a volcano sinks below the surface of the ocean."

"We're on a volcano?"

He smirked just slightly. "Not an active one."

I shook my head, trying to understand. So, I was on a deserted volcano-turned-island with Liam Montgomery? What was *happening?* It felt like something out of a cheesy fan fiction.

"What about our cell phones?" I asked.

He shook his head. "No service on either of them. I did use some palm branches to write an S.O.S. on the beach, though." He pointed toward the sand. "In case someone flies over."

I followed his gesture to the impressively large letters across the ground. "Wow, so you've done all this, and I've just been laying here out cold?"

"You were hurt pretty badly. Like I said, I wasn't sure you'd wake up at all."

I looked at the gash on his face. "Are you ok?"

He touched it gently and winced. "Yeah, it's fine."

I focused on the water again. It met the sky in a straight line across the expansive distance. There was an endless horizon as far as I could see. "How long…do you think…" I gulped. "Before…they find us?"

Liam followed my gaze. "Hours, hopefully. Days, maybe."

Days. Stranded alone. Did people last days on deserted islands? Surely not people like me. I scanned the skies and then shifted my attention to the vegetation around us. "What will we eat?"

Liam looked at the tree above me. "I'm going to try and get us some coconuts."

I craned my neck, feeling the ache in my head again as I caught sight of a small bunch of green coconuts at the base of the tree's leaves. They were almost twenty feet off the ground.

"But how will you get to them?" I asked.

He shrugged, squinting into the sunlight. "I'll try to climb. I saw some shorter trees further inland."

I let my eyes travel down his torso. He was impressively fit. As dancing was half his career, I was sure he had an expensive personal trainer to keep him in shape. His grey t-shirt pulled across his broad, muscled shoulders in just the right way.

I looked down at my own clothing; the same items I'd been wearing on the flight. There were stains of blood on my shirt and across the right leg of my pants.

Liam noticed my observation. "I grabbed a few suitcases and threw them into the boat. My own, and a couple from your area. I hope maybe I found yours." He pointed toward a stack of two suitcases and a bag next to the boat. "I know you'd probably like to wash up and change."

"That's mine." I pointed toward a navy-blue suitcase in the pile.

He pulled it toward me, and I unzipped it, revealing all of my clothes and toiletries. I paused and looked up at him. "So both engines just….?"

"Both engines," he echoed sadly.

I shook my head in a grief that was more shock than anything else. "There must have been more than 200 people on that plane."

Liam frowned and looked down at his hands. "Most of the plane was on fire. But I checked as many as I could for pulses."

"So, it sank?"

When he nodded, there was immense pain in his expression. I couldn't imagine moving from person to person, only to find out they were dead. It was horrific, really.

We were both silent for a moment before I spoke again. "Were you traveling with anyone?"

"No, I was alone. Was meant to meet with my agent and a producer this morning in Auckland to discuss a new project," he sighed.

"Well, at least Kate is safe back in L.A.?" The words flew out of my mouth before I had a chance to filter them. I brought my hand to my cheek in embarrassment. His life, or the life that the media shared about him, was common knowledge to me, and I forgot for a moment that it was probably strange to ask him something so personal.

He looked up and studied my face for a few seconds. "Kate's fine. Yeah, she's probably…ugh, I don't even want to think about how she's feeling right now," he frowned.

I decided to stay silent, afraid I'd say something humiliating again.

"They'll find us soon." He said it with confidence, but I could see right through his façade. He was worried too.

He leaned back on his hands and watched me for a moment. "So, you know about my girlfriend? You've done your research." He raised his eyebrow lightheartedly.

My cheeks grew warm. I didn't know what to say. But it was clear now that neither I nor my turkey sandwiches had made *that* much of an impression on him yesterday if he didn't remember me now.

Liam chuckled softly and began to stand up. "Sorry, I'll let you change. I'll go investigate the coconut situation."

I watched as he walked away, all tall and poised. A surge of butterflies grew in my stomach, but a thousand other thoughts rushed through my mind in tandem. Hundreds of people had died today. I'd almost been one of them. News had definitely reached home by now. Rescue crews were scrambling. Friends and relatives were mourning.

My family was finding out I'd gone down with the plane. Imagining the looks on their faces brought the painful knot back to my throat. And Tess... Tess was supposed to have been on the flight too. If she had been, would she have survived? I squeezed my eyes shut as I realized how close she'd come to boarding the plane and sitting right next to me, in a seat which now held a dead passenger, probably at the bottom of the ocean. A tear escaped the corner of my eye and rolled down my cheek.

I wiped it away and reached into my suitcase, finding a sleeveless top and a pair of jean shorts. When I could no longer see Liam in the distant trees, I slowly pulled off my bloodied clothes and replaced them with clean ones. My left knee ached painfully as I bent it to change, but other than that and my throbbing head, my body felt miraculously unharmed.

I pulled out my bag of toiletries and opened a small mirror. My reflection startled me. I looked like an absolute mess. There was a long shallow cut across my forehead, and the area around it was swollen and becoming black and blue. There was smeared mascara beneath my blue-green eyes, and my hair was even more of a rat's nest than usual.

I fumbled through the bag and took out a small tube of antibacterial ointment. Placing a dab on my finger, I rubbed it gently on my cut. Then I used a makeup remover wipe under my eyes, and I ran a brush through my hair. When I looked at myself again in the mirror, I still looked disheveled, but not as frightening.

I snapped the mirror shut just as Liam reappeared from the trees.

"How is your head feeling?" he asked as he sat down in front of me.

I looked at the gash on the side of his face. It was much deeper than mine. I was surprised he hadn't lost a significant amount of blood. "I'm ok. But your face. You look like you almost need stitches. You should probably get that bandaged up."

"Oh, it's not that bad." He waved me off.

"I think it really is. Here, I've got some ointment." I pulled out the tube I'd used on my own face.

He pondered for a moment and then took it from me, putting a small dab on his finger and staring at it for a few seconds. "How much do I…?"

I half-grinned at his naivety. "Do you want me to?"

He looked up gratefully and handed the tube back to me. "Yes, could you?"

I scooted closer to him and inspected his cut. It was about five inches long and ran down the right side of his face, unsettlingly close to his eye. He watched me as I studied him. I tried not to meet his eyes, but I felt my gaze wander toward them a couple of times. "Did you wash this out yet?"

"Yes, a few hours ago," he replied.

I tentatively reached my hand toward his face and smoothed a stray curl away so that I could get a better look. My heart skipped a beat as my fingers made contact with the strands.

They were even softer than I'd imagined in my countless fantasies.

The gash was deep. Without stitches, it would definitely scar, but we didn't have much of a choice. His nose and forehead were pink and burned already. I may have been lucky to rest under the shade of a tree, but he'd been exploring the island alone in the beating sun for the last twenty-four hours waiting for me to wake up. Already, he looked exhausted compared to yesterday at the studio. It felt like so long ago.

Wiping the ointment from his finger onto mine and recapping the tube, I took a deep breath. It was clear that I was going to have to remind him that we'd already met before things got *really* awkward. "So, did you enjoy your *tossed* salad yesterday?" I bravely asked.

His thick, dark brows furrowed at my comment, but the recognition spread quickly across his face. "Oh, wow, the catering. That was you, wasn't it?"

I nodded as I dabbed some cream along the line of his cut. "It was."

"I can't believe I didn't recognize you."

I can.

"Well, I was in and out pretty quickly," I replied, pretending like I didn't mind.

"Those turkey sandwiches…" He closed his eyes. "I could go for one of those right now. You're a fantastic chef."

Cool, so he remembered the sandwiches, but not me.

"Thank you," I replied, taking one of the shirts from my suitcase and tearing it into strips to fasten them around his head.

"What an insane coincidence that we're here together now." He tilted his head as he watched me.

"Yeah, it's crazy, right?" I replied, scooting away and averting my gaze. "Well, it's gonna scar if you don't get stitches soon, but that's as good as we can do for now."

Liam smiled at me. "Help will come soon. Thank you, Cora."

I looked out at the turquoise blue waves again that covered the horizon as far as the eye could see. I wanted to believe him, but there was still a frightening anxiety at the pit of my stomach that had me fearing that surviving until now would be the easy part.

FOUR

I massaged my aching knee as I watched the sparkling current crash gently on the shore. "What about a nearby island? Could we take the lifeboat out?"

Liam traced random lines through the sand as he shook his head. "I've been around the perimeter of the island and I can't see anything in any direction. I think we'll be safer if we stay put."

I wanted to agree with him, but I already felt useless sitting and waiting for a rescue. "What about fresh water?"

He took a deep breath and reached into one of the suitcases, taking out four mini water bottles. "I grabbed these from the plane, but it's all we'll have until it rains. Then we can catch some more."

I remembered the long gulps I'd taken from the bottle he'd held to my lips when I'd first woken up. My eyes widened. "Why did you let me drink so much just then?"

His face softened. "You were dehydrated. You needed it."

I ignored his sympathy, doing the math to figure out how much water we'd need per day, *each*, to survive without rain. The answer was *a lot*. We had barely enough for even a few days. If no one found us for weeks, would we already be dead? I wondered what it would feel like to die from dehydration or malnutrition. Is that how it would end?

Liam watched me with remorse as my mind raced. The realities of our predicament were finally sinking in. This wasn't a casual vacation on the beach. This was quickly becoming a test of survival.

Panic washed over me, and I tightened my lips, fighting back the urge to cry. I looked down, trying to hide my feelings, but as hard as I attempted to hold them in, a stray tear dropped down onto my shirt, leaving a dark, wet mark where it landed.

"Hey, hey…" Liam said softly. He slid toward me and placed his hand on my back. "It's going to be ok."

I sniffled and tried to wipe my eyes, but the tears fell more steadily, and I started to tremble. I shook my head, unable to form words amongst my sobs. As if a floodgate opened, I finally understood the immense danger I found myself in.

Liam's touch was warm and reassuring on my back, and there was some comfort there, but my nerves couldn't be completely consoled.

"Cora…" He moved his hand to my shoulder. "Hey, look at me." His voice was not much more than a whisper.

I blinked, trying to clear my eyes, and slowly lifted my gaze to his. He reached up to wipe my cheek. Even through my veil of fear and despair, my heart lurched at his touch.

"We're going to get through this." His eyes held mine steadily.

"I'm not going to let anything happen to us. We're going to get off this island, and we're both going to be fine."

I sniffled and attempted to slow my breathing. "How are you so calm about all this?"

He smiled softly. "I've been exploring this island for a full day now. I've already been through the shock." He paused, frowning like he was remembering his first moments of disbelief too, but then he smiled again. "We've made it this far. We're strong. Right?"

I wiped the remaining tears from my face and nodded slowly.

"They'll find us soon." He patted my shoulder and stood up. "But in the meantime, we need to get a fire going. Do you happen to have a mirror?"

I nodded again, still trying to regain my composure. I reached into my bag, pulled out my small compact mirror, and handed it to him.

"I tried to start a fire earlier." He pointed toward a pile of wood and kindling a few yards away. "But didn't have much success. I think the mirror might do the trick. Do you think you can stand?" He extended his hand to me.

I placed mine in his and he slowly pulled me up to my feet. I winced, feeling a jolt of pain in my knee.

"Are you alright?" Liam watched me, concerned.

I forced a brave face. "Yeah, my knee just hurts a bit when I put weight on it."

He looked down at my leg. "It doesn't look swollen. Can you walk?"

I continued to hold his hand as I took a few small, tentative steps. It was painful, but I could do it. I nodded and took a few more.

Liam was patient as we walked out from under the canopy of the trees, and he helped me sit down again in the sand next to the wood. He knelt and began to rearrange it, forming a small teepee.

I watched his fingers as he steadied the sticks and pushed dried grasses into the center of the pile. "Do you know how to do this?" I asked.

"Well, I know the sun is beating down on us, and if I can focus it at the kindling, we should be able to generate enough heat." He held my mirror at varying angles, finding a strong cast of light and directing it at the center of the pile. "I'm not a pro, but I think this should work."

I was again impressed by his calm disposition. My heart was still beating heavily in my chest, but his hands held the mirror perfectly steady.

We both stared at the bright spot on the dried grasses for many minutes before the tiniest bit of smoke spiraled into the air. There was a brief sense of relief as Liam pulled the mirror away and blew gently into the teepee, but no flames resulted.

He cursed under his breath.

Finally, a chink in his ultra-composed armor.

"It's alright," I reassured him. "I think you almost had it."

He sat back and stared at the smoking pile of wood, setting his jaw.

"Maybe hold the light there longer this time?"

He readjusted his grip on the mirror and leaned in again, focusing the light on the kindling once more. We watched as the grass began to smoke again, but this time, Liam held the mirror there longer. His hand shook slightly, and the tip of his tongue stuck out near the corner of his mouth as he concentrated.

It was only a few more moments before a tiny orange flame flickered to life. Liam carefully bent down to blow again into the pile as the flames multiplied slowly and a steady fire stood before us.

He wiped his brow with the back of his hand and relaxed. "Alright, fire. We have fire."

"Good work," I nodded as relief washed over me. "We should get a stockpile of wood to keep it going."

"Yes, and I also need to get working on a shelter before nightfall. I tried to sleep in the boat last night, but who knows when it might rain and we'll need to be covered." He stood up and looked around, rubbing his forehead. "Ah, what I would do for a machete or an ax right now."

"Have you checked the other suitcases? Maybe they were traveling with one?" I smirked, surprising myself with the humor I was still able to muster up.

He grinned at me with a twinkle in his eye. "Well, why don't I bring one of the bags over to you and you'll have a look?"

I beamed, basking in the knowledge that I'd successfully amused Liam Montgomery.

When he turned on his heel and retreated toward the bags, I stared into the fire, watching the wood hiss and snap as the flames began to engulf it. The sound was comforting, reminding me of childhood campfires, s'mores, and sparklers on the Fourth of July. But this was not a holiday. This was no party. We needed this fire to survive, and to *eat* if they didn't find us soon.

I closed my eyes and listened to the sound of the waves, the wind, the crackle of the flames. It was a strange kind of peace in the face of the terrifying unknown. Focusing on the sounds allowed me to think clearly. The sea, the breeze, and the fire created a melody that calmed my senses.

I listened for a while, trying to slow my heart rate while Liam retrieved the suitcases. I imagined the fanfare that might ensue if we made it home. The world would fixate on the story, simply because Liam was involved. But I'd forever be part of the tale too, his nameless companion. *That one girl from L.A. who was stranded with Liam Montgomery*—that's how I'd be known.

With a deep breath, I cleared my mind and focused on the calming sounds again, until another one joined the mix. It didn't fit. It was a faint, low-pitched hum that was gradually growing louder. My head shot up and my eyes flew open. I scanned the skies, squinting across the horizon until I spotted a tiny silver speck in the distance, wavy in the heat. A surge of adrenaline coursed through my veins as my head snapped back toward Liam.

"Liam, a plane!" I yelled, scrambling to push myself to my feet.

He'd heard it too. He was staring at the same spot in the sky, eyes pulled wide and his mouth hanging open. But it was only a moment before he jumped into action and ran out onto the beach.

"Hurry, get the flames as big as you can make them!" He dashed toward the S.O.S. lettering he'd crafted and began adjusting their legibility.

Spinning around to the fire, I tried to figure out what would catch quickly. I spotted some fallen palm fronds a few yards away and painfully limped toward them. They were large and cumbersome in my grip, but I managed to pick them up and throw them onto the flames.

Once they'd caught, I looked back at the sky. The plane was getting closer. I could make out the wings now. I turned to Liam, breathing hard. "Will they see us?"

He was laser-focused on the plane. "They've got to. They will, *they will.*" He began to wave his arms over his head.

I threw my arms into the air too, trying to flag down the tiny speck.

"They're coming…" Liam spoke breathlessly. "They're coming this way…"

A blur of emotions erupted within me as I watched it grow from a tiny dot to a recognizable shape. It was a propeller plane, flying close to the water. Searching for debris, or bodies maybe? It was still miles away, but we watched it increase in proximity, headed straight toward us.

I jumped up and down, waving my arms and ignoring the stabbing pain in my knee. Rescue was on the horizon, and that was all that mattered now. We were *saved.*

But as if fate had heard my thoughts and decided otherwise, the plane began to bank left, altering its path away from us.

"WAIT! NO…" Liam splashed into the water, still waving frantically.

My heart dropped. The plane had banked fast, and it was becoming a speck again, disappearing into the distance. Liam stood at the edge of the sea and dropped his arms to his sides. I let out an exhausted breath and sank to the sand. My gaze lost focus as I stared at the languid waves.

Liam slowly turned around and walked back to the fire. He stopped and gazed blankly into the flames. "We weren't prepared enough…"

I rested my elbow on my knee with a sigh. "Maybe they saw us? Maybe they turned around to go get help?"

Liam closed his eyes and tensed his jaw. "I should have started the fire *hours* ago. It wasn't big enough."

"I bet they saw us," I repeated, trying to believe it myself.

"They didn't get close enough." He shook his head, looking away.

"Maybe they'll be back," I suggested with forced enthusiasm.

"I'm sorry…" He stepped back from the fire and walked alone into the trees.

I studied the empty horizon once more before pushing myself up and stretching my aching knee. Liam was so quick to blame our failure on himself, even though I was the one who'd been unconscious for a full day, contributing absolutely nothing. I wanted to believe that we'd been seen; that the plane was headed back to civilization to alert rescue crews to come get us. That was the scenario I wanted to trust inside my mind, but I couldn't help but fear that we may have missed a vital opportunity.

I sat down next to my suitcase and examined its contents, trying to distract myself. There were lots of clothes. Why had I packed so many clothes? I pushed them to the side and opened my bag of toiletries again. There was some sunscreen that I knew would come in handy, all of my makeup, toothpaste, and a bottle of mouthwash. I also had my laptop, which was now basically a brick without access to power or wifi, and some charging cords. Those could be used as ties, so I set them aside.

I looked at the other bags. One was a black duffle bag I'd seen Liam dig into, and the other was a brown suitcase. I took the latter and unzipped it, making a wish that it would be full of non-perishables and tools. But my eyes were met by more clothes. Wishes didn't always come true. I unfolded the articles gently. There were both men's and women's styles. I touched a lace-embroidered blouse and thought of the couple who had been seated in my row. These must have been theirs. My fingers froze on the soft fabric as their fate sank in. I blinked back new tears and placed it neatly to the side.

Next, I found a small, canvas bag. I untied it and reached in, pulling out bottles of pills and checking the labels. Most were vitamins, and I smiled, realizing that these would actually come in handy if we were faced with a lack of nutrition.

As I reached further into the bag, I found a long, green, rubber resistance band, rolled into a tight ball. It looked like something used to stretch or exercise an injured muscle. I set it to the side with the bag.

As I lifted out a pair of men's jeans, my fingers felt the weight of a small, smooth object in one of the pockets. I furrowed my brow as I pulled it out, and my breathing stopped as I stared into the palm of my hand, realizing what it was. I made out the familiar white cross centered in the shape of a shield on a red background.

A Swiss Army knife.

My jaw dropped. How was this even allowed on the plane? I carefully fanned open its tools. Three different knives, scissors, a corkscrew, a can opener, a small saw, and a hook. I turned it around in my hands, trying to understand how it had passed security and the restrictions on carry-ons.

There was rustling in the leaves behind me, and I turned to squint, searching for Liam. He was on his way back, dragging long palm branches behind him.

My expression must have been that of shock because he dropped them and walked swiftly toward me. "What's wrong?"

I silently held up the knife.

His eyes grew wide when he saw it. "How in the world...?"

"It was in the other suitcase." I handed it to him. "I don't know how it got past security."

He studied each tool carefully, shaking his head in awe. "This is incredible…what brilliant luck…"

I thought about the couple who had died. The elderly man probably hadn't even realized he'd made the mistake of carrying it on the plane. But little did they know, they'd packed a survival tool that might just save our lives. I thought of the security personnel who had missed the knife during the screening process. Little did they know, they'd allowed a tool onto that plane that could add *days* of survival to our time on this island. Those would be days we might need if our rescue didn't come soon enough.

"This'll be perfect for cutting bamboo." Liam flipped to the largest knife. He pointed to the palm fronds he'd dropped on the ground. "Can you work on splitting these down the middle? That way, we can lay them as a shingling system for the roof of our shelter."

He showed me how to tear them down the stem as I watched him in astonishment. "How do you know this?"

He grinned slightly. "Alright, so have you seen those *Primitive Technology* videos on YouTube? I got into a long kick watching those last year. Actually retained a few of the skills. Who would have thought they'd come in handy?"

His knowledge continued to impress me. As it turned out,

he was more than just a handsome face.

I took a long branch and began to split it like he'd shown me, grateful for him now in more ways than one.

FIVE

Over the next few hours, Liam built us a lean-to shelter against a large tree. Its structure was made from the bamboo he cut down and covered in dozens of palm fronds I'd split. By the time we'd finished, the sun was sinking lower into the sky, casting longer shadows across the beach. As Liam stood back and surveyed his work, his chest heaved up and down beneath his damp t-shirt, and his forehead sparkled with sweat. He looked up at the sparse clouds for about the millionth time and I knew he was searching for a return of the plane.

"You need some water," I encouraged, holding out a bottle in an attempt to distract him.

He glanced at it briefly and then waved it off. "No, I'm fine."

I set it down and gripped one of the supports of the lean-to, checking its strength. "This is really sturdy. I think it will work well."

He sighed and walked past me toward the fire. "Yeah, for now." He placed more wood on the flames before turning back to the trees. "I need to figure out how to get some coconuts before nightfall."

"I can help." I stood up from the ground, trying not to wince at the pain in my knee.

"You're in no state to be climbing trees." He gestured toward my leg with a frown.

"I *am* in a state to make sure you don't fall out of one in the process," I replied with determination.

He let out a tense breath as if he might argue, but then shrugged and motioned for me to follow him. "Alright, I saw a decent one this way."

We walked through the tropical groundcover, weaving between smooth tree trunks until we came to a mid-sized palm that leaned slightly toward the open beach. There was a large bunch of coconuts at the top near the base of its leaves. Liam removed his shoes and wiped the sand from his hands before gripping onto the trunk.

"Are you sure you can do this?" I stepped toward him nervously.

He didn't answer as he began to climb, muscles flexing as he ascended the tree slowly. His bare feet gripped the trunk and his fingers spread widely around the smooth bark. The tree's slight angle made the climbing easier I assumed, but I was still impressed by his strength. My own hands began to sweat as I watched.

When he made it to the top, he looked down at me. "Stand clear."

I backed away from the tree as he pulled one of the coconuts free. It dropped to the ground with a loud thud, and then he pulled four more off by the time I noticed his legs begin to shake.

"Be careful," I shouted up to him, blinking away visions of his arms and legs flying through the air as he tumbled fatally to the ground, leaving me alone on the island.

He pulled two more coconuts and then began his descent. Halfway down, his feet slid and lost traction. He gripped his arms tighter and regained his control, but my heart had already stopped. It didn't start back up again until he made it safely to the ground.

"Well, I'm impressed." I began to help him pick up the coconuts.

He wiped his brow. "I'm extra grateful for my personal trainer right now."

I knew it. And so was I.

"So how do we get into these?" I asked, turning a coconut around in my hands.

He loaded them all into his arms. "Let's bring them back to the beach. We'll need a sharp rock."

When we found the rock for the job, Liam turned it on the ground, finding its sharpest edge. He took a coconut and crashed it against the point, splitting it open so that he could tear the husk off. Once the process revealed the inner shell, he reached into his pocket and pulled out the knife. Carefully, he cut a hole in the top and then handed it to me.

"You want to try first?"

I studied it briefly before placing my mouth on the opening and tilting my head back until a sweet liquid touched my lips and ran onto my tongue. It was almost like water, but even more refreshing.

It was *delicious.*

After a small sip, I tried to hand it back to him.

"No, you can have that one. I'll work on another." He repeated the same process with a second coconut and when he took a gulp, the reaction on his face told me he enjoyed it just as much as I did.

We each drank three coconuts and then Liam cracked the shells open on the sharp rock and we ate the bright white flesh. With each bite, I realized I was hungrier than I thought, and just about anything would probably taste good to me at this point.

And we'd only been here thirty-six hours.

Twilight had fallen and the flickering fire began to illuminate Liam's face. As he stared silently into the flames, his eyes reflected the sparks that floated into the air. I was struck by the familiarity of his expression. It was reminiscent of the brooding character he'd played in the film I'd watched too many times. Somehow, I felt like I already knew how to read him.

As we sat in mostly silence, I had a hard time tearing my eyes from him. It was as if I was seeing him in front of me for the first time again. By some twist of fate, he'd been on my plane, and the two of us—*just the two of us*—had been the sole survivors. Now that evening had fallen, and I had nothing else to occupy me, the reality of his presence had my nerves racing again. It *really* was him. It was *Liam*, sitting next to me.

I must have been staring at him with an unexpected intensity because when he looked up, his eyes met mine with question.

"What is it?" Concern crossed his face.

I blinked and shook my head, looking away. "Oh, it's nothing." But I peered back up at him through my eyelashes. "This is all just a lot to take in."

He cocked his head. "Being stranded like this?"

I bit my lip and tried to hide the redness that was forming on my cheeks.

He recognized my bashfulness and shrugged, pushing the logs around beneath the fire. "I'm really not that interesting. I'm just your average bloke, struggling to make sense of this just like you are. The last thing I want is for you to be too nervous to really speak to me."

I took in a trembling breath. "It's gonna take me a minute. And I definitely wouldn't call you *average.*"

"Pfft..." he scoffed. "You'd be surprised."

"Well, you make the nerves inevitable."

He crinkled his nose and smiled. "Well, it's my job to calm those nerves then."

My cheeks still felt warm, but I smiled at his kind reassurance.

He shifted his body to face mine. "Since you seem to already know so much about me, how about I ask you a few questions?"

"Sure." I nodded carefully.

"You're American?"

"Yes, I live in Burbank."

"Why were you headed to New Zealand?" He tilted his head curiously.

"I was going there with my friend for a vacation. She actually got shifted last minute to a different flight."

"It's a beautiful country," Liam responded. "And L.A.'s fantastic too. A bit congested, but then again, it's difficult to suffer from boredom there," he chuckled.

"I'd love to get out of L.A.," I replied. "Too much pressure and too many expectations. I'd prefer a less populated, less hectic city. Something more remote I guess."

Liam gestured to the empty beach around us. "Is this remote enough for you?"

I grinned. "Maybe a step too far."

He smirked.

I considered the countless questions I had for him, trying to decide which to ask first. "I can't imagine doing what you do. How do you handle all the attention? Doesn't it get exhausting?"

"Incredibly," he exhaled. "But it's alright. It's worth it to do what I love."

I smiled. "Well, you're fantastic at what you do."

"I appreciate it," he replied, not looking at me.

I leaned back on my hands. "You know, this has got to be all over the news back home."

"I wonder what they're speculating at this point?" He rested his chin on his palm.

"I can picture it now." I ran my fingers in a line in front of me as if tracing a headline. "New Zealand bound flight disappears—200 onboard including *Until Dawn* star, Liam Montgomery."

He sighed deeply. "I wish they wouldn't single me out. The 200 who perished deserve loads more respect."

I looked out at the crashing waves, picturing the bodies still strapped into their seats as the wreckage sank to the bottom of the sea. My stomach turned at the thought. I shivered as the wind picked up, but I was more distraught than I was cold. Barely a day ago, I'd been fretting about turkey sandwiches and Liam Montgomery.

Today…well, today I still fretted about Liam Montgomery, but now I was worried about water and shelter, and each hour that passed without rescue.

Would I die here on this island? Would I have to watch Liam die here on this island? What kind of cruelties would we have to endure? My parents' grieving faces came to mind again. Did they think I was dead? Yeah, probably.

I wrapped my arms around myself, wishing I could be home with them.

Liam noticed my shaking and stood up quickly. "You're cold. Hang on." He stepped away into the dark for a moment and then returned with his black leather jacket—the same one I'd seen him in on the plane. "Here, take this."

I thanked him and took it gratefully. It was much too large for me, but I slid my arms through the sleeves and pulled it tightly around my shoulders. As the collar brushed my face, I breathed in his scent; clean and crisp, with a hint of woods and spice. It was *marvelous.* I'd unabashedly pondered what he might smell like, or what cologne he might wear. And now, here I was, wrapped in his jacket—wrapped in his scent.

Liam returned to his spot next to me. "So, how long have you worked for the catering company?"

"Since I was fifteen. It's my father's business. He has me lined up to inherit it when he retires." I watched the sparks from the fire dissolve as they drifted down to the ground.

"Is that what you want?"

I looked up at him and shrugged. "I guess. I don't *hate* it. I really do enjoy cooking."

He cocked his head, watching me intently. It was nice to be listened to, so I continued. "It can definitely be stressful, but I think you're going to get that with any career choice. I think I'd like to open a restaurant someday."

"You should." He nodded. "You'd be brilliant."

I shrugged again.

Liam turned his gaze to the waves. "Hmm, it certainly is peaceful here, if nothing else."

Night had fallen completely now, and the moon reflected in shiny ripples on the water's surface. I rubbed my eyes, feeling exhaustion creeping in.

"How is your head feeling?" Liam asked.

"Better…I think," I replied, stretching my neck and yawning.

"You should probably try to sleep if you can."

I assessed his weary eyes too. "What about you? Aren't you tired?"

"I'm going to keep the fire going a bit longer, just so that it's strong enough to hold its heat when I do sleep." He poked at the flames and yawned.

I pursed my lips.

He smiled softly. "It's ok. You can go. I'll be alright."

As much as I hated to leave him awake all alone, my eyelids were becoming increasingly heavy. I started to get up, but in my periphery, I noticed tiny crabs scurrying along the water's edge and burying themselves in the ground.

"Um," I gulped, glaring toward them. "Do you think they'll…bother us?"

Liam followed my gaze and smiled. "Nah, they've got better things to do. Besides, that's why I built the platform at the floor of our shelter to keep us off the ground."

I couldn't take my eyes off the crabs. They skittered around like oversized spiders, and I grimaced.

Liam chuckled. "They won't getcha."

I gave him a sidelong look and stepped away. "They'd better not."

"Get some sleep, Cora. I'll be in soon." He smiled and turned back to the fire.

The way my name rolled off his tongue brought a warm, tingly feeling to my chest, and it lingered as I hobbled to the shelter. I had no idea if I'd be able to sleep here, in a strange place, exposed to the elements and the creepy-crawly crabs, but I placed a few large shirts for padding on the bamboo platform and laid down. The space under the roof of the shelter was not much larger than a queen-sized bed—just enough room for the two of us. I shifted as far as I could to one side, allowing space for Liam when he eventually decided to sleep.

Even with the shirts, the ground was hard and cool. I pulled Liam's jacket tighter around my shoulders and stared out across the beach at him. He sat at the fire with his back toward me, and the light from the flames silhouetted his figure. The edges of his wild, curly hair glowed against the rich, black night.

I wondered how Kate was coping. I didn't have a significant other to miss me and grieve in that way. I imagined being in her shoes, helpless to know if her Liam was alive, and I felt a touch of guilt, wishing there was some way I could tell her he was ok. I wished I could put her at ease.

If we didn't make it, would I be the last to ever see him alive? Would she be jealous that I'd spent his last moments with him? He was driven and skilled, but I saw the worry behind his confident façade. He was vulnerable too.

I was sure she cared deeply about him. I needed to care for him, for her, while she couldn't.

I closed my eyes. As helpless as I felt—stranded and unable to let anyone know I had survived—I did have control over two things. First, I had to keep myself alive until our rescue. That was simply a matter of being smart and motivated. Second, I had to keep Liam encouraged. If that plane truly *hadn't* seen us, it was unlikely it would return. It would be a difficult truth for him to swallow. He felt responsible for being unable to start the fire earlier, so I had to keep his spirits up. To do that, I'd have to remain positive. I knew it wouldn't be easy, but if he could be strong physically, I could be strong mentally.

I felt the sand around me crunch quietly, and I cracked open my eyes to see Liam crawl into the shelter and lay down beside me. His proximity—mere inches away—made my heart beat a little faster. He laid on his back, not noticing I was still awake, and stared blankly at the palm fronds above us for a moment before finally closing his eyes.

I closed my own and tried not to linger on the butterfly-inducing reality that I was laying down to sleep next to him.

Sleeping was all we were doing after all, *Cora*.

Instead, I focused on the fortunate reality that I wasn't alone. I had a partner in survival. I didn't have to do any of this on my own.

SIX

I tried my best to sleep, but the new and strange sounds of the island kept me from ever fully going under. Every time my eyes flew open, I held my breath, checking the space around me for crabs or other island-dwelling creatures. And every time I did briefly fall asleep, they assaulted me in my dreams anyway.

Liam was tossing and turning too. I'd forgotten to ask him if he'd really gotten any sleep the night before when I'd been unconscious. I had to give him credit for spending his first full day practically alone.

At one point during the night, I woke up from what was likely only a few minutes of continuous slumber to an itch on my leg. I touched my skin and felt a small, raised bump.

Mosquitos.

I moved my hand to the left. Another bump.

There was a small sting on my cheek, and I clapped my hand down onto a large mosquito trying to make me its midnight snack.

Liam sat up next to me and slapped his own arm in frustration at the same time. "Ugh, bloody bugs," he hissed, crawling out from the shelter and slumping down next to the fire.

I rubbed my eyes and reached for my suitcase, pulling out a pair of sweatpants and a pink t-shirt. As I tugged the pants up my legs, they gently grazed the bites, cueing the itchy irritation. I used all of my willpower to not scratch them as I wrapped the shirt around my face and let out a frustrated grunt as I laid back down on the ground. Now that I had every inch of my skin covered to the best of my ability, I closed my eyes and desperately tried to find sleep again.

***

I breathed in deep, hot, thick air as I opened my eyes to bright, fluorescent pink, and I momentarily questioned where I was. In the hospital? Why was this hospital so hot, and *so pink*?

I reached my hand to my head and felt the soft fabric laying across my face. I quickly remembered the purpose of the shirt and pulled it off with a sigh. I rolled over, squinting into the morning sun, which was already bright and blistering on my face as I yawned and stretched my joints.

Liam wasn't next to me, so I peered out at the beach. The soft waves sparkled as they washed ashore, and a few yards into the water, Liam's shirtless figure was standing waist-deep, facing the horizon. His thick, dark curls tousled softly in the breeze as he cupped the water in his hands, splashing it against his bare skin.

I crept closer to the edge of our shelter, trying to catch a better view. He took a deep breath and sank below the surface. I watched intently until he emerged again, and the water ran down his bare back and dripped from the now elongated strands on his head.

I was entranced by him, forgetting for a moment to worry about anything else. But when he spun around to face the beach, I shrunk back into the shadows of the shelter and turned to busy myself, hoping he hadn't noticed my gawking.

"Did you manage to get any sleep?" He asked from behind me a short moment later.

I unzipped my suitcase, pretending to be occupied. "Not really," I sighed. "The bugs…"

"Yeah. They're murder," he replied. "Hungry?"

I turned to see him straightening a t-shirt he'd just pulled over his head. His shorts were still dripping, and his hair was slicked back from his bandaged face. He held a coconut out in my direction.

I received it from him gratefully and took a swig. Once I'd drained it, he cracked it open on a rock and handed it back to me. I picked at the white coconut flesh, trying to savor every last bit, and my stomach gurgled. How long would I last on coconuts alone?

Liam was quiet, and when I lifted my gaze to his, he was staring down at me with a furrowed brow. "We need real food."

I turned to the ocean. "Fish?"

He scratched his head. "I suppose spearfishing is our best bet. Or maybe if we had some sort of net."

A thought popped into my head, and I rifled through my suitcase to pull out a mesh laundry bag. "What about this?"

He nodded in approval. "That might actually work." He placed his hands on his hips and looked over the trees to the west, where darker clouds were forming in the sky. "It looks like there is a storm brewing."

"I'll see if I can create something to collect water," I suggested.

He still looked uneasy, but he picked up the bag and started his trek into the trees. "Good. That'll be good. Water is good."

I sighed as I watched him walk away. I could tell he had one of those type-A personalities—always on the move, always looking for some problem he could solve. It was something I hadn't picked up on until meeting him in person. Clearly, his thoughts were on one thing: survival. And that's where my mind needed to be too.

I pulled out my compact mirror and studied my forehead. My cut looked a bit better, and the swelling was down slightly. After pulling my hair up into a ponytail, I stretched my legs and stood up. My knee hurt considerably less today, so I walked over to the fire and tossed some of Liam's stockpiled wood onto it. Then, I looked at our bottles of water. Only one was still full. I picked it up and examined the crystal-clear liquid inside. My throat stung with dryness, but I set it gently next to Liam's suitcase. Then, I took the empty ones and lodged them partway in the sand under the open sky.

With my hands on my hips, I frowned. Their small openings were unlikely to catch rainwater very quickly, so I looked to the foliage at the edge of the tree line. There was a plant with large, smooth leaves, so I snapped one off and funneled it into the opening of one of the bottles, creating more surface area for the water to trickle in. I did the same with the other three, and then I took all of the half-coconuts we'd eaten from and settled them into the sand as well.

I stood back and studied my work. If all the containers and coconuts filled up one time, they would get us through maybe a day and a half if we were lucky. I tapped my foot, glaring at the sad display. That wasn't going to cut it. It probably wouldn't rain every day. We needed to stockpile more.

Out of the corner of my eye, I noticed the bright yellow lifeboat. It was made of shiny plastic, meant to repel water, but I was sure it would catch water well too, so I pulled it out onto the open beach. It was heavier than I expected, and it took a few grunts to tug it into position, but I managed.

The sun beat down on my neck, threatening to blister and burn me to a crisp, so I applied some of my sunscreen from the tiny, travel-sized bottle that I knew wouldn't last. I gazed down at my arms. They were a deep shade of pink already.

I supposed looking like a lobster was inevitable.

When I turned toward the trees, Liam still wasn't back, and since I hadn't explored the island myself yet, I stretched my knee and stepped over tropical grasses and fallen logs, weaving my way inland. The trees and bushes were denser as the ocean disappeared behind me, but after a few minutes, the vegetation dispersed again to reveal a wide-open expanse of shallow, pale turquoise water, completely surrounded by land. *An island shaped like a ring.* Liam's description made sense now. At the center of this 'atoll' was the most picturesque lagoon I'd ever seen. All the way across, the water looked to be no more than waist-deep. It was calm and teeming with tiny silver fish, reflecting the sun as they skittered about.

I scanned the water to the other side until I found Liam sitting on a large boulder, staring down at the sparkling surface. On his lap, he held a long stick of bamboo with my mesh laundry bag attached to one end.

I circled my way around the lagoon, slowly approaching. He didn't see me at first, and I feared that he would dislike my intrusion into his solitude. His posture oozed defeat, but he glanced up at me as I grew closer.

"Do you want some company?" I asked quietly, stopping next to his rock.

"Couldn't hurt." His response was devoid of any animation or inflection, and he turned his tired expression away toward the water again.

I climbed up onto the boulder and sat down a few feet from him, staring across the lagoon in silence. At the other end was an inlet from the ocean, where the water flowed freely in and out to sea. I could see all the way to the open horizon beyond.

Liam was much quieter today, especially after he'd watched me eat my coconut this morning. Apparently, I didn't hide my hunger well. I wished I could lift his spirits, but I hardly knew how to raise them when mine weren't high to begin with.

I cleared my throat, eying his makeshift net. "That looks like it should work."

"It doesn't," he replied without emotion.

I blinked in confusion. "Did you try it?"

He looked up at the sky and exhaled loudly. "Ok, the net would probably work if someone *skilled* used it. But I've had no luck."

I frowned. "You probably just need to practice more." But as I said it, my stomach growled loud enough for both of us to hear.

He tossed the net to the ground with a huff. "We don't have time to practice. It's been forty-eight hours since the plane went down. We can't survive on coconuts alone."

"So, I'll try too. We'll get the hang of it." I hopped off the rock and picked up the net, studying his craftsmanship.

He squinted out across the inlet at the horizon again. "They should be here by now...if that plane saw us, they'd be back already."

I took a breath, slumping back down onto the rock. "Even if that plane didn't see us, someone else will come. They won't stop looking for us this quickly."

"If they found the plane wreckage, they have no reason to keep searching. They'll have assumed we perished as well." His voice broke on the last few words.

A chill ran down my spine. I didn't want to admit that he was right. He'd been sleep-deprived for two nights now and I knew he was not in a place to see the positives. But part of me was terrified that he *was* right.

I decided to change the subject instead. "What's the first thing you'll do when you get back?"

"Sleep," he replied without hesitation.

I was surprised Kate wasn't the first thing on his mind. But I supposed sleep deprivation trumped all else.

As if he'd read my thoughts, he spoke up. "*And Kate*, I need to see Kate. She's probably a mess right now."

"I'm sure she misses you terribly," I said quietly.

He scratched the hair on his chin, which was quickly becoming more than just stubble, and looked at me out of the corner of his eye. He let out a long breath. "We didn't part on the best of terms."

I gulped at his admission and focused on my fingers tracing across the net, trying not to seem too interested.

"We're still together of course, but we've been struggling lately," he continued. "Well, at least, *I* have. I miss her, but I've been questioning things."

I bit my lip, trying to figure out if he wanted me to respond. When I looked up, he was staring at the water again, so I sat forward. "Do you think you'll be able to mend things with her when you return?"

He ran his hand through his hair. "I want to, I think. She's great. But we're looking for different things. I'm thirty-two. But I feel like I'm going on forty-eight. I'm done with the games and the casual dating. Acting is still a high priority for me, but settling down with someone has begun to climb the charts. Kate is still very much young at heart. She'd rather be at a party until the wee hours of the morning than really working on our relationship."

Appreciation warmed me as I listened to him. To the public, he was so private about his personal life. I felt extremely privileged to hear him divulge some of his innermost thoughts. "How old is Kate?"

"She's thirty."

I wrinkled my nose. I was *younger* than she was, yet I'd left my days of partying far in the past already. If Kate was still there at thirty, I could see why Liam was bothered.

He spoke up again. "I don't mean to speak ill of her. She's really wonderful. She's beautiful, funny, smart." He paused with a sigh. "We get on great, but we have a lot to work through."

I could hear the pain in his voice, but there was uncertainty there too. "Maybe this whole situation will be a wake-up call for her," I suggested. "I'm sure she couldn't bear to lose you."

He smiled without humor. "Thanks for your confidence."

I couldn't stop the smirk that formed on my face. "What? you're a catch. I'm sure if she knew how you were feeling, she'd change her ways."

He shook his head and turned to face me. "What about you? Is there someone special who's missing you?"

I stretched my arms and leaned back. "Nope, it's just been me for the last year." I gazed into the tired brown eyes that waited for me to continue. I didn't love to talk about my personal life either, but I forced my anxieties to the side. "His name was Jacob. We dated for a year. It was rocky for all but maybe the first month."

"What happened?" he asked.

I sighed, replaying the disaster in my head. While it had started out all roses and rainbows, he'd quickly grown tired of me. At first, I'd endured it, resorting to the reality where I wasn't worth his time, but I began to see that I was never his priority, and it was too difficult to make him mine if he wasn't giving anything back. The turning point had been the night I got my rejection letter from the culinary school of my dreams. When I'd told Jacob, he'd shrugged it off and then proceeded to leave me alone while he went out for drinks with his sports buddies without so much as a consoling hug. I'd spent most of that night in tears, wondering if I'd expected too much from him.

We'd bitterly parted ways not too long after that. There was plenty to tell, but I gave Liam the abridged version. "We were on different pages. I don't think he was ever that into me, and we just grew apart. Unreturned calls, missed dates, you name it." In a failed attempt, I tried to laugh it off.

Liam scrunched his nose. "What a git."

"In the beginning, I put my all into that relationship. I wanted that strong bond, you know?" I sighed. "Commitment, someone who'd make me a priority, and I'd make him one too… But I can't be with someone who doesn't feel the same." I thought for a moment and then laughed genuinely. "I must sound really high-maintenance right now."

Liam laughed too. "No, not at all. You sound perfectly sensible." He studied me for a moment. "How old are you?"

I tried to stifle a blush, knowing I was younger than his apparently immature girlfriend. "Twenty-eight."

He raised his eyebrows. "You seem mature for your age."

I peered at him with playful offense. "Thanks?"

He chuckled and shook his head. "No, no, it's a good thing. You seem like you know what you want, and what you need. That's very impressive."

I smiled with a shrug. "I guess that's just the way it's always been with me. I don't ever remember *not* thinking that way."

Liam rested back on his hands. "Oh, *I* do. A committed relationship was the last thing on my mind through most of my twenties."

"What changed?" I asked.

"Just time passing," he mused. "Getting that early-twenties lifestyle out of my system. Then I realized it wasn't all that fulfilling after a while."

I nodded. "I think most people have that epiphany, eventually."

Liam smiled, focusing on me again. "Some of us fail to see it into our thirties, and others, like you, apparently catch on quite quickly."

"Well, it hasn't done me any favors yet. Just a handful of

failed relationships."

"You're still young, and you have a great mindset." He lifted the net from my lap and began to fiddle with it. "Your time will come."

"I've been telling myself that since I was about three," I laughed.

Liam smiled at me, but I diverted my gaze to my empty hands and clasped them together in my lap. Even though he still made my heart race, he was oddly easy to talk to, now that I'd gotten past the initial shock of meeting him. And it was strange, sitting here by a picturesque blue lagoon, pouring my heart out to a man who, just days prior, had been nothing more than a fantasy to me.

SEVEN

You can't truly understand exhaustion until you've spent three days stranded on a deserted island, I thought to myself as I practically collapsed onto the ground of our shelter at the end of the day. The sun was barely touching the horizon, but we were both ready to pass out again. Liam had spent a few more hours trying to fish with absolutely no luck. He was beyond frustrated, and as a result, not in a great mood. I'd sorted out the rest of the items from the suitcases, hoping to find something helpful. But instead of machetes and protein bars, I found clothes, makeup, and electronics that didn't work.

The dark clouds had slowly increased in proximity over the course of the afternoon, and I knew the skies would soon open up. The bottles, coconuts, and lifeboat were all poised to collect as much water as possible. Liam had built a makeshift roof over the fire in preparation for the probable downpour, and when he was finished, he climbed into the shelter and laid down next to me.

"Maybe the rain will keep the mosquitos at bay," he suggested as he rested an arm across his eyes and yawned deeply.

"I'll welcome the rain on any terms as long as I can get a drink," I responded. My mouth was dry and sticky as I said the words. Liam had insisted I take the last bottle of water, and since then, we'd been surviving off coconut water all day. It kept us mildly hydrated, but it never fully satisfied.

I stared up at the palm fronds above us, slowly rustling in the breeze. "Do you think the roof will leak?" I asked.

When I didn't receive a response, I turned to look at Liam. His eyes were closed, and his lips were parted slightly as his chest rose and fell. I was glad that he'd found sleep, even for just this moment. It was peaceful to see someone else at ease. At the very least, I could allow myself to feel the sensation vicariously. I smiled and rolled over, adjusting my position on the unforgiving bamboo floor so that I could try to let sleep grant me that sweet ease as well.

***

My ease was short-lived.

Soon after I'd fallen asleep, I was awoken by a wet, misty breeze blowing over my face. I ran my hand across my damp forehead and looked to my left.

Outside the shelter, steady streams of rain pelted the beach, the palm trees were blowing wildly, and the wind was beginning to pick up. The roof Liam had built over the fire was whipping chaotically, and the flames were dancing drunkenly in search of oxygen.

I gasped and sat up, turning to Liam. Somehow, through

the sound of the penetrating rain and the beating wind, he was still asleep, and I didn't want to wake him, but something had to be done about the fire. It was choking rapidly.

"Liam..." I coaxed gently, nudging his shoulder.

He sniffed but didn't wake.

"Liam..." I repeated, this time a bit louder. "Liam, the fire..."

He opened his eyes and blinked slowly before focusing on me.

"The fire..." I said again, pointing out into the rain.

He suddenly understood me and sat up, looking out at the dying flames. "Oh, shit..."

He jumped to his feet and darted outside to adjust the protective roof. I stepped into the downpour too, grabbing as many palm fronds as I could and adding them to the structure. The rain pelted my face in tiny stings as each drop made contact.

We were both drenched to the bone as we fumbled. Liam tried to add more wood to the fire to increase the heat, but the new wood was soaking wet and would not catch. The flames continued to fail as the storm grew in strength, and Liam's soaking wet hair whipped in the wind as he struggled.

As we wrestled with the branches, a strong gust blew across the beach, completely dislodging the entire roof over the fire in an instant. It blew away in a tumbling mess down the beach and splashed into the tumultuous waves. Liam stopped his work immediately and dropped his arms heavily to his sides. I hung my head as the last of the sputtering flames were quickly extinguished.

Neither of us moved. We both stared at the wet logs where the fire once roared. I sighed as the rain dripped down my face, and without a word, we both accepted defeat and made our way back to the shelter.

We crawled in and laid back down, still soaked. I didn't want to say anything, for fear that he might be on the edge of a frustrated outburst, so we both laid silently, staring at our makeshift roof. I wondered if this one would blow down the beach too.

Almost instantly, the winds increased again and the palm fronds above us started to detach one by one, leaving small cracks where the rain began to drip in.

Drip, drop, drip, drop.

They fell like heavy tears onto my skin. I let out a frustrated huff and draped my arm over my face, trying to shield it from the torture. But it was no use, the streams became steadier until the ground beneath us began to pool.

"This is ridiculous," Liam growled from beside me, sitting up and running his hand through his wet hair.

I pulled myself up too and watched him with a misery of my own. He pushed on the inside of the roof, and a waterfall of pooled rain came splashing down onto him. He cursed and scrambled out of the way as my teeth chattered.

Liam reached into his bag to grab his jacket and then took my hand. "Come on."

He pulled me to my feet and led me out of the shelter and into the vegetation. The rain was slightly less driving under the canopy of trees, but the heavy drops still pelted the ground around us in loud splats. We found a tree that had fallen, and Liam climbed up onto its horizontal trunk off the ground. I sat down next to him and continued to shiver as the dampness soaked into my body.

"Here, put this on." Liam handed me his jacket. "It'll repel the rain a little."

I looked quizzically at him. "But what about you?"

"I'll be ok," he replied. "Here, take it."

He pushed the jacket further toward me again, and after a moment of hesitation, I took it and wrapped it around my shoulders as I shivered. He was right, it did help a bit.

"Thank you," I whispered.

Liam shook slightly, hunched over in his spot on the log, about a foot away from me. As my teeth continued to chatter, I looked down at the empty space between us, pondering the idea of moving closer. Surely shared body heat would help us both, but I didn't want to give the wrong impression. I bit my lip and stared at the space for another moment, contemplating the implications of such a bold move, but another gust of wind brought splatters of cold rain down on us and I instinctively pulled his jacket tighter and scooted a few inches toward him.

To my grateful surprise, he had the same reaction, closing the distance from his own side until we were pressed against each other. I immediately felt his heat in the spots where we touched, and a chill of a different kind sent new goosebumps across my skin.

I closed my eyes and buried my face in the collar of his leather jacket, inhaling his scent once again as I tried to stifle my shivers.

***

While I had never casually wondered if it was possible to sleep sitting up in the pouring rain, I knew now that the answer was a resounding no.

The last leg of the storm began to slow just as the light of a new day crept through the trees. I was still hunched over with my face buried in my knees, pressed into Liam on my left side when I opened my eyes slowly from my state of limbo. I wasn't really asleep, but I wasn't really awake either. My head felt heavy and my body lethargic. The jacket Liam had lent me was now completely waterlogged, and I let the heels of my feet fall to the ground as I turned to look at him.

Leaning against me slightly, his shoulders were slumped, and he didn't move.

"I think it's finally over," I croaked quietly as I began to peel the jacket from my shoulders.

Liam grunted and lifted his head. His eyes were swollen and red as he peered around. He ran his hand through his hair, took a deep breath, and stood up, putting an aching distance between us again. He didn't say anything as he stumbled away toward the beach.

With shaking legs, I managed to get to my feet, feeling like a drowned zombie. I took a shuddering breath and followed Liam out into the open. He was already recreating our SOS lettering from the branches that were now strewn across the beach. I walked to the bottles and coconuts I'd lined up to collect water. They were each filled to the brim. I picked up a coconut and poured the water into my mouth, gulping it hungrily as the cool liquid ran down my throat and coated my mouth in welcome moisture. The lifeboat was filled nearly halfway with water too. I let out a breath of relief. We'd be set for a few days. At least the storm had given us that.

I drained another half coconut and then walked one of the

bottles to Liam. He gratefully gulped the entire thing before handing it back to me.

"Another?" I asked.

He shook his head. "Perhaps in a bit."

I took a step back. "Do you need help?" I watched him drag the branches into place.

"I'm fine." His voice was short and clipped, and his movements were calculated and purposeful as he focused solely on his work.

I frowned and turned away, walking to the pile of logs where our fire had once been. Bending down, I touched my fingers to the wood. It was completely drenched. We'd have no chance of starting it back up until it dried out. But the rain had completely ceased, and the clouds were beginning to part. The sun would rejoin us soon.

Our shelter was a complete mess. During the night, the roof had mostly blown off, leaving just the bare structure, and there were puddles everywhere. We needed something sturdier.

I walked to the water's edge and sat down in the sand, running my hands across my damp, sunburnt skin. The tide kissed my toes gently with each surge, and there were hundreds of shells strewn around me that had washed up with the storm. I picked up a few, turning them around in my fingers and studying their intricacies. In another time, I would have loved to walk the beach, collecting these treasures as keepsakes. But here, they were just part of the landscape; small reminders that we were in a place of beauty, yet utter desolation.

My eyelids began to droop as I sat in silence, feeling the peek of sun start to warm me from the outside in. But I rubbed my forehead, knowing I needed to stay awake if Liam was too.

I turned to see him struggling with the wood for the fire, so I pulled myself up and crossed over to him.

"The wood is too wet to light," I said quietly.

"We need fire," he replied simply.

"You need sleep. The fire can wait."

He didn't look at me, but continued to stack the wood with exhausted, shaking hands as he knelt in the sand. "No, sleep can wait. We need fire, we need a new shelter, we need food. You're going to be skin and bones soon."

I looked down at my body. I could tell I'd lost weight since we'd been here, and I was already thin to begin with, but I hadn't realized it was that noticeable to him too.

"You have to sleep," I pleaded, ignoring the blush that tried to creep onto my cheeks.

When he looked up at me, his eyes were angry. "Look, Cora. We can't just sit around idly like this. We're not going to survive if we don't get these things done." He used an imposing, forceful tone that I hadn't heard from him yet, and it gave me pause.

I held his gaze for a moment before taking a breath and kneeling next to him. I touched my hand to his shaking one. "Liam, listen to me. You're exhausted, I'm exhausted." I pointed at my chest. "We aren't going to be successful with any of these tasks until we've slept. Look, the sand is drying. You should lay down and let your body rest. Let the sun dry out the wood, and then you can build a fire."

His frustrated eyes bore into mine, laced with redness and fatigue. He clenched his jaw, weighing the options in his head until finally, he dropped his hands from the wood.

"Just a short nap," he exhaled.

As he spoke, I noticed the bandage that wrapped around his wound was becoming discolored from his strenuous routine.

"Let me change that first," I pointed toward his head.

When he didn't object, I walked to the suitcases, tore a new strip of clothing, and grabbed the antibacterial ointment. When I returned, he closed his eyes as I untied his old bandage and pulled it slowly from his wound. He winced slightly as I removed it, and the deep cut was far from healed, but it didn't appear to be infected. I placed a dab of ointment on my finger and gently applied it to the gash. Liam never opened his eyes as I worked. His shoulders rose and fell evenly under his dirtied shirt, and I wondered if maybe he'd dozed off. But when I tied the new bandage, he finally opened them again and looked directly at me.

"Thank you," he said quietly, almost apologetically.

I tried to smile, but I was so tired, the muscles in my face barely worked. We both stood up and walked back to the shelter. The floor was damp, but not drenched. We grabbed a few stray palm fronds and threw them over the roof for shade and then we collapsed onto the unforgiving bamboo. The second my head touched the ground, I felt sleep finally take me captive.

***

The next thing I knew, I was waking up from a dreamless sleep. I blinked and stretched, turning my head toward the water to see that the sun hung close to the horizon. Was it still morning, or had I slept all day? When I remembered that the sun had set on this side of the island last night, I knew it must be evening again.

My brain felt slightly less cloudy as I sat up and peered at Liam, who still slept soundly next to me. He laid on his back with his dark hair sprawled messily around his head. His chest rose and fell rhythmically, and I allowed myself the moment to admire him. He was ruggedly handsome, with dark features and a pensive brow that gave him an edge that others didn't have. And now, his beard, which was coming in thick and fast, tipped him into a new level of manly charm.

I blinked and shook my head, tearing my eyes from him. I crept out of the shelter as quietly as I could and walked to check the pile of firewood again. To my delight, it was dry now, so I set to work starting a new fire. It was a patient job as I mimicked what I saw Liam do before. I sat with the mirror aimed at the kindling for many frustrating minutes until I realized that the heat from the low-hanging sun must not be enough to generate a flame. Liam had been right that getting the fire lit was top priority. Our daylight was now gone, and we'd have to wait until tomorrow. I threw the mirror to the ground with a huff and looked back at Liam, who was still unmoving.

I sighed and stood up, placing my hands on my hips as I studied our makeshift campsite. There was nothing for me to do other than sit and wait for a disgruntled Liam to wake up, so instead, I decided to explore the island.

I walked around its perimeter slowly, letting the waves graze my bare feet. Just as he had confirmed, there was no land to be seen on any horizon. We were really, truly alone.

About halfway around, I turned inward toward the lagoon and came upon the rocks where Liam and I had sat the night before. I climbed up onto a larger one and pulled my knees to my chest as unrestrained strands of my hair blew in the soft breeze. The growling of my stomach was now so common that I barely felt it. But when I sat in silence, I couldn't tear my focus from my ailments. Physically, I was bruised and scratched. I was famished, exhausted, and sunburnt. I couldn't hold my hands steady, and my head felt like it weighed a million pounds. My knee was getting better, but emotionally, I'd lost a lot of hope. It had now been three days since we'd seen the plane fly nearby. Five days on the island. Surely, if they'd seen us, they would have returned by now. Maybe Liam was right; they'd found the wreckage and assumed us dead as well, lost to the depths of the ocean.

I closed my eyes and breathed in the fresh sea air. In any other situation, I would have welcomed a calming trip to the beach. It could truly be relaxing and rejuvenating…in any other situation. But here, nature was only taking from us. It gave us nothing in return.

I thought about Tess. If she knew I was stranded on an island with Liam Montgomery, she'd say something comical, as if I were living out a cliché fantasy. But in our threatening state of hunger, this wasn't a tale of a lucky fan and her incredible encounter. This was a tragedy. Danger lurked around every corner. Death was closer than it had ever been. With a gulp, I let that awareness sink in as I gazed across the lagoon and out toward the sea, watching the burning sun set over the horizon.

EIGHT

"I was wondering where you'd wandered off to." Liam's deep voice startled me from behind.

I closed my eyes, waiting for the inevitable outburst I was sure was coming. But he quietly climbed up next to me on the rock and stared across the lagoon.

"I'm sorry for being short with you earlier." He spoke gently.

I was caught off guard by his apology, but I shrugged. "We're both exhausted. I understood."

"Well, I shouldn't have taken it out on you."

I turned my gaze to him. "I didn't see it that way."

He met my eyes briefly and then looked back to the water. "Fair enough. But I *am* sorry."

Neither of us spoke for a long moment. I rubbed my hands up and down my face and yawned. Somehow, I was tired already, even though I'd woken up just over an hour ago. Lethargy and fatigue were creeping in, and I knew it was because I'd barely eaten anything in almost a week.

I stifled a second yawn as I turned back to Liam. "So, the firewood should be dry enough in the morning to light."

Liam closed his eyes. "Let's not talk about the fire right now."

I shut my mouth quickly. *Nope, not time to bring that up yet.* "Ok, do you feel more rested after sleeping?"

He massaged the bridge of his nose. "I do feel a tad better, but I'd rather not talk about that either. Can we just, for a moment, pretend like we're not stranded, starving, and miserable?"

I tensed at his clipped tone and frowned. How could I pretend not to be stranded, starving, and miserable, if that's all I could think about?

But, with a sigh, I understood. This whole situation was taking its toll on us not only physically, but emotionally too. Our days were spent stocking wood and coconuts, and failing at our fishing attempts, over, and over, and over again. A break from our survival-charged reality sounded like a welcome distraction.

It was time for me to capitalize on the mental strength I'd promised myself.

I sat up straighter and brushed the sand from my hands. "Ok, I'll play along. If we weren't stuck here in the middle of nowhere, maybe right now I'd be delivering another catered meal to you on set? And hopefully, I'd have enough guts to ask you for an autograph this time."

The corner of his mouth twitched up. "Would you like my autograph?"

I smirked. "Well, I think we're kinda past that now."

“Are you sure? I think I have paper and a pen in my bag.” He pointed back toward our campsite with a wink.

I laughed. “I’ll tell you what. If we make it through this and get back home, then you can give me that autograph.”

He nodded, but a frown took the place of his smile. I’d brought up our reality again by mistake.

Darn.

I cleared my throat and continued. “So, if I did meet you that second time, I would probably have said something like, ‘I’m such a fan of your work. Tell me, where did you learn to dance like that?’”

A faint twinkle reappeared in his eye as he turned to me. “Well, I started dancing when I was five. My mum dragged me to my older sister’s classes, and I’d watch her practice, mimicking the steps from the corner of the room.”

I beamed at him, picturing little Liam dancing across the floor.

“Mum finally enrolled me in some of my own classes. I eventually settled on modern ballroom, and the rest was history.”

I couldn’t help but smile as he divulged the little details about his life. Fame or not, he was just like the rest of us, following dreams and goals he’d developed in childhood.

“Do you dance?” Liam asked.

I practically snorted. “No. I prefer to trip over my own feet instead.”

He laughed.

“What else do you like to do?” I asked.

“Well, I draw. Though I’m wildly untalented at it,” he chuckled.

"That, I doubt," I replied. "What do you draw?"

"Landscapes mostly. You'd be surprised at my level of incoordination with a pencil though," he laughed again. "I'd do best to stick with dancing and acting."

"I think that's what the world would want." I feigned seriousness, but broke a grin.

When he smiled back, he shifted himself on the rock so that he was directly facing me. "What do you do when you're not crafting delicious turkey sandwich recipes?"

I rolled my eyes. "You're still thinking about that, aren't you?"

"Sure as hell, I am."

I scratched my temple, peering up at the stars that were beginning to show in the evening sky. "Well, I run. It clears my head. And I read."

"What do you read?"

"Anything and everything. My parents used to have to force me to rejoin the real world when I'd spend my entire day with my nose inside a book."

"It's a great way to escape," he agreed. His eyes raked over my face.

I smiled and tucked a few strands of hair behind my ear as he watched me. "Do you read?"

"A little." He pulled his bottom lip between his teeth as he held my gaze for a little too long. "You know, your eyes are the *exact* color of the ocean."

I blushed. Compliments always made me uncomfortable.

"It's a really beautiful color." He smiled.

"Thanks," I replied quietly, focusing on dislodging a bit of sand trapped beneath my fingernail.

Thankfully, he didn't say anything more, but when I looked

up at him again, he'd pressed his lips together and dropped his eyes to the ground. "Tomorrow, we'll be better rested. We'll build a new fire, a stronger shelter, and we'll work on the fishing again."

I sighed at the conversation's change in direction, wishing it didn't have to. For just a few moments, we'd escaped. We'd gone somewhere else together—somewhere we could be at peace. But reality had sprung to the forefront again.

Liam climbed down off the rock. "We should head back and get some more sleep."

As I stepped down too, he grabbed my hand to steady me, but as soon as my feet touched the ground, he let go quickly.

And just like that, we were stranded again.

***

The mosquitoes were ten times worse at night. While I'd slept decently during the light of day, the darkness brought sharp stings and an onslaught of itching bumps. Even through our clothing, we were getting bit nonstop. It was enough to drive us crazy, and the frustration was becoming overwhelming.

When the sun finally peeked through the trees, Liam sat up and rubbed his forehead. "We have *got* to figure out this bug situation. I'm about to lose my mind."

I sighed and pulled myself up too, scratching a large bump on my knee and trying to ignore the gnawing hunger in my stomach.

He took a deep breath and stood up. "We'd do best to make use of our daylight." He looked around the beach, now dimly lit by the rising sun. He pushed his tangled curls off his forehead and tightened the bandage around his head. "If we're going to make it through another storm, we need a better shelter. Maybe a different location out of the wind."

My legs felt weaker today as I got to my feet, and I had to pause for a moment as the edges of my vision threatened to close in. I reached for a coconut, trying to disguise my frailty, and cracked it open on a rock. I'd perfected the skill now, and I bit into the white interior as we began a walk along the sand.

"I want to stay close to the beach. The bugs will relent more here than deep in the trees, but at the same time, the winds are brutal out in the open," Liam explained.

We walked almost halfway around the island's perimeter until we came upon a small, smooth sandy beach situated between a gathering of large boulders.

"Hang on." He stopped and squinted toward the tree line.

I followed his gaze. This part of the island had a rocky façade that opened up to a small tree-spotted beach.

"Is that a cave?" He began walking toward the formation. "How did I miss that before?"

What I saw could barely be described as a cave, but rather a section of rock that hung over a small alcove, maybe eight feet in diameter. The ground was smooth and flat, sloping gently down onto the beach.

"This is perfect," Liam said eagerly as we crossed toward it. "The water won't pool, and we can lean a wall of bamboo and palm fronds against this edge." He extended his arms, envisioning his plan.

"And the fire could go here." I pointed at a sandy spot between two large boulders out of the wind.

"Yep, you're right. This will do well," Liam replied, placing his hands on his hips and surveying the area like he was buying a plot of land.

I wiped my already damp forehead as my stomach growled loudly. It was an empty, ringing, helpless feeling, and I leaned against one of the boulders for support, still nibbling my coconut. I stared at the rocky opening with a sigh. This was home. For now, at least. I longed for my innerspring mattress and a slice of pizza, but wishes weren't coming true today.

What followed was a long morning of transporting our belongings to this side of the island and gathering materials for our new shelter. We occasionally stopped to eat coconuts or drink from our supply of lifeboat rainwater, but mostly we worked together to craft our new 'residence.' I took more breaks than Liam did, pausing to rest my weak, hungry body, but I was successful in splitting and laying palm fronds across the floor and the outside wall of the structure. He held the pieces while I secured them tightly with vines and long leaves. Liam did all the heavy lifting and even crafted a door-like panel that we could close to ward off any rain.

It was much sturdier and more weatherproof than the makeshift lean-to we'd started with, and when I stood back and studied it, I felt a sense of pride. But there was also a gnawing anxiety within me as I realized that we'd finally resorted to building something more permanent. We'd been stranded for the better part of a week now, and I was beginning to fear that we'd be here much longer.

At noon, when the sun was at its strongest, Liam successfully started a new fire between the wind-blocking boulders. He seemed in better spirits once we'd finished these tasks, and we sat by the flames while he whittled down the tip of a long stick, crafting a fishing spear.

"Alright, I think I'm going to give it a go." He pushed himself to his feet.

"I'd like to help," I said, standing up too quickly and needing to rest my hands on my knees for a moment.

"Are you sure? You should rest." Liam furrowed his brow.

When my head cleared, I stood up straight and took a deep breath. "No, no, I'm fine. I want to help."

He watched me with concern. "Alright...here, you take this one. I'll make another."

I took the spear and made my way in toward the lagoon. Stepping into the warm tide, I eyed the small fish that swam nearby and positioned myself with the tip aimed and ready. I had no idea what I was doing, but the emptiness in my stomach urged me to try.

The fish were not large by any stretch of the imagination, and I knew they'd be difficult to pierce, but after a few moments, when nothing bigger came along, I flung the spear at one of them. It wobbled as it flew and missed the fleeing fish by a good yard. I sucked in an agitated breath and walked to retrieve it, by which the rest of the fish scattered as well. I reset my position and waited again.

My second and third attempts were the same failure, and by then, Liam had appeared behind me with his new spear.

"Any luck?" he asked.

"None whatsoever," I replied.

"That's alright, keep at it." He waded into the shallow lagoon and chose a position twenty feet away for himself.

We worked for what felt like an hour, spearing, and then resetting and waiting, each time coming up empty. I stood back and watched him a few times. He was better at it than I was—more patient, and he threw his spear faster. I watched him to learn, but I also watched him because he was wearing a sleeveless shirt that showed off his flexed arms as he threw. My mind began to wander, wondering how those firm muscles would feel under my fingers, or if they would flex the same if they were wrapped around me. But as I studied him, I noticed the bones on his shoulders protruded more so than they had a few days ago. He was struggling with his hunger too, but hiding it much better. I hadn't really noticed until now.

I glared into the water, wishing I weren't so obviously weak.

As the blistering sun beat down on the back of my neck, my stomach grumbled again, and I felt a wave of sweat suddenly wash over me. I squinted at the swimming fish, trying to pick my next target, but they danced in my vision and my focus wavered. Soon, my ears were ringing and the lapping waves at my feet began to throw me off balance.

I stumbled slightly, trying to keep my footing, but the world went fuzzy, and I dropped my spear as I brought my hand to my damp forehead. A swarm of fish skittered past my ankle, startling me, and I tripped, falling to my knees in the shallow water.

"Whoa!" Liam called from nearby, dropping his own spear and dashing toward me. "Cora, are you alright?" He looped his arms under mine and helped me to my feet.

I continued to hold my forehead, suddenly very out of breath. "Yeah, I'm fine."

He released his grip on my arms, but my legs would not hold my weight and I fell again, this time directly into his chest. He grasped my elbows, holding me up against him.

"Ok, time to get out of the sun." He spoke gently as he wrapped his arm around my back, supporting me almost completely as he helped me limp up the beach.

"I'm fine…" I whispered again through shallow breaths.

"No, you're not." He sat me down under the shade of a low palm. I hung my head between my knees, trying to regain full consciousness.

"What's wrong?" He crouched down next to me.

I squinted my eyes, trying and failing to find the answer myself. "I don't know. I got chills and then felt like I was gonna faint. I don't know what came over me."

"You're not getting enough to eat. Combine that with the hard work and beating sun, and your body can't take it."

I frowned. "But *you're* doing just fine."

"Well, that's not true. I'm ravenous."

I wished I was *only* ravenous. I pursed my lips and shook my head. "I'm sorry."

"Sorry for what?"

I peered up at him and gestured to myself. "I want to help. I'm sorry I'm so pathetic."

"What you need to do right now is regain your energy." He handed me another coconut and a bottle of water. "I'll continue to fish, and you can rest."

I sighed.

"Do you need anything else?" he asked.

A new body and a cheeseburger. Not necessarily in that order.

"I'm fine," I responded defeatedly.

He let me be, and for the rest of the afternoon, I sat on the beach, sipping my water and nibbling my coconut like a child in time-out, watching Liam struggle with his spear. He moved up and down the lagoon, trying over and over again without success. He even moved to the open ocean and spent a few hours in the shallow waters there. I wondered how much longer he'd last before he gave up. At what point would his patience crumble?

As evening fell, I sat by the fire, absorbing its warmth. Shivering was another symptom of my extreme hunger. I was only cold half the time, but I couldn't seem to cease the chattering in my teeth, and my hands constantly trembled.

When it was too dark to see anymore, Liam walked slowly back toward me, his shoulders and face red from the sun. I cracked open a coconut and handed it to him as he sat down with a thud.

"Ugh, I'm wrecked. What am I not doing right?" His deep voice pierced the quiet of the night. "There has to be some trick or technique I'm just not getting."

"I'm sure there is something," I agreed. "But no one expects you to be an expert spearfisher immediately."

Liam scoffed. "I've been at it all day, and yesterday with the net. You'd expect I could catch at least *one* measly fish."

I frowned. I didn't want to upset him, but I was worried too. Without protein, we wouldn't survive. We'd been taking some of the vitamins I'd found in the elderly couple's suitcase, but they didn't replace real nutrition, and they would only last so long. Eventually, the coconuts wouldn't get us by on their own.

I thought back to a documentary I'd once watched about a plane crash in the Atlantic. Had the rescue crews searched for more than a few days? I thought maybe they did, but that was because they hadn't found the wreckage. Would they have any reason to keep searching if they thought we were dead? I imagined my parents planning my funeral, the tears falling from my mother's eyes, the trembling lip of my father, the hugs between my friends. I wanted to scream out to them that I was alive.

I'm here! But I'm struggling to survive.

My eyebrows pulled together as a lump formed in my throat again. I wanted to be home, cozy and warm, safe and sound. I couldn't believe how quickly I'd lost my motivation. I was losing myself more each day, each *hour*. I could feel my body slowly failing me. How long until we reached the point of no return?

I pulled my knees to my chest and rested my forehead on them. "They're not looking for us anymore, are they?" I asked quietly, not wanting a response, but hoping there would be encouragement in his words.

Liam was quiet for a moment before he sighed. "No, Cora, I don't think they are."

Shock. I felt it immediately. I hadn't expected him to agree so easily. I kept my face shielded from him as I stifled a sob. Hearing him concur without hesitation terrified me more than anything.

"What about vi…visitors to the island? Someone has to own it, right?" My breath caught in a quiet sniffle as I spoke, but Liam didn't notice.

"Have you *seen* any evidence of humanity here?" His words came out agitated. "It's not exactly a tourist destination."

I squeezed my eyes shut as a tear dropped onto the sand beneath my legs. "So, is this it?"

The anger in his voice didn't lift. "I don't know. I'm sure this island won't go untouched forever, but by the time someone finds us, it might be too late."

His response stung me with fear, and I brought my hand to my mouth, pressed between my face and my knees as I stifled a heavier sob.

"I'm obviously incapable of providing a decent food supply, so that'll probably be our demise." His voice was wrought with self-loathing. "We apparently aren't skilled enough for this challenge, and we'll pay the price."

I felt the guilt, *hard.* I wanted to be strong for him, to boost his confidence, but I was the worst companion. I was another mouth to feed who couldn't pull her own weight.

It all crashed around me in an instant, and I broke down. My body shook as I let the tears fall, accepting our failure.

Liam scooted toward me. "Ahh, that was thick of me. I'm sorry, Cora."

I kept my head buried. "You're right though. We can't do this."

"Of course we can, of course we can," he cooed, pushing a strand of hair from my forehead. The line where his finger traced my skin felt like fire to the icy fear in my soul.

"I didn't mean what I said," he continued. "I'm shattered and not thinking clearly. But I haven't lost hope yet."

I lifted my head and squinted at him through puffy eyes. I didn't believe him. "You should be home with Kate. If she finds out you tried so hard and then didn't survive..." I choked on my words.

He watched me with knitted brows. "Look, we have a dry place to sleep tonight. We're doing this. If we stick with it, we'll get better at it."

"I'm losing hope." My voice was a strained whisper.

His warm brown eyes stared deeply into mine, and he

paused before he spoke. "I promise you I will not stop trying. *If* you promise *me* you won't stop either." He scooted even closer and wrapped his arm around my back, pulling me into him.

I obliged, letting myself collapse into his chest. "Ok..."

He drew me in until I was locked in his full embrace, and he whispered into my hair. "I promise."

With my face pressed into his shirt, his chest slowly rose and fell, and my sobs began to slow. His strength wrapped around me, engulfing me in a warmth that brought forth a calm I couldn't find on my own. I'd tried so long to comfort myself, but there was a security in his embrace that made me feel like I could really depend on him.

"I don't want to die." I finally whispered the words we'd both been holding so close to our hearts. Because admitting the fear only made it more real.

"You're not going to die." His lips brushed against my hair as he spoke, hugging me tighter. "I won't let that happen."

NINE

After a slightly better night of sleep in our new shelter, the next morning went much the same. I stayed by the fire, resting and throwing an occasional new log onto the flames while Liam went out to fish. In an attempt to be useful, I busied myself with figuring out how to weave palm leaves into softer floor mats for the cold stone of our shelter. I had just finished a decent prototype when Liam returned. He was empty-handed again.

I passed him a coconut as he sat down in the sand next to me. He drank the water in long gulps. "I have a new plan."

I eyed him hesitantly. "What's that?"

He licked the coconut water from his lips and wiped the back of his hand across his growing beard. He looked down at his spear, which he'd been tinkering with all day. After lots of trial and error, he'd figured out how to attach the green resistance band I'd found in the suitcase to one end. When he pulled it taut, he could sling the spear more quickly through the water than when he simply threw it.

"I think I've been in the wrong place. The fish I'm trying to spear near shore are too small to target. I think I need to swim out further to find bigger ones."

I gulped. "Deeper into the ocean? Are you a good swimmer?"

"Yeah, I can swim just fine," he replied, taking a confident bite from his coconut.

I knew we needed real food more than anything else right now, and Liam was probably right about the larger fish further offshore, but the ocean was strong and unpredictable.

I peered out at the expanse. The wind was gentler today and the waves were fairly calm. Our options were limited. We could either sit back and wait to die of malnourishment, or take a risk to turn our predicament around.

But, if something happened to Liam… I'd be left all alone. The thought sent a painful knot to my throat. I knew I couldn't survive by myself.

Nevertheless, I knew what had to be done.

"I think you should try it." I forced the words out, my conviction fueled mostly by my grumbling stomach.

He nodded and stood up immediately, making me wonder what he would have done if I'd tried to stop him. Was my approval what ultimately made his decision? I didn't take well to that kind of responsibility. But before I had a chance to backtrack, he grabbed the hem of his shirt and pulled it over his head, revealing his broad and chiseled torso as he picked up his spear.

My mouth threatened to drop open, but I held it shut as my

eyes traveled across his chest, sparsely covered in dark curls that trailed in a line all the way down to the dip of his hips where they met his shorts. I'd seen him shirtless when he went out to wash, but that was always from a great distance. This was the first time I'd had a front-row seat.

"Please...be careful," I managed to squeak out.

"I will," he replied, clearly not noticing my gawking as he turned to walk away.

I watched him retreat, admiring his wide, muscular back as I swallowed my accumulated saliva. But I managed to snap myself back to focus and call after him. "Hey, Liam..."

He stopped and turned to face me as he balanced the spear on his bare shoulder.

I tried to keep my eyes on his face. "The ocean is stronger than you think. Be smart. Don't risk your life for one fish."

A compassionate grin formed on his face. "I'll be careful, I promise. Don't sit and fret about me."

I frowned, letting my eyes dip to his chest once more, but just for an instant. "It's unlikely that I'll be able to think of anything else."

He cocked his head in sympathy. "I'll be back before you know it. Get those hot coals ready. We're dining on fish tonight."

And with that, he turned on his heel and disappeared beyond the shelter of rocks that surrounded our beach and into the salty, unforgiving waves.

I rested my chin on my hand, fretting exactly like he'd told me not to. Had I really just let him go? Was my hunger worth the risk? How long would it take him? I began to panic as I realized I had no way to keep track of time. I briefly imagined sharks circling and strong waves crashing into immovable boulders, but I shook my head, pushing my anxieties away. He was confident. I could see that today. I needed to let him try.

My mind wandered to his bare chest again and then drifted to the memory of last night when he'd cradled me in his arms, promising me that he wouldn't give up. I'd been embarrassed by my tears, but he'd had the unique ability to make me feel secure. I could still feel his warm embrace and his fingers brushing across my hair. A smile touched my lips as I imagined his strong hands around my arms, caressing my back, tracing the curve of my neck…

Not now, Cora.

I stopped my fantasy in its tracks. Last night, all he'd been doing was comforting my sadness. That was it. Nothing more. He had a girlfriend. Kate was home grieving as if he'd died, and I was here, starving to death while fantasizing about his bare chest. It was disrespectful, and also shockingly delusional.

Maybe I was losing my mind too.

A deep breath of the clean ocean air helped me to stand up slowly. My head thumped painfully, but I set off to distract myself. I started by tightening the palm fronds that were secured to the outer wall of our shelter. Then I added my handwoven pads to the ground on the interior. When I stepped back out into the sun, I stopped to check our lifeboat. The water was getting low. As much as I hated to admit it, we needed another storm.

Quickly becoming exhausted by my small tasks, I found a shady spot in the sand and laid down on my back, gazing up at the clouds. Today, they were large, fluffy, and bright white. I remembered, as a child, I would search for shapes I recognized.

It was a fun, carefree game and I wondered if I could go there again today. I studied the formations, searching for familiarity.

First, I found a hamburger.

I blinked, clearly distracted by my stomach.

Next, I spotted a slice of cheesecake.

I sighed.

When I'd located a pile of mashed potatoes and gravy, I closed my eyes in despair, helpless to my agony.

My stomach clenched painfully on its emptiness, my head was swimming, and I felt disoriented even when laying down, so I focused again on the only other thing that could divert me: Liam.

He'd been gone for at least an hour, maybe two. I knew he was just as famished as I was, yet he carried on, pushing himself hard to provide for us. There was luck in having him by my side.

I thought about everyone else on the plane who'd perished. Would they have had the persistence and motivation that he did? I could see that he was a fighter, even when he was down on himself. He was tougher than he probably knew, and he was so selfless. He'd stopped to search the burning plane for anyone alive before saving himself. I surely would have died if he hadn't hauled my limp body from the wreckage.

I would have died.

An overwhelming sense of gratitude gripped me. Had I really thanked him enough for what he'd done? I made a mental note to make sure I did.

A soft breeze blew across my hair, sending wispy blonde strands across my forehead. I forced my overly cluttered mind to become blank as I lay on the ground at the mercy of nature's attempts to defeat me.

"Ready to eat?"

My eyes flew open, and I blinked into the sunlight. Liam was standing over me, glistening with drops of ocean water that were splattered across his bare chest. His curls hung in damp strands around his face and his wet shorts clung to his legs. On his face was a cheeky grin and in his hands were two shiny, plump fish.

I sat up so quickly I almost toppled over. "Oh my..." I stared in disbelief. And then I lurched to my feet as if my fatigue was instantly cured. "Liam...you did it!"

He grinned widely as he set the fish on a nearby rock, and before I had a chance to stop myself, I crossed the distance between us and flung my arms around his neck. He stumbled backward, surprised by my hug. But with barely a second of hesitation, he wrapped his arms around me too.

"Sorry, I'm a bit wet," he laughed.

"I don't even care," I breathed as I pulled away from him, looking up into his sparkling eyes. "I can't believe you did it."

His expression turned to playful offense. "What? You didn't think I could do it?"

I smirked, taking another step back and wringing my hands together. "No, of course I knew you could." I blushed, suddenly embarrassed by my physical display of gratitude. I turned my eyes to the fish, eyeing them hungrily.

"We've surely earned this meal." He picked up two sturdy sticks and pierced them through the fish before taking them to the fire and positioning them over the flames.

I followed him, straightening my now-damp shirt as I sat down. Liam disappeared into the shelter briefly and then returned, pulling on a white t-shirt, much to my dismay.

"Was it difficult?" I asked as we cooked. "Once you swam deeper, I mean."

"It took me a bit to find the right spot, but once I did, there were loads of fish. It was so simple, Cora." He smiled, laughing at himself. "I wasted so much time close to shore."

I sighed happily, watching the fish start to sizzle above the heat. "So, you think it's repeatable?"

"Oh, most definitely," he nodded.

For the first time since we'd been stranded, a true sense of hope coursed through my veins, like water released from a kink in a hose. If we had food—real food—we could do this. If we could eat, we could survive.

"I'm *so* excited," I almost squealed as I watched our meal cook.

Liam simply beamed at me as he turned the fish on their sticks.

Once they were done, we removed them from the fire and pulled the white, flaky nourishment from the bones. The first bite was heaven. As soon as it hit my empty, suffering stomach, I became ravenous. I couldn't imagine I'd ever tasted something so buttery smooth and flavorful as this unseasoned mystery-fish delicacy. I stuffed bite after bite into my mouth until only the bare bones remained. When I came up for air, I glanced at Liam, who had also licked his clean.

I breathed a sigh of contentment, leaned back on my elbows, and closed my eyes, basking in my fullness. My stomach was so shrunken that one small fish was enough to satisfy my hunger for the moment. And immediately, I could think clearer. When I opened my eyes again, Liam was staring at me with a crooked smile.

"What?" I raised a playful eyebrow.

He continued to grin. "I'm just glad you're feeling better."

"*So* much better," I agreed, pulling myself up to sit again and eying him sincerely. "Thank you."

He shrugged. "I was worried about you. I made a decision that I wasn't coming back without fish today."

I smiled. The sun was now hanging low in the sky, sending deep pink hues across the horizon. The flames danced across Liam's features, flickering and casting shadows down his nose and lips. I watched him for a moment as I remembered my thoughts from earlier.

"I don't think I ever properly thanked you for saving my life…" I paused. "And now you've essentially just done it again. You never had to carry me off that plane. I could have gone with the rest of them…"

"Cora…" he began softly.

"I don't know how to repay you," I finished.

His eyes were laced with an emotion I didn't quite recognize. "I wasn't going to leave you to die. And I'm so grateful you've survived." He paused. "For you, of course, but also because I can't imagine being alone out here. There is a comfort in having someone to lean on."

I looked down at my thin, useless hands. "I don't think I'm much to lean on."

"Sure you are." He smiled. "I would have lost my sanity if you weren't here with me. I don't do well with complete solitude. And you've been so encouraging. I needed that."

I took a deep, undecided breath. "I suppose you're right. Together we're stronger. We have to work together as a team and support each other."

When I looked back up at him, his eyes were still locked on mine as he nodded his head, and then he sat back and let out a weary chuckle.

"What's funny about that?" I asked, wrinkling my nose.

He wiped his hand down his face. "Life is just interesting..." He paused. "I wish Kate shared your thoughts."

I cocked my head to the side. "She doesn't?"

Liam scratched his head, shrugging and tossing his fish bones onto the fire. "With her, it's kind of always the 'Kate Show.'" He used air quotes with his fingers. "If she's not happy, no one can be happy. And if *I'm* not happy, she's usually mad at me for not being more positive."

I frowned slightly at his description, carefully crafting my next words. "Don't take offense, but...you don't seem to have a lot of good things to say about her. Why are you still together?"

Liam took a deep breath as if he already knew the question was coming. "I don't know if I have a clear answer for that." He scratched his cheek. "We have a lot of fun. Or at least, we used to. But we struggle a lot now. I think I'm just always hoping she'll change. Hoping maybe she'll grow up a bit." He looked at me with guilt. "I know, that's not the way to go about it."

I forced a smile. "People change. That's not out of the question."

Liam watched the flames. "Eh, everyone's got a base personality though. I think I've started to see hers."

I tightened my lips. I wanted to press further, but I wasn't going to sit here and talk Liam out of his relationship, especially when I knew Kate was grieving him as we spoke. Plus, I didn't know the whole story, and it wasn't my place for an opinion.

He seemed to be content with my silence and changed the

subject. "So, how was the fish?"

I laughed. "I can confidently say that after today, fish is now my favorite food."

"Yeah, it's shot to the top of my list too." He smiled.

I shifted my gaze to the sunset, which hung at its lowest point, almost completely obscured by the horizon, and the gentle sea breeze blew across my face as I took a deep, cleansing breath. "You know, I haven't really had a chance to appreciate this place. "With a full belly and a little bit of hope, you could actually call it beautiful."

In my periphery, I saw Liam respond, but he wasn't looking at the sunset. His eyes were on me. "You're right, but the beauty has always been there. You just have to open your eyes to see it."

TEN

Palm leaves blowing in the breeze.

Crisp, clear, fresh mornings.

Tree climbing and coconut hauling.

Parched thirst before cleansing rainstorms.

Cool sips of freshly pooled water.

Nervous anticipation of fishing trips in dangerous waves.

Relief upon a safe return.

Crackling flames on silent evenings.

Savory, flaky, white fish.

Full bellies and thoughtful conversations.

Burning red sunsets.

A companionship growing.

For the first time since the crash, I was finding beauty in our circumstance. The island had poetry to it, ebbing and flowing like the wind and the waves, reminding us that our lives were hanging on the edge, but we had the tools to sustain us if we looked hard enough.

It had been five days since we'd dined on our first real meal. Liam now had spearfishing down to a science and he was able to provide multiple fish for us every evening. It was a luxury neither of us had expected, and it was amazing how easily my strength returned after a few nourishing meals.

Liam was in better spirits too. I started to see bits and pieces of his true personality; the part of him he'd kept hidden beneath his anxiety until now. The results were in: he was cheeky and sarcastic—much less serious than he'd been during our first week, and much friendlier than he'd ever let the media see.

I often found myself entranced by him. He was so multi-faceted. One minute, he was making me laugh, and then next, we were diving into a deep and heartfelt conversation. We were starting to become more comfortable with each other, and we were finding out that we got along incredibly well.

Even though our struggles were still far from easy, and we longed for the comforts of home and the faces of our loved ones, I found myself realizing that there was a whole lot of joy and fun hiding in our daily routine. At almost two weeks since the crash, every day was still a fight for survival, but we weren't slowly fading away anymore. We were working harder than ever before, but we were *living*.

Liam spoke of Kate only occasionally. Mostly, he wondered whether she was ok, and he hated the idea that she thought he was dead. I didn't blame him. He was in a horrible position, helplessly unable to assure and console her.

I usually kept my mouth shut when he spoke about her. When he asked me direct questions, I answered, but otherwise, I let him navigate his thoughts on his own. I had my own guilt to deal with. Images of my grieving family flashed before my eyes more often than I could bear.

Our biggest struggle currently was the nightly bugs. We still hadn't figured out how to keep them at bay, and we spent our nights covered from head to toe in clothing, trying to ward them off. It made for hot and uncomfortable sleep, but it was better than the itchy alternative.

This morning, I awoke from another night of broken slumber and pulled the shirt from my face. I laid still for a moment, sprawled on the floor of our cave, counting the tick marks we'd etched onto the stone wall to record the days we'd been stranded. It was still hard to believe we'd been here so long.

Liam appeared in the doorway, blocking the rising sun with his tall figure. "The tide is calm this morning. Fancy a walk?"

I rubbed my eyes and sat up. "Yeah, sure. Give me a sec."

"Sure. I'll meet you down there." He smiled and retreated outside.

I stretched my joints, releasing the tension from my agitated sleep, and I ran my hands up and down my thin arms with a yawn. I was still underweight compared to the way I'd arrived on the island, but it was no longer a steady decline. I seemed to be maintaining now that I wasn't constantly starving.

Reaching into my suitcase, I felt around for my toothbrush. I dabbed the tiniest bit of toothpaste onto the bristles and began to scrub at my teeth. I was rationing the travel-sized tube as much as I could, but I still tried to brush once a day. I'd seen

Castaway. I didn't need a tooth infection to add to my list of hardships, thank you very much.

After I was finished, I pulled my hair up into a bun and stepped outside. Liam was right, it was a calm morning, perfect for a walk along the sand. We took walks frequently since we didn't have much else to entertain us. Sometimes we stayed silent, locked in our own minds. Sometimes we talked. But it passed the time and helped us get more acquainted while learning the ins and outs of the island.

Liam was leaning against a large rock with his arms crossed, staring out at the horizon when I met him. His dark curls twisted softly in the gusts of wind, unhindered by the bandage that he'd stopped wearing a few days ago. Now just a small pink scar traced the right side of his face until it disappeared beneath the thick hair of his beard. I took a moment to admire him. He was still as handsome as the first time I'd laid eyes on him—maybe more now that I knew him on a new level.

When he sensed my approach, he uncrossed his arms and turned to me as a genuine smile formed on his face.

"Ready?" he asked.

"How did you sleep?" I smiled back at him, taking a few steps down the beach, avoiding his gorgeous and penetrating hazel eyes.

He followed alongside me. "Terribly as usual. You?"

"Same," I sighed. "I'm not sure we'll ever outsmart the bugs it seems."

"Maybe eventually we'll learn to welcome their tiny little stings," Liam suggested.

I eyed him sideways and saw that he was grinning at his own joke.

When he met my gaze, he let out a chuckle. He reached down and picked up a seashell and turned it around in his fingers. "You said that it was six months ago that you and Jacob split?"

I gulped as I responded tentatively. "Yes." We hadn't talked about Jacob since the first time I'd brought him up. I was surprised Liam even remembered his name.

"Do you think he's worried about you?"

I thought for a moment, remembering quickly how much Jacob had taken our relationship for granted. "I'm sure he was shocked by the news, but we haven't spoken since we split."

"How did you meet?" Liam asked.

I let my mind travel back to a year and a half ago. I could still see Jacob sitting nervously across from me at the café table, his hands clasped tightly in front of him. It was probably the most invested he'd ever been in me.

"We were set up on a blind date by a mutual friend."

"Did you hit it off right away?"

"Well," I began. "He was handsome, for starters. That pulled me in *real* quick. So, there was an instant attraction there, but he also made me laugh and he said the right things. He was a really smooth talker."

"Ah, the smooth talker," Liam scrunched his nose.

I shoved his arm playfully. "Hey, you're a pretty smooth talker yourself, Mister."

He looked at me with wide, spirited eyes. "What? I am *not*."

I chortled. "Pfft… you should hear yourself. With that accent, you're liable to knock any woman off her feet."

"You like the accent, do you?" Liam responded impishly with a wink.

Realizing I'd quickly dug myself into a hole far too deep to climb out of, I teasingly narrowed my eyes at him without a reply.

He answered with a grin that touched the corners of his eyes and made them sparkle.

I bit my lip and skipped ahead of him, splashing my toes through the water as I went. "You have to know what your accent does to your fans, right?" I called behind me as I went.

When I stopped and turned around to face him, he was watching me with a mischievous smirk.

"I know a bit." He stopped in front of me. "And I believe you confirmed earlier that you *are* a fan, did you not?"

I looked up at him, melting under his cheeky expression, and he stared down at me with playful patience, waiting for my response.

I bit my lip again, wishing I could produce another comeback, but I wasn't quick-witted enough. *"I might have."* My voice came out quiet, but I raised an eyebrow at him and turned again to keep walking.

He kept up with me this time as I tried to hide my face and the blush I knew was there.

"I rest my case," he stated simply.

"What case?" I laughed.

"The one that confirms you've got a bit of a thing for me, Miss Cora."

I dropped my jaw in mock astonishment. "I think you're a little full of yourself, *Mister* Liam."

He cracked up at that one, stepping past me with a smirk. "I'm just glad you can speak to me without fumbling over your words anymore."

I grinned into the wind. *Shoot,* had I been that bad? And had he really just accused me of the very real truth I was trying to hide from him? I loved his playful personality, but this time he was trying to get a confession out of me, and it roused the butterflies in my stomach that I'd long tried to repress.

Thankfully, he didn't say anything more, and we walked for a few silent moments until we reached a particularly vegetation-thick portion of the beach.

"Hey, will you teach me to climb?" I pointed toward a small coconut palm.

He eyed me carefully. "Are you sure you feel up to it?"

I nodded and set my hands on my hips. "Yeah, I feel fine now."

He pursed his lips, looked at the tree, and then back at me. "Alright."

I skipped over to the tree with Liam at my heels. He shook the trunk to test its strength, and then he brushed the sand from his bare feet and showed me how to grip onto the bark.

"The trick is to keep steady pressure and use your body weight as much as you can," he explained.

Stepping up to it, I gripped as high as I could on the trunk and pulled myself up so that my feet rested near the base. Even with the first step, I felt my muscles shake and burn under my own weight.

"Wow, it's so slippery." I hesitated as I tried to pull myself further.

"Try another step. I've got you." He placed his hands at my waist to steady me.

I twisted my head to look back at him. His fingers were firm on my hips as his eyes met mine. Immediately, I knew that I could not make it to the top. I'd expected it to be difficult, but my practically nonexistent muscles were now even more weakened after so many days of malnourishment. I squinted up at the coconuts. *Not a chance.* But I didn't want to admit my failure yet.

"You've got this," he encouraged.

I pushed with the full strength of my legs as Liam stood safely behind me. I managed one more step up until my feet slipped and I came tumbling down into him.

My back slammed against his chest as he looped his arms around my waist, hoisting me away from the tree and easily lowering me to the ground.

When my feet found the sand, I looked down at the inside of my calves, which were streaked with mild scratches. "Well, darn."

"You did good for a first try."

I eyed him skeptically. "You don't have to sugar coat your comments. I realize I failed."

The corner of his mouth turned up. "Ok, so maybe climbing's not your thing. But that's alright. I can handle the coconut-gathering."

With a sigh, I turned and began to walk back out to the beach. If I didn't have Liam with me, I surely would have died already. That reality was both disheartening and a blessing at the same time.

As I walked, I began to smell something familiar. The scent reminded me of a lemon surface cleaner my mother always used in our kitchen. I wiggled my nose, trying to find the source until I reached a bush with long thin leaves. As I leaned toward it, I confirmed the citrus scent.

"Liam," I called out to him. "Have you seen this plant before?"

He joined me and stuck his nose into the leaves, pulling his eyebrows together. "Lemon? Maybe lemongrass?"

I studied it for a moment. "It's a strong scent. I wonder if it might deter the bugs?"

He nodded in approval. "That's a decent thought, and worth a try." Pulling out the knife, he reached down and sliced a bunch of leaves from the plant and handed them to me. Then he sliced off a bunch for himself.

"Should we put them in the cave?" I asked.

"Couldn't hurt. They smell pleasant anyway," he replied with a smirk. "They'll spruce up the place."

"A little home décor?" I joked, eliciting another grin from him.

"Decorate away," he waved his hand toward me. "It could certainly use your feminine touch."

I smiled to myself, feeling useful for once, even if just for my *feminine touch.*

***

That evening, after we'd gorged ourselves on fish, we sat by the fire as I weaved baskets with palm leaves, a pastime I'd come to enjoy. Liam was sharpening his spear when he glanced up at me.

"Are you full enough?" he asked, studying me out of the corner of his eye.

"Oh yes, plenty," I replied. "I've been feeling so much better."

"I hated seeing you withering away like that."

"I'd still be in that state if it weren't for you."

"You don't think you could have learned to spear?" he asked, raising an eyebrow. "I have confidence in you."

My mouth pulled up at one corner. "Thanks for your confidence. But my skills paled in comparison to yours, and I don't think I was strong enough."

He studied his spear point carefully as he sharpened "Well, regardless of that, I think mentally, you're stronger than I am."

I pressed my lips together. "Yeah, I don't know."

"You've got a good head on your shoulders, Cora. You know what you want in life, and you're making it happen. Finding your way through the madness that is L.A., leaving a relationship that wasn't healthy for you. A lot of people wouldn't have had the guts."

I tucked a leaf into the rim of my current basket, finishing the loop. "My mom taught me to never settle for something that didn't make me happy."

"And I admire that about you."

I met his gaze and found that he was staring at me now. I breathed slowly, but my heart thumped loudly. *He* admired something about *me?* That was backward, and I didn't know how to respond.

But as I replayed my own words in my head, I realized that I really wasn't following my mother's advice at all. I wasn't happy working for my father. Not completely, at least. The truth was, I *was* settling.

"What are some of the things that make you happiest?" Liam asked, saving me from the awkward silence.

I rubbed my chin. "Family, friends, bike rides, autumn leaves…chocolate truffles." I smirked at the last one.

Liam smiled softly. "Ah yes, truffles indeed are the root of all happiness."

"And you?" I asked. "What do you love?"

He tilted his head back and gazed up at the darkening sky, thinking to himself. "Well, as you said, family, friends, and truffles top the list." He glanced at me with a wink. "But also, I love to meet new people and visit new places, and I love to draw, and dance of course."

My eyes lit up. "I should hope that dancing is one of your sources of happiness."

He laughed. "Yes, I miss it already, actually." This time, he stopped sharpening his spear as he watched me curiously.

I felt self-conscious under his inquisitive stare.

"I could teach you a few steps," he suggested quietly, almost with hesitation.

I gaped at him breathlessly, not believing he could possibly be asking me to dance. "Right here?"

He seemed to relax when I didn't immediately decline him. "Yes, right here."

"But there's no music." I felt my cheeks burn.

He stood up and extended his hand to me. "We don't need any."

I didn't budge for a moment, looking up at his smirking face as he waited for me to oblige. "I don't know…" I gulped. "I told you before… I'll just trip over myself."

"I won't let you fall." He waited patiently, still presenting his hand.

Oh dear, was this actually happening?

I knew I was about to make a major fool of myself, but I took a deep, shaking breath and placed my hand in his. He pulled me to my feet and guided me toward an open sandy area a few yards from the fire.

When he stopped and stood in front of me, he squeezed my hand gently. "Have you danced before?"

"No, not really," I replied. My mouth was drier than it was before our first rainstorm.

"Well, I'll teach you a bit of the Waltz, then. It's the easiest to learn, in my opinion." His voice grew steadier as he fell easily into his comfort zone. "The Waltz is based on a count of three… One two three. One two three. One two three." He spoke slowly, holding my gaze. "Keep that rhythm in your head."

I swallowed and nodded nervously.

"The basic step is the box step. We'll start with that." He stepped toward me, and as he took a visible breath, I watched his Adam's apple slip up his throat and then back down again.

Was he nervous too? Surely not. He'd danced with more women than I could probably count.

"So, you'll place your left hand on my shoulder," he said, and I tried desperately not to blush as I let him guide my hand there, feeling his broad, firm muscles under my fingertips.

Liam took his right hand and placed it on my back and then took my right hand in his left. "Now, keep your elbows high." He smiled and took another step toward me. He was so close I could feel the heat of his chest almost against mine. I wondered if he could hear my heart. It was pounding in my ears.

"Ok, follow my lead. First, you'll step your right foot back." He inched his left foot forward, guiding my foot backward. "Now, step out with your left and then follow with your right." We did so in unison. "Next, step forward with your left."

I felt his hand on my back, pulling me gently forward in his direction. I stumbled slightly and had to grip his shoulder tighter, and I dropped my head, laughing in disgrace.

"It's alright, it's alright." He squeezed my hand again.

When I looked up at him, his eyes were kind as he let me find my footing again. But there was also amusement there as he watched me.

"Ok, now step out with your left, and follow with your right…that's it." He paused and smiled at me. "And that's the step. That's all there is. Shall we try a few in a row?"

I took a deep breath, hardly remembering any of what we'd just rehearsed. But I decided to go all in. "Sure, why not?"

He nodded. "Ok, remember to start with bringing your right foot back. One…two…three… One…two…three."

We completed the full series of steps two more times. His body was rigid and controlled as he led me. His movements were clean and smooth, and even as I stumbled and made mistakes, he swept me back into the rhythm effortlessly each time, as if he didn't mind my errors at all.

"I'm sure I'm the most uncoordinated partner you've ever had the pleasure of dancing with," I laughed, looking at his chest as he gripped my hand tightly.

"You're actually doing really well, Cora." He beamed. "Do you want to try a few more steps?"

I was giddy at the feel of his hands on me and couldn't imagine saying no, so I nodded happily.

I'd watched his films how many times? Too many to count. And now, here I was, dancing with Liam Montgomery myself.

Alone on a deserted island.

I wasn't sure which part was more outlandish.

We continued the box step as Liam recited the numbers, and eventually the movements formed in my muscle memory and he was able to stop counting. I bravely looked up into his eyes, which were deep brown in the dark of the evening.

"Want to try a spin?" He looked purely joyful to be in his element.

"Do I?" I asked, unsure if I trusted myself not to fall flat on my face.

He grinned and grasped my right hand tighter. "Just follow my lead."

He released my back and swung me away from him, twisting me under his arm as I went. When his arm fully extended, he pulled me back and my body rotated easily into place in front of him again. It was as if I'd done it a million times with perfect precision. He led me so flawlessly and effortlessly, I felt my heart skip a beat again.

I could tell my face was flushed when I looked up at him once more, and all I could say in my flustered state was, "Whew..."

He grinned proudly at me, stepping away. "You did wonderfully. A true natural."

I snorted quietly. "Yeah...I think you pretty much made all of that happen."

He laughed. "You actually caught on really quickly."

"That's only because you're a great teacher." I smiled.

He crinkled his nose and smirked again. "Maybe I'll teach you some more, another day. It would be a good way to pass the time."

Um, yes please.

I could still feel his hands at my waist and my back, even when they were no longer there. My answer came without pause. “I’d like that.”

Liam beamed at me. “It’s a plan then. By the time we leave this island, you’ll be a pro.” He squeezed my hand again gently. I was beginning to really love that little reassurance.

“We’ll have to be here for quite a long time for me to go pro,” I laughed. But the humor faded quickly as I realized the underlying reality of what I’d said. Neither of us knew just how long we’d remain.

Liam dropped my hand as I looked up past his shoulder into the dark night sky, searching for the blinking red light of a passing plane. But the light of a thousand stars was all I saw. The silence of our little island was deafening, as if every sound we made was that much more piercing and vibrant. We were giving this quiet place a life it had probably never known.

Letting my gaze turn back to Liam again, I found him watching me, and I smiled. “Thank you for the dance.”

His lips pulled up into a warm grin. “It was my pleasure, Miss Cora.”

ELEVEN

The distant sounds of the crashing waves woke me gently the next morning. I'd slept without a shirt over my head for the first time in weeks, and I smiled contentedly, realizing that the lemongrass had worked. We'd tied bunches of it to our bamboo wall, and the entire enclosure now smelled of crisp citrus. I scratched one of my day-old bug bites and breathed a sigh of relief.

I turned my head to glance at the spot next to me where Liam slept. He wasn't there, but then again, he almost always woke before I did. I ran my fingers through my hair, replaying the previous night in my head. After we'd danced, we were both so tired we went to bed almost immediately, chatting only for a bit when we'd laid down. He told me stories from his dancing career and how it had led him to eventually star in his first movie eight years ago.

He'd been in such a positive mood last night, talking about

a passion that meant so much to him. I could have listened to him reminisce for hours, but we'd both eventually drifted off, too tired to keep our eyes open any longer.

I was beginning to distinguish between the Liam I'd perceived through the lens of the media and the real Liam I knew now. He'd been mysterious then. A bit closed off. Charming, of course, but untouchable and unreadable. But I could see him clearly now. He wasn't an enigmatic fantasy. He was perfectly human like the rest of us, struggling and thriving in his own unique ways.

The thing that caught me off guard the most was that even though I'd discovered many of his flaws over the last two weeks, I actually admired him even more because of them. There was something about his humanity that made this all very real.

And through that realization, inevitable feelings started to grow. They appeared slowly, replacing my fangirl crush with actual reasons for admiring him as a person and not just a swoon-worthy idol on my TV screen. It didn't feel like I was falling for the Liam I knew before the crash. This Liam was very real to me now; the man whom I'd shared the last two weeks of my life with. He was so kind to me and so inquisitive about my goals and aspirations. He concentrated so intently when I told stories. And when he shared his, I could tell he genuinely appreciated my advice. He was responsible and motivated, and he was always a gentleman. I rarely saw him as 'Liam, the actor' anymore. He was 'Liam, my friend' now, and I could feel the bond strengthening between us each day.

Last night, when he'd asked me to dance, I couldn't help but wonder where that suggestion had come from. He didn't *have* to dance with me. No one had forced him to offer. Was he just desperate to dance with whoever was convenient and available? He'd made it clear that he missed it immensely. Had that been the only reason, or had he asked me because he wanted to dance with *me?*

I sat up in our cave and rubbed my eyes, shaking my head. I knew my thoughts were just wishful thinking. He had a girlfriend, and in his eyes, I was just a silly fangirl, 'Miss Cora.' He probably thought he'd humor me with a dance. That was the more reasonable explanation, and dwelling on a fantasy in the midst of life-or-death survival would do me no good.

I shook my head again and pushed open the door, stepping into the morning sunlight. The fire crackled a few yards away and a pile of fresh coconuts was visible nearby. Liam had been busy already. I scanned the beach but didn't see him anywhere. Maybe he took a walk? He occasionally did so alone, but after yesterday, I thought he might be eager for a stroll together again. And typically, he was around when I woke up.

I picked up the coconuts and placed them in one of the larger baskets I'd weaved, and then I took one and ate it quietly by the fire. Had he told me where he'd be this morning? Maybe I'd forgotten? Was I supposed to meet him somewhere?

When I'd finished eating, I tossed my empty coconut into the flames and stood up, rising to my toes and peering up and over the rocks, but he was nowhere in sight. Pursing my lips, I realized I had nothing else to occupy me, so I decided to take a walk by myself. Maybe I'd run into him.

I ambled along the edge of the water, watching the waves rise and fall across the shore in small, gentle surges. The tide had a rhythm and a promise of coming back again and again. It was sometimes unpredictable, but it always returned. I was growing fond of the calming effect it had on me.

I'd been walking for twenty minutes and had made it all the way to the other side of the island before I saw Liam. He was sitting in the sand, a few yards from the edge of the water. His arm rested on his knee as he stared out at the horizon.

I smiled, excited to see him again and eager at the prospect of another day of jokes and dancing. I had the pep in my step of a giddy schoolgirl as I walked over to him.

He didn't see me at first, but when he did, he met my eyes briefly, smiled mildly, and then turned back to the water.

"Sleep well?" he asked.

I crossed my legs and sat down next to him. "That lemongrass really did the trick."

"It did, didn't it?" he mused quietly. "I might try transplanting an entire bush to just outside the door."

"That's a great idea." I smiled and glanced at him, but he still did not look at me. Not missing a beat though, I continued. "I'd love to help."

His expression didn't change. "That would be great. Thanks Cora."

I frowned. Where was the jovial Liam who spun me around on the sand last night?

I spoke up again. "I wondered where you'd gone this morning. What have you been doing out here?"

He blinked and quickly looked over at me, almost as if he'd already forgotten I was there. "Oh, sorry, yeah I just needed a walk."

I nodded slowly as he turned back to the waves.

He continued, "I've been thinking about Kate."

Oh.

I looked away from him quickly, focusing on a broken seashell in the sand in front of me.

"I just wish I could tell her I'm ok. I hate that I can't even give her that." He paused. "Especially after the way we left things."

I touched the rough, jagged edge of the shell, tracing it with my finger. "You miss her," I stated simply.

Liam nodded. "I do miss her." He took a breath. "But differently than I thought I would."

I looked out at the bright blue sky and mentally scolded myself. Liam was sitting here missing his girlfriend while I'd been daydreaming that he might have feelings for me.

Shame on you, Cora.

I took a deep, guilty breath and quickly turned my thoughts to the day ahead. "It looks like it's going to be a beautiful day. What should we do first?"

Liam glanced over at me again and smiled tightly. I didn't like it. It was too forced.

"I think I'm going to rest until later when I fish for dinner," he responded.

I assessed him quietly for a moment. I wanted to ask him if anything was wrong, but I already knew what was, having taken for granted the fact that I didn't have a partner to miss so deeply at home like he did. *Of course* he was in turmoil and longing to be with her. Was I really so cold-hearted to not have considered that?

We sat in silence for a while. I wasn't sure what he was thinking, and I wondered if he'd rather I just let him be.

A greyish-green bird with a white head flew out of a tree behind us and came to land on the sand a few yards away. It reminded me of the pigeons I'd seen on a trip to New York City. Liam shifted his focus, watching it preen its feathers.

"I've never seen any of them fly off the island," I commented. "They seem to stay put here. So, that tells me there probably aren't any other islands nearby."

Liam was still looking at the bird, but then he frowned and dropped his gaze to the sand in front of him again.

I couldn't help it anymore. I had to speak up. "Liam, are you ok?"

When he lifted his eyes to my concerned ones, his face turned sympathetic. "Oh, yeah I'm fine." He failed at pretending to smile. "I'm just a bit lost in my mind today. Don't worry about me."

I blinked at him for a moment, giving him the chance to elaborate, but when he didn't, I sighed and stood up from my spot. My sudden movement startled the bird, and it flew back into the trees. "I'm going to gather more leaves for my baskets. See you in a bit?" I eyed him cautiously.

His smile was more genuine this time. "Ok, be careful."

"I always am." I nodded and turned from him, walking toward the trees. I ran my hand down my face in an attempt to wipe off the uncomfortable exchange. I wanted to slap myself, realizing I'd disrespected him so deeply with my own growing feelings. He didn't know that, but *I* did.

I weaved in and out of the plants, searching for dropped palm fronds and placing them on my back. The ground was soft and moist from a recent rain and I frowned at my wet, sandy, bare feet. I hadn't been wearing shoes often, and my skin was beginning to toughen up against nature. My hands were rough too from carrying branches and coconuts and climbing across rocks. My body was adapting to the island and this new way of life. That wasn't going to change. Not as long as we were still here.

Out of nowhere, a bird flew out from a low tree, making me jump. After the initial startle, I steadied myself as I watched it disappear into a distant bush. It looked like the same bird we'd seen on the beach. I peered into the tree it had flown from and spotted a mess of small twigs and straw just at eye level. I crept in closer, standing on my toes to get a better look. Nestled gently in the center of the twigs were six small eggs.

My heart skipped a beat. Eggs! We could *eat* these. My mouth began to water in anticipation as I reached in and took them out, one by one.

Nearby, the mother bird was squawking loudly at me. She screeched and flapped her wings as she stared me down in a flustered panic. I ignored her at first, going about my work to gather the eggs, but I stopped abruptly before I took the last one. I slowly studied the five in my hands. They were a fair bit smaller than the average chicken egg, and they were still warm. I pursed my lips and looked at the angry mother, feeling an overwhelming sense of sympathy as I realized what they meant to her.

But… Liam and I needed the nutrition. It felt silly to contemplate the morals of a bird's short life when we were in such a dire condition, but the frenzied screeching rang through my ears too loudly. I left the last egg untouched. Sacrifices had to be made, but today my heart went out to that angry, protective, squawking mother.

"Thank you…" I whispered to her as I tiptoed away from the nest, five eggs in my cupped hands.

When I brought them back to the campsite, Liam was sitting by the fire. I walked up to him, arms outstretched with my discovery.

His eyes lit up when he saw them. "Eggs! Where did you find them?" He took one from me and turned it around in his fingers.

"There was a nest not too deep into the trees. I think they came from the same bird we saw on the beach." I smiled, glad to see him happy.

"Wow, and five? That's great!" He beamed.

I bit my lip. "Yeah, well…there were actually six, but I left one behind."

He looked up at me, clearly confused. "Why?"

I continued to chew on my lip as I looked down at the eggs in my hands. "Well, the mother was nearby…" I gulped. "And she was yelling at me. I couldn't take them all. They're hers and I'm sure they would have hatched eventually."

When Liam didn't immediately respond, I peered up at him through my lashes. He was watching me with amusement while trying to stifle a smile.

I nodded my head guiltily. "I know, I know, it's stupid, but I just couldn't."

"You're adorable," he replied quietly, still trying to hold back his smirk.

My cheeks grew warm as he observed me with that expression. He thought I was adorable?

No.

He thought that leaving an egg for its bird mother while we were practically starving was adorable. But in fact, it wasn't adorable at all. It was stupid.

"I can go back and get it…" I started to suggest.

"Let's get these fried up." His words overpowered mine as he got to his feet without another glance.

I stood with the remaining eggs in my hands, wondering if I should go back and retrieve the sixth. Would that mean I wasn't adorable anymore? Was that the better or the worse alternative?

In the end, I decided to stay adorable.

We fried the eggs on a thin stone perched on a support system of branches over the fire. Watching them slowly turn white and sizzle in the heat brought back a nostalgic feeling of simpler breakfasts at home. I mixed the fried eggs with freshly caught fish and we felt like we were eating at a five-star restaurant. It was astonishingly cathartic, serving up a delicious meal to Liam. I missed the rush of preparing new recipes and seeing them being enjoyed.

Plus, it was amazing how much I didn't even miss extra flavors and spices anymore. My taste buds were becoming much more sensitive to the muted flavors of the few foods we did eat.

After we'd finished, we leaned back on our elbows, relaxing in the warm sunshine. I watched Liam pull something from his pocket and turn it around in his fingers. It looked like a small, triangular-shaped stone.

"What is that?" I asked, leaning toward him and studying it closer.

"A shark tooth," he replied, examining it carefully. "I found it on the beach this morning."

"Wow…" I breathed. "What are you gonna do with it?"

"It's quite sharp. I'll keep thinking on it." He turned it over one last time in his palm and then placed it back in his pocket. "In the meantime, that meal was fantastic. Those eggs were a great find."

I took one of the empty eggshells in my hand and nodded. "Yeah, eggs are so versatile too. They went well with the fish, I think."

He peered at me with a frown. "You miss your job, I bet? Not much room to be creative out here with these limited options."

I tossed the eggshell aside. "I miss cooking, yeah. Don't necessarily miss the job though."

"Too stressful?"

I shrugged. "It's just not really what I want to do."

Liam sat up and shifted his posture toward me. "You said you want to open your own restaurant though, didn't you?"

With a small nod, I traced a circle around the discarded eggshell in the sand.

"So why haven't you?"

My shoulders slumped. "My dad needs the help, and working for him is the safe option. I'd probably fail if I tried to start my own thing."

"Well, that mindset's no good. I think you'd be brilliant."

I waved him off. "Nah, the locals just like my dishes because they're familiar. Not because they're actually any good."

"If the rest of what you make is as good as that sandwich, then I beg to differ."

I glanced up to see him studying me with a furrowed brow, so I averted my gaze again. "Eh, I'll probably just inherit my dad's company. Eventually, I'll be able to run it the way I want to."

"But your dream is to own a restaurant, not a catering company." He said the words like he knew they were true.

They were.

I took a long, deep breath. "Yes, but if I try and fail, I'll be furious at myself, and my dad will say 'I told you so.'"

"But if you don't try, then what?"

I met his eyes again. They were gentle yet piercing as they watched mine.

He raised his brows when I didn't respond. "Then you'll always wonder what could have been."

"First-time restaurateurs fail like eighty percent of the time," I said quietly.

"Who told you that?"

"My dad." I grabbed a handful of sand and poured it over the eggshell, covering it completely.

"Prove him wrong." Liam's gaze was unwavering.

I set my jaw. "It costs a lot of money, and I'd probably never make a profit anyway."

"Did your dad tell you that too?"

I gulped. "No. Jacob did."

"Bloody hell, does anyone you know actually care a lick about your aspirations?" Liam shook his head and leaned back on his hands again.

Wincing, I pressed my palm into the mound of sand I'd made, crushing the eggshell beneath its surface. "They're just trying to protect me."

Liam didn't respond, and when I glanced at him again, he had laid back with his eyes closed and his hands behind his head.

"I'm fine. I'm happy with what I do," I said quietly, trying to make it sound convincing.

"Alright," Liam replied simply, not opening his eyes.

I pursed my lips and sighed, laying back too and staring up

at the bright blue sky. I knew he was right. I knew I should stand up for myself and follow my dreams. That wasn't the surprise. The surprise was that when he told me I could achieve them, I actually believed him.

TWELVE

Liam reached around his neck and pulled the sweat-drenched strands of hair away from his skin as he sat up. "My hair is getting a bit unruly for this heat. Before long, I'm gonna have to start borrowing your elastic hair bands."

I touched my own wild waves, which were messily tucked into a bun. I'd already considered chopping mine off multiple times when I'd been working in the hot, unforgiving sun, but I couldn't bring myself to let go of them.

Gazing at Liam's dark, loose curls, I considered the option for him. "There's a set of scissors in the swiss army knife..." I suggested.

He tugged his bottom lip between his teeth. "I was supposed to keep it growing for the *Until Dawn* sequel. Filming was set to start next month, but I think being stranded on an island is a good enough excuse." He glanced at me. "Would you...cut it?"

I blinked in shock. "Hang on, there's going to be a sequel?"

He chuckled and nodded.

"Well, dang. I wouldn't want to get you in trouble." I paused. "Plus, I don't have the slightest idea how to cut hair."

He laughed again. "I don't think anyone here is going to judge your work. I just want it shorter. The producers will have to deal with it."

I looked at my hands. "I've never… I'll mess it up…"

"I don't think I'm coordinated enough to do it myself." His eyes pleaded gently. "Please, will you try?"

I stared at him for a moment. I was almost positive I'd butcher it, but saying yes meant I'd get to run my fingers through those curls, and if anything motivated me forward, that would be it.

"I can give it a try…" I replied tentatively.

"Great." He grinned. "How about you give it a go now?"

I took a deep breath and raised an eyebrow. "Are you prepared to say goodbye to a decent haircut?"

He smirked. "You'll do fine. I trust you."

"Be careful with that trust," I replied sarcastically as he handed me the folded knife set. I knelt in front of him and flipped open the scissors. "So, how do you want it?"

"However you see fit." He smiled at me.

I squinted at him skeptically. "However *I* see fit? It's *your* hair."

"Yes, but you're the one who has to look at it," he winked.

I cracked a grin. He was all too right.

I scooted closer so that I could assess him straight on. Even though I avoided his gaze, I could feel his eyes on me, and my hands started to shake. I bravely smoothed the sides of his hair back, envisioning a style. "Maybe shorter on the sides and a bit longer on top?"

"Sounds great," he responded easily.

I envied his ability to remain so carefree about his hair. *What a typical man.* My fingers traced his soft curls as I pinned them backward. I sensed a tension in the air between us as I touched him, and I wondered if he felt it too. Or maybe I imagined a connection that wasn't really there. That was the rational explanation.

When I briefly glanced into his eyes, my heart skipped a beat. The sunlight was bright this afternoon and it made his irises seem much lighter, like honey dripping from a spoon. I took a deep breath and pulled my hands away.

I picked up the small scissors and took a lock of his hair between my fingers. With a pause, I positioned them against the strands. "Are you sure about this?"

He chuckled. "Yes. It's just hair. It will grow back."

It was an obvious truth that too many women had yet to grasp.

I took a deep breath and closed the scissors over the lock of hair and watched as a chunk of dark curls fell to the ground.

"No going back now," I laughed.

Liam smirked and closed his eyes patiently.

I took the opportunity to admire his face. His dark eyebrows pointed toward a straight nose, and his perfect lips were surrounded by what was now a short, thick beard. And even through that, I could see his strong, angular jawline. His skin was tanned and smooth, and his long dark lashes laid gently across the tops of his cheeks.

I began to cut, making my way around his head. It was much easier when he had his eyes closed. I felt less distracted, and I was surprised to find that it was a cathartic experience creating something new. Each dark lock that tumbled onto the sand represented one of my old observations of him before I knew him so personally. They fell to the ground like old memories, ill-formed and underestimated. The Liam that sat with me now was someone I'd grown close to, and I cared for him in a way I'd never be able to erase.

"So, I've got two questions for you." Liam grinned, keeping his eyes shut.

"Oh, *do* you?" I raised my brow.

"Yeah, I'm curious. What do you think has been the best part about being here so far?"

The best part? We'd focused so long on the negatives, it was disorienting to try and flip my judgment. I paused my cutting and watched him for a moment, trying to decide how to answer. The best part, hands down, had been the fact that he was here with me. I wondered what he'd think of that.

I decided to play it off as a joke. "Apart from *you?*"

The grin that spread across his face immediately made it worth it.

I returned to my trimming. "I'd have to say…the peace, the calm, not having to deal with the stresses of normal life. Sure, we have our own to deal with, but somehow, they're almost more manageable."

"Good answer." He smiled. "You're very right. It's almost like these struggles are more worth our time."

I nodded and tugged gently at a section of his hair to test its length.

"But you miss home?" he continued.

I shrugged. "Of course, and I hate to know that everyone

thinks we're dead."

His expression became grim. "Yeah, well, a lot of people *are* dead."

"Yes," I replied, pausing.

"I carried you off that plane so fast. I sometimes wonder if I would have stayed and continued to look…"

"Then you probably wouldn't have made it out alive," I finished his sentence for him. "You did more than enough, Liam."

He squeezed his eyes shut tighter. "I just can't help but picture someone strapped into their seat, still alive, sinking with the plane, because I didn't go back to help them."

I touched his shoulder gently. "You can't put that responsibility on yourself."

He shook his head. "We'll see…when we return. I'm sure the media will have something to say about it."

"Well, I think what you did was amazing, and I'm really glad you were on that plane."

He shrugged. "I almost wasn't."

I furrowed my brow. "What do you mean?"

"The date for the meeting in Auckland changed at the last minute. I had to plead with the airline to get a spot on that flight." He grimaced. "I kinda can't believe I'd begged my way onto a flight that would crash."

The wheels spun in my head as I listened to him explain. He'd convinced them to give him a spot on the flight at the last minute? The dots connected. That meant…

"I know." He laughed lightly. "I'm not at all proud of using my celebrity status to sweet talk them into shifting things around for me, but I was desperate."

My mouth hung open. "You're the reason Tess got bumped

off the flight..."

He raised an eyebrow. "Tess? Your friend?"

I nodded. "They shifted her to a later flight at the last minute." I watched him in awe. "She was *so mad*."

This time *his* mouth dropped open. "She was supposed to be on our flight?"

"Yeah, we bought our tickets months ago. But they told her at the gate that she'd been shifted. I didn't even know they could do that."

Guilt spread across his face. "I guess that's my fault."

"No..." I sat back from him with wide eyes. "If she'd been on the flight, she would have sat next to me. Odds are, she wouldn't have sur..." I gulped. "...survived."

"Wow..." He blinked out at the ocean. "It's like a domino effect."

"So, you've not only saved my life now, but retrospectively, you've technically also saved hers."

As he nodded, he frowned, and a thousand thoughts flew across his features. "I wish I could have done more."

I wished he knew how much he *did* do, but I took a deep breath and continued to work, knowing it wouldn't be so easy for him to see that. "You have a lot of special people waiting for you at home. I don't have anyone like Kate. I can't imagine how painful this is for her...and for you."

Liam visibly swallowed, pausing a moment before he spoke. "I was going to break up with her," he admitted.

My fingers stuttered on his hair as I cut the next piece.

"I was going to do it as soon as I got back from New Zealand..." He sighed. "She likely has no idea..."

He still hadn't opened his eyes, so I let my cheeks fill with a silent whoosh of breath. "I thought you said you wanted to try and work things out with her?"

With a grimace, he sighed again. "I've been telling myself that, but the decision is too hard to make without seeing her again...especially after all this."

I moved around to the back of his head, blinking up at the bright sky with extreme unease. I was *not* the person he should be divulging these truths to.

"I'm sorry," he said quickly as if reading my mind. "You probably don't want to hear about my relationship drama."

I gulped, desperate to change the topic. "What was your second question for me?"

He waited a beat before responding. "Is there anything I can do to make life here easier for you?"

I stared at the back of his head quizzically. "Liam, you already do so much. What do you mean?"

"I mean...because..." he stumbled over his words. "We're stuck out here with only each other. I'm all you have right now. Is there anything I can do to make you happier?"

What? The offer came from a place of such selflessness that I hardly knew how to respond. "I don't know...I'm not sure. You don't have to do anything for me." As I cut, I was slowly rotating back around to the front of his head again.

"You don't know?" he replied, opening his eyes to look at me once I faced him. "You can't think of anything?"

What was he getting at? Why did he care so much about my happiness? Was he looking for an honest response? Because, if I were being honest, he could *take me* right here on the beach and fulfill every want and need I'd had for almost the last year, but I was sure that was far from the answer he was expecting.

And it was even further from what he *needed* right now as he grieved his failing relationship with Kate.

"Do you think I'm not happy?" I asked cautiously.

"I think you miss your family and your friends. I think you're scared that we'll be stranded for too long." His kind gaze peered into mine. "I can't fix those things, but I'm asking you what I can do to help ease the stress a little."

I couldn't tear my eyes away from his. The compassion there was unmatched. "No, I just…" I paused. My voice was quiet and unsure. "No one has ever asked me anything like that before."

Confusion spread across his face. "Surely that's not the case? Of course Jacob must have…"

I shook my head. "Jacob didn't care. He was too busy with work and his own hobbies. I was too overbearing. I pushed him away."

He pulled his brows together and closed his eyes. "There's no way that's true."

I shrugged, touching my fingers to his hair, running them through it, and pulling gently on some of the strands to evaluate their length again. One of his curls cascaded onto his forehead and he suddenly opened his eyes to meet mine. I blinked and looked back toward his hair quickly, realizing he'd caught me staring.

I cleared my throat. "I think this looks good."

He raised his hands to his head and ran them through his new cut, testing it out. "I think it feels great. Thank you, Cora." He smiled at me.

I sat back and observed my work. I actually hadn't done half-bad. The shorter look suited him, and I was surprisingly content with the results.

"You're welcome," I replied, slipping the scissors back into their slot.

"I don't know what I'd do without you," he continued.

I sighed as I stood up. "You'd have longer hair and a lot more fish to yourself."

"Hey." He took hold of my arm and tugged me back down to the ground. "Why do you always do that?"

"Do what?" I frowned, tracing a small stone through the sand as he held me there.

"Disregard yourself like that," he clarified. "You talk about yourself like you're a burden to me."

I gazed up at him slowly, but I didn't respond.

Liam eyed me with puzzlement. "You actually think you're a burden to me, don't you?"

I shrugged.

He shook his head and let go of my arm. "That's the furthest thing from the truth. Cora, you have to know that."

Flashes of Kate came to my mind. I wondered how it would have been if she were his companion on this island instead. I pictured him spinning *her* around in the sand. In my head, they were in love, and they were content, and they were free. But the harsh bite of reality reminded me that they were stressed, and grieving, and very much apart.

Maybe if Liam would have been safely back in L.A. by now, he would have reconsidered his emotions and stayed together with her after all. I knew his concerns weren't my fault, but there was still a persistent strain of guilt that coursed through me. I felt guilty in the face of Kate too, knowing that I had to rely on Liam so heavily when he was not mine. My hidden feelings for him didn't help matters either.

This time, when I stood up, he didn't grab me. "No, you're right. Of course I'm not a burden." I pointed toward the lagoon. "I'm going to go wash up. I'll see you in a bit?"

Peering over my shoulder for just a second, I saw him nod from his spot on the ground. But I didn't let my gaze linger. Lingering on Liam meant admitting my feelings for him, and that was a very enticing, yet terribly dangerous trap.

THIRTEEN

Another full week passed. I was beginning to forget what it felt like to live with modern conveniences. It had been almost a month since I'd stood in front of the stove at *Dales Catering*. It had been almost a month since I'd sat on the floor with Tess eating greasy pizza and binging reality TV. It had been almost a month since I'd felt the warmth of my mother's embrace. And it had been almost a month since I'd watched my father's eyes light up with pride at the sight of one of my new recipes.

Here on our island, in our own little world, we struggled daily, but we also thrived in a way I'd never expected. While we didn't eat much, we ate clean, and I felt my body growing stronger. With fish, coconuts, the addition of occasional eggs, as well as a green leafy seaweed we'd discovered, our diets were becoming quite well-rounded.

Even though I felt healthier, I also felt physically drained to an extent I'd never experienced before. It was amazing what hard work did to the body. Every night, we both collapsed onto the ground of our cave, falling asleep almost immediately.

The mornings and the evenings were my favorite. Liam and I usually spent time sitting by the fire, chatting and watching the sun rise and set. I shared stories from my childhood in Burbank, and he encouraged me to talk about my dreams of opening a restaurant where I could serve dishes on my own terms and craft a menu of comfort food staples.

We talked about food *a lot.*

He also told me what it was like to film *Until Dawn*, filling me in on secrets and stories from behind the scenes. It was shot almost exclusively in and around Paris, following his character, James, and his begrudging dance partner, Cherise, as they stepped in at the last minute to compete in an international dance competition. He talked about his castmates like family, and it was easy to tell that he missed them dearly.

Liam vibrantly described the beauty of Paris, where he'd spent so much time, but also the rich history of Greece, and the crazed fans of the Philippines. He shared stories of Canterbury, England too, the town where he'd grown up. Just east of London, it was home to ancient cathedrals and cobblestone streets. It sounded magical, and his eyes lit up with nostalgia as he reminisced.

I was intrigued, watching him intently as he talked about his life. It was so much grander than mine. He'd been around the globe and had met so many amazing people. Apart from New Zealand, I'd barely been out of the country. But somehow, we found common ground on the things that mattered. I was beginning to feel like I'd known him for months, not weeks.

Time passed differently here on the island. The days were long, but our companionship grew at the speed of light.

Liam's mood had varied during the last week. Sometimes, I would see a glimmer of something in his eyes when he looked at me, just like when he'd told me I was adorable for leaving one egg behind like an idiot—I added the 'idiot' part. But we hadn't danced again, and I tried not to think about it too much. He'd occasionally talk about Kate, and I could sense how badly he was struggling. I'd like to have said, for her sake, that I felt better when he was being more introspective, thinking about her, but I was beginning to admit to myself that I wanted nothing more than for him to develop feelings for me instead.

It was wrong. It was shameful. But it was true.

This morning, I watched as he etched another mark onto our cave wall. When he'd finished, he sighed. "Three weeks. Hard to believe."

I stood small next to his tall frame and stared at the ticks. "I never would have thought we'd be here this long."

Liam tossed his etching stone to the floor and then turned to leave the cave, but he winked over his shoulder as he went. "Sorry you're stuck with me."

I caught the hint of mischief in his voice as I followed him out. "I know, such a *pain.*"

He sat down by the fire and looked up at me with a grin. "For the record, I'd rather be stuck with you than most people."

I smirked and sat down next to him. "I can't say I disagree."

"Am I much like you expected?"

I tilted my head, studying him. "Yes and no. You're…" I paused, trying to find the right words. "You're more…real."

He smiled warmly at me. "Did I seem fake?"

Shaking my head quickly, I pushed a log around in the fire. "No, no. Not like that. It's just, you know…you seemed kind of like a mirage. Kind of untouchable."

He considered my words with a twinkle in his eye. "Is that why you barely said a word to me at the studio when you catered? Was I just a *mirage* to you then?"

I laughed as I tried to hide the pink I knew was growing on my cheeks. "You're lucky I've been stuck with you for three weeks, or else you might not have *ever* gotten another word out of me."

Liam grinned and leaned back on his hands. "Guess that's one good consequence of being here so long."

"I think we make a pretty good team." I smiled.

"I think we do too."

I pressed my lips together, thinking in silence for a moment. "What if they never find us?"

"They'll find us," he responded softly.

"But what if it's not for a long time? What if we're here for months… or years?" It terrified me to even say it.

Liam frowned as he rubbed his jaw. "Then we'll figure things out as they come. We've made it this far. It won't be *years* though."

I took a deep breath and pulled my knees to my chest, resting my chin on them.

We sat quietly like that for a long stretch of time before I peered over at him again. He was staring at the flames, unblinking. I longed to know what was deep inside his head. He did that a lot—staring like he was searching an abyss. I probably did the same thing myself.

I decided to dig a little. "I love how quiet it is here. Do you miss the rush of your career?"

He lifted his chin and bit his lip in contemplation. "Had I never had this experience, I might have a different answer. But now that I'm here, it's proven to be more cathartic than I would have expected."

I watched him carefully, seeing more on his mind and waiting for him to continue.

He traced his finger through the sand slowly. "I'm usually busy all the time. I tend to push myself to take on more projects than I can handle. And…" He paused. "I put my all into them. But it takes a toll. I'd forgotten what it was like to let myself relax and reflect. There is a lot of thinking to be done."

I gazed at him. "Have you come to any new realizations?"

He looked at me briefly, blinking quickly, and then he turned back toward the fire. "I think I was already beginning to realize this before. I need to slow down. Being here, away from it all, really puts things into perspective. I already avoid social media and that whole spectacle when I can, but I let other things get to me too easily. The press is relentless. There are lots of expectations. But I'm not interested in a drama-filled, extravagant lifestyle."

I knew what he was thinking before he said it. "But Kate is."

He rubbed his forehead and sighed. "She is. She always has been."

"What drew you to her in the first place then?"

He exhaled heavily. "Well, back then, last autumn when we met, I thought I still wanted that type of life." He paused and looked at me. "I did it for a while in my twenties. It was fun for a bit. Parties, expensive gifts…" He waited a beat. "Women."

I gulped and looked down at my hands.

"I think I thought I could still find joy that way. But I quickly found out I was wrong. It's massively unfulfilling." He shook his head and laughed, lifting his eyes to me. "I'm sorry, I'm rambling."

I felt bad that he was laughing at himself. These were serious emotions he was uncovering, and I respected him deeply. "No, no, I appreciate you sharing with me." I smiled at him sincerely. "I can sympathize. I did the "party" thing for a bit, but it was short-lived. Not really my thing. Besides, I was too busy in the kitchen with my dad." I laughed at myself now. "Pffft, I always wanted to go live in the mountains of Colorado, open my quaint local restaurant, and otherwise stay away from the world."

Liam's eyes were kind and thoughtful as he listened to me. "I know you do. That stunned me the first time you told me… to know that you've always envied a simpler living like that. I'm, what, almost five years older than you and I'm just now discovering those aspirations? You've been on that page your whole life."

I felt my heart thump a little as he complimented me so kindly. It was flattering to hear him say such nice things about me.

We gazed at each other for a moment before he continued. "So, in your happy little future in the Colorado mountains, do you have a family? A dog? A cat? What's the dream for you?"

I chewed on my lip. Now it was my turn to be honest. "I want all of it." I smiled. "A marriage, a family, a home… I just want to grow old with someone I can call my best friend." I paused and smiled to myself. "It's a bit boring and traditional-sounding, I suppose."

Liam was watching me intently with his chin resting on his palm as if I were telling the most enthralling story. "I don't think it sounds boring at all. I think when I started to gain fame, I wrote off any sense of normalcy in my life, but I don't think I realized it could still be attainable. I'd like to settle down with the right person too, and develop the kind of connection you can only get from spending decades together." He took a deep breath. "Someday, when I have it, it'll be a balance, of course. I don't want to give up acting. I have such a passion for it now. But I think I could make both dreams work with the right priorities."

I smiled. "So, maybe if you get out of here safely, this won't have been such a bad experience for you? You seem to have learned a lot about yourself."

He grinned. "Yeah, I have."

I beamed back at him. It was fascinating to hear him expose his dreams; dreams *he* didn't even know he had. But it was even more interesting to hear that many of his dreams were the same as mine.

Liam took a deep breath and pushed himself up from the ground. "One thing I already knew about myself though was that I like to be creative." He stepped over behind one of the large boulders surrounding our beach. "I have something to show you."

I watched him curiously until he appeared agin, holding a long, thin, straight stick. On one end were three feathers, tied tightly and evenly, and on the other end was the pointed shark tooth he'd found last week. He also pulled out a larger, curved stick, thicker than the last one, with a long drawstring connecting the ends.

My eyes widened as I realized what he'd made. "A bow and arrow…"

He smiled proudly and turned the bow around in his hands, admiring his work.

"The shark tooth…" I mused. "Can I see?"

He handed the arrow to me, and I studied the craftsmanship. He'd fastened the tooth tightly to the end of the stick with strands of dental floss. I touched my finger to it. The point was sharp and strong.

I passed it back to him. "This is impressive. What are you going to hunt?"

"Have you seen those larger birds that wander around in the lagoon?"

I nodded.

"I've been studying their habits. They're quite slow. I think I might get a hit on one of them."

"Have you tried yet?"

"No. I've been practicing though." He pressed on the tip of the arrow, testing its hold.

"Do you know how to use it?"

He chuckled. "I'm a little rusty, but luckily, I have some experience." His eyes met mine with a twinkle.

I blinked eagerly. "You're an archer?

He laughed again. "I hardly deserve that title. But I used to be in a club in my teens. It's been a bit of time since then, of course, but I still remember enough."

My mouth hung slightly agape, picturing him with a real bow, aiming and shooting like some sort of hunky fantasy character. "Can I see…?"

I desperately needed to see.

Liam's eyes crinkled. "Sure, come on." He motioned for me to follow him out past the large rocks and onto an adjacent, wider, sandy beach.

He took a large piece of soft driftwood and placed it in the sand. Then he used his knife to trace a bullseye in the center. Next, he backed up a dozen or so yards and positioned the arrow onto the crude bow and neatly between his fingers. He closed one eye and lifted the bow into the air.

I was giddy as I watched him take his stance, line up his target, and slowly pull the arrow backward. His shoulders were tight and strong as he held the string taut, and he took a focused and calculated last breath before releasing the arrow. It flew through the air and buried itself into the driftwood, right inside the third ring of his bullseye.

I clapped as he relaxed his stance. "That was great!"

He walked to the arrow and pulled it free, touching the sharp tip. "Eh, it was alright. I'll need to be more accurate to make a kill."

I eyed the contraption in his hands. "I'm sure it's difficult with a handmade bow?"

He glanced up at me as an idea flashed past his eyes. "Do you want to try?"

I hesitated, taking a step back nervously. "I don't think I'd be very good at it."

He held the bow toward me. "It's alright, I'll show you."

I raised an eyebrow at him and took a tiny, reluctant step in his direction. "I don't want to break it."

He laughed. "You won't break it."

He passed it over and stepped up behind me. I inhaled sharply as he touched his hands to my arms, helping me position the bow correctly. Each time his fingers grazed my skin, my heart skipped a beat. Every nerve where we connected felt bright-white and alive.

When my hands were in place, he set the arrow between my fingers. I took a deep breath, trying to concentrate but failing miserably as the heat of his chest against my back sent my brain into a cloud of inappropriate lust.

"Ok, line it up…right there." His face was inches from my cheek, and his breath was on my ear with every word. Shivers poured down my spine and goosebumps rose on my neck. I prayed he didn't notice. He lifted my arms and helped me to aim at the bullseye. I could almost hear my pounding heart. Focusing on anything other than him was out of the question at this point.

"Close one eye and get your aim right," Liam said quietly as he backed away from me.

Aim? What aim? I'm about to melt into a puddle in the sand.

"Take a breath and release the arrow as you release your breath."

I squinted and attempted to line the arrow up with the target. Inhaling deeply, I poised myself to release it, and then let out my breath as I pulled my fingers from the string. The arrow soared through the air, and for a moment I thought it might make contact, but instead, it flew completely over the driftwood and landed softly in the sand beyond it.

I dropped the bow to my side and laughed, shaking my head.

Liam placed his hand on my shoulder as he walked past me. "Hey, that was really close!"

I looked up at him with skepticism, but he was grinning.

"You were a little high, but horizontally, you lined it up perfectly." He pointed his hand at the target to demonstrate. "You'll be a pro in no time."

"You're funny." I laughed sarcastically, handing him back the bow.

"And *you* don't give yourself enough credit." He retrieved the arrow and positioned it in his own hands again to take another shot.

"No, I just give you a lot more credit than me."

"And I haven't the faintest idea why." He kept his gaze on the target as he aimed.

"I think it's pretty clear," I sighed.

He pulled back and released the arrow, which landed in the second ring this time, and then he took a deep breath and turned toward me. His smile had faded. "Cora, if someone had asked you three weeks ago how long you thought you'd survive here, what would you have said?"

I shrugged. "I don't know, a week, maybe."

"Then aren't you even just a *little* bit proud of yourself for making it this far?"

"But without you, I wouldn't—"

Liam dropped his bow to his side and turned to face me fully, annoyance written all over his face. "Do you not *want* my help?"

Taken aback by his hardened features, I shrunk slightly. "Well, yes, but—"

"Because I can go set up camp on the other side of the island and you can do your own fishing and your own gathering, and I won't bother you at all." He narrowed his eyes.

Well, shoot.

I gulped and met his gaze cautiously. "If that's what you want…"

"No. Cora." He let out an exasperated sigh. "That's not what I want. Is that what you want?"

"No." My voice was smaller than it had ever been.

"Then I need you to stop being so damn unsure of yourself." He held my gaze firmly. "It's putting unnecessary stress on the both of us."

"I'm sorry. I just…I don't feel like I'm pulling my own weight."

He shook his head. "You gather almost half of the fallen coconuts now, you do *all* the cooking, you keep watch of the fire, you make my baskets to store the caught fish, I get *way* better sleep with the lemongrass you found and those mats you made for the cave floor, and I hardly think I need to remind you how grateful I am to have you to talk with. Either one of us would have gone a bit batty out here all alone."

I started to speak, but he stopped me with his hand as he continued. "And just because I do the fishing, and the building, and the heavy lifting doesn't mean I'm pulling more weight than you are. It means I have different strengths, and because of that, we make a good team. You said that yourself."

He was right. Of course he was right. But the tone of his voice still stung. There was annoyance heavily laden in it, and it burned me at my core. I was more of a burden to him in *thinking I was a burden* than I actually was a burden.

I ran my hand through my hair and tried to shake away my uncertainty. "No, you're right. I just want to be worth the effort you made to save me."

His face softened quickly, and he stepped toward me. "I

didn't save you because I felt some sort of obligation to. I saved you just like I would have saved anyone else on that plane who was still alive. But the thing is, you're not just 'anyone' to me anymore. I care a great deal about you now that I've gotten to know you for this long."

My heart thumped so hard I almost reached up to grasp my chest. *He cared a great deal.* It was shocking to hear him say that. But he was right. If the tables were turned, it wouldn't matter to me if he were contributing nothing while *I* pulled all the weight. I'd do it with a smile on my face because I cared about him too. It was easy for me to feel that within myself, but difficult to come to terms with the fact that he could possibly feel the same way about me.

And he was right about another thing too. I was too *damn* unsure of myself. It was a fault I'd struggled with all my life. I couldn't even stand up for myself in the face of my father and follow my own dreams, for fear I'd fail and disappoint him.

I silently walked over to the target and retrieved the arrow, and then I returned and placed it in Liam's hand. Looking up into his eyes, I nodded with a heartfelt smile. I couldn't bring myself to reciprocate his words yet. They were too true to admit, but I hoped my eyes could convey it instead.

The warmth in his expression told me he understood, and he placed his hand gently on my arm. "So, I fully expect you'll be cooking us up something absolutely delicious with the first bird I get."

I grinned. "Oh, it'll be so good, it'll rival those turkey sandwiches."

He beamed at me. "Well, I'd better get practicing then."

I nodded, forcing myself to break our gaze, and then I

walked a few yards from him and plopped myself down in the sand, poised to watch.

He caught me from the corner of his eye. "You're going to watch me practice?"

I smiled, clasping my hands in front of me. "Yeah, why not?"

A lopsided grin graced his face. "Alright, if that's what makes ya happy."

"It does, indeed." With a playful smirk, I locked eyes intentionally with his. He didn't look away, and I saw the realization in his expression. He knew I wanted to watch him, and I was glad he did.

FOURTEEN

Real meat was beyond incredible. After a few days of unsuccessful attempts, Liam finally shot one of the plump birds he'd expected to be so slow and lazy. Turns out, they weren't as lazy as he'd thought. Plus, his makeshift bow proved difficult to be accurate with, especially on a moving target. But one day, he came back to the campsite holding his catch proudly out to me.

I plucked it and cooked it over the fire that morning and we dined like kings. The meat tasted like chicken, and I watched him finish every bit off the bones before licking his lips and grinning widely at me. With that giddy expression on his face, he looked about five years old, and I couldn't help but beam at him.

He sat back, throwing the last of the bones onto the fire. "That was…exquisite."

I laughed. "As good as the turkey sandwiches?"

He closed his eyes and shook his head.

I grinned. "I'm super impressed. Think what you could do if you had a proper bow."

"I'm sure going to appreciate the proper things in life when we return. Might go out and buy myself a spear and a new archery set."

I swallowed nervously. When he spoke of leaving the island, he always used words like "when" instead of "if." I wished my confidence were on par with his. I knew that the odds said we'd be discovered eventually, but between now and then, there were too many unknown dangers. We had no doctors and no first aid, apart from the partial tube of antibiotic ointment we savored like gold. It wouldn't last forever, and it wouldn't save us from anything worse than a scrape or a cut.

Liam scratched his dark beard, staring up toward the bright sun. It was an extraordinarily hot day with almost no breeze, and we were both sweating through our shirts. I was about five shades tanner than I'd been when we'd washed ashore, and my skin no longer burned as easily, but the heat was still often inescapable.

"I'm gonna to go for a swim in the lagoon," I said, stripping down to my swimsuit as I stood up.

When I met his eyes, they were focused nowhere near my face—far below it in fact—and I stifled a smirk. I liked knowing I wasn't the only one with a wandering gaze. He'd seen me in my swimsuit dozens of times, yet he never failed to give me an extra glance, no matter how well he thought he was hiding it. It gave me a surge of confidence, and *goodness*, I needed that with him. As well as I knew him now, he was still massively untouchable in my eyes, so I felt a bit smug, knowing I could attract his attention, even if just for a moment.

"Mind if I join?" he asked, clearing his throat. "It's bloody hot today."

His accent came out extra strong, and I smirked as I responded. "Sure, we'll have a *bloody* swim in the lagoon, *mate*."

But he burst into laughter as he got to his feet. "See, when you say it like that, it just sounds like we're about to go dive into a literal pool of blood."

I scrunched my nose. "Gosh, that sounds like a massacre, doesn't it? How do I say it right?"

He walked past me, pulling his shirt over his head. "Maybe just stick to your own American English."

I stuck my tongue out at him when he couldn't see and then skipped across the sand to catch up. "Do you like *my* accent?"

He waded into the water as he turned his lighthearted face to mine. "You don't sound like you're from L.A. at all."

I raised an eyebrow. "Where do I sound like I'm from?"

"I don't know." He scratched his beard. "Typical America, I guess."

"*Typical* America?" I chuckled.

"Well, you certainly don't sound like a stereotypical Valley Girl." He pretended to flick his hair over his shoulder and smack his lips. *"Oh my Godddd, take a chill pill…gag me with a spoon."*

I burst into laughter at his horrible impression. "Wow, ok, we don't sound like that."

"*You* don't." He shrugged with a grin, and then dove under the surface and propelled himself away toward the center of the lagoon.

As my laughter faded, I stepped into the crystal-clear, turquoise waters, wiggling my toes. My gaze trailed up my thin, tanned legs and I frowned at the wispy blonde hair that was left unshaved. I'd cursed myself so many times now for not packing a razor, but I thanked mother nature for blessing me with genes for bleach-blonde hair. With Liam's growing beard and my lack of hair maintenance supplies, we were both giving true meaning to the term, 'au naturale.' It should have been embarrassing, but it was surprisingly freeing.

When I'd been with Jacob, he'd barely even seen me without makeup. If I were in bed with him and realized I'd missed one hair on my leg, my self-consciousness would have skyrocketed and ruined the moment. He never gave me reason to feel that way, yet I never felt confident enough in his affections that something trivial like that might not turn him off.

In the year we'd been together, I wasn't even sure we'd spoken as deeply as Liam and I had already. Jacob had his sweeter moments, but more often than not, his main interests lied in the upcoming football game or his next beer with 'the guys.'

I shook my head, trying to remember what I saw in him in the first place.

Once I'd waded in up to my waist, I traced my fingers across the glass surface of the water. Liam swam back to me and reemerged to run his hand through his slick hair. The water lapped at his collar bone as he watched me continue to tiptoe. "You coming in, or what?"

I sank into the cool relief of the sea, moving closer to him. Drops of water hung from his beard and his eyelashes, both sparkling in the sun. His full lips pulled into a smirk, and I couldn't stop myself from staring.

"You don't leave your hair down very often." He studied my

ponytail as he bobbed slowly in front of me.

I touched it and shrugged. "No, not really."

"Why not?"

"The same reason you cut all yours off." I eyed him with an accusatory grin.

"Fair enough. But you're in the water now."

"Keen observation," I teased.

"You should take it down." He stepped forward and reached around to give my ponytail a playful tug.

I gulped. "Why?"

He rolled his eyes with a chuckle and ran his hand through his wet hair again. "I don't know, from the few times I've seen, you look really pretty with it down."

Thump, thump, thump. My heart heard the words before my brain could comprehend them.

I held his gaze as I reached up to release my hair from its elastic binding. It tumbled down onto my shoulders in messy waves.

I shrugged nervously as the soft current guided me closer to him. "It kind of has a mind of its own."

He watched me with a warm smile. "I like it."

God, he was gorgeous. The sun shimmered in his eyes, bringing out little specks of green buried against the brown. I would have been content to stare into them all day, but I blushed and looked down into the clear waters. I could see my hands, clasped together nervously at my waist. He'd had that effect on me since the beginning, but now that he was pulling out compliments like this, an entirely different breed of butterflies erupted within me.

"So, the English accent really does it for you, huh?" he said.

I failed to stifle my smile and responded by quickly pushing a surge of water in his direction. It splashed up onto his face and he blinked, shocked by my bravery.

"*You* are a tease, Mr. Montgomery." I grinned.

"Mr. Montgomery is my father," he replied. "And is this how you want to play it?" His tone was sarcastically stern as he caught me off guard, sending back a much smaller splash of water my way.

I wiped my face and laughed. "Oh come on, is that all you've got?"

"Is that a challenge?" He raised an amused brow.

I held his gaze defiantly, not believing he'd do it again, but when he suddenly stepped toward me, I squealed and tried to back up. He grabbed my hand and pulled me further into the water as he sent another splash my way.

Our laughter echoed in the silence of the vast lagoon around us, and I sent a larger surge back toward him, completely re-soaking his hair. He sank below the surface briefly to smooth his curls, and when he returned, his face was only a few inches from mine.

I was still laughing as his hand held onto mine, warm and firm in its grip, but I soon began to realize that he was quiet, staring directly at me with an expression I hadn't seen from him yet. I stopped laughing and cleared my throat nervously, struggling with myself not to look away.

My breathing came shallowly as I stared quietly at the drops that trailed down his face. It was as if the waters were coaxing us closer, trying to bring forth the fantasy in my head. I wished that maybe they could, but I also knew it was exactly that; just a fantasy. I glanced down at his lips, which still glistened with beads of seawater. I wondered what they'd feel like against mine. I wondered if I'd be able to taste the salt on them with my tongue.

When I lifted my eyes to his again, he was breathing slowly and deliberately, searching my face like he was waiting for an answer. But I didn't know what the question was.

Right? I didn't know.

I gulped.

Wait, did I?

My mind went numb and fired on a million cylinders at the same time as he let the waves press him nearer to me. His chest grazed mine, and I stopped breathing entirely when I felt the heat of his breath against my lips. We paused like that for what felt like an eternity. His eyes darted back and forth between mine, filled with a lust that set off a jolt of something deep within me. My own thumping heartbeat was all I could hear in the silence of our deserted lagoon.

The gears whirred in my head as I tried to understand his intentions. The waves coaxed us once more, and the tip of his nose touched mine. He didn't back away, but he didn't move in either.

I suddenly realized what was happening. He'd made his move and started to close the distance between us. He was waiting for me to fill in the rest.

Oh God, he was waiting for me to kiss him.

Looking back and forth between his eyes one last time, I summoned up every ounce of courage within me and began to lean in. But just before our lips touched, he tilted his head down and rested his forehead against mine. He closed his eyes and pulled his brows together.

"I'm sorry..." he whispered. "I can't..."

I blinked and backed up, instantly embarrassed. *Shoot,* I knew I'd read him wrong.

He retreated slowly, shaking his head. "I just...I can't..." When he looked at me, there was a sort of tortured pain there.

I ran my hand through my hair as my voice shook. "Oh, um...I'm sorry."

"No, no, this isn't your fault." He turned to the shore and began wading up to the beach.

I hesitated, immensely confused and out of sorts. It had seemed like he wanted to kiss me, right? What had I done wrong? Reluctantly, I followed him, wringing my hands together.

He walked up the beach and leaned against one of the boulders, running his hand around the back of his neck. "That was unfair to you, Cora, I'm sorry." He turned his eyes to mine with remorse.

I stopped next to him and leaned against the same rock, looking up into his face as images of Kate flooded my mind.

He wiped his hand down his cheek. "This is...this is very difficult for me. I..." He paused. "You..."

He didn't have to say it. I knew.

But he took a breath and continued. "I want to...But Kate..."

I could feel the butterflies in my stomach slowly disintegrating, one by one.

"She's out there thinking I'm dead..." He gestured loosely toward the sea. "She's still grieving...I know I already had one foot out the door on that relationship, but this is not fair to her. There was no closure. As far as she's concerned, if I'm alive, we're very much still together." The distress was evident in his eyes as he looked at me. "And…this is so unfair toward you too. I let my feelings grow. I shouldn't have led you on. I'm so sorry."

Feelings. He had feelings? No, I didn't want to hear it.

I barely knew how to respond, but when he gazed pleadingly at me, I took a deep breath and replied in the best way I could. "Liam…you already have way too much to stress about. I don't want to add another reason to the list. I respect you for respecting Kate, and I would never ask you to adjust your morals for my sake. So please do not be sorry."

When his shoulders slumped and he frowned at me, I realized that what I had to say next was not the truth, but that it must be said. "I'll be fine. Please don't worry about me. I knew it was a long shot from the start anyway. You're a good friend now, and I'm happy for that."

He closed his eyes for a moment, but when he opened them again, he quickly dropped them to the ground. I gulped, trying to swallow the lie I'd just told. I was completely crushed to pieces. After having this opportunity handed to me and then ripped away in just a few seconds, I wasn't sure how I'd recover, but I couldn't let Liam wrestle with his guilt like this. Just as he'd been so kind and supportive to me, I had to do the same for him and ensure that he needn't worry about my feelings.

"Cora, I—"

"It's ok, really," I whispered, feeling like the wind had been knocked out of me. I gently placed my hand on his shoulder and forced myself to smile encouragingly, before stepping away and leaving him to his own thoughts.

I walked methodically into the trees. The sorrow, the guilt, and the jealousy bubbled strongly within me. There is a specific kind of pain you feel when your deepest desires are almost reached, only to be pulled from you so quickly. It feels like drowning in a pool of molasses. You've just reached the surface and then it sucks you down into its sticky depths again.

I stumbled over a few branches as I tried to contain my emotions, but when I knew I was deep enough into the island that he wouldn't find me easily, my body gave up and I fell to my knees and brought my hand to my mouth, blinking back tears.

I was embarrassed. For knowing Kate existed and still reciprocating Liam's flirtations and leading him on. For not shutting him down sooner. For leaning into him when I knew he was losing restraint.

I was heartbroken. For the closeness we'd almost shared. The closeness that we would now surely never experience again. For the pain that he was going through. For the guilt he had to suffer.

I was scared. For our unknown future on this island. For the inevitable awkwardness that would remain between us. For the torture I'd have to endure every time his eyes would meet mine, knowing we had been so close…

Wiping my eyes, I took a deep, shaking breath. It was silly, really, crying over something that I never even had. But I hung my head, knowing that regardless, it would take me a while to recover. And with Liam in my presence every day, he was the only person I could interact with, and I knew it would take me that much longer.

Just moments ago in the water, his face told me there was no question that his feelings were real. I closed my eyes and imagined how it might have felt if he hadn't changed his mind, and his lips *had* touched mine. Oh, I'd wanted it so badly. We'd grown so close during the last three weeks. I wanted even more than just that kiss. I wanted *all of him*.

I sighed and leaned my head against a tree. The crisscross of branches above me weaved in and out of one another, just like our lives, connecting and disconnecting, sometimes almost touching, but never quite catching hold.

Nearby, I spotted a coconut on the ground. It sparked a thirst within me, and I crawled over to it, tore off the husk, and then dug a sharp rock into the shell. I brought it to my lips and drained it into my mouth, just like I always did, but this time, something wasn't right. I spewed the foul liquid onto the ground in front of me and gagged. This coconut was *far* from fresh. I coughed and spat, trying to clear the taste from my mouth and scolding myself for being so careless. I'd swallowed some of it before the taste had registered, and just knowing it was in my stomach made me queasy.

I leaned back against the tree again and pulled my knees up to my chest. Trying to put the bad taste out of my mind, I thought about anything that could distract me. Unfortunately, the first thing that came to mind was Liam's relationship with Kate. He'd told me he had plans to break up with her, but did those plans change now that he'd almost lost his life? I didn't really know. He was clearly questioning their relationship more now, and I wondered if he would ever be able to let her go.

I hated to admit it to myself, but I had to give him credit. He was being incredibly respectful in the way he wanted to stay faithful to her, but ultimately, it made my heart ache for him even more. He was a good man. I saw that so clearly now.

I wanted him to stay true to his word, but at the same time, I desperately longed for him to change his mind.

Did that make me a bad person? No, that just made me an imperfect human falling for another imperfect one. The part that made me a bad person was the fact that I would have absolutely kissed him back, all while knowing that his girlfriend was home grieving his supposed death.

I hung my head. I needed to be on my own for a bit to collect my thoughts and move forward in a way in which I could support him. I'd gone completely off the rails.

A swarm of mosquitoes migrated in my direction, and I stood up, deciding to go somewhere else to think before I became their dinner. Rubbing my now uncomfortable stomach, I walked back toward the lagoon. Before I stepped out from the trees, I peered around to make sure Liam wasn't there, and when I didn't see him, I walked out onto the beach and sat down at the edge of the water, letting my toes just barely touch the shallow waves.

I drug my finger through the sand, aimlessly tracing a heart into its surface. I thought about how much had changed since I'd boarded that plane a month ago. I'd arrived at the airport, still giddy from meeting Liam the day before and craving the chance to meet him just once more. Yet here I was, having spent many weeks alone with him. I'd learned who he truly was in the deepest parts of his character, and I'd developed real, genuine feelings for him. And most shockingly, by some sort of miracle or sheer luck, he had developed feelings for me too.

Yet, he couldn't act on them.

A wave rippled up the shore right over the heart I'd drawn, and when it receded, the sand was perfectly smooth, as if the heart had never been there.

I stared blankly at the spot where it had been. What would we do now? How would we go on as a team after that awkward *disaster?* I dug my toes into the wet sand, watching the water pool around them, realizing that we *couldn't*. It would never be the same. Everything was ruined.

At some point while I sat in contemplation, I sensed a presence behind me, and then Liam quietly sat down to my left. I didn't look at him right away. I continued to stare out at the water in silence. We stayed like that for a few minutes, both in our own thoughts, connected only by a shared sense of bittersweet sorrow. It was sticky and raw, and I wasn't ready to face the reality yet.

When he finally spoke up, his voice was quiet. "You must think me an absolute jerk right now."

I took a deep, labored breath. "No, I don't think that at all."

"I wish I could explain…"

I interrupted him gently. "You don't need to explain. I understand completely."

He sighed. "This wasn't what I was expecting at all. I like you very much, Cora. If this were any other situation, I would be speaking to Kate right now, sorting this out."

I closed my eyes hopelessly. I really didn't want to hear it. "If this were any other setting, things would have never gone this far. This whole…*thing,"* I gestured between us, "couldn't be duplicated anywhere else."

He was quiet for a moment before he spoke. "I think I would have grown to feel this way about you no matter what."

I turned to look at him with skepticism. "I highly doubt that."

You didn't even remember me. I made you that turkey sandwich, but you forgot about me.

He frowned, sorrowful contemplation in his eyes. "If we weren't forced into being stranded together like this, you're right, things would have been different. I've really gotten to know you so much better than I would have otherwise..." He blinked at the ground.

I breathed slowly, watching him try to explain his feelings. But I didn't want to hear them because I couldn't bear the pain of knowing how strongly he thought he felt. He'd said it himself; we were *forced* into this. I didn't want to be the object of his affection if I was his only option. No one wanted that.

However, he continued. "But, regardless of whether or not I would have gotten to know you this well in another version of this life, it *has* happened here. And it's caught me off guard in ways I wasn't expecting. I only wish the circumstances were different."

"But they're not." I completed his train of thought, looking back at my feet. "And I've accepted that. I even respect that. When I think of Kate, I realize how much she must miss you. I understand her. I understand what she sees in you." I looked up at him again to see that he was watching me sincerely.

Liam frowned. "I hope you know how much I wish…"

"Please, just don't say anything more." I stopped him again, tortured by the prospect of hearing the rest. "We're going to be here alone for who knows how much longer. I can't bear to hear any more." I paused, locking eyes with him. "I'll be honest. I'm envious of her. You're a really good guy, Liam. I can see that so clearly now."

When his expression carried an even deeper level of sympathy, I shifted mine to a more hopeful one. "But, we're a good team, and I think we can still be if we let this go. You deserve a clear conscience, and I don't want to do anything to jeopardize that."

"Cora, I—"

"You asked me what you could do to make me happier..." I interrupted. "I don't want to be the cause of any extra stress for you. We need to focus on our survival. I'll be happy if you're happy. So, if staying faithful to Kate is what makes you happiest, then...you keep at it, and I'll follow your lead."

Liam closed his eyes and leaned his head back on his shoulders, clearly at a loss for words. He looked genuinely torn, but I didn't let myself linger on his grief. I had to be strong, at least on the outside.

After a moment, he tilted his head back down and looked at me. He hesitated before whispering softly. "Thank you..."

I nodded, recognizing his response as confirmation that he had truly chosen to remain faithful to Kate. I had to accept that, just as I'd promised, so I replied with a tight-lipped smile as I got up from my spot. "Well, I'm going to go get something to eat. I'm not hungry, but I know I should."

Liam stood slowly behind me. "I haven't much of an appetite either, but you're right. Are you ok with fish today? I'm not sure I have the patience for hunting."

I turned to face him, wishing he could really see how much I appreciated him. "Of course, Liam, I'm always grateful for whatever you're able to provide us." I forced a genuine smile. But on the inside, I fought the knot in my throat that threatened to erupt into the worst kind of heartache.

FIFTEEN

Later that evening, after a quick dinner and too much silence, we both laid down on the floor of our cave. We usually chatted briefly before falling asleep, but tonight, we didn't say a word.

I hated it.

I hated every second of the awkwardness that had plagued us throughout the day. We didn't know how to exist around each other anymore. Ever since we'd arrived, our relationship had slowly built into something more than friendship. A little more teasing, a little more flirting, a few more affectionate glances each day. But shifting from that to cordial friends in the span of a few minutes was not an easy transition. It was terribly depressing.

Plus, my stomach hurt. I wondered if my emotions were so high that my body was interpreting them as physical pain. I turned to look at Liam. He was laying on his back, staring at the ceiling. The moonlight that peeked through the cracks in the door fell across his eyes, illuminating them softly. I let out a soundless sigh and closed my own, trying to think of anything other than the imaginary sensation of his lips on mine. But all I could focus my sleepy thoughts on was the memory of his face so close to mine, the soft waves coaxing us together, and that look of desire in his eyes. How many times had I imagined that same look in my foolish fantasies before I'd even met him? *Too many times*. Seeing it in the flesh set off a cascade of desires and emotions within me that I couldn't halt.

But I *had* to try.

After a while, I managed to finally drift into a restless sleep.

And the next time my eyes flew open, I looked over at Liam, who was now rolled over, facing away from me. I furrowed my brow, trying to figure out why I had woken up so abruptly, when a wave of pain pierced my abdomen. I sat up, clutching my stomach and wincing at the deep, frightening, ringing sensation.

And then the nausea hit.

I reached my other hand up to clasp my mouth as my gut clenched, and I groaned, struggling to my feet. I burst out through the door, faintly noticing Liam stir as I left.

The pain was almost unbearable. It was a shocking, piercing agony. This wasn't right. Something was very wrong. Making it barely to the edge of the tree line, I fell onto my knees and emptied the contents of my stomach violently onto the sand.

Seconds later, warm hands touched my back and pulled the hair from my face as I continued to lean over, trying to stop my heaves.

"Cora, are you ok?" Liam's concerned voice came from behind me.

"I don't know..." I gasped for air.

I coughed and wiped my mouth, trying to take deep breaths, but failing miserably. My stomach continued to convulse, and I grabbed my abdomen again, hunching over stiffly on the ground.

Liam was still holding my hair as I turned to glance at him briefly. Even in the dark of night, I could see thc fear in his expression.

"I think I drank a bad coconut," I choked. The wave of nausea passed for a moment, and I sat back on my heels, taking deep breaths.

"How long ago was that?" he asked, releasing my hair.

I pushed myself up off the ground, wanting to move away from the mess. "A few hours."

"Hmmm..." Liam held my arm and guided me slowly. "Maybe it'll pass. Let's get you back inside to rest." He supported me as we walked back to the shelter.

Inside, I tried to lay down, but the pain only increased when I did, so I leaned my back against the wall. "Ugh, this is horrible..." I moaned, rubbing my stomach.

His eyes were wide with concern as sat down next to me, but I could barely look at him. Embarrassment, anxiety, and the grief from yesterday mingled with the excruciating pain and nausea that now overwhelmed me.

"Man, what was in that coconut?" I groaned.

"Nothing good, it seems," he answered with a sigh. "Is there anything I can do?"

I leaned my head back against the wall, trying to breathe through the misery as I shook my head.

"You should drink," Liam suggested, reaching over and

grabbing a bottle of rainwater.

I frowned.

"You don't want to get dehydrated..." Liam spoke softly as he pushed the bottle toward me.

Reluctantly, I took it and forced myself to take a few sips. But as soon as the water reached my stomach, another wave of nausea hit. I covered my mouth and quickly stumbled out of the shelter to throw up again.

I hung my head over the sand with my eyes shut tightly. There wasn't anything left in my stomach, yet the nausea remained relentless.

Feeling Liam's presence behind me again, I shook my head in shame. "You don't have to watch this."

"Well, I'm not just going to leave you out here all alone puking your guts out." He rubbed my back gently. "I wouldn't do that to you."

I leaned my back against a nearby tree and closed my eyes again, trying to encourage my body to relax. I knew Liam's words came from a good place, but I really didn't want him to see me like this. Not in any circumstance, but especially not after yesterday.

"I'm sorry I woke you," I breathed with my eyes still shut.

He sat down beside me. "You don't need to apologize."

"Ughhhhh..." I winced at the pain again, peering at Liam through half-lidded eyes. "This is unlike anything I've ever felt." I could barely focus on his face. The pain was deep and sharp, like someone was grabbing my stomach and twisting it tightly.

"Maybe it would help if you walked?" he suggested.

I nodded, willing to try anything. Liam took my hand and pulled me to my feet again. I brushed the sweaty strands of hair from my face and looked out at the dark beach. There was already a hint of daylight on the horizon as we made our way out toward the water.

"This is so stupid..." I groaned between waves of pain, gripping his arm. "I can't believe I drank it without checking first. It was just lying on the ground...it wasn't fresh."

"You didn't know," Liam consoled me quietly. "Have you had food poisoning before?"

"Yes, but not like this—owww..." I held my stomach again. "It feels like someone is trying to tear out my guts."

"Is walking helping the pain at all?" he asked.

I wrapped my arm around myself, feeling the chill of the sea air. "Not really...Are you cold? I'm cold," I groaned.

Liam stopped and turned to me. He placed his hand on my forehead. His skin felt icy against mine.

"Jeez, Cora, you're burning up." His face contorted with concern.

I shivered, but it was only a brief distraction from the pain and nausea. I could barely focus on anything else now. My mind was beginning to wander and dip between conscious thoughts. This was more than a typical stomachache. Whatever I'd ingested, my body was rejecting it violently. I wondered how much of it had already soaked into my system...

Facing Liam, I let my hand rest on my hip as I took deep, labored breaths. "I think I need to lay down."

"Ok, let's try that." He immediately took my hand again and turned me back toward the shelter.

He supported me as we walked and helped me lay down on the palm-padded floor. He rolled up a shirt and placed it under my head as a pillow.

Still wincing, I looked up to see his dark, knitted brows. I brought a hand up to my forehead, embarrassed that I was causing such a scene. "You don't have to stay with me…"

He frowned and pondered my request for a moment. "Ok, um, yeah, maybe you'd like to get some sleep…I'll, uh…" He looked around blankly. "I'll go work on the fire…" He slowly turned to exit the cave but glanced at me one last time. "Call out if you need me, I'll be right outside." And then his face turned sympathetic. "Hang in there…"

I feigned a smile, but I knew I was failing to fool him.

Once he'd left me alone, I pulled my knees up to my chest and rolled over on my side, squeezing my eyes shut and trying to fight through the pain. I'd suffered food poisoning before, but who knew what kinds of bacteria were festering on this island? Was my body prepared for that kind of battle?

Burying my head in the balled-up shirt, the pain subsided slightly. But my nerves were tingling and aching, numb and on fire at the same time. Slowly, I felt my overwhelmed brain slip out of consciousness. I wasn't sure if it was from exhaustion, or if my body was just using oblivion as a coping mechanism.

***

Sleep was peaceful. Sleep was painless. Sleep was escape.

I reluctantly opened my eyes to see Liam's blurry figure sitting next to me. He was holding a bottle of water on his lap, turning it around in his hands silently. His eyes were motionless as he stared down at it.

The numbness that came with sleep began to subside and was replaced by the same sharp pain I'd experienced before. I shivered. Every inch of my skin felt cold and sensitive.

My movement caught Liam's attention and he quickly turned to me. "How are you feeling?"

I rubbed my eyes and grimaced. "The same…"

He scooted toward me and placed his hand on my forehead again. "You're still feverish. Do you want to try to drink again?"

I glared at the bottle of water, fearing the consequence, but when I looked up at Liam, I could see that he was worried about me. So, I hoisted myself up on my elbows and took the bottle from him.

I tried a few small sips, and at first, the liquid was welcome to my parched mouth, but after the fourth, the nausea returned.

I slammed the bottle down and scrambled to my feet again. "Nope. Nope. Not yet…" I stumbled out of the shelter and bent over my knees, emptying those few sips of water onto the sand.

Liam was behind me shortly after, placing his jacket around my shivering shoulders.

I pulled it around me tightly, groaning through chattering teeth. "Ugh, what can I even do right now?"

Liam watched me nervously. "I think you'll just have to let it pass."

It wasn't the answer I wanted to hear, but I knew it was true. I peered up at the sky. The sun was rising quickly, casting long shadows across the beach. My head started to pound, and I rested my forehead in my palm. My muscles were fatigued, and it was becoming harder to stand. "How long was I asleep?"

"A few hours, I think," Liam responded.

The pounding grew stronger and I winced, pulling his jacket even tighter around myself. As I looked at the ground with my hands still braced on my knees, the corners of my vision began to cloud, and my fingers started to tingle. I breathed in and out through my nose, but I couldn't fight the sensation. "Liam..." I whimpered. "I don't feel well...I don't know what's wrong...I don't..." And then I fell forward.

Liam caught me before I hit the ground, but consciousness was eluding me, and my eyelids began to drift shut.

"Cora..." Liam's voice came stiff and concerned as he held me. I could hear him, but I couldn't open my eyes to look at him. "Cora, can you hear me?"

Drowning in my own illness, my ability to respond was gone. The pain, the fatigue; it was too much, and I began to slip away. Through the fog that hung around me, I felt myself being lifted from the ground, carried some distance, and then placed back down on another surface. I sensed the leaves against my back. I was in our cave again.

Fingers brushed the hair gently from my face. "Cora...are you ok?" Liam's voice traveled to my brain in a muffled murmur.

In this temporary state, I was no longer in pain. My body had chosen to check out for the moment; to give me a break. I saw lights and colors, sometimes mingling to form familiar faces or noises. Mostly it was Liam's face that morphed from the mess of shapes behind my eyelids. Sometimes he was looking directly at me, and other times he was staring off into the distance, just like he'd done when he was thinking about Kate.

I sank in and out of deep unconsciousness, sometimes rising back to the surface and almost opening my eyes, but never fully waking up. I had no idea how long I'd been out, but each time I reached the surface, I sensed bits and pieces of the real world around me. Occasionally, I'd feel a cool hand on my forehead, or a finger trail gently down my arm.

Once, I heard a voice, and I knew it was Liam's.

"Cora...can you hear me?" His tone was more strained this time, more worried. I wanted to respond, but I couldn't.

I felt a cool, wet cloth press against my forehead. I winced and shook my head, trying to avoid it. I was so cold already.

"You're getting too hot. I'm sorry. I have to keep you cool." Liam's voice was soft and kind as he continued to touch it to my head.

The new sensation momentarily brought me up from my unconsciousness, and I opened my eyes to see him leaning over me, his face filled with concern.

When he saw that I'd woken, he touched his hand to the side of my face. "Can you hear me?"

I blinked quickly, trying to stay awake, but the pain returned and all I could do was respond in a mumble. "Mmmhmmm..."

Liam rubbed my shoulder gently. "Just keep fighting this. It's gonna pass...It's gonna pass..." His voice, laced with fearful undertones, trailed off again into the cloud of fog.

I focused on his face for as long as I could. His deep brown eyes watched me with weary distress. In my wakeful state, I began to realize the nausea was subsiding, but the deep pounding in my head prevented me from forming coherent words to tell him my symptoms were changing.

He trailed his hand down my cheek again. "I'm right here. I'll be right here."

I closed my eyes. Even if there wasn't much he could do, there was security in his presence. I wished I was capable of speaking, to tell him not to worry, but the thick haze took over once more and I let myself go under again into the escape.

SIXTEEN

The air was fresh and warm the next time I opened my eyes. I breathed it deeply into my lungs. I tensed for the return of pain, but this time, it did not come. I brought my hand to my forehead to find it damp and cool. I wasn't shivering anymore.

The sounds of the waves crashing outside sent a soothing nostalgia through me, and the calls of the birds indicated morning. I laid still for a moment, still waiting for my symptoms to return, but when they didn't, I turned my head to see Liam sitting nearby. He was leaned against the cave wall, slumped over, and sound asleep. His lips were parted slightly as he breathed evenly, and in his lap was the water bottle and a damp rag, cradled in his hands. The longer curls on top of his head hung down, almost touching his closed eyes. It was clear that he hadn't even laid down last night. He'd fallen asleep sitting, watching me.

I tilted my head slightly, sorry that I'd put him through the ordeal. I couldn't have imagined seeing him in my place, dipping in and out of consciousness, not knowing when he'd wake up. The gratitude I felt was overwhelming. He'd been with me all night. He hadn't left my side.

I placed my hand lightly on his forearm. He sniffed and closed his mouth, lifting his head and blinking slowly as he took in his surroundings.

When his eyes met mine, he sat forward and anxiety sparked across his face again. "Cora…how are you feeling?" He placed his hand on my forehead, paused, and then expelled a deep breath. "Your fever broke…"

I nodded, watching his fear recede. "I'm feeling better, I think."

He relaxed back against the wall and wiped his hand across his brow. "My God, Cora, you had me so worried."

I frowned and tried to sit up.

He grabbed my arm in support. "Hang on, are you sure you can sit?"

I continued to hoist myself up until I was leaning against the wall next to him.

"Do you feel nauseous? Are you in any pain?" Liam questioned insistently, still holding onto my arm.

I swallowed carefully and assessed my symptoms. Apart from being a bit tired, I felt completely fine.

"Not at all. That's all gone." I smiled gently at him.

He let out an exhausted breath again, but his gaze held mine tentatively. "You were not well. Do you remember any of yesterday?"

I searched my foggy memories. "I remember…throwing

up…and I remember the pain…and I remember you. I'm so sorry I had you so worried."

As he assessed me, there was a deeper emotion behind his gaze as if he'd been through his own mental war last night. "You were tossing and turning, breathing hard, not responsive…" He looked down at his lap. "I wasn't sure…I couldn't tell if you were getting worse…"

I leaned forward, trying to meet his eyes. He raised his line of sight to mine, and in his expression, I saw how much he cared. I showed him my gratitude with a smile. "But I didn't. I'm here, I'm ok. I'm better. Thank you for taking such good care of me."

He stared at me for a moment before turning his focus to the bottle in his hands. He extended it to me. "You should drink some water."

I took a long breath and brought the bottle to my lips, hoping it wouldn't reignite the sickness. After a few sips, I lowered it from my mouth and waited. When the nausea stayed at bay, I took a few more sips and then set the bottle down next to me.

I looked up at Liam, who was watching me intently again. "Did you even eat yesterday?" I asked.

"What?" He blinked as if in a daze, and then fumbled with the rag in his hands, folding it neatly. "Oh, no I'm fine."

"You need to eat," I coaxed, feeling the guilt immensely.

He frowned. "I wasn't going to leave you alone to go hunt or fish. I did eat a bit of coconut, I think, at some point."

"Well, I'm feeling better now. You shouldn't let yourself starve on my account just because I stupidly ate a rotten coconut." I grimaced.

He looked down at his hands. "I can't help but think maybe you weren't in the right state of mind to have been paying much attention to that coconut…" When his eyes met mine again, they were grim. "And I blame myself for that."

My heart dropped as I realized he thought he was responsible for my sickness; that somehow the sadness I'd felt after our almost-kiss yesterday had caused me to make the mistake. I gave him a disapproving look. I could never imagine putting *any* of the blame on him. It was my fault, and mine alone.

"Liam…" I whispered. "This has nothing to do with anything you said or did yesterday. It was just a stupid mistake. A mistake that I will not make again."

His eyes lingered on mine for another moment before he closed them and nodded.

I placed my hand on his knee. "I'm a little hungry, and I know you are too." I tried to insert positivity into my weary voice, hoping that his spirits would be lifted if he knew he could provide something.

He looked down at my hand briefly and then up at me. "Yes, of course. I'll head out now." He quickly stood up. "Do you need anything else?"

I shook my head, but as he stepped through the door, I spoke up. "Liam, thank you, really."

As he turned to me, his expression softened. He gave me a nod before dutifully exiting the cave and disappearing from view.

***

When the sun hung just past midday, Liam returned with five fish in one of the palm leaf baskets I'd made for him. I'd brushed my teeth, changed my clothes, and come out to sit by the fire, feeling so much better after resting my body throughout the morning.

He quietly sat down next to me, pierced the fish with sticks, and placed them over the fire. "Are you still feeling alright?"

I nodded, taking one from him. "Yes, even better. I think I'm pretty much back to normal."

"I'm glad," he responded gently, not meeting my gaze.

I focused intently on my fish, positioning it above the hot coals and rotating it as it began to sizzle. Fortunately, my bout of sickness had allowed us to put our awkward almost-kiss on the back burner. This new, even more significant episode had given us something else to put our attention to, and it was a welcome distraction.

As I turned my stick slowly, I thought about what I would have done if he'd been in such a terrible condition. My mind would have immediately predicted the worst: a future alone on this island. I wondered if he thought I'd almost died. *Did* I almost die? I doubted that, but if I would have kept getting worse... Goosebumps rose on my arms as I realized how tragic this could have been. He'd spent the entire night fretting about me, which meant that he was probably no longer thinking about his feelings for me, but instead about the fact that he'd need to be on the lookout for any more stupid mistakes I might make.

I frowned, internally scolding myself for being so careless. We were a team, and I couldn't leave him alone out here. That's what he'd told me he feared the most. I had to stay strong for him. There was no room for thoughtless errors. Until we were rescued and would leave this island, I had to be his partner, his companion, and his teammate.

I let out a long breath, wishing I could be those things to him *after* we left this island too.

Sensing that my fish was fully cooked, I lifted my gaze to Liam, finding that he was already staring at me. His tight brows were serious, but his eyes were laced with emotion.

I blinked at him, confused. "What is it?"

His jaw tensed. "I just keep expecting you to grab your stomach again."

"I think it's all in the past now." I pulled the fish from my stick. "We'll see how this sits with me though."

When I glanced back up, he was still staring at me like I might keel over at any minute. I nervously focused back on my dinner and began to pull the meat from the bones. He was unnaturally distracted by me, and I didn't quite know why.

"You gonna eat your fish?" I asked.

In my periphery, I saw him shift and pick up his stick. "Oh, yes, of course…" His voice trailed off.

We ate in silence. He was usually quite chatty, but tonight he didn't say a word, and I was starting to fear the worst. Maybe he *did* resent me for my carelessness. Maybe my mistake had hurt our relationship even more than I'd thought.

When we were both finished, Liam threw his last bone onto the fire and took a deep breath. I watched him cautiously, waiting for his lecture on taking better care of myself.

He looked up at me, chewing on his lip. "Do you want to take a walk?"

I nodded hesitantly because I knew this wouldn't be *just* a walk. He was preparing to divulge whatever was on his mind. Probably either a speech about safety or even worse, his next explanation as to why he felt he needed to remain faithful to Kate.

Neither option sounded very appetizing.

He waited for me to get to my feet, and then we made our way toward the open beach.

"Sorry, do you feel strong enough for a walk?" he asked quickly after we took a few steps, suddenly sounding very concerned again.

I chuckled softly. "Yes, I feel fine now."

As we strolled, his arm was mere inches from mine, threatening to brush against it with every sway of his body. I glanced over and saw that his gaze was trained directly ahead. His jaw was tight, and his eyebrows were pulled firmly together. I swallowed nervously, waiting for him to speak.

"I was so worried about you, Cora." His voice was tense.

"I know, I'm sorry…" I slumped my shoulders with a sigh.

"No, no, I'm not trying to reprimand you," he said quickly. "But…seeing you like that made me realize how much I care about you."

"Of course," I replied. "You would be miserable here all alone. I get that. And I'm sorry I put you through that anxiety."

"It's not just that…" He inhaled slowly. "It's more than just the fear of being alone…"

I turned toward him, questioning his train of thought, but he hadn't looked at me yet.

"I didn't realize it before; the extent of my feelings," he continued. "But when I was watching you, sick like that, I realized that I wasn't worried about losing you just because I'd be left alone out here. I was worried about losing you *altogether,* and that's when I knew my feelings were deeper than I'd thought."

My heart thumped twice in quick succession as the words

left his mouth. I turned back to the sea, which was calm and rhythmic, just as it always was on quiet nights like this. It comforted me. It was predictable.

Liam was not. His thoughts and feelings were all over the place and I was having a hard time keeping up.

Unexpectedly, he grabbed my hand and stopped in place, turning to face me. I jumped at his touch, but I gradually lifted my eyes to his.

He gulped. "I was so focused on doing what I felt was proper, and not what I really needed, or what I really wanted. While you were unconscious, I thought long and hard about it. Things were never going to work with Kate, and I've always known that. We weren't right for each other, and if I were home now, it would have been over already." He gulped again as his gaze pierced deeply into mine. "How could I stand here and repress my true feelings? The ones I have for you?"

No, no... You have Kate. I recited her name over and over in my head, trying to ignore the seemingly genuine emotion in his eyes. His warm hand still gripped mine, and the place where our skin touched burned like the fire that I'd tried so long to stifle.

I wanted to speak up—to tell him it was ok. It was ok for him to want her instead. But I couldn't get the words out.

"Whether we're here for weeks, months, or longer..." he continued. "I can't deny the way I feel about you anymore."

My breath hitched in my throat. This admission was the last thing I expected from him after what we'd been through. But he took hold of my other hand and stepped even closer to me. He searched my expression as if trying to read my thoughts, though I doubted he could. I couldn't even understand them *myself.*

"Liam…I…"

"I know…" he interrupted me. "But you've made me realize things I never knew about myself and things I want in my life…" He swallowed. "…like you."

My heart was bouncing around in my chest in all sorts of directions. Here he was, finally expressing his change of heart, and I didn't even know how to react. Until now, I'd only heard his words in my wildest dreams.

The wind tangled my hair, sending a strand across my face, and Liam reached out to slowly tuck it behind my ear. I waited for him to drop his fingers, but he let them rest on the side of my face, surging with electricity in the spots where they connected.

He shook his head. "I tried to pretend like my feelings weren't there. I really did. But I can't lie to myself." He let out a shallow breath. "And I don't want to hide them anymore."

His eyes watched mine, burning with an ache that felt almost forbidden. I hardly wanted to believe him. He'd caught me completely off guard, and I feared he wasn't thinking clearly.

But my honesty escaped in barely a whisper. "I can't hide mine either…" I said it so quietly I wasn't sure he even heard me.

A small smile touched the corners of his mouth as he laid his palm on my cheek. And then, almost without pause, he leaned in and touched his lips softly to mine.

The sea, the sun, the sounds of the calling birds—they all disappeared. I lost all will to doubt him, and instead, I let myself *feel*, taking a small step toward him and pressing my lips deeper into his.

At my response, he dropped his hands to my waist and

pulled me into his firm body as he parted his lips against mine, all hesitation dissolving from them. As many times as I'd imagined this moment, it never felt as real and as raw as it did right now. I grasped the front of his shirt, holding him close as the tension released from me like the tide going out to sea. Because in that moment, something changed. Something beautiful and new began between us, and nothing would ever be the same.

In the gentle breeze of the late afternoon, on a beach we called our own, Liam and I embraced in a kiss so tender, yet so fueled by the passion we'd long suppressed, that the entire world vanished. I didn't know up from down or right from left. All I knew was that I was where I wanted to be, where I *needed* to be, finally able to liberate my feelings, and more at peace than I'd ever been—even before our plane had fallen from the sky.

SEVENTEEN

My heart pounded as Liam slowly broke our kiss and rested his cheek against mine. His beard was soft against my skin, and I smiled at the sensation, having imagined it for so long. When his eyes met mine again, they were filled with a relief that I reciprocated in equal measure. He tilted his chin up and pressed his lips softly to my forehead.

"I've wanted to do that for a long time..." he said.

I gazed up at his still smiling face. "Oh, you have *no* idea." I smirked, knowing full well that I'd dreamed of it much longer than he had.

He laughed and stepped back, taking my hands in his again, a grin spreading across his face and touching the corners of his eyes. It was the first real smile I'd seen from him since before I got sick. It was perfect and gorgeous, and I still couldn't handle how adorable he was. I returned it with one of my own, and then I giggled softly, casting my eyes to my feet.

"Come 'ere." He pulled me into a hug, wrapping his arms around my back and pressing his lips to my hair. I buried my face in his shirt, clinging to him tightly. This man had saved my life, and now, on this tiny island alone with him, he was my *everything.*

Neither of us spoke, even when he stepped to the side and coaxed me back into our walk. I interlaced my fingers with his as he squeezed gently; reassuringly. It felt like a dream. I could barely believe my life had taken such a drastic turn, not just once, but now *twice.* Surely things like this only happened in fairytales?

There was something so innocent and sweet about walking hand in hand with him; connected as we navigated our path. We'd felt like partners before, but with the snap of a finger, there was a new depth to our companionship. I grinned again, overwhelmed with joy.

Liam nudged me playfully. "So, I take it I did the right thing in telling you?"

I looked up at him, catching his sparkling gaze. "I believe you did more than just *tell* me."

He smirked and leaned down to kiss me once more, and I smiled against his perfect lips—the ones I'd get to kiss over and over again.

But when he pulled away, I eyed him nervously. "I still have a few questions though…What made you change your mind?"

Liam strolled slowly next to me, finding his words. "That dodgy coconut made me realize a few things. Like I said, if I were home right now, I'd call things off with Kate immediately." The mention of her name made me tense, but he looked me in the eye with sincerity. "Only, I'm not home, and I don't know when I ever will be. It's been an entire month, and we both agree it feels like much longer. But I've already let go of her, and because I have absolutely zero way to tell her, I decided that I can't let myself miss out on the chance with you."

I watched the waves as we walked, thinking about how betrayed she'd feel. I cringed as I realized I was the woman who'd pulled them apart. It was a nasty position to be in. But Liam had a point. He had no other choice.

Except to ignore his feelings for me.

My heart dropped as I considered what that would have meant for us. He'd been so decided on remaining faithful to her, and I tried to understand his change in mindset. He'd said all the right things, but were they true?

"But you were so..." I furrowed my brow. "Sorry, I'm just trying to understand."

He sighed. "It wasn't an easy choice, I assure you. I'm not the kind of bloke to be unfaithful. And that may sound like a line to you. But I'm being completely honest. This situation is just...different." He turned to me, watching me closely. "I like you a lot, Cora. What other option do we have?"

I knew the other option, but I didn't want to entertain it. If he was done holding back, I was too.

I studied his face, trying to believe his words. I wanted to, but they were so incredible that I almost couldn't. Did he actually care that deeply about me? Or would he have fallen for any pretty girl he was stranded with? There were so many variables. I couldn't make sense of them.

How could I be sure that he wouldn't forget about me and run back to Kate as soon as we made it home? I wondered if a short time on an island in a passionate relationship with Liam would be worth it if everything went south once we returned?

The snap response was *yes*.

As I sucked in a long breath, Liam stopped walking again and turned to face me. "I know what you're thinking, but you have my word…you're not just a distraction to pass the time while I'm stranded and away from Kate." He grimaced. "You're far from that. It took me a while to come to terms with the fact that I can't literally break things off with her. But I see something in you that I didn't realize I needed. I'm so…drawn to you." He paused, looking closely at me. "Kate no longer fits in my life. I know it may take a while for you to believe me, but I'm willing to do whatever it takes to get there."

I smiled lightly, entranced by his words, but they almost sounded too good to be true. I squeezed his hand gently, but I knew I'd have to fight to protect myself and stay reserved before I fell in too deep.

"I *told* you that you were a smooth talker…" I grinned, starting to walk again.

He took a long stride to catch up and then stepped in front of me, making pointed eye contact again. "I'm going to prove it to you. I want you to know you can trust me."

I stopped and looked up into his eyes. They were light and semi-transparent in the warm rays of the setting sun. "I do trust you…this is just an odd situation, and I'm trying to be careful."

He smiled gently. "I don't blame you…and that's one of the things I admire about you; you're smart like that."

I blushed. "It's nice to hear that you admire a few things."

A mischievous smirk spread across his face as he took a step closer to me. "There are *many* things I admire about you, Cora."

He placed his hands on my waist and pulled me into him.

My chest collided with his as he leaned in without hesitation, kissing me firmly and deeply again. I wrapped my arms around his neck, hugging him as the warmth of our embrace shattered the cool silence of the empty beach around us, sending my worries to the distant corners of my mind.

***

Later that evening, we sat by the fire, full and satisfied from a bird Liam had shot just before the sun went down. In the hour he'd been gone, I'd gathered some of the edible seaweed and prepared it for cooking. All the while, I grinned like a fool, still feeling Liam's kiss on my lips, and continually pinching myself to see if it was all a dream.

"I think I'll fish tomorrow," Liam suggested, tossing another log onto the fire. "I'm dying for a good swim."

"Could you show me how to spearfish?" I asked, blinking happily at him.

He scratched his beard. "I suppose I could. But you'll have to be very careful. The tide can be strong."

I smiled at his irony. "I believe *I* said the same things to you when you first went out."

He chuckled. "I know, but I worry about you."

I nudged him. "Hey, I'm stronger than you think. I survived that coconut, didn't I?"

His smile turned to a frown quicker than I'd expected. Clearly, it was too soon to make jokes. I placed a gentle kiss on his shoulder in the form of an apology, and he wrapped his arm around my back and pulled me closer.

"I'm feeling completely fine now," I reminded him, resting my head in the crook of his neck.

We watched the flames as they danced around the logs, sending sparks flying gently through the air. Eventually, I closed my eyes and snuggled in closer, savoring the butterflies that still fluttered through my stomach. If magic existed, it had been unleashed tonight.

"So, I'm curious," Liam began.

"Mmm?" I murmured. But when he didn't speak, I lifted my head to look at him.

He smiled warmly. "I've never dated a fan before. I should probably know what I'm getting myself into. Before you met me, were you like a…crazed fanatic, or…?"

I bit my lip and smirked. "I was not *crazed*."

Liam rubbed my back and laughed. "Ok, but for example, did you just casually watch my films, or…if your phone had a charge right now and I opened it, would I find my picture of myself saved somewhere?"

I buried my face into his sleeve and laughed, shocked that he was really asking me this. "Oh, God…I hope not…but maybe…"

He pried me off him, looking me in the eye and grinning mischievously.

I gazed up at him through my eyelashes, feeling my cheeks growing warm. "There may be one or two…" I whispered, completely mortified.

He smirked. "I actually think that's a bit sweet."

"You do not!" I shot back. I didn't believe him for a second.

"What?" he laughed. "You got to know me before we even met. I'm a touch jealous."

"Yeah, but…" I took a breath. "I don't want you to think I'm infatuated with you because of how I felt before we met… You mean so much more to me now."

"You're *infatuated* with me?" Liam's grin was so cheeky that I pushed his arm with a force that knocked him off balance.

"Liam…" I pleaded, giggling and hiding my face.

"Ok, ok." He smirked, righting himself and holding up his hands in defeat. "Ok, I'll listen."

I bit my tongue, watching him with a tight-lipped smile as I tried to figure out how to play his game. He stared back at me with a playfully expectant expression, but I knew he was going to let me speak now. It was my turn to expose my true feelings.

I took a deep breath. "Ok, so yes, last year I…became a fan…God, that sounds weird now." I laughed. "And sure, you caught my eye in more ways than one." I smirked as his grin grew. "But you're like a different person to me now. I can see the real you."

As he watched me patiently, I had trouble meeting his eyes. "You're so selfless and driven. You're thoughtful too. Every time you ask me how you can make me happier, I don't know what to say. I've never had someone ask me those things." I blushed again. "You make me laugh, you take care of me, you've saved my life *multiple times*, and I think we've both discovered that we want a lot of the same things in life." I paused and gazed deeply into his eyes, which had grown serious as he listened to my words. "You mean so much to me."

Liam's mouth curled into a soft grin, and he leaned in, placing a tender kiss on my lips. "Thank you for telling me those things."

I traced my finger down the now mostly healed scar on his

cheek. "They're true." I dropped my head to his shoulder again as he ran his fingers through my hair. "How did we even get here?" I mused.

Liam's chest rose and fell deeply as he gazed across the flames. "Some chance of fate, I suppose."

"Looking around at where we are, it says a lot that I think fate has been kind to us," I said quietly.

"Fate *has* been kind to us," he agreed. "We walked off that plane…well, *I* walked off that plane and carried you," he corrected himself with a chuckle.

I laughed and then blinked slowly, letting out a slow yawn. I hadn't realized I was so tired, yet the sun had set hours ago.

He rubbed my back again. "We should get some sleep."

I nodded drowsily and pushed myself to my feet. Liam tossed a few more logs onto the fire and then followed me into our cave. As we both laid down on our palm mats, I replayed the last twenty-four hours in my head. What a whirlwind of a day it had been. When I'd gone to bed last night, I'd been on the brink of serious illness, and now, here I was, lying next to Liam with an entirely new outlook on our relationship.

We laid close like this every night, but it was always completely platonic. What would happen now? We were both quiet as we stared at the stone ceiling. He was breathing gently next to me, unmoving, and I wasn't sure what he expected from me. I'd dreamed of lying in his arms for so long, but I wasn't confident enough to make the first move.

Thankfully, I didn't need to. Liam turned to me and smiled tenderly. "Come here…" he whispered, coaxing me toward him.

I grinned and rolled into his shoulder, placing my hand on

his slowly rising and falling chest. He wrapped his arm around me and planted a soft kiss on my forehead.

It felt right, laying with him like this. His fingers trailed slowly up and down my arm, leaving goosebumps in their wake. We fit together perfectly. It almost felt like a dream, yet the warmth of him was very real.

Finally.

His embrace was comforting and reassuring, and for the first time since the crash, I actually felt *safe.* Slowly, I drifted from consciousness, having just lived the most terrifying, yet *perfect* day—one I could have never predicted; not in a million years.

EIGHTEEN

The sounds of calling birds coaxed me awake the next morning. I breathed deeply, rolling over and rubbing my eyes. Waking up in a cave was no longer a surprise to me anymore. It was home for now, and I was used to the sights and sounds that were once so foreign to me. Except, today there was something different to remember; something new and sweet. My cheeks grew warm as the memories of the previous day flooded my mind.

I turned to find Liam fast asleep next to me, and I studied his face; his relaxed eyebrows, those long, dark eyelashes, his soft beard, those lips that had kissed me so tenderly... He was painfully handsome, and I couldn't believe this man had feelings for *me*.

I didn't want to wake him when he looked so peaceful, but I couldn't help myself. I scooted toward him and nuzzled my face into the crook of his neck, breathing in his comforting scent. He stirred slightly, and then slowly wrapped his arms around me, pulling me even closer.

"Good morning, love," he said gently into the silence, running his fingers through my unrestrained hair.

My heart skipped a beat at his affectionate term. Hearing it from his lips, so sweet and so easily rolling off his tongue, made me grin widely.

"Good morning," I sighed happily, kissing the warm skin of his neck

"Did you sleep well?" he asked.

"Mhmm…" I murmured. "You?"

"Quite well, yes."

We stayed like that for a few moments, slowly waking up, wrapped in each other's arms. Each breath I felt from him was a reminder that he was very real and alive here with me. It was a glorious way to start the day, and I hoped that many more would follow.

"I should check the fire," Liam whispered into my hair.

I groaned and hugged him tighter, but he kissed the top of my head and pulled his arm from underneath me.

"It'll just take a minute." He smiled before standing and exiting the cave.

I slowly sat up, stretching my joints and reaching into my suitcase to grab my toothbrush. Today, more than ever, I felt the urge to make sure I was fresh. I was glad I'd rationed the minty toothpaste.

After brushing my teeth, I pushed open the door to our shelter to see Liam carrying a pile of new logs. I spotted the swiss army knife lying on a rock nearby, so I grabbed it and prepared a coconut. I tentatively sniffed it, now extremely careful to check for freshness, and then walked it over to Liam.

"Need a drink?" I asked, holding it out.

"Thanks." He took it and smiled as he gulped down a long swig. "You still want to learn to spearfish today?"

"If you're still willing to teach me," I replied, leaning against a boulder and crossing one leg in front of the other casually. I watched him as he cracked open his coconut and continued to stoke the fire. Under his grey t-shirt, his shoulder muscles rippled as he moved the logs around. He licked a stray piece of coconut from his lips, and I swallowed slowly, completely entranced by him.

"Of course I am," he replied. "The fish are most active in the early morning and late evening. Do you want to go out now?"

I pulled my eyes from him and threw my own coconut shell onto the fire. "Sure, let me go pull my hair up."

I turned toward the shelter to head for my suitcase, but before I even took two steps, Liam had grabbed my waist and spun me around, leaning in and pressing his heated lips into mine. I was so caught off guard that I almost squealed, but in his firm grip, I quickly relaxed into him and grasped his upper arms, pulling myself closer.

When he finally broke the kiss, he stepped back and lifted a hand to trace it through my long, loose hair, tucking it behind my ear with admiration. Then he returned his fingers to my waist, holding me in place. "Ok, now you can go put your hair up."

"Are you sure?" I smirked, rendered motionless by his hold on me.

He pressed his lips together with a touch of humor as he pondered my question. "Hmmm…" he mused. His eyes met mine with a twinkle. "Yeah, I suppose not." He leaned in and planted another deep kiss on my lips; long and slow, filled with yearning.

The feel of his hands on me, holding me close to him set the depths of my core ablaze. *Oh God,* I needed him. I wanted more.

But when he stepped back again, he let go of my waist this time. "Ok, *now* you can go."

I raised an eyebrow, hoping maybe he was teasing me again, but he grinned and nodded, so I turned on my heel and headed toward my suitcase.

***

When we stood on the beach, Liam set his spear on the ground for a moment to pull his t-shirt over his head, and I couldn't help but stare. He was definitely thinner than he'd been when we'd arrived on the island, but wow, he was still some sort of Adonis of a man. I internally thanked his personal trainer again.

"Ready?" he asked, picking up his spear.

I pulled my eyes from his chest to look back up at him with a nod.

We waded into the water and began to swim into the current. Liam pulled a basket behind him, attached to a phone charging cord he'd tied to his wrist. His spear was the only one that had a rubber loop, which helped with its propulsion through the water, so we didn't bring mine.

I hadn't been out this far from shore yet, and I felt a jolt of anxiety as I turned to look at the beach in our wake. The waves rose and fell around us, obstructing it from our view at times. But soon, we made it to the spot where Liam said he'd had the most success. He showed me how to dive and let my eyes adjust so that I could see underwater and aim for the larger fish. There were multiple kinds swimming among the coral and rocks, but I was quickly able to pick out the shiny silver ones that Liam always brought back for dinner.

It was exhausting work, holding my breath and releasing the spear through the water with enough force and accuracy. I was starting to appreciate Liam even more, knowing what he went through to provide for us.

We alternated turns, and after a half-hour, he'd caught three fish and I was still empty-handed. I paused, treading water and catching my breath as I watched the dozens of elusive fish swim beneath me in the crystal-clear waters. With the spear in my hand, I looked down and spotted a particularly large one meandering between some brightly colored coral, so I took a deep breath and sank slowly into the water, trying not to startle it.

I opened my eyes, making out the blurry shapes underwater, and I saw the fish again, a few yards away, moving slowly. I crept toward it with my spear poised and ready, trying to predict its path. When I felt confident, and just before it inched too far away, I shot the spear through the water.

To my surprise, it made contact, sending the pierced fish to the sandy bottom. I dove after to retrieve it and pulled it up to the surface with a proud grin. It was flopping wildly, still very much alive as I fought with it in my arms.

"Liam…" I sputtered, taking deep, labored breaths and trying to keep the fish from escaping.

"Brilliant work!" He swam to me quickly, taking it from my

arms and wrestling it into the basket.

I bit back my own elated smirk, pleased with my success.

"I think we have enough for lunch now." He closed the basket and pulled it toward him. "And you deserve a rest."

I gazed back to the beach, examining our island from a new angle. It was bright and green, drastically contrasting the turquoise blue waters that surrounded us. The trees waved lazily in the breeze and the sand sparkled in the sun. This place we presently called home was becoming more beautiful each day.

Once we reached the shore and waded up to the beach, Liam tossed the basket and spear to the sand. I sat down in the shallow tide, completely spent, and he lowered himself down next to me, resting his elbows on his bent knees as he breathed heavily. "Hard work, isn't it?"

I caught my breath and leaned back on my hands as my heart rate returned to normal. "I don't know how you do this almost every day."

"It's not so bad after a little practice." He shrugged. "And the look on your face every time I come back with a fresh catch is worth it." He trailed his gaze down to my rising and falling chest.

I noticed him linger there just for a second or two before he met my stare again, and his expression was a bit darker—dark in a way that made my eyes fall to my hands, at the mercy of the same shyness I'd struggled with all along.

"Kinda like the look on your face when you ate my turkey sandwich?" I asked, sneaking a glance at him.

He'd moved an inch closer to me. "Mhmm…"

I bravely held eye contact, smiling bashfully as the gentle waves lapped around us in the shallow waters. Wet curls hung over his forehead and beads of water dripped from his beard onto his bare chest. His expression told me where his thoughts were, and I felt myself breathing harder again, developing the same thirst in my own eyes.

He closed the last of the distance between us, touching his lips to mine, slowly at first. But the feelings inside me were thoroughly roused and I placed my hand on the back of his neck, tangling my fingers in his hair and pulling him closer. His tongue traced my lower lip just slightly, begging for entrance, and I obliged, parting my lips and tasting him for the first time. He was sea, and salt, and sweet like the coconut he'd eaten this morning.

If only I could bottle him up and keep him forever…

Soon, he was pushing me down onto the sand. The cool water pooled around my back as he traced his hand through my hair and down along my arm, eliciting a shallow exhale from my lips. My heart was beating out of my chest, and every nerve on my body heightened as our mouths moved hungrily together. He was a fantastic kisser, and I felt myself losing control under his expert and passionate lips. But just as fast as it had begun, he pulled away and pressed his forehead into my own, breathing hard.

We both laid still, Liam partially on top of me as the gentle waves caressed our skin. He opened his eyes, revealing a hint of tortured desire behind them as he looked at me, and then he leaned back and took my hand, pulling me up to sit again. I rested my head on his shoulder, regaining my breath as he ran his fingers through my hair.

I knew that I had to guard myself carefully, but all I longed to do was show him how strongly I felt, over and over again.

I closed my eyes and smiled. "I know it's crazy to say this, but I'm *so* glad we were both on that plane."

He kissed my forehead gently. "I know…me too."

***

Later that evening, after we'd eaten, we laid on the soft sand, staring up at the stars. They were so much brighter here than I'd ever seen them in L.A. With all the light pollution there, they had been merely dim specks in the sky. Here, they were multiplied by the thousands and sparkling impressively above us.

There was something about these moments that made our time here so profound. We were frequently busy keeping ourselves alive, but in the evenings we could *really* rest. We didn't have the weight of the world on our shoulders. We had the weight of the *island* on our shoulders, but on days like today, it felt like a cakewalk. It was just the two of us, our growing feelings, and the un-numbered days ahead of us.

As it frequently did, my mind wandered to Kate and the guilt that gnawed at my heart. As utterly blissful as I was, knowing that Liam felt things for me, and I was able to kiss him, and touch him, and hold him, I couldn't help but feel like I was the "other woman." As much as I didn't want to think about it, I knew that eventually, once we both made it home—*if* we both made it home—I'd have to face her. How would I explain myself? And what would Liam do? Would he have to choose between us? I grimaced at the thought. He'd told me that he was done with Kate, but what would happen when he saw her in front of him again and the memories came flooding back? Would his perspective change?

I closed my eyes and frowned. As much as he told me otherwise, I still wasn't confident that he actually cared for me enough for this to last longer than our time here. I was his only option, so of course he was interested, *for now*. I sighed. He'd forget about me once he remembered how exciting his life was before all this.

"Everything alright?" Liam asked, turning his head toward me.

I opened my eyes and looked back at the stars, deep in thought. "Do you think…" I paused, trying to formulate my question. "Do you think you would have felt the same way about me if we'd gotten to know each other somewhere else?"

He rolled toward me and brushed his fingers along the side of my face. When I turned to look at him, he was smiling gently. "You're really worried about that, aren't you?"

I rolled over to face him. "Well, I mean, you don't have many choices out here in the middle of nowhere, and sometimes I wonder."

He tucked a stray strand of hair behind my ear as he studied me sympathetically. "I wish I could show you inside my mind so that you wouldn't have to doubt me."

"Do I *want* to see inside your mind?" I cracked a smile.

He bit his lip and grinned back. "Ah, true. Depends on what you might or might not be expecting." And then he laughed his wonderful laugh that I now knew so well.

I smirked and shook my head, loving how playful we could be with one another, even during our deeper conversations like this.

Liam spoke again. "I can tell you this. I absolutely would

have noticed you under any circumstances." He rested his warm hand on my arm.

I narrowed my eyes. "*Did* you, though?"

He smiled. "That day on set, I thought you were absolutely adorable. That sweet little blush when you realized you'd sent those tongs flying across the room."

I laughed. "You know the blush was because of *you,* right? Not the tongs."

The corners of his mouth turned up, and I studied him closely, feeling brave enough to ask the obvious.

I bit my lip nervously. "If you thought I was so adorable, why didn't you recognize me when you pulled me off the plane?"

Compassion crossed his features, and he softened his expression. "Because your face was covered in blood, and you had a giant gash across your forehead."

Oh, true.

He caressed my shoulder gently. "But regardless of that, our first meeting was so short. Now that I've gotten to know you, I see you in a new light." He paused. "And you're absolutely beautiful, Cora."

Realizing that this was the first time he'd said that to me, I let my gaze fall shyly to his chest. His words were so sweet, yet a nagging voice in the corner of my mind reminded me that they could all be fake.

"And if I'd had a chance to speak with you more that day and get to know you better, I bet I would have seen some of the same qualities that I admire today. If I knew we'd both be in town for a bit, I'd likely have asked to see you again," he said confidently.

My doubts dissolved once more and I couldn't hide my grin.

"Where would you take me?"

He brought a finger to his chin. "Well, there is a quaint little pub downtown L.A. It's very reminiscent of a pub in my hometown of Canterbury, actually. So, I might have taken you there, because I'd feel comfortable, and therefore more likely to sweep you off your feet." He winked.

"Oh, *would* you?" I smirked, loving that he was painting this little picture. "Would we spend the whole evening there?"

"I think, after we ate, we'd take a nice stroll, just chatting and getting acquainted. Nothing too extravagant. I'd know a bit about you by then and I'd realize that you'd enjoy something simple."

I grinned. He was so thoughtful and perceptive, even in his imagination.

He continued. "At the end of the night, I'd drop you back at your flat, and I'd fumble with my car keys as I walked you to your door…" He paused and his eyes crinkled. "Just like the movies. And then I'd wait to see if you went right inside, and if you didn't…" He inched closer to me and his deep brown eyes stared into mine. "…then I'd lean in and give you a short, sweet kiss…" He touched his lips to mine, softly and chastely, and then pulled away. "Because I'd want to show you that I'm a gentleman. And then we'd say goodnight, and I'd think about you the entire drive back to my hotel, wondering if I'd left too soon."

A foolish grin spread across my face as he told his story. His ability to be completely adorable knew no bounds, and I wondered how I could possibly ever resist him if he kept up like this. He had a way about him that pulled me in, inch by inch, day by day, slowly sending me to the brink of deeper feelings that I could hardly believe were becoming my reality.

I lifted my hand and traced the soft, dark curls that framed his face. They had an unruliness to them that made me smile.

Only lit by the stars, we laid in silence, savoring the moment, and the prospect of many more moments like this to follow.

NINETEEN

A few more days passed.

A few more days filled with blissful kisses and cuddles and moonlight strolls, coupled with deep conversations and enough flirting to make us forget we were stranded in the middle of nowhere. It felt like life couldn't get any better in our unique adventure. The fish were plentiful, occasional morning rainstorms gave us our drinking water, and our bodies were stronger now and more adapted to our environment.

I tried to live in the moment, but I couldn't help but wonder when our luck might run out. Even though we'd cleared our first hurdles and were thriving now, I couldn't rely on life continuing to be so kind to us.

Having finally expressed our feelings for each other, Liam and I slowly began to explore what that meant for our relationship. 'Slowly' was the operative word, because firstly, I was shy. I always had been. I always would be. That was my nature, and

I got a sense that Liam knew that about me. I wasn't the kind of person to dive right into something so intimate so fast, and he seemed to easily respect that. And I also had an extra guard up, knowing that Kate was still part of the equation. She posed an entirely different set of roadblocks for me.

But almost as much as I was cautious, I was also starting to lose my sense of restraint. The closer we grew, the more I longed to throw myself at him and give in to the desires that had built up within me for so long. Plus, he was downright *irresistible.* My word, this man could tease and flirt and smooth talk any woman into a puddle of goo at his feet. And as his newest victim, I found it harder and harder to hold myself together.

One evening, as we sat by the fire digesting our dinner, Liam was leaning against one of the large boulders and I sat between his legs resting my back against his chest. His arms were wrapped around me and he gently kissed my temple.

"Did you get enough to eat?" he asked quietly.

"Mhmm…" I sighed, closing my eyes and laying my head on his shoulder.

"What's the first food you'll eat when we get back?" he asked.

"Hmm…" I pondered, wondering if there was anything I *wouldn't* eat right now. "How about a juicy burger? No, wait, maybe some pasta? Ooh, chocolate cake…" I giggled, shutting my mouth to stop myself from going on.

Liam chuckled and kissed me again. "That all sounds delicious, but I'll tell you what, I could go for a nice whisky right now."

I smirked and trailed my finger up and down his forearm, tracing the dark hairs that grew there. "Well, we'll just have to get you one when we get back."

I tilted my head and looked up at him, grinning and wondering what it would be like to sit down with him at a bar, in the real world, like a normal couple.

"I'd like that very much," he responded.

I nestled my head back onto his shoulder and watched the flames of the fire twist and disappear into the air.

"So…" Liam began. "Might I be so lucky as to get a second dance with you?"

The butterflies fluttered to life as I looked up at him again. "I do think you promised to teach me some more."

Liam unwrapped his arms from around me and stood up, holding out his hand. "Then, may I have this dance?"

I placed my hand in his and let him pull me to my feet. Brushing the sand from my shorts, I glanced down at my sad display of clothing, which looked like it hadn't been washed in days, and, well…it hadn't…

An idea popped into my head. "Hang on…I'll be right back."

Confusion crossed his face as I pulled my hand from his, but I gave him a reassuring grin before disappearing into our shelter. I knelt and unzipped my suitcase, revealing the items inside. There were a few pieces of clothing that I hadn't worn yet because they just weren't practical for life on a deserted island. I dug through the fabric, searching for a specific article. When I found it, I slid the soft cotton between my fingers and pulled it out. It was a simple, elegant, yellow sundress. Thin straps led to a lace bodice that was fitted through the waist and then flowed freely the rest of the way down.

I bit back a smile, remembering how much I loved the dress and how confident I felt in it. It was cute and comfortable, with just a hint of sexiness as it left a bit of skin exposed. I pulled off my shorts and t-shirt and stepped into the dress, smoothing it around my figure. It still fit well and hugged my torso in the right places. It was crisp and clean, and it still smelled of the flowery detergent from home. I twirled once, letting the skirt flutter away from my bare legs, and then I reached to the back of my head and released my hair from its elastic band, letting it fall loosely over my shoulders. For the first time in over a month, I actually felt pretty.

I slowly stepped out of our shelter and began to return to Liam, who was standing with his back to me, studying the fire. When he heard me coming, he turned around with hands in his pockets, and his eyes immediately dropped to my dress.

I grinned as his expression turned fiery and his gaze roamed up and down my body. He took a step toward me and placed his hands on my waist, tracing the smooth lace.

"You look…" he breathed. "…stunning….and…" he swallowed. "Wow…" His eyes rose to meet mine as he trailed his palms up and down my sides.

I smirked. "I figured if we were to have a proper dance, I should look the part."

His hands continued to touch my waist as he bit his lip and took a shaking breath. He didn't speak as he grasped my hand and led me slowly toward the open beach. There was a sensual, wanting look in his eyes as he stopped in front of me, sending my heart rate skyrocketing.

He slid his hands up to my bare arms, leaving a trail of warmth as he stroked them gently, not saying a word

I gulped. "So…which dance will you teach me tonight?"

He reached up to push a stray strand of hair from my forehead. "I'm not sure I have the focus to teach you something new tonight. Do you remember what we practiced before?" There was a new, gruff tone to his voice.

I admired his face, perfectly lit by the flicker of the nearby fire. His eyes were dark, but laced with a touch of kindness and warmth. Slowly, I placed one hand in his and the other on his shoulder, just as he'd shown me before.

He took a deep breath, lifted his elbow, and began to count slowly. "One, two, three…one, two, three…"

I let him lead me effortlessly around the sand, watching him as he watched me. With each round, he stepped closer and closer, closing the distance between us. Eventually, he stopped counting and his cheek fell to the side of my neck. His breath fanned my hair as our chests touched. We slowly moved together, and I closed my eyes, completely entranced by the moment.

Soon, his lips were on the column of my throat, trailing tender kisses underneath my jaw and down to my shoulders. My skin tingled at his touch, and I tilted my head back, giving him more access. Then his lips were moving featherlight across my cheek until they met mine, thick with an unsuppressed need.

Every hair stood on end as I kissed him back fervently, breathing him in and wrapping my arms around his neck as I pulled myself impossibly closer. His arms snaked around my waist, encapsulating me with his warmth and strength.

Kissing Liam was like sinking into a scorching hot tub after a long chilly day. It was like wrapping yourself in a fluffy blanket at the close of a stressful night. It was relief, and safety, and comfort. But kissing Liam was also something else. Every nerve ending within me was burning with a repressed yearning, and all I wanted to do was rip the shirt from his chest and become one with every part of him.

His demeanor shifted and he moved his hand roughly to the small of my back, holding me to him as he guided us down onto the soft sand. Straddling my legs, he kissed me deeply as he trailed his hand down my neck to the exposed skin of my collarbone. I was euphoric, forgetting all restraint as I slid my hands down his muscled arms, wanting to touch him wherever I could.

His mouth was everywhere. First at my cheek, and then at my ear, his hot breath sending shivers down my spine. And trailing one hand down along the fabric of the skirt of my dress, he found the edge and pushed it slowly up my leg.

My breath hitched in my throat as his touch traveled higher and higher. I almost let it happen, but I squeezed my eyes shut and reminded myself that we needed to discuss something first. It took every ounce of my being to pull away from him.

"Liam…" I whispered.

"Mmhmm…" he responded, sending vibrations into my neck.

"Liam…we have to…" More urgently this time. "We have to talk about this…"

He paused and lifted his head to look at me. His eyes still burned with desire, but they grew tentative and cautious when they found mine. I caught my breath as I stared up at him, complete putty in his hands as I tried to regain my coherent thought.

He removed his hand from my leg and lifted his body from mine slowly, coming to his knees in front of me. "I um…I'm sorry, Cora."

I sat up and touched the side of his face, smiling gently.

"No...don't be sorry. Please...that's not what I meant."

He curiously gazed into my eyes as his chest continued to heavily rise and fall.

I ran my fingers through my hair, taking a deep breath. "As badly as I didn't want you to stop, I..." I paused, searching for the right words. "We have to talk about this...before it goes... too far."

He bit his lip and looked down, resting his palms on his legs. "I know..."

I knew. *He* knew. This relationship wouldn't play out the way a typical one could. We couldn't just hop over to the corner drugstore and pick up a box of condoms. And I hadn't been on birth control since I'd broken up with Jacob.

I slid my fingers through the hair on the side of his head and looked up at him, trying to get him to meet my eyes. "We have to be smart about this. We don't have...protection..." I blushed. "At least...*I* don't." I watched him closely, hoping he had a better response.

But he lifted his remorseful eyes to mine and shook his head. I took a disappointed breath and rested my hand on his arm. "I just don't want us to do something we'll regret. We don't know how long we'll be here, and we *cannot*..." I put an emphasis on the word. "...bring a child onto this island..." The words came out of my mouth evenly and clearly, but inside I couldn't believe that this was a conversation we were really having.

"The reason I stopped you now..." I continued. "...was because we needed to talk about it with clear heads before... you know, things went too far."

He frowned. "No, you're right. And I've thought of that too. I'm sorry, I lost a bit of control just then..."

"Losing a *bit* of control is not the problem." I smirked. "Lose every little *bit* of control you want."

He took a long, measured breath. "I shouldn't have… I mean, I don't want to make you uncomfortable. That's my fault."

I touched his cheek again. "I'm sorry I've only brought it up now. I should have said something earlier…"

"No, Cora, you're perfectly fine." He scooted closer to me. Our legs weaved between each other as he grasped my hands gently. "It's been a bit of an elephant in the room, and it needed to be discussed. This is all very real, and there are serious consequences." He leaned in and affectionately touched his lips to mine. "Making sure you're comfortable is most important." He finally smiled. "I'll be glad that we've been responsible about it." His gaze traveled down my body again, growing darker. "But that dress…might be dangerous."

I grinned and kissed him again, deeply and with heartfelt emotion. "I can go change…" I chuckled.

"No, *no*…please don't." His eyes were fiery as he leaned back to admire me. "Wear that every day please…"

I laughed and leaned in to press my lips firmly to his neck. "If that's what makes you happy…" My voice came in a soft and intimate whisper.

He responded deep and rough. "It does indeed."

***

Three days later, I waded through the shallow, rocky waters in the area near our campsite, searching for the leafy green seaweed that we sometimes included in our meals. My culinary background had me loving the color it added to our metaphorical 'plates,' but it was scarce lately, and I was lucky to find even just a little bit of it. Nevertheless, I searched anyway, scanning the waters closely and watching the tiny fish scatter with every step I took.

I pondered the few days that had passed since Liam and I had talked about the roadblocks for our intimacy. That night, I'd made a joke, telling him he could lose a *bit* of control, and I'd thought he had understood me, but since then, he'd had *all* the control in the world.

He kissed me, he held me in his arms, and he whispered sweet words in my ear as we drifted to sleep each night, but the fire that had once darkened his eyes was missing. It was as if it had simply disappeared, or he'd put up an internal wall to hold it back.

Just last evening, we'd been cuddled up in our cave, winding down for the night after a long day. Liam's eyes had been closed peacefully when I'd leaned in and softly kissed his lips.

"Mmm…" he'd murmured, kissing me back gently.

Perched on my elbow, I'd trailed my fingers through his dark hair, watching him open his eyes, filled with warmth and contentment. "These curls…" I'd mused, twisting one of them around my finger affectionately.

Liam had rubbed his hand gently up my arm. "You like them?"

"Very much…" I'd whispered, moving on to touch another.

"Then why did you agree to cut them?" He'd smiled.

I'd leaned down and kissed his jaw through his full beard. "Because you said you were too hot, and I wanted you to be comfortable."

Liam chuckled. "I can grow it out again, if you'd like."

I'd leaned back and grinned at him. "But then you really will have to start stealing my hair bands."

He'd taken a deep breath and lifted his hand, trailing it along the side of my face toward my ear. "Well, I hope we aren't here long enough for it to get to that point."

"I wish I had your confidence..." I'd whispered sadly.

"We'll make it off this island, Cora... Don't worry."

"Well, while we're here, we can at least make the most of it..." I'd leaned down again to kiss him deeply, and he'd responded in earnest, snaking his arm around my waist and pulling me closer to him.

His hand had rested on my back, warm and insistent, holding me to him tightly. I'd let my lips leave his mouth and had just begun trailing kisses down his neck when I'd heard him take a deep breath.

"We should get some sleep," he'd said quietly. "I have the big task tomorrow of replacing some of the supports for the wall."

I'd stopped my assault on his neck and raised my head to look at him. He'd smiled and placed a chaste kiss on my lips before pulling me down onto his shoulder and wrapping his arms around me in the position we'd often fallen asleep in.

That night, along with the others that had passed since our conversation about accidental pregnancy, left me a bit troubled and with more questions than answers.

Back in the present, I wondered if our pregnancy conversation had felt too awkward to him, or if maybe my fears were a turn-off. Had I ruined the mood altogether? Or maybe he was too afraid of losing his own control.

I sighed. Could he have had a change of heart and realized that going much further with me would be even more of a disrespect to Kate? I scrunched my nose, sincerely hoping that wasn't the case. Yet, a nagging voice in my head told me it was a possibility. I hated that. I needed him to pick a side. I wouldn't let myself settle for only part of his heart. That would be unfair to both Kate and to me. It was already bad enough that I was the "other woman."

I wanted to talk to him about it again, but I wasn't sure how I'd ask without inflicting some sort of offense. It was clear that something made him take a step back. But if it was pregnancy, why had he decided to shut down any advance in our intimacy at all? We could still have plenty of fun in other ways. It didn't make sense.

I lowered myself down onto a smooth rock and closed my eyes. The fact that I was even sitting here, contemplating the possibility and consequences of getting pregnant by Liam Montgomery made me chuckle ironically for a moment.

I was briefly transported back to our introduction on the Universal Studios set. It felt like an eternity ago, and my life had changed so drastically since then. I thought about the tiny apartment I shared with Tess and the paycheck I received that barely even allowed me to afford that. Regardless of the extreme danger I faced in becoming pregnant on a deserted island, I was also far from ready to raise a child, and I had a feeling Liam wasn't ready either. Plus, we'd known each other for less than two months now. Jacob and I hadn't even slept together until we'd been dating for four months. Yet, I already felt a thousand times closer with Liam. The trials and tribulations we'd been through had brought us together on a level that only we could understand. But one simple moment of passion could change everything in an instant. It wasn't worth the risk. Even though I'd been undernourished, my period had still come last month—which was just a joy to deal with on a deserted island—and so I knew I couldn't take any chances. This was not a game. This was real life.

Keeping my eyes closed, I laid down onto the rock and retroactively examined Liam's recent behavior. He wasn't necessarily *less* affectionate. He was just…unchanged. It was like our conversation had put a halt on any progression of our intimacy. We'd hit a wall. Maybe it was for the best? Was I expecting too much, too soon? He'd had this intense hold on me since long before we'd even met. But for him, his feelings were much newer. Maybe he needed more time. Or maybe he realized he'd made a mistake.

"Working hard, or hardly working?" Liam's voice startled me, and I sat up quickly. He was grinning as he took a seat next to me. He placed a quick kiss on my lips and then rested his hand on my back; an apology for scaring me.

"There is literally, like, *none* of that seaweed left…" I frowned.

"Hmmm…" he replied, looking out into the water. "Well, we still have other things to eat at least. We can look again when maybe it's grown back."

"I suppose so…" I sighed, pulling my knees to my chest and wrapping my arms around them. I watched the sea silently, sulking.

"Is anything else the matter?" Liam asked gently.

I gazed at him for a moment, searching his hazel eyes for some type of explanation for his bewildering behavior. But the look he returned was entirely curious about my mood and not a bit aware of his own.

I set my jaw. "How have *you* been these past few days?"

"I've been perfectly fine." His eyes never left mine as he spoke with what appeared to be complete sincerity.

I raised an eyebrow. "Nothing on your mind?"

He frowned. "Cora, are you sure nothing is the matter?"

I took a deep breath, realizing that I was going to have to outright explain it to him, and I dreaded the probability of feeling embarrassed.

I held eye contact for a moment, considering my words. "Ever since we talked about..."

But I stopped speaking because Liam was now staring over my head with wide, stunned eyes as if he'd seen a ghost, or a comet, or...

"A plane..." he gasped.

TWENTY

"A *plane…*" This time Liam's voice was louder as he rose from the rock.

I swung my head around, looking up into the sky to find a tiny silver speck, much like the one we'd seen weeks ago, slowly approaching in the distance.

"A plane, Cora, A PLANE!" He was almost yelling now as he sprinted from the rocks toward the fire.

I scrambled to my feet and ran through the sand after him.

"Get anything you can find! Throw it on the fire!" he shouted in a frenzied panic.

The blood was rapidly rushing from my head as the adrenaline coursed to my hands and feet, carrying me toward fallen palm fronds and stray driftwood.

My eyes darted to the SOS we'd formed on the sand. It was still perfectly legible, so I worked with Liam to throw every last piece of anything we could find onto the fire. The flames quickly grew to be taller than us both, crackling and winding wildly in the breeze. But it was midday, and the light they cast was surely much less noticeable than it would be in the dusk of evening.

We stood next to each other, eyes locked on the plane, chests rising and falling as we tried to catch our breaths. Words eluded us as we watched it approach just like the first one had. And then it was even *closer*. It stayed true to its course, closing in on us slowly. The tension in the air was achingly palpable as we both waited for an answer to a question we were afraid to ask.

My mind flooded with images of my parents running toward me, enveloping me in their arms as they discovered I was still alive. God, I missed them so much. More than anything, I needed them to know I was safe.

Maybe we'd done it. Maybe we could finally return home and say that we survived. I'd dine on pasta and cake, take a hot shower, and curl up on the sofa with Tess to watch *Dirty Dancing*, reciting every line and grinning like a teenager when Johnny told them not to 'put Baby in a corner.'

A tear sprung to my eye as my heart swelled and I began to rejoice, but in the same second, the tiny silver speck caught the light and banked to the left.

No…

I stared in disbelief as it diverged from our island and retreated. My fists clenched and my chest burned as I hung my head and sank to the ground, finally, *truly* out of hope. The warm afternoon air blew through my hair, and I took long, trembling breaths, holding back the scream of frustration that was lodged in my throat.

Liam swore loudly next to me and I closed my eyes, bracing myself for the reality that still had us in its grips. I stood up and silently shifted the logs apart to bring the fire back down to a manageable level.

"Two planes in a WHOLE month. What kind of dead zone are we in?" Liam's loud voice snarled. In his rage, he kicked a basket of coconuts onto the ground, grabbed one, and whipped it as hard as he could into the ocean. "Why are they not flying directly overhead!?"

I continued stirring the logs in silence, having nothing productive to contribute.

"We're never going to get off this godforsaken island," he growled, sinking to the sand with a loud thud and throwing his arm roughly over his knee.

I slowly walked past him to pick up the disturbed coconuts and place them back in the basket neatly. "We will someday," I said gently, trying and failing to use his own confidence to reassure him.

"Not like this we won't." His voice was edging toward intimidating. "Not if they can't be arsed to fly directly overhead and see us! How far could we possibly be from the crash site? Why haven't they searched here?" He threw one hand into the air defeatedly and then wiped both of them down his face and up through his hair. "God, we can't be stuck here forever together."

I watched his crushed figure quietly. I wasn't sure how he'd meant the words to be taken, but they *stung*. Deep, aching pain shot straight to my heart. Maybe I had been right. Maybe he was done with me.

"I'm sure there are many people you'd rather be seeing back at home than me..." The words left my lips, dead and emotionless before I had a chance to stop them.

With his hands still in his hair, he looked up at me with angry eyes. *"What?"*

I held the basket of coconuts in my arms, playing with a stray leaf that had come loose. "I'm sure you're eager to get back and make sure Kate is ok. The longer you're here, the further away from you she'll grow. If you stay out here with me, there'll be less chance she'll take you back."

Liam was still looking at me in disbelief, but his expression quickly turned to disgust. "You can't be serious. You know that's not why I want us to get rescued, Cora."

The coldness in his voice upset me, but I continued. "You've never been able to really end things with her, so maybe you'd like to get back and make sure you actually want that door closed."

"What are you even talking about? Why would you think that?" His voice was thick with distaste.

I shook my head and gritted my teeth as I set the basket down hard on the ground, looking directly at him. "Oh, I don't know Liam, maybe because you've barely *touched* me ever since that conversation we had…DAYS AGO."

My level of anger surprised me as it bubbled up so fast, fueled by the extreme disappointment we'd just endured with the plane. I glared down at him and set my jaw. He stared back at me with narrowed eyes, but then his brows pulled together in confusion.

I saw right through his bewilderment, though. I knew he was fully aware of his actions, or lack thereof. He had a reason for his change in demeanor, and I was almost positive now that it had to do with Kate.

When a small hint of realization crossed his features, I glared again. "Yeah, that's right, I noticed..."

I turned from him quickly, before he could respond, retreating toward the emotional safety of the overhang of trees. I pushed branches out of my way, trying to get as far from the uncomfortable situation as possible. I found a fallen tree and sat down hard onto the trunk, letting out a frustrated groan as I rubbed the bridge of my nose.

I knew my words had been harsh, but they came from a place I couldn't ignore. Liam wanted us off the island for our safety. That was obvious. But the way he'd worded it, saying he didn't want to be stuck here 'forever together' made me wince. That combination of words had affirmed doubts in my mind that I'd tried to ignore for weeks.

I'd have liked to believe those doubts were untrue, but I was starting to realize that I may never be able to debunk them until Liam had his closure with Kate. It was naïve of me to think he could let her go this quickly. And his recent chaste behavior with me was just adding insult to injury. Was he losing interest? It sure seemed like it. The look of realization in his eyes stung in my memory.

He knew.

That meant he was keeping something from me.

My feelings for him had grown so swiftly in the last month, and I was beginning to actually picture a future with him. But what if he didn't feel the same way? Would this time on our island be the only time we had together? This small glimpse of euphoria; was it all just temporary? Surely, everything would change if we were ever rescued, but would those changes mean saying goodbye to him forever?

The knot in my throat returned, and my heart ached at the thought of losing him. Even though I'd only really *had* him for a few days, he'd been my entire life for the last month and a half. First my savior, then my protector, always my companion, and eventually my best friend. What would my world look like without him?

I let my head drop to my hands, replaying the last few moments through my mind. How had I let myself speak so harshly to someone I cared about so much?

I felt bad.

I shouldn't have accused Liam of still having feelings for Kate without letting him speak for himself. My emotions had been high after the plane passed, and I'd lost control of my outburst. We would have been so much more productive if I'd let myself cool down instead of saying something so reckless.

His hurt expression when I'd accused him of wanting to return to Kate still played behind my eyelids. It was an awful thing to see. He had a way of contorting his face so deeply that I felt physical pain, knowing I'd caused it. I squeezed my eyes tighter, trying to wipe it from my memory bank.

I clasped my hands down on the sides of my head, massaging my temples, ashamed of what I'd said.

Then, I heard the crack of a branch nearby.

I glanced up to see Liam walking toward me, irritation still written on his face. I took a breath and let my eyes flutter closed briefly.

When I opened them again, he had come to a stop a few yards away. There was a deep crease in his forehead where his eyebrows were pulled together.

"Cora…" he began. His voice was deep and imposing. "My

reason for wanting to leave this island has *nothing* to do with Kate. You must know that."

I breathed slowly, observing his body language as he spoke. His stance was wide and rigid, and his hands were clenched at his sides. He was still on edge. I held his gaze, but I did not respond.

"I've told you, she's in my past now. It's over with her. I don't know why you still can't see that." His jaw was tight, and I knew he was on the brink of another outburst.

I hated to see him like this, and I knew it was my fault. I was afraid that he might raise his voice again, and my bottom lip began to tremble. "But how *could* I see that?" I whispered softly, unable to use my full voice, and wishing he could understand how uneasy I felt.

"How could you *not?*" His tone was still constricted, but he took a small step toward me. "I don't understand. You said just then that I haven't touched you lately, but I'm confused. I can barely *stop* touching you, and I've done nothing but express my feelings for you over these last few weeks. I can't even remember ever bringing up her name. Why are you still lingering on that?"

I hid my troubled expression so well, and I could tell that he had no idea that I was on the verge of tears because his words were still cold and harsh. I thought he knew what he'd done, but he was clearly very perplexed, and now I desperately wanted to just reverse time and restart the whole conversation.

I swallowed as a tear began to well in my eye. "Can't you see?"

"See *what?*" Liam extended his arms out in frustrated bewilderment.

My lower lip quivered even more, and I closed my eyes, allowing tears to spill down my cheeks. I didn't know what to think anymore. Was I blowing this whole thing out of proportion? Was my mind making up doubts that weren't even there?

"I don't know…I'm sorry…" A sob escaped as I started to wish I hadn't brought anything up in the first place.

"Cora…" His voice was instantly soft as he came to sit down next to me. "Look, I'm not angry with you. I'm just on edge right now. Please, tell me what's the matter."

I opened my eyes to find his gentle ones staring back at me. Through my tears, his blurry face was exhausted and sad as he waited for my answer.

"Everything is just a disaster…" I choked softly. "We're stuck on this dumb island, and you don't even want to be here with me…"

"Hang on, *what?*" Liam sat back, puzzlement written all over his expression. "When did I say that?"

I sniffed. "You said…you said you didn't want to be stuck here forever…together."

"Did I say that?" Liam blinked. It was a second before the realization dawned on him and he frowned again. "Ugh, I didn't mean it that way, Cora, I was shattered back there. I wasn't thinking clearly. What I meant was that I wished we could get off this island *together*. I still want to be with you, but I want you safe."

I looked up at him through wet eyelashes and furrowed my brow. "That's not how it sounded."

"I'm so sorry. That's my fault." His voice was quieter now, more sympathetic.

I wiped my nose and looked down, away from him. His

apology wasn't helping to ease my doubts.

Liam shifted next to me. "Cora..." His voice was soft. "Look at me."

I slowly raised my eyes to his again, but another tear dropped down my cheek. I was a mess, and beyond any chance of getting control of my emotions at this point. I'd given up on that.

But there was no longer any anger in his eyes, just uncertainty and sympathy. He took my face gently in his hands and wiped the tears from my cheeks with his thumbs. "You still don't believe me." It wasn't a question; it was a statement. He knew I wasn't there yet.

I swallowed with some difficulty. "I *want* to."

He dropped his hands to mine and held them gently in my lap, palms warm and comforting against my skin. "I know you may never completely believe me until we leave this island... *if*...we leave this island." He corrected himself.

It was the first time in weeks that I'd heard him question our chances of rescue, and it made me nervous. He was usually so confident. His was the last bit of hope I could hold onto.

His eyes pleaded with me. "But, please tell me what I can do to ease your worries a bit."

I watched him silently, afraid of what to say. My chest still trembled with lingering sobs. *Could* he do anything to ease my worries? I hardly knew.

He rubbed his thumb across my knuckles gently. "You said I've barely touched you lately...but I'm not sure what you meant by that."

I stared at him, disbelieving. Was he really still that clueless? If he didn't know what I'd meant, then maybe it *was* all in my head.

He tucked a strand of hair behind my ear. "Look, I know you feel like I'm keeping some big secret from you, but you're going to have to tell me what I'm doing wrong here. Because I'm at a loss."

I really was going to have to explain this all to him, whether or not I embarrassed myself in the process. I took a deep breath and looked up into his inquisitive eyes. "You remember the conversation we had last week about…boundaries?"

"Of course I do." His eyes never left mine, calm and reassuring.

"Do you remember what I said about…" I swallowed nervously. "…not losing all control, but just a *bit* of control?"

"Yes…" he replied tentatively.

I was hoping that he'd understand, and I wouldn't have to make a fool of myself explaining my silly emotions to him. But when he didn't speak, I had to continue. "Well…the thing is…you've only barely kissed me since then, and…" I looked at him pleadingly. "…Please don't make me keep explaining this…"

He squeezed my hand and sat forward, his eyes softening. "*That's* what you meant by saying I hadn't touched you?"

I nodded shyly as my cheeks grew warm. I was starting to feel like I probably looked like some sort of nymphomaniac to him, craving his touch more than he was willing to give it.

He shook his head and wiped his hand down his face. "Wow, well that plan backfired…"

I eyed him quizzically.

A hint of a smile formed on his lips as he took my hands in his again. "Cora…" He almost seemed amused. "Don't you for one second think that I'm not wanting to be touching you…"

He chuckled lightly. "That is the furthest thing from the truth."

I watched his expression with my own bewilderment, trying to understand where his emotions were.

"The reason I took a step back after our talk was because I didn't want to make you uncomfortable," he said softly.

I gaped at him. "Why did you think that would make me uncomfortable?"

He smiled again and closed his hands around mine. "You seemed pretty concerned about the risks, which I don't blame you for, and I wanted to make sure you felt like I was recognizing that. I didn't want to push you too far."

Tension released from my shoulders as he revealed his reasons, which were actually quite genuine and sweet. How had we been on such drastically different pages?

"I'm sorry," he said quietly. "I hadn't realized this was affecting you so much. In perfect honesty, I was just trying to be respectful."

I still watched him in disbelief, trying to figure out where our lines had gotten crossed. "But…then, what did you think I meant by 'losing a *bit* of control?'"

"I don't know…but, apparently not what you were thinking." He started to smirk again.

"Oh, God…" I covered my face and started to stand up to get away from him, completely, over the top embarrassed about our miscommunication and what he must think of me.

Liam grabbed my arm and pulled me back, laughing. "Cora, hey, come here."

I reluctantly sat back down next to him and stared at my knees, mortified.

"Hey…" His voice was kind as he placed his finger under

my chin, lifting my gaze to his. I was greeted by a wide smirk and a set of sparkling, amused eyes—a far cry from the irritation he'd displayed at the start of our conversation.

He spoke again. "I can assure you that my mind would have been in the same place as yours, had I let it go there, but you're so quiet and reserved. I thought you were content with sticking around first base for a bit. So, that's where I stayed."

I blushed again. "Am I that hard to read?"

Liam's smile warmed. "Well, we've only known each other for six weeks, so yes, I'm still learning." He chuckled.

"I suppose you're right," I replied, frowning. "But it feels like so much longer…"

"It does…" Liam agreed. "Time moves differently out here."

I sighed as I realized he saw me as some sort of quiet, delicate flower, which, admittedly, I was in some sense. But that didn't mean I didn't have desires. Who *wouldn't* desire Liam?

But now, if he was so surprised to know that I was already craving a more intimate relationship with him, was I coming off as overly eager?

I wrinkled my nose. "I'm a bit mortified that my mind was in that place. I don't know what you must think of me…"

Liam placed his hands on my shoulders. "I'll tell you what I think of you." His eyes twinkled. "Knowing you were thinking of those things has got me feeling a certain way, and maybe I've underestimated you."

I watched his mischievous face as his gaze began to burn a bit darker again. I replied bravely, "Maybe you have…"

He gripped me tightly and leaned in, planting a firm, emotional kiss on my lips. I sank into it, spent from our argument but relieved that he'd responded so positively.

When he pulled back, his expression lightened. "It seems we need to do a better job of communicating."

I smiled. "We'll have to work on that."

As he dropped his hands, his eyes were once again serious. "And again, I'm very sorry that I made you question my feelings. That's the last thing I wanted. I was really trying to do the exact opposite."

I placed my hand in his. "Look, I'm sorry too about what I said back there on the beach about Kate. That was out of line. I feel really bad…" I took a deep breath. "But I'm also not going to deny that I still have doubts…and none of those are your fault," I added quickly. "But as you said, I don't know if I'll be able to dissolve them unless we are rescued, and I can see for myself that you've had closure with her. I mean, who knows what kind of reaction she's going to have when she finds out. For all I know, you could change your mind if she tries to get you back."

He squeezed my hand and tried to speak, but I kept on before he had a chance. "And if we stay together…if we leave… we haven't even begun to talk about what that would mean. I live a fairly uneventful and simple life in L.A. You travel the world, you're away for long periods, your life is under a microscope. I wouldn't know how I'd fit into that…"

He blinked at me for a moment, chewing on the inside of his cheek. I waited for him to say something comforting, assuring me that my fears weren't warranted. But he pressed his lips together and stated simply, "You're right."

I frowned. It wasn't the reassurance I was looking for.

"You're right to have those doubts," he continued. "They all make perfect sense. But I can tell you this…" He paused.

"No matter what Kate thinks about us, it's not going to change the way I feel about you. My feelings for you are already much stronger than they ever were for her. There is not a question in my mind about that." He watched me sympathetically. "So, if you can try to work on putting any of your doubts to rest, that's the one."

I nodded, wondering if I could simply *choose* to believe him and have it come to be.

Liam took a deep breath. "In terms of how we'll navigate our relationship when we get back, I can't be sure. It will be an entirely different adventure…for the both of us. I think about it sometimes. We don't know each other in the 'real world.'" He used air quotes. "It'll be almost like we're meeting again for the first time…"

I dropped my gaze from his, concerned that he was right. I had no idea what he'd be like when faced with the distractions of his old life. And he didn't know what to expect from me either. Maybe we were wildly incompatible outside of our little island sanctuary. Maybe we'd eventually grow apart and realize it wouldn't work.

Liam touched my arm gently. "Our situation is unique, for sure, but we have something here, Cora. I know you feel it too."

"I do," I whispered.

"Then all we can do is keep moving in the same direction while we're here, and if that day comes and we get off this island, we'll remember our foundation and build upon it."

I lifted my eyes to his and saw that he was regarding me with an expression of hope, and of comfort, and almost of something else. But I didn't dare let myself explore that thought.

Not yet.

TWENTY-ONE

I stared down at the lifeboat with my hands on my hips. There was less than an inch of water at the bottom—not enough for more than a day. I sighed and rubbed my forehead. I could barely remember the last time it had rained, which was unusual in this tropical climate.

In the distance, Liam was walking toward me across the beach, lit by the setting sun with his bow slung over his shoulder. He'd gone out to hunt after our chat earlier in the afternoon, eager to get his mind off the irritatingly close call with the plane. But he was returning empty-handed.

As he arrived in front of me, he tossed his bow to the ground. "Have you noticed that the birds are becoming scarce?"

I furrowed my brow. "You know, you're right…come to think of it, I haven't seen many at all lately."

"The last time I went out hunting, I barely managed to find even one. Today, I couldn't find any. I've seen a few smaller ones in the trees, but none of those that are large enough to eat." He sighed.

I gestured toward the lifeboat. "Our water is low too… It seems like it hasn't rained in forever."

Liam glared at the boat and the small pool that remained. "It's been five days at least? Maybe the birds know something we don't…"

I looked at him with wide eyes, dreading the worst. "You think, like…a drought?"

"I don't know…I hope not…" He bent down to stoke the fire.

I watched him breathlessly, wondering what kind of treacherous conditions lay ahead of us.

"It's getting too dark to fish now. It'll have to be coconuts tonight." He peered up at the evening sky, exhaling loudly.

I glanced at our basket. There was only one left. "I can go get some more…"

"No, no. You stay put. I'll take care of it," he replied, turning from me and heading into the trees.

I sat down next to the fire and rubbed my grumbling stomach. It had been weeks since we'd been without meat, and coconuts didn't satisfy the same way. If the birds were leaving the island, then there must be another one close by. But in which direction, and how close really? The thought of leaving on our own was an option we'd discussed, but if we tried to leave, how would we even begin to decide which direction to search? I shivered, thinking about being stuck on a raft in the middle of the Pacific, with no land in sight in any direction. That risk was certainly not the answer to our problems.

Looking back at our lifeboat, I thought about the last time we'd been without drinking water before our very first storm when desperation had set in. I swallowed nervously, remembering how weak I'd become. Since then, rainstorms had been plentiful—until now. Without water, it wouldn't matter if we had birds to eat. Nothing else mattered if we couldn't stay hydrated…

I shifted the hot embers around aimlessly. At least Liam and I had made positive headway in our relationship today. The last thing we needed was for a dark veil of hopelessness to hang over us once again. It was amazing what a deep, healing conversation did to my already growing feelings for him. To know that we'd argued, and then come out on the other side stronger for it gave me hope for our future.

But at the same time, Liam had admitted to sharing my fears about continuing our relationship in the real world. Would our lifestyles be compatible at all? Kate was a dancer, so she was used to being in the public eye. I knew nothing of the sort. My ten seconds of fame happened when I was five years old, and the local news crew interviewed me on the spot about a brand-new playground at the city park. I'd been so nervous I cried. How would I respond to my life being turned upside down if I stayed with Liam? Paparazzi, journalists, angry fans?

I sighed. It was all so far away. I was getting ahead of myself.

Water. Water was what I needed to be worried about right now.

Eventually, Liam came back through the trees with a basketful of fresh coconuts. He prepared one and handed it to me. I drank it gratefully. It wouldn't be very filling, but it was food.

I cleared my throat and looked at him. "Well, even if the birds aren't around right now, we still have fish."

He smiled tightly. "Yes, we still have fish." His response

lacked animation, and I didn't blame him. We were on the brink of a potentially life-threatening situation if a drought was imminent. The birds were leaving, and I'd come to learn that animals usually knew more than we did.

"Do you think there'll be enough coconuts to keep us hydrated?" I asked quietly.

"We're on a tropical island. It has to rain soon…" Liam responded, throwing his empty shell onto the fire.

I chewed nervously on my lip but decided to change the subject to put our minds at ease. I scooted closer to him. "You know, I'm really glad we talked this afternoon."

His expression softened. "Me too."

"It felt good to be so honest. We should do that more often."

"Yes, and I also learned that I apparently need to pay more attention to your subtle signals." He laughed, touching his fingers to the ends of my hair. I kept it down more often now, knowing how much he liked it.

I grinned. "My apologies for being so cryptic."

His eyes twinkled. "Well, now I know a bit more of what's going on in that mind of yours."

I studied his perfect face, illuminated by the gentle flames nearby. He was watching me with amusement, and my heart began to beat faster. I longed to be close to him again.

"Would you like to dance?" I asked, smiling coyly.

"I don't want to dance," he responded as his eyes bore into mine, burning a bit deeper. He placed his hand firmly on my hip and pulled me toward him, guiding me up and over his legs so that I was facing him, straddling his lap.

I traced my fingers across the sides of his neck, feeling the soft whiskers there. "Ok, we don't have to dance," I whispered.

His palms found my back, pulling me closer into a kiss. After all we'd been through today, there was a new intimacy in the way his lips felt against mine. My fingers curled around his head, tangling in his hair as our mouths moved together.

When I pulled back briefly, he was gazing up fixedly at me. "Do you realize how absolutely beautiful you are?"

I blushed. "I think you're drunk on that coconut."

He smiled slightly, tucking my hair behind my ear. "I'm really not sure what I did to deserve you..."

I found it hard to believe that he could feel as lucky with me as I did with him. "Well, for starters, you saved my life. I wouldn't be here if it weren't for you..."

His eyes roamed my face, and then he took it in his hands, pulling me back to his lips. His kiss was deep and emotional. I could almost taste his sincerity. And when his mouth found my neck, I let my head fall back, giving his soft lips access to the delicate skin there.

A flutter of desire burned between my thighs as his fingers trailed up my sides, leaving paths of heat as they went, and then his large palms were brushing feather-light across my chest. Through the thin fabric of my shirt, I could feel the rough, coarse skin of his hands—hands that were hardworking, providing for us every day.

His touch was deliberate and assertive, yet it was tender too, as he kneaded and caressed, sending jolts of electricity down to the part of me that could now feel him firm beneath me as I straddled his lap. He was eager too.

I let out a shallow sigh and then crashed my lips back into his, sliding my tongue between them, and clutching the collar of his shirt.

We kissed feverishly, breathing heavily against each other, and succumbing to the passion between us until a sudden loud crackling and a bright flash of light lit up the fire behind me. We both jumped a foot into the air, and I spun around to see an array of sparks dancing up into the sky and glowing embers flying in all directions. The logs must have been teetering delicately because they had collapsed in on themselves.

I brought my hand to my chest, and I started to grin, briefly amused by such a silly interruption to our passionate moment, but then Liam's body tensed, and he urgently lifted me off him.

"Oh, shit…" He swore as he jumped to his feet, eyes wide as he looked past the fire.

I spun around again and saw that one of the sparks had landed precariously on the lemongrass bushes we'd planted outside our shelter. On the leaf that it touched, a small flame was beginning to form, singeing a hole and dropping burning pieces onto the rest of the plant below it.

Liam dashed over to the bush and quickly stomped the flaming embers with his foot, choking them of oxygen and extinguishing them quickly. I stood up with my hand still on my heart, which was now beating fast for an entirely different reason.

He looked at me with wide eyes. "These bushes are too dry…that's why it caught so quickly."

I gaped at him for a moment, grateful for his quick thinking. But a thousand scenarios flew through my mind. "What if we'd been sleeping?" I breathed, imagining waking up to inextinguishable flames and heat. It would have definitely continued to spread, and without rain, it would have dug into our supply of coconuts, and maybe rendered this island completely uninhabitable.

"I think I'll have to let the fire burn completely out tonight. We can't take any chances," Liam said, taking a stick and spreading out the remaining logs.

I walked toward him and touched his arm. I was worried he was on edge again, but he turned to me and smiled.

"Well, that was a bit of a jolt, wasn't it?" He wrapped his free arm around me, and I rested my forehead on his chest. Our passionate moment was gone, but I didn't mind much. The warmth of his body and his protective embrace helped to slow my heart rate, and I relaxed into him, closing my eyes.

"Tired?" he whispered, kissing the top of my head.

"Mhmm…" I replied softly, surprised that I was so sleepy after our scare. But it was as if this last shock was all my mind needed to finally succumb to the exhaustion of the day.

"You can go ahead and go to bed," he whispered. "I'll stay out here and watch the fire burn out."

I yawned. "No, I'll stay with you."

He didn't argue, but sat again, leaning against the rock as I lowered myself down next to him and rested my head on his shoulder. We both watched the small flames lick at the red-hot coals that remained, slowly cooling and disappearing. The gentle crackle, mingled with the sound of the waves nearby, was incredibly calming.

As my eyes began to flutter shut, Liam spoke up softly. "It's kind of amazing how connected I feel with you after all we've been through…"

He was becoming introspective, and I loved that part of him, but I could barely keep my eyelids open. "Mhmm…" I managed to reply.

"I've never really felt this before." He paused. "I thought

I had. But I don't think I ever knew what it meant to rely on someone so strongly. We really need each other. And I adore that. It's really something special."

"*You're* special," I mumbled in my half-awake state.

Liam's shoulder shook as he chuckled softly, and I smiled, feeling at peace knowing that he was happy.

He tucked his fingers into my hair and trailed them softly through the strands, lulling me even deeper from consciousness. I let my eyes fully shut as I relished in the warmth of his shoulder, and the gentle strokes of his fingers finally soothed me to sleep.

***

The next morning, after Liam had started the fire again—it was easy now that the kindling was bone-dry—he left to fish for breakfast. We were both hungry after having eaten so little last night, and I eagerly awaited his return.

It was a bright and sunny day without a cloud in the sky, but I scowled, wishing to see any indication of an approaching storm. When the fire was stable, I took a walk toward the shore to see if I could catch a glimpse of Liam. I liked to watch him skillfully bobbing up out of the water, occasionally placing a fresh catch into the basket, never giving up until he had enough for a meal.

I made my way toward the boulders that marked the part of the beach where he always began his swim and smiled, planning to perch myself atop one of the rocks and enjoy the show. Except, the smile quickly fell from my face when I heard a sound that chilled me to the bone.

"ARGHHHAHHH." Liam's pained yell echoed from behind a boulder.

My heart dropped, and my feet moved quickly, propelling me around the massive stone, afraid of what I might find. When Liam came into view, I was horrified to see that he was laying on the wet sand, clutching his leg and moaning in pain. Bright red blood swirled in the bit of water around him, originating from the spot on his leg where his hands held tightly.

My head went numb, and my mouth ran dry as shock singed through me. "Oh my God…what happened?!" I scrambled to the ground next to him and tried to look at his leg, but his hands were holding it too tightly.

"UGH… ARGHHH… caught on… the coral…" he moaned again.

"Liam… move your hands. Let me see," I said urgently, trying to keep my wits about me and avoiding going into a full panic.

I looked at his face, which was twisted with pain and distress. He squeezed his eyes shut, breathing heavily as he moved his hands slightly, revealing something even worse than I'd expected. There was a deep, long gash along the side of his calf—much deeper than the one he'd sustained on his face in the plane crash. My stomach turned, and I covered my mouth. The blood hadn't done it, but the depth of the wound was extremely unsettling. Now that he'd released it, the quantity of blood had increased instantly. I pulled my t-shirt up over my swimsuit and off my head, wrapping it around his leg.

"Ok, ok, put your hands back. Hold it tightly," I squeaked, looking around and trying to figure out what my next move was. The water around him was now a deep red. He was bound to bleed out if we didn't act quickly.

Instinct kicked in. "A belt, Liam, do you have a belt?" I gasped, horribly out of breath.

"My… UGHHH…. my bag… in my bag…" he groaned, holding his leg tightly again.

I touched his shoulder. "Ok, hang on. Hang on…I'll be right back. Don't move. Keep pressure on it." And then I stood up with every ounce of effort and left him on the beach in a pool of his own blood.

I ran at full speed, purely fueled by adrenaline, back to our shelter and tore inside, falling to the ground in front of his leather bag and fumbling with the zipper nervously. When my fingers finally cooperated with me and I had it open, I dug through its contents, feeling around until my hands came in contact with the smooth, stiff leather of a belt. I yanked it out and then shifted to my own suitcase. I pulled it open and threw the items from my cosmetics pouch onto the ground, searching for the antibiotic ointment. But when I picked up the small tube, I could immediately tell that it was completely empty. I flipped open the cap and squeezed with every ounce of effort, but nothing came out.

I wasn't one to swear, but I did so—loudly into the quiet of our shelter—and slammed the empty tube to the ground. For an instant, I stared at it blankly, trying to sort through my panicked thoughts. But I shook my head and quickly remembered the small emergency sewing kit I'd seen in the elderly couple's bag. I found it and also grabbed one of my t-shirts before standing up and dashing back outside and toward the beach again.

As I ran, I did my best to even my breathing. I didn't have any medical skills, but I did know that if we didn't stop the bleeding and close up the wound, he would only continue to get worse.

I rounded the boulder again, praying that Liam was still conscious, and I was relieved to see that he was. He continued to clutch his leg, but his face was paler, and his groans had turned to labored breathing instead. I collapsed to my knees next to him and looped the belt under his leg, just above his knee. I pulled it as tightly as I possibly could as he winced at the pressure.

"I know, I know…" I said gently. "But we have to stop the bleeding."

I looked at his contorted face again. His lips were pasty-white as his tortured eyes stared into mine. I took a deep breath and set my jaw, trying to prepare for what I would have to do next. I held the t-shirt out to him. "Bite down on this."

His eyes widened, but he took it from me, stuffed it into his mouth, and then leaned his head back onto the sand and squeezed his eyes shut.

When he released his other hand from his leg, the bleeding was less, and when I untied the t-shirt I'd wrapped around it, I was able to get a better look at the gash. It was deep, *really deep,* and I swallowed hard again, not sure if I could stomach it. But now wasn't the time to hesitate. I took a deep breath and opened the sewing kit. With shaking fingers, I selected a needle and spool of thread. I held them up to my eye, trying to push the thread through the tiny hole. It took me a few frustrating tries, but when I finally had success, I positioned the sharp point next to his skin, at the edge of his wound, and took a deep, trembling breath. I had no clue how to do this.

But I had no other choice.

TWENTY-TWO

"Ok, hold still," I said through gritted teeth, with the needle poised against his skin. I squinted my eyes shut for a second, dreading the task in front of me, But I managed to calm my nerves, open my eyes, and slowly make the first stitch.

"UGHH…" Liam moaned into the shirt in his mouth. His leg jerked underneath my hands.

"I know, I'm sorry. But you have to hold still," I replied firmly. I used my left hand to hold his leg in place as I continued with the next stitch.

Liam breathed hard, and his fists clenched at his sides, but his leg remained still this time as he fought through it.

I tried to pretend like I was working on some sort of demented art project, and not a real leg, as I continued the stitches, closing up his wound tightly. Liam continued to wince, but he stayed still enough that I could finish the job to the best of my unskilled abilities. When his skin was pulled together, I tied a knot, finishing the last stitch, and then sat back on my heels, studying my work. It wasn't pretty, but the gash was now held closed.

"Ok, I'm done..." I wiped the back of my hand across my brow.

Liam opened his eyes and lifted his head to look at his leg. He grimaced when he saw it, took the t-shirt out of his mouth, and handed it back to me. I tore it into long strips and tied them around his leg as I'd done with his wound on his face, and then I slowly released the pressure of the belt above his knee.

He groaned in pain again as the blood returned to his leg. I scooted toward his head and placed my hand on the side of his face, brushing his hair out of his eyes.

"How are you doing?" I asked, watching him closely.

His lips were still white, and his breathing remained labored. "How bad is it?" he whispered.

I frowned, not wanting to be honest. "You're going to be ok..." I nodded, but I wasn't sure how much truth was in that wishful thinking. It was a deep wound, and without antibiotic ointment, I didn't know how likely it was to become infected.

"Let's get you up onto the shore and out of the water," I said, looping my arm under his and helping him scoot backward, away from the blood-stained tide that surrounded him. His body was heavy, and he could only just barely help push himself along, but I managed to lean him against a large rock.

When I looked at his leg, there were spots of red soaking through the makeshift bandage, but the heavy bleeding seemed to be under control.

Liam spoke in a mumble, pointing out toward the water.

"The fish…the basket…it's still out there…I have to…" He started to try and push himself up from the ground.

I pressed down firmly on his shoulder. "No, you're not going back out there right now. You lost too much blood. You need to rest."

"But the basket…" His words came out garbled and slurred.

I turned to squint at the ocean waves. There was no sign of the basket as far as I could see. I stroked his arm. "It's gone, Liam. But that's ok…we'll get more fish and I'll make a new basket."

He let his head fall back against the rock in defeat. "Is my spear at least…?"

I saw it laying on the beach next to us, safe from the tide. "Yes, your spear is here."

He exhaled slowly as the afternoon breeze picked up, sending his wet curls blowing gently, and then he shivered.

"We should really get you back to the fire if we can, but I want you to sit and rest here for a bit. Are you cold?" I asked gently.

His eyes were still closed as he nodded. The pained grimace never left his face.

"Ok, hang on, I'll be right back." I stood up quickly and then studied him for a moment. His body was limp from exhaustion as he slumped against the boulder, and his chest heaved up and down. I glanced at his bloody leg and felt my heart begin to beat faster again. Would it heal? Our water reserves were officially depleted. We didn't have anything to wash it with. This injury couldn't have come at a more inopportune time.

I turned from him and walked to our shelter. My legs felt numb, carrying me forward on their own accord without much command from my brain. When I reached the cave and stepped inside, I was greeted by the mess I'd made in my frenzy to find Liam's belt and the sewing kit. I spotted his black leather jacket strewn on the floor and I knelt down to pick it up. But as I did, my fingers began to tingle and my shoulders started to shake. I braced my hands on my knees and closed my eyes, trying to stop my trembling, but my heart was racing faster, and I felt the blood rushing from my head. I leaned forward and placed my forehead in my hands, trying to take deep breaths.

"Get it together, Cora..." I whispered to myself.

What if I hadn't gone to watch Liam fish this morning? Without me, would he have bled out, right there on the beach? What if he hadn't had the strength to make it back to shore? Would he have drowned, surrendered to the sea forever? And what if now he'd already lost too much blood and his body couldn't fight? What if his wound became infected, and instead of healing, it only got worse...until...?

I squeezed my eyes shut tightly.

No. There had to be something I could do.

Lingering in our cave and worrying would do me no good. And it wouldn't do Liam any good either. It was my turn to support him and to do everything in my power to get him through this. So, with shaking hands, I took his jacket and stood up.

I jogged back to Liam and saw that he still sat, white-lipped against the rock with his eyes closed. When he sensed my presence, he opened one eyelid slightly.

"Here, let's get this on you." I held out the jacket. He sat forward, wincing as I helped him slip his shivering arms through the sleeves. He pulled the collar tightly around his neck, and I placed my palm on his forehead. It was cold and clammy.

"How badly does it hurt?" I asked quietly.

He took a deep, shuddering breath. "I'm so numb right now, I can barely feel it. I feel tingly and lightheaded."

"Do you feel like you're going to pass out?" I asked anxiously.

He closed his eyes again and frowned. "Maybe..." His words were barely a mumble as he continued to shiver, despite wearing his coat now.

I surveyed his position. He should really have his legs elevated to keep good blood flow to his head. And it would be ideal to get him closer to the fire. But I knew he could not stand, and I was far from strong enough to even think about carrying him or dragging his dead weight.

I considered bringing the fire to him, but it was windy down by the water, and I wanted him back at our campsite. As my brain scanned through our items, trying to figure out what might help me, my mind landed on the now-empty lifeboat. I remembered tugging it through the sand to collect rainwater. It wasn't easy, and it would be even more difficult with him inside it, but the bottom was smooth and would slide better across the sand. After many weeks of hard work on the island, I knew I was stronger now than I'd been the first time I'd moved it.

Feeling a surge of motivation, I stood up again. "I'll be right back."

I walked with forced confidence up the beach toward the boat, which was now bone-dry, and grasped one of the handles firmly. I expected a strong resistance, but to my surprise, I was able to pull it easily across the sand. I *was* stronger.

When I made it back to Liam, I tugged it beside him. "Ok, we're going to get you up next to the fire. You'll be warmer.

Do you think you can help me get you inside the boat?" I pointed toward it.

"What…are you doing?" he slurred.

I put my hands on my hips. "I'm going to drag you back up shore."

"Cora…" Even in his half-conscious state, I could still hear the doubt in his voice.

"I'm getting you up there somehow…and this is the best idea I've got," I said firmly. I looped my arms under his again and tried to lift him. "Ok, here we go."

He was able to help me slightly, but most of his body was limp as I hoisted him over the edge of the boat. I watched his injured leg carefully, making sure not to bump it as I helped him to lay down. Once he was in, he closed his eyes and grimaced.

"Ok. I can do this," I whispered to myself with forced conviction. I grabbed one of the handles with both hands and pulled as hard as I could.

The boat moved about two feet.

I let out a deep breath and turned to the fire in the distance. This was going to take a while.

Almost allowing myself to feel defeated, I looked down at Liam again. He was still so pale, and he had his arms wrapped around himself as he shivered. I needed to do this, no matter how long it would take. He needed that heat. So, I dug my feet into the sand and grabbed the handle again, pulling with every effort I could muster. The boat moved a few more feet.

I continued this slow progression for about ten minutes, stopping to breathe, and then pulling it another two or three feet.

Eventually out of breath, I stopped to assess how far we'd come. There was a smooth path in the sand where I'd dragged the boat. It reminded me of the tracks that saucer-shaped sleds had created in the snow during a winter family vacation to Wisconsin. The contrast of those carefree moments against this one was alarming.

I looked back at the fire, gauging the distance. It seemed like I was about halfway there. I wiped my brow, which was hot and sweaty from the sun, and then my gaze fell to Liam again. He was still trembling, and his colorless lips were parted slightly, but he wasn't grimacing anymore. He looked less in pain, but also further removed from reality.

I gritted my teeth and took hold of the handle again, grunting as I pulled the boat another small distance, prepared to fight through sore muscles and lack of breath.

After another fifteen minutes, I pulled the boat one last time, coming to a stop next to the fire. I collapsed to the ground and ran my hands through my hair, completely exhausted and drenched with sweat.

"Ok, let's get you out of there and next to the fire," I said to Liam, reaching my hand out to him, but he didn't move. My heart stopped briefly, but then I saw that his chest was still rising and falling.

"Liam, can you hear me?" I asked tentatively.

No response.

His body must have shut down due to lack of blood. I took a few short, terrified breaths, but I swallowed the lump in my throat and placed my hand on his forehead again. It was still cold and clammy.

I massaged my fingers between my eyes, and then I stepped

into the boat behind his head and shoved my hands under his shoulders to grasp him under his arms.

"Alright, Liam, let's go," I said to his non-responsive form.

Then, with a surge of effort, I lifted his limp body into a sitting position. Without any of his help, he was *heavy.* He wasn't a huge guy, but he was certainly much larger than I was, and his dead weight was a lot to handle.

I grunted, pulling him to the edge of the boat. His head hung to the side as I stepped out and braced my legs in the sand. I heaved him clumsily over the inflated wall and down onto the ground with a thud. All the while, he remained unconscious.

I laid him down gently, close to the fire, and placed a balled-up shirt under his head. I could immediately feel the heat from the flames. I was sweating profusely from all I had done, but I hoped that the warmth would help Liam regain some blood flow. He laid there in his crimson-stained shorts, limp and unresponsive, and I couldn't look away. I wanted him so badly to wake up—to tell me that he was ok. But his body was trying to heal, and all I could do was wait and keep him warm.

I curled up in the sand next to him and pushed the damp hair from his forehead. He was oddly peaceful in his wounded state, but his brows were pulled together slightly, which told me that he was in there, fighting. I trailed my fingers across his jacket, feeling his chest rise and fall. I needed him to fight. I needed him to fight *hard*, because I wouldn't survive out here on my own. And I also needed him to fight because over the last few days, I'd realized that I could no longer deny a new and deeper emotion that had snuck into my heart so quietly I'd barely even noticed it.

I loved him.

It was the full and complete truth, staring me in the face, clear as day. It was something I hadn't expected, but it felt so natural now. Every time he was introspective or deep in thought, every time he stepped up to provide for us without hesitation, every time a grin spread wide across his face, crinkling his eyes because of something that amused him, I fell further and deeper into a genuine and passionate kind of love. I wanted to know every part of him, and I wanted to experience everything new and beautiful in the world together. I wanted to discover a life with him.

I pressed my hands to my face, trying to prevent the tears from falling. I couldn't bear to think that he might leave me now after I'd finally realized that I *loved* him. We'd tried too hard already. We'd come so far. He couldn't die. I wouldn't let him.

I laid next to him for many hours, watching the sun make its way across the sky, thinking about what I would do to thank the universe if he pulled through this. I felt helpless knowing I could only do so much. Eventually, a tear escaped, dripping down my cheek onto the sand. I had no idea how I'd cope if I was left alone. I'd quickly lose motivation to continue on, knowing that he had lost his fight. It was a horribly painful emotion to have to imagine, and another tear fell as I scooted closer to him and laid my head on his chest.

Through his jacket, I heard his heart beating quickly, trying to replenish his blood supply, and undoubtedly struggling. But each beat, as fast as they came, was a reminder that he was still here with me, and I knew somewhere, deep inside his head, he was fighting to stay with me too.

TWENTY-THREE

I awoke with a start, blinking the sleep from my eyes and trying to get my bearings, but it was dark, apart from the flickering of the fire nearby, and my neck was cramped and sore. The warmth beneath my cheek reminded me that I was laying on Liam's chest, and the awkward position was causing the painful strain.

Dread filled my heart as the memories of yesterday flooded my mind, but just as I was about to lift my head, he took a deep breath. I instantly shot up and squinted closely at him through the dark. I couldn't believe I'd fallen asleep, and I panicked briefly, worried that he may have gotten worse. But he blinked a few times and grimaced before turning his head slowly to me.

His lips were still pale, but I placed my hand on his forehead to find that it was warm and dry.

"Liam…" I exhaled. "How are you feeling?"

He squeezed his eyes shut. "In A LOT of pain…"

I rested my hand gently on his cheek. Seeing him awake gradually slowed my heart, but the emotions within me still burned strong. The words I was too afraid to say echoed over and over in my head.

I love you, I love you, I love you.

"I can't believe I was so stupid," he groaned angrily.

"It could have happened to anyone," I whispered, touching his chest, his arm, his cheek—all warm with life.

He opened one eye and glanced down at his leg. "Is it clean?"

I sucked in a deep breath. "I'm still trying to figure out how to be sure of that, but I didn't see any debris when I was…" I gulped. "…sewing it up."

"You must have guts of steel," he winced.

I rubbed my thumb soothingly along his forearm. I didn't know how I did it either, but somehow, in that moment, nothing else had mattered but saving his life.

"Did you put any ointment on it?" he asked, closing his eyes.

I swallowed nervously. "We're out."

He peered at me through one eye again. "It's gone?"

"We've used it on small scrapes so much, there is none left…" I solemnly replied.

He regarded me for a few drawn-out seconds. "It's gonna get infected," he stated simply, looking away. "I'm so sorry."

I placed both hands on his cheeks and leaned over his face, looking closely at him until he returned my gaze. When he did, I shook my head. "No, it's not, Liam. You're going to fight this."

He pressed his trembling lips together. "I can't help it if it gets infected. We have no fresh water to clean it with. There will be nothing we can do."

My eyes darted between his, not wanting to hear the reality of his words. I wouldn't let them be true. When I bent down and kissed him, he responded, but just barely. "It's not going to get infected…" I whispered.

He let out a long sigh and closed his eyes again. I sat back, staring blankly at the wisping orange flames. He *had* to pull through this. He was speaking to me, here and now, showing signs of improvement. He was moving in the right direction.

When I surveyed his limp figure again, sprawled out on the ground, my heart broke. He'd always been so strong in my eyes, finding a solution for everything. There was nothing he couldn't do. Yet now he laid here, practically helpless without me. It was a different dynamic, and I could finally see a vulnerability in him. He needed me just as much as I needed him.

Realizing that my feelings had deepened and admitting to myself that I loved him—who he truly was on the inside—I knew I would do anything and everything to keep him alive. If I could find some way to pull the blood from my own veins and feed it into his, I would.

Liam shivered again, so I added a few more logs to the fire. The bandage on his leg still hadn't bled through completely, so my stitches must have been somewhat successful. I prepared a coconut and helped him raise his head so that he could take a sip. He was still shaking, and some of the liquid escaped and dribbled down his beard.

"You should get some more sleep," I wiped the droplets from his chin and lowered his head to the ground.

"Hmmm," he mumbled.

"You're gonna be ok," I whispered, laying down next to him

again and resting my head on his shoulder as he wrapped his trembling arm around me. It was a small gesture, but knowing that he was in so much pain, yet still had the mind to be affectionate made my heart swell.

***

I didn't get a wink of sleep for the rest of the night. The hours passed, but all I could do was think about any possible method of cleaning his wound. Without fresh, clean water, even soap would be useless. For what felt like hours, I mentally ran through the items in our suitcases, trying to find a solution. Just when I was about to give up and I was desperately considering the antibacterial qualities of toothpaste, my mind landed on the bright blue travel-sized antiseptic mouthwash that I hadn't touched since we'd arrived.

I sat straight up. How had it taken me so long to remember it? It was literally made for killing bacteria.

Excitement surged through me, but I bit my lip, realizing it was filled with alcohol and imagining the horrible kind of pain it would likely cause him. But it could work. It *would* work.

My heart beat faster again. I wasn't sure why I hadn't used it for its original purpose yet, but I was beyond grateful that I hadn't.

I stood up quietly, tiptoed to our shelter, and knelt down, gathering the items strewn across the floor. At the corner of the cave was the unopened bottle of blue liquid. I turned it around in my hands carefully as if it were gold.

I grabbed another t-shirt and slowly returned to Liam. The sky was now a soft, pale blue as the morning crept in. He was still sound asleep, so I sat down and leaned against a nearby rock. I crossed my legs and stared at him, holding the bottle securely in my grip. I considered waking him, but he seemed like he was finally sleeping well, and I wanted to leave him alone for a little while longer. I was hopeful now with this possible lifesaver in my hands, and I could breathe a bit easier.

In the dim light of the new day, a small amount of color was returning to his face. I sat anxiously, impatiently waiting for him to open his eyes, and when he finally did, I gripped the bottle even tighter in my sweaty fingers.

He lifted his hand and rubbed his forehead, turning toward me. "Hmm…" he grumbled.

I stared back at him, biting my cheek. "I think I know how to clean it…"

He knitted his brows briefly, and his gaze fell to the bottle in my hands. I turned the label toward him and saw the realization set in. He looked back at the sky and closed his eyes with a gulp. "Do it."

I swallowed the knot in my throat and crawled over to him.

"Can I bite down on that shirt again?" he asked, breathing a little harder now.

"Of course," I said quietly, handing it to him.

"Don't use it all in one go." His voice was strained. "We should save some to repeat this a few times."

"I know, I won't." I hated that I was going to have to cause him more pain. "Are you going to be ok?"

"Yep. Just do it." His voice was clipped, but resolute. He stuffed the shirt in his mouth and took a deep breath.

I gulped, and with shaking hands, began to untie the bandage. Liam twitched a few times as I peered under the wrapping. The area around the wound was a bit swollen, but it was pink. It didn't look infected yet. My unskilled stitches were holding together, and the bleeding had stopped. I relaxed a bit, relieved that he wasn't worse off than when he started.

I uncapped the bottle and tried to determine the best way to apply it to the wound. I needed it to soak in and reach all the potential bacteria, so I figured that pouring just a little directly onto the gash would be my best bet.

I bit my lip and looked up at Liam, who still had his eyes shut and the shirt stuffed in his mouth. "Ok, ready?" I asked.

He nodded and squeezed his eyelids even tighter.

I took a deep breath and hesitated one last time before dropping a few teaspoons of the blue liquid onto the stitches.

Liam's face contorted as he yelled loudly into the t-shirt, fists clenching and tensing at his sides.

Tears sprung to the corners of my eyes as he twisted his neck and moaned in agony. I rubbed his arm gently, trying to distract him, but the tendons beneath his jaw pulled taut as he strained and fought through the pain. All I could do was watch helplessly and wait for it to subside.

"I'm sorry, I'm sorry…" I whispered the whole time.

Slowly, his body began to relax again, and he finally spat the shirt out onto his chest. He opened his eyes to look at me with a gasp. There was immense pain behind his gaze. "That was ten times worse than the actual injury."

I pushed the sweaty hair from his forehead. "I know, I'm sorry."

"Don't apologize…" he groaned through labored breaths.

I picked up the t-shirt from his chest and tore it into strips like I had the last one, and then I fastened them around his leg, being as gentle as I could.

When I was finished, I checked his face again. "How does that feel?"

"I'm just glad it's clean," he winced.

I ran my thumb across his cheek. "You should eat some coconut. You need your strength."

He nodded.

"Do you think you can sit up?"

He placed his hands firmly on the ground and began to push himself upward. I rushed to grab his elbow, supporting some of his weight. "Let's get you leaned up against something," I said, helping him scoot backward so that he could prop himself against a large rock. "You feel ok?" I asked, looking him in the eye to make sure he wasn't going to faint.

He nodded as he leaned his head back.

I stepped away and grabbed two coconuts out of the basket. I peeled and carved a hole into the first one and passed it to him. He took it with shaking hands and brought it to his lips, taking a tentative sip. He did better this time and didn't let any of the liquid escape down his chin. I drank the other quickly, realizing I was parched since I hadn't had anything to drink since yesterday.

I took Liam's coconut when he was finished, cracked it open, and then handed it back.

"Thanks," he replied with a drawn-out sigh. "I'm sorry to put you through this and have you waiting on me…"

I set my coconut down. "All I want you to focus on right now is resting and healing. I'll take care of everything else." I pushed myself to my feet. "Actually, right now, I'm going to go fish for something more substantial for you to eat."

"Whoa, what?" Liam said hurriedly, grabbing my arm. "You are *not* going out there."

I turned around to face him. I knew he'd protest, but I'd been thinking on it all night, and I'd come to the conclusion that I had to go out there on my own. "Yes, I am. There are no birds, thus there are no eggs. There is no seaweed, and you are not going to heal on coconuts alone. You showed me how. Now I'm going to go get you some real food."

"Cora…" he pleaded. "It's too dangerous. I won't be there if something happens…"

His hand still gripped my wrist, but I took a deep breath. "Nothing is more dangerous than the possibility of you never recovering because you didn't get enough to eat." I held eye contact with him, defiantly. "I'm going out there. And I'm coming back with fish."

He stared at me for a few seconds, and I could tell he was thinking about trying to stop me again, but I was prepared to stand my ground. He took a deep breath and pulled gently on my wrist, drawing me down to him. He lifted his chin and placed a light kiss on my lips. "Watch the waves, and don't drift too far out…Remember what I showed you." His eyes gazed achingly into mine. "Come back to me…"

I will. Because I love you…

"I'll always come back to you," I replied quietly, holding back the words I wanted so badly to say.

Liam's expression softened, and then he slowly let go of my wrist and allowed me to stand back up again. I grabbed two more coconuts and prepared them, and then I placed them down next to him in the sand. "Keep drinking."

I found a small basket I had woven weeks ago, and I picked

up another charging cord and tied it to the edge. Then, I grabbed Liam's spear and walked confidently toward the shore.

When I came to the spot where I'd found him lying yesterday, my heart skipped a beat. But the blood was gone now, washed away with the tide as if it had never happened.

I looked down at my clothes, which had not forgotten the ordeal. There were still splatters of blood across my shorts. I peeled them off, and then bravely waded into the water in my swimsuit, pulling the basket behind me.

I swam out into the open ocean, breathing deeply and evenly. My muscles were lethargic from lack of food and sleep, but I pushed myself further from the shore until I felt like I was in the same place Liam had brought me before.

I thought about him, sitting back by the fire, probably worried about me and feeling useless. I remembered having the same emotions early on in our journey when I had to sit and rest while Liam was trying desperately to spear a fish so that I didn't starve. This situation was almost an exact mirror image of that one.

It was my turn.

Looking into the clear waters, I saw dozens of fish swimming underneath. I bobbed up and down with the current, trying to find its rhythm. The waves were larger today than the first time I'd been out here with him. It was harder to accurately pinpoint the fish. But I took a deep breath and sank beneath the surface.

When I opened my eyes, I spotted a large one a few feet away, and I crept closer to it, spear poised and ready. But when I shot the pole through the water, the fish was too quick and made its escape just in time. I retrieved the spear and swam back to the surface, pulling oxygen roughly into my lungs as the waves splattered into the side of my face.

I went down again, and again, and again, coming back empty each time. But every time I failed, I reminded myself I was not going back without fish. My success might mean life or death for Liam, and if I had anything to say about it, life would win.

An exceptionally large surge crashed over my head, and I coughed and choked, taking in water. My eyes teared and my nose burned from the salt as desperation crept in. But I gritted my teeth and dove in again. This time, directly in front of me was a small, silver fish. It was motionless as its beady eye stared back at me. For a moment, I felt a connection with this small creature, almost as if it were presenting itself to me. I pulled the elastic band back and drove the spear forward, perfectly piercing it into the sand below. My heart leapt, and I dragged it back to the surface, sputtering and coughing as I placed it in my basket.

Ok, good enough.

After what was probably more than an hour, one fish was all I could manage today, and I chose to accept that. My muscles seared as I pushed myself back toward shore, pulling the basket along with me. When I reached the sand, I stumbled out of the waves and fell to my knees. I was lightheaded and my vision was blurry, but I took long, calculated breaths. If spearfishing was going to be this difficult every time, I was going to have to step up my endurance.

After a few moments of rest, I got to my feet and carried the basket back to our campsite. When I came around the last boulder, my eyes found Liam, who was sitting against the rock staring blankly at the flames. When he saw me, the worry receded from his expression, and he let out a long breath.

I smiled tightly and set the basket down next to him. He looked inside, and then back up at me with a warm smile. "You did great."

I slumped to the ground in defeat.

He placed his hand on my back and rubbed gently. "You caught a fish, *and* you're back safe…that's a success in my book."

I sighed and pierced a stick through the fish, holding it over the flames without responding. I wasn't exactly proud of myself for this sad display.

He continued. "Look, your dad might not give you the recognition you deserve for pushing yourself and going out on your own to achieve something impressive, but I do. And I *will* when you eventually take the plunge and open up that restaurant of yours."

I stared fixedly at a red-hot coal, wishing it were as easy as he made it seem.

"I'm proud of you." Liam spoke up again.

I remained silent.

He cleared his throat. "I think the resting has helped me. I'm a bit better. I don't feel like I'm about to pass out anymore."

I turned to look at him. There was much more color in his face. I smiled. "Your blood is returning."

He took a deep breath. "Hopefully soon, I can get out there with you and fish, but…"

"You can't submerge that leg until it's healed over," I interrupted him. "Who knows what's in that seawater."

"I know," he replied sadly, focusing on his hands in his lap.

"I can keep going back out," I assured him. "It's really not that hard." It was a lie, but a necessary one.

Liam didn't respond. He knew how important my help was.

After we watched the single fish cook, I pulled it from the fire, placed it in a coconut bowl, and handed it to him.

"Aren't you going to split it up?" he asked, confused.

I picked up a fresh coconut and began to eat it slowly. "No, it's yours."

"Come on, Cora. You should take half of it."

I eyed him warily. "*I* can survive off coconuts right now. *You* cannot."

He gazed down at the fish for a short moment, and then his eyes met mine again. "Just one bite?"

He was so generous, even in this state, and I couldn't resist him. I sighed and held out my hand. He pulled a piece of meat from the bones and placed it in my palm. I popped it in my mouth, which instantly watered in gratitude.

"Thank you." I smiled softly.

"I wish I could be of more help," Liam sighed.

I looked closely at him, making sure that he would understand my words well. "The best help you can be to me now is to heal." I paused with a gulp. "Without you, I'm nothing. Alone, without you, I couldn't continue on."

His expression fell. "But…you know you would have to… right? You're strong, Cora."

I held his gaze. I wanted so badly to reveal my heart—to tell him that I loved him—that going on without him would be impossible. But not knowing how he felt, I couldn't bring myself to do it. So, instead, I chose a response with less gravity. "Strength is different than happiness. Without you, I would be miserable, and I know I wouldn't see the purpose in trying any longer."

Liam frowned and leaned in, gently touching his warm lips to mine. When he pulled back, he watched me with compassion. "I would argue with you, but…I felt the same way when you were sick…so I understand…"

I placed my hand on his cheek and pulled him in again, resting my forehead against his for a moment. My love for him had grown tenfold, even since yesterday. I wished I could feed him my thoughts through osmosis since I couldn't bring myself to say them out loud.

***

Three days passed.

Each morning, I poured a small amount of mouthwash onto Liam's wound, and every time, he bit down on a shirt in agony. It was torture for us both. He had to endure the physical pain, and I had to deal with the mental anguish, knowing that I was the inflictor. But there were still no signs of infection, and each day, the wound looked a bit better. The area around the gash had turned black and blue, but the edges of his skin that were pulled together by the stitches were beginning to seal.

I was beyond grateful that he seemed to be turning a corner, and I grasped onto hope again, despite the drought we were facing. His recovery gave me the motivation to push forward.

Liam had begun to try walking again. He couldn't put any weight on his injured leg, but with the help of a large bamboo pole, he could hop around our campsite, tending to the fire and fortifying the shelter. He was in better spirits now that he was no longer in constant pain, but I could see that he was struggling to let me take on the role of 'provider' for this time.

I'd been back out to fish twice. On both occasions, I'd returned with two fish. It wasn't a lot, but it was enough to keep us alive. Since it still hadn't rained, I spent most of my time finding low-hanging trees and collecting coconuts. It was the lone source of hydration we had, and each one only held a few ounces of water, so I literally spent multiple hours a day scouring the island for as many as I could find. I was even beginning to learn how to climb the shorter trees, and we now had accumulated a decent stockpile.

Today, I hauled a suitcase full of them back to our campsite, wiping my brow as I emptied them into our raft.

"Looks like you had some luck today?" Liam asked from behind me.

I turned around to nod at him but saw that he was sitting with his hands behind his back, grinning at me.

I raised a skeptical eyebrow with a laugh. "What's with *that* face?"

"Come 'ere." He continued to grin and nodded at the ground in front of him.

I smirked as I walked tentatively in his direction. "What's going on?"

"Just sit down," he chuckled.

I lowered myself to the ground in front of him and crossed my legs, searching his expression for an explanation.

He still had his hands behind his back. "Ok, hold out your hands and close your eyes."

I blinked at him.

"Just do it," he laughed again. His eyes twinkled, letting me know that this was all fun.

I took a deep breath, shut my eyes, and positioned my palms

up in front of me. After a pause, I felt something lightweight and soft being placed on them.

"Ok, you can open your eyes," Liam said softly.

When I did, they landed on an oddly shaped object, wrapped in a piece of red fabric, and tied up with a green palm frond. It looked like a present.

I peered up at him. "What's this?"

"So, I've been counting the ticks on our cave wall and doing the math…" A bright smile spread across his face. "It turns out…I think today is Christmas."

My mouth hung open, barely believing that I could let a date like Christmas fly by without even noticing. And the fact that Liam had counted the days, *and* had taken the time to give me something, made my eyes well up.

"So, Merry Christmas…" He continued to smirk.

I held the gift gingerly in my hands and gazed at him with complete and utter love. The words almost slipped from my lips, but I gulped and held them in. This man continued to astound me as I fell deeper and deeper for him.

I leaned in and kissed him tenderly, beyond grateful that he was alive and still here with me. When I leaned back, I was speechless, and almost forgot about the gift in my hands until Liam spoke up again.

"Well, aren't ya gonna open it up?" he chuckled.

I blinked quickly. "Oh, yes, of course…" I pulled my eyes from his and focused my attention on untying the palm leaf while he watched me intently.

When it came free, I unfolded the red fabric to reveal a piece of deep brown wood, about five inches wide, and endearingly carved into the shape of a heart. Tears welled in my eyes again as I ran my thumb over its smooth edges.

"I know, it's not much, and it's kind of childish and silly, but…" he began.

"It's *perfect,"* I breathed, smiling widely and throwing my arms around him, burying my face in his neck. "Thank you…I love…I love it."

I love you.

He kissed my cheek. "I've had a lot of time to myself, so I've been perfecting my whittling skills," he laughed. "No idea what you'll do with it."

I sat back and placed the wooden heart over my own, clasping it to my chest. I imagined him, carving away at this precious gift while I was out gathering coconuts. "I'll save it forever…"

He beamed at me as his dark hair blew in the wind, framing his breathtaking face.

But I frowned and laughed. "I'm sorry, I didn't get you anything."

Liam placed his hand on mine. "You *being* here is the best present you could give me."

I moved in to kiss him again. "Merry Christmas, Liam."

"Merry Christmas, Cora," his warm lips replied against mine.

TWENTY-FOUR

It had been over a week since Liam's accident, and each day he showed another sign of improvement. His leg wasn't in pain anymore unless disturbed, and he was able to walk without the aid of the bamboo pole. He wasn't in a state to fish again yet, but he helped me carry coconuts and we took evening strolls together. He was officially out of the woods, and I was beyond relieved.

The birds had not returned, and thirst was now our main concern. We were both dehydrated. We weren't as active as we used to be, and I found myself suffering from daily headaches. Though, I was getting better at fishing—well, if better meant spearing an average of two tiny fish per day. It was not enough to fully satisfy, but it was enough to keep us from starving.

Ever since his injury, Liam and I hadn't shared more than sweet kisses and cuddles. Up until a day or two ago, he'd still been in a fair amount of pain, and we were busy most of our hours, trying to keep ourselves alive during the drought. By the time we returned to our shelter each night, we were so exhausted that we fell asleep within minutes. I longed to feel him so intimately again, but my mind was so focused on providing for him and helping him heal that I didn't have as much time to linger on those thoughts.

However, this morning, as I was tidying up our shelter, butterflies found their way into my stomach again as I adjusted the carved wooden heart carefully in the corner. It was one of the first things I saw each morning when I opened my eyes, and it reminded me how deeply he cared. Whether or not his feelings were as strong as mine, I knew they were there, and that was a special motivation that helped me push through each day. I still remembered the heated look in his eyes and the way his hands had felt on me in front of the fire over a week ago. I recognized that maybe now that he was feeling better, I wouldn't need to feel guilty being extra affectionate with him, and maybe we could get a little closer again.

Liam was quiet when I met him outside the shelter and sat down to untie the bandage on his leg. The bruising now held more of a yellowish-green tint, and his skin had completely fused at the cut line.

I studied it carefully. "I think it might be time to remove the stitches..."

Liam sighed, leaning forward and looking closely at it as well. "You think?"

"It looks pretty closed up now. You don't need them anymore." I frowned, knowing he'd have to endure more pain again.

He took a deep breath and nodded. "Might as well get it over with."

I stood up and grabbed the Swiss Army knife, flipping it open to the mini set of scissors. "Do you want a shirt to bite on?"

He shook his head. "No, I think I can take it." He braced his hands in the sand and clenched his jaw.

I leaned in to get a good look at his wound. The small strands of thread were barely visible, but I was able to gently slip one of the scissor blades under a loop to make the first snip. Liam didn't wince at that part, but after I'd cut all the loops and began pulling the threads out, his face contorted.

"You alright?" I asked when I was halfway through.

"Yep. Just keep going," he replied tensely, not opening his eyes.

When I'd pulled the last thread free, I took the bottle of mouthwash and poised it over the wound. "Ok, I'm going to clean it now."

He nodded and balled his fists.

As I poured a bit of the liquid onto his skin, he let out a low growl, but it was a welcome change from the yelling he'd done when I'd cleaned it the first few times.

The removal of his stitches had caused some bleeding again, so I wrapped new strips of fabric around his leg tightly. "Ok, you're good to go."

Liam sighed and touched his fingers to the bandage. "Thanks, hopefully I won't be a hindrance to you much longer."

I placed my hand on his. "It's been nice to take care of you for once. Having the tables turned is not the worst thing."

He looked blankly at the fire, giving no response.

"We have to be strong for each other. This was one of those times I needed to be strong for you." I wished he didn't feel like such a burden.

Liam lifted his eyes and placed his other hand on top of mine. "Cora, regardless of whether or not we're strong for each other, things are still going to happen. This place we're living…" He gestured to the island around us. "It's unforgiving. Accidents happen. Droughts happen. One of these days, we aren't going to be able to fight back, no matter how strong we are."

It was a morbid thought, and I peered back at him with unease, not sure what to say. He was right, but I didn't want to believe him. I wanted to believe, in my fantasy world, that we would either be rescued or that we would live out some kind of magical forever here together.

But Liam's sad eyes still studied mine. "We can't be sure we'll ever be found, and we don't know what dangers lie around the next corner. It's terrifying." He pressed his lips together.

I could see that he was struggling, maybe even more than I was. My heart went out to him, and I rubbed my thumb gently across his knuckles, swallowing the sticky dryness in my throat. "Someone will find us."

"But what if they don't?" He gulped. "It's been two months now. Our chances aren't getting any better."

He was right, and it was distressing. I knew they had probably stopped looking by now. I'd known that for a while, but the thought hit me hard in the gut every time.

"Do you think they've held the funerals?" I asked quietly.

"Undoubtedly."

Did they bury empty caskets? They didn't even have proof of our deaths. Was that allowed? My mind wandered to Kate, wondering if she'd started to move on yet, but I quickly pulled myself away from that thought and returned my focus to Liam instead.

He emptied a coconut into his mouth, and then went immediately for another.

"We really need water..." I stared blankly at the pile of spent shells in front of us.

His face was grim as he nodded.

"How long before..." I started.

"Before we die?"

I sucked in a short breath, shooting him a wide-eyed look. "Liam..."

"A few more months...I don't know." He sighed. "And that's if we don't get hurt again. I mean, look at what just happened to me. Had you not found me when you did, I wouldn't be here right now."

I stared into his eyes for a beat. "Surely we have more than months?"

He looked out at the sea. "I honestly don't know. I think, eventually, I'll have to take the raft out to try and find some help, and then come back to you. It probably will be my demise, but I want to at least die trying."

His figure grew wavy beyond the tears that sprung to my eyes. "No..." I whispered. "No. I can't lose you."

When he lifted his gaze to mine again, the edges of his eyes were red. "We won't survive if the drought continues. I'm gonna have to do something..." He pressed his trembling lips together.

I scooted into him and laid my head on his shoulder. "No...I need you." I shuddered.

He was silent and stiff beneath me, but he wrapped his arm around my back and kissed the top of my head. "I know. I'm right here..."

***

Later that evening, before the sun had gone down, we relaxed by the fire after splitting one small fish I'd speared. After our conversation earlier, we'd spent most of the afternoon practically joined at the hip. As soon as he'd suggested that he might take the lifeboat out to search for help if things got dire enough, all I could picture was his helpless form, sprawled under the beating sun, floating around in the middle of the Pacific with no land in sight. In my book, that wasn't an option, and now I didn't want to let him out of my sight for fear that I might miss out on a moment with him that I'd never get back.

Trying to distract myself, I watched the horizon, observing the beautiful colors of the setting sun. Pinks and oranges swirled with blues and purples, lighting up the sky.

"Kinda beautiful tonight, isn't it?" I mused.

"Mhmm," Liam said quietly next to me.

When I turned to him, he wasn't looking at the horizon, but instead at me. "I'm talking about the sky." I smirked.

"I'm not," Liam replied, straight-faced, and still not tearing his eyes from me.

I blushed and looked back at the array of colors. No matter how many times he complimented me, I still couldn't get used to it. There was something about him that made my heart flutter wildly, even after months alone together.

Liam pushed to his feet and extended his hand. "Dance with me…"

I placed my hand in his warm one, and his fingers wrapped around mine tightly as he pulled me up from the ground.

When my eyes met his, they were a brilliant amber in the light of the setting sun. He led me away from the fire, touching the small of my back and pulling me closer to him. His heartbeat was warm and alive against my chest.

"It's been a while. Can you remind me how?" I said quietly, looking up into his face as my spine tingled where he touched me so gently.

"No counting..." he replied softly. "...just dance with me."

I admired his face, which was filled with emotion, deeper than I'd seen from him before. It wasn't the lust he'd watched me with when I'd put on my yellow dress. It was something different, something more profound.

I turned my head and laid it on his shoulder as he began to sway gently to an imaginary rhythm, chest rising and falling evenly against mine. There may not have been any audible music, but there was a symphony of feelings inside my head. Liam was different from the rest. He was my greatest dream and my deepest desire come to life here in front of me. Everything just felt *right* with him.

"I'd like to spend eternity, right here in this moment, with you..." Liam spoke close to my head.

I closed my eyes and focused on the sensation of his hand on my back, and his breath in my hair. "I could live with that."

"I can't imagine my life without you anymore. You're the reason I wake up every day, and you're my favorite part about going to sleep, knowing you're right there next to me, safe," he said quietly.

I touched my lips to his neck, feeling the heat beneath his soft skin. He threaded his fingers through mine, holding our hands close to our bodies as we swayed.

"When that plane went down," he continued, "I knew my life would be turned upside down, but I had no idea what that would mean, and I never dreamed that something like this would happen." He paused. "You're everything to me now, Cora."

My heart skipped a beat, and I lifted my head to look at him. When his eyes met mine, they were vast hazel pools of deep emotion that seemed to have no end.

He pushed a strand of hair from my forehead. "Nothing..." He choked on the word. "*Nothing* matters more to me than keeping you safe. I don't know what tomorrow will bring. All I can be certain of is the 'right now.' We can only live in the moment. And in this moment, it's you. *You* are my moment."

I swallowed anxiously, wanting to say the same things to him. Because they were all true. Each and every one of them.

He squeezed my hand tightly, and with a shallow exhale, he smiled. "I love you."

My heart leapt into my throat as I gazed into his eyes, barely believing that he'd finally said the words that mirrored my own.

In the quietest whisper, because I could hardly speak, I responded, "I love you too."

Joy danced across his expression as he leaned in to kiss me, deeply and with heartfelt passion.

He loved me.

And I loved him.

Nothing else mattered. Not the drought. Not his leg. Not our grumbling stomachs.

"I love you..." I repeated as he broke the kiss and rested his forehead against mine. I wanted to say it over and over again until I felt like the words had been done justice, but I knew that would never be possible.

Liam pulled me deeper into his arms and buried his head in my neck. "Thank you," he whispered.

I grinned into his shoulder. "For loving you?"

His eyes crinkled as he leaned back and took my hands in his. "For taking care of me. There is nothing more precious than saving someone's life and having yours saved in return."

I kissed him again, slowly and firmly, memorizing the way his lips felt against mine. I realized once more how easily I could have lost him. Dread threatened to fill my bursting heart.

"I don't know what I'd do without you," I whispered against his lips.

"I'm right here…" He took my hand and placed it over his heart. "With every ounce of effort I have, I'm going to be right here. I'm not going anywhere."

But his eyes betrayed him. He knew he could never promise me that. Neither of us had any idea what tomorrow held, and it was an unspoken fear that pierced the silent air between us.

He stared at me for a long moment, holding my hand against his chest. I could feel the warm beat of his heart, thumping beneath my fingers. I lowered my gaze to his shirt, slid my hand from his, and trailed it down across his navel to the waistband of his shorts.

I bit my lip as a new heat built within me.

After a silent pause, he took my hand again and pulled me gently in the direction of our shelter. I followed eagerly, blind to everything but him. He opened the makeshift door and led me inside, and when he'd walked a few steps away, he turned around to face me, and our eyes locked.

"Cora..." he sighed.

"I know…" I whispered, recognizing the battle behind his expression.

I understood. The drought was weakening us, day by day. If the rain continued to hold off, we would eventually grow too weak to fish—to stay alive. Time was elusive and frightening.

My eyes raked slowly down his body and then back up again, the same battle raging in my own head.

"I'm torn…" he said, still standing on the other side of our small room. "I know we said we'd be careful, but *God,"* He paused. "I love you so much Cora, and I'm so afraid of losing you." The pain on his face shot straight to my heart.

I took a deep breath, watching him struggle, all the while, bouncing back and forth between our options in my own mind. The familiar flutter between my thighs returned, and I chewed on my lip.

I was always so responsible. It wasn't usually this difficult for me. But I wanted him. I *needed* him. The consequences began to blur in front of me.

Liam watched me closely, quietly. "We don't have to—"

"Please." The word dropped from my lips with a shallow exhale—a plea for him to give in.

Liam stared at me, breathlessly, unmoving. I thought maybe I'd said the wrong thing, that maybe he was counting on my restraint. But suddenly, he closed the distance between us in barely a second, crashing his lips into mine and almost knocking me over.

He snaked his arms around my waist and pulled me into him, supporting my lost balance with his own strength. There was a desperation in the way he held me, and I felt it within myself too. I needed him more than I needed *rain.*

He pushed me backward into the wall of the cave, pressing his body against mine. Open-mouthed kisses and frantic breathing assaulted my senses, leaving me completely raw and vulnerable. My hands reached to his hair, curling the loose strands around my fingers firmly and urgently. Without breaking his lips from mine, he found the hem of my shirt and traveled his fingers ravenously under it and up my back.

My palms trailed down his neck to his broad shoulders, and then across his torso until I felt the edge of his t-shirt. I slid my fingers under, lifting it slowly, feeling his burning hot skin and the bits of hair that covered his lower abdomen. He broke our kiss and pulled his shirt over his head, revealing his tanned chest, rising and falling heavily. His eyes still held mine, scorching and hungry, sincere and passionate.

He didn't miss a beat, lifting my shirt off and wrapping his arms around me again, guiding us both easily down to the ground. The palm leaves were cool against my back, deeply contrasted by the warmth of his body.

He reached behind me to untie the knots that held my swimsuit together, letting it fall to the floor next to us. I blushed as I watched his eyes scan across my chest.

"You're so beautiful…" he whispered, leaning down to press his lips to my collar bone, and then across the swell of one of my breasts. They were sensual, sultry kisses that made me wonder how I'd ever had the restraint before.

I arched my back as my fingers slid through his hair, and I tried to remember why I should stop him, but my nerves were aflame, and my mind was numb.

I grasped at his arms, his shoulders, his hips, until I slid my fingers to the waistband of his shorts, and he rose up to remove them in one quick motion until he was bare in front of me.

My eyes caught sight of him. Firm, stiff, ready.

I took a deep, shaking breath.

I shimmied out of my swimsuit bottoms and tossed them to the side. His dark gaze traveled down my body slowly, and his hands followed the same path, touching and caressing as they made their way to the apex of my thighs. His fingers were like electricity, sweeping featherlight across my heated flesh. I couldn't hold back the breathless sound that escaped my lips.

He covered my sigh with his mouth, kissing me urgently and nudging my knees apart as he lowered himself between them. And I felt him there, firmly pressed against me.

He was still as his mouth was at my ear. "We shouldn't do this…"

"Yes…but we *should*…" I gasped back, having already forfeited any chance of stopping myself. I trailed my hand further down across his abs, causing him to breathe even heavier into the crook of my neck.

"I need you so badly." His voice came in a husky whisper.

"Yes…we can be…careful…" I panted, though I knew it would be Liam alone who would need all the restraint.

"Yes, I can stop before…" Liam trailed off, growling into my neck and sending vibrations through my skin.

"Are you sure?" I asked, involuntarily pressing my hips up into his.

"I don't know…" He moved his mouth down my collarbone and onto my bare chest again, sending a new round of pleasure coursing through my veins.

I closed my eyes, realizing that we were now far past any chance of self-control. I traced my hand down his stomach again, continuing my descent through the thicker dark hair below.

As I slid my fingers around him, he groaned into my chest. "Ok, yes...I'm sure…"

He was velvety smooth and pulsing under my touch, and I sighed again at the feel of him in my hand. Maybe just this would be enough…

But when he lifted his head to look at me, I saw his love there, deeper rooted than even his impassioned hunger. Love was what was ultimately bringing us together, and I was at peace with that truth.

I dug my fingers into the skin of his back and pulled him closer. He kissed me again as he finally pushed slowly into me, taking his time as I adjusted. I sucked in a deep breath, overcome by the sensation.

Liam lifted his head, and we locked eyes, understanding the gravity of our decision. But neither of us spoke. Words didn't matter. Our eyes did the talking as he slowly began to move.

Every desperate need I'd had, to feel him pressed into me and to see him wholly undone was fulfilled in our long-awaited, euphoric exchange of passion. Every breath I drew was a plea for more, to which he indulged each time, sending me higher and higher. It was as if nothing else in the world mattered, or even existed, as we finally moved together as one.

Our passion overflowed into a mess of tangled limbs and breaths of ecstasy. Tender touches led to frenzied hunger, and all that existed between us was our mutual desire, our love, and every ounce of me that craved every ounce of him.

As the pressure built to a crescendo, his name slid from my lips and he picked up his pace, sending me over the edge. The world around me burst into bright arrays of exploding color, and the sounds that followed pierced the air of our once quiet cave as he held me tight.

His movements grew erratic, and he pressed his teeth into my shoulder with a groan as he pulled out and found his own release.

I lay there panting as I came back to Earth and the flashes of light faded from my eyes. Liam collapsed almost fully on top of me, breathing heavily against my neck as he tried to support himself on his arms.

I kissed my way down his taut shoulder and ran my fingers through his hair. He grunted and pushed himself up onto his elbows. His caramel eyes stared deeply into mine. "I love you."

"I love you, *so much,"* I replied. And I meant it more than I'd ever meant any other words that had ever left my mouth.

His warm and exhausted lips found mine, kissing me with an unyielding devotion. And in that moment, I was no longer afraid, because there was one thing I was sure of: no matter what would happen tomorrow, I knew I would be loved.

TWENTY-FIVE

A ray of sun peeked through the leaves of our shelter wall the next morning, and my gaze followed the glimmer of light down to where it landed across Liam's face. I blinked slowly, admiring how peaceful he looked as he slept. Where the light touched his dark hair, bits of gold and amber shimmered through. His thick beard looked soft and inviting, and I wanted to reach out and touch it—to touch him, in any and every way.

I couldn't believe that *he* loved me. While I had surprised myself with my own growing feelings, at least I understood how they came to be. I saw how incredible he was and how easy it was to fall for him. But to know that he felt the same way about me was almost unfathomable.

Last night, I'd watched him give into a primal passion that he could not contain, and it was a breathtaking montage of moments that I couldn't have created in my own imagination if I'd tried. Afterward, we'd laid peacefully together, basking in an afterglow that seemed to never end and chatting deep into the night. I'd fallen asleep in his arms, safe and content.

The only regret that weighed on my mind was that we'd gone as far as we did. We could have stopped short and explored our intimacy in other ways, but in the moment, that hadn't seemed like an option. All coherent thought had left me as soon as he'd led me into our cave. The fear of losing each other seemed to push any other reasoning aside. But even though we'd been so careful, we'd still taken a risk, and it was bound to worry me for at least the next few weeks.

I rolled over and wiped my hand down my face. I was *so* thirsty. Coconut water was just barely life-sustaining. We were alive, but our bodies craved what they did not have enough of.

Liam stirred next to me, smacking his lips and blinking into the daylight. When his gaze met mine, his eyes sparkled, and his mouth turned up into a warm grin. He wrapped his arm around me and pulled me into his chest, burying his face in my hair.

"Good morning, my love," he sighed.

"Mmm…good morning," I replied, smiling into his bare skin.

"Did you sleep well?" he asked.

"Marvelously." I grinned.

He leaned back and assessed me eagerly. "God, I love waking up next to you…"

I touched my lips to his. "If I went back in time and told the version of myself two months ago that this is where I'd be now, she'd laugh me out of the room, and then probably pass out when she realized it was true."

Liam raised a playful eyebrow. "Wanted me that bad, did ya?"

I smirked and nudged his shoulder.

"So, did I do myself justice?" he asked with a wink.

I blinked affectionately at him. "Reality is always better than dreams."

"Reality…" Liam echoed, absently running his fingers through my hair as his face turned serious. When he looked at me, I melted. I could stare into those expressive brown eyes for forever and an eternity.

He tucked a strand of hair behind my ear. "How do you feel about what happened last night…honestly?"

I studied him for a moment before taking a deep breath. "I have a few thoughts…"

Liam propped himself up on his elbow and looked intently at me.

"First…" I began. "And I'm surprised by this, but I don't regret anything. It was perfect, and…mmmm…" I remembered the vivid details as shivers trailed down my spine. "Yeah, it was pretty much perfect." I grinned.

Liam smirked with a twinkle of pride.

"But…" I took another deep breath. "It can't happen again." I watched him closely to gauge his reaction.

He tightened his lips. There was disappointment there, but he nodded.

"It's too much of a risk," I continued. "You know it as well as I do. We have to be smart. When I'm able to think clearly about it, I know that it's probably not worth the danger."

Liam sighed. "I would almost say that last night shouldn't have happened at all, but I'm with you—I don't regret it. It was something that…almost *needed* to happen. I might have lost my mind if it didn't," he chuckled.

I grinned and placed my hand on his chest, feeling his heartbeat beneath my fingers.

"But I also feel a bit guilty," he confessed. "I should have had the mind to stop it before it happened. I don't know what I'll do if…" He trailed off.

"Hey..." I responded gently. "It'll be ok. We were careful."

He chewed apprehensively on his cheek. "Well, for now, as difficult as it may be, we'll take one step back in the name of caution. We're gonna get rescued. It'll happen. And when that day comes, we'll have access to all of the contraception we could ever need." He smirked. "Until then, we'll hold off."

I sighed, wishing I could have him again, right here, and right now. But he was right. We'd be more careful from now on.

I let out a disgruntled breath, but as the air passed over my throat, I coughed at the dry, sticky feeling that lingered. "Ugh, I'm so thirsty…"

Liam frowned. "I know, we've gotta up our coconut intake. Hang on, I'll get you one."

I grasped his arm tightly so he couldn't get up. "Stay a little longer…"

He regarded me for a moment with a sympathetic smile, and started to relax back into me, but at the same time, a rumble resounded from outside. We looked at each other in surprise, recognizing the familiar sound.

"A storm…" he inhaled.

My heart jumped. We needed rain *so* badly. We needed those birds back, and we needed the hydration. Liam leaned in and kissed me fully on the lips, and then he slid his arm from my hand, stood up, and got dressed.

"I'm going to go check it out and see what we're in for."

I reached out and grasped tightly onto his hand again. I missed him already.

He leaned down to kiss me. "I'll be back, love."

I let his fingers slip from mine as he exited the shelter, and I flopped onto my back, grinning at the ceiling. I loved him so much, I felt like I was about to burst. Yes, the thought of imminent rain left me thirsty, but the thought of imminent Liam left me parched.

I tugged my own shorts on and pulled my shirt over my head, and then I turned to etch a new mark into the cave wall.

Sixty-four days.

More than two months.

Sometimes it felt like such a short flash of time, and other times it felt like an eternity. The hours and the days passed differently here without the distractions of our old lives. And during these two months, I felt like I'd gotten to know Liam even better than the friends I'd known for years.

Once upon a time, I'd played a silly game with those friends, where we'd question each other on how we'd survive on a deserted island, what we'd bring with us, and who we'd want to be stranded with. Somehow, I was indeed surviving, I'd brought enough to keep myself alive, and I was stranded with the person who would have probably topped my list if I'd been presented with that game months ago.

The odds of our situation were shocking. If the plane had never gone down, Liam would have safely disembarked in New Zealand, exiting the cabin far ahead of me, and I would have never even confirmed that he'd been the man I'd seen in first class. We would have gone our separate ways, and most likely never had the chance to meet again.

A lump formed in my throat. We'd have never fallen in love…

Life was so intricate, hanging on the edge of small choices and small mistakes, completely altering the path of the future, and laying the foundation for moments and lifetimes of joy that would have been unattainable otherwise.

That plane had failed either because of mechanical neglect, or maybe just by chance, and both Liam and I had somehow survived. We were thrust into this adventure together, and we'd taken it and made the most of it. We'd turned a tragic act of fate into an epic journey toward love.

Other than saving the lives of the other souls on board, I wouldn't have changed a thing. All the hardships we'd faced, and the close calls that almost took our lives were worth it if it meant we had been brought together like this.

I sighed and turned to peer out the door onto the beach. The skies were becoming dark with clouds, so I decided to join Liam to watch their arrival. He was standing by the water, assessing the waves as they picked up speed in the growing wind. I stopped quietly next to him and slipped my hand into his.

He quickly looked down at me and squeezed my fingers affectionately. "Looks like the drought might finally be over."

I laid my head on his shoulder as we watched the storm roll in.

"Are the containers still set out?" Liam asked me.

"Yep."

"Well, then let's just watch it happen," he said, lowering himself to the ground and pulling me down with him.

I sat between his legs, and he wrapped his arms around me. In the distance, the darkness increased and the clouds expanded; becoming larger and larger. It was like watching the small plane inching closer to our island, except in this case, the storm was too large to miss us, and we could anticipate it confidently.

Liam turned to kiss my temple. "So, I'm curious. When did you know that your feelings for me had grown?"

I smiled, remembering the way my love for him had come slowly, over the course of a few days. "It was sometime between our conversation when I learned that you were trying to be respectful of me, and when I watched you struggling to stay alive after your accident." I paused and frowned. "I realized how much I couldn't bear to lose you…"

He pressed his lips to my shoulder. "I had thought that my flub-up about respecting you had been a net loss."

I smiled. "No, I appreciated that you were trying to take care of me. It was very kind."

Liam interlocked his fingers with mine in my lap. "I just want you to be happy."

"I am," I replied with a smile, and then I laughed, remembering our first few days on the island. "Remember when I could barely speak to you, early on?"

He chuckled. "You were adorable."

I rested my head against his shoulder as I gazed out at the rough ocean waves. "So, when did you know?"

"It was when I saw you in that yellow dress."

I blushed and looked down at our hands. That was a long time ago.

"But it wasn't just because of how beautiful you looked," he added quickly. "I was so touched that you'd taken the time to doll yourself up like that for me. I could tell that you really cared. You did it for me. That meant a lot."

I smiled into the breeze, remembering the look on his face when he'd seen me in that dress for the first time. That moment had been special to me too.

"And then," he continued, "when you saved my life, and spent so much time taking care of me, I knew I had to tell you." He touched his lips to my cheek, but I turned to kiss him fully.

His lips were soft and warm, reminding me that his body was no longer struggling from lack of blood. He was thirsty now, but soon, once the storm hit, he'd be healthy again. I didn't know what I'd done to deserve him, but I never wanted to let him go.

As we kissed, small pelts of water began to dot my bare arms.

Rain.

We both looked up at the sky, blinking against the drops that fell down onto us. Liam got to his feet, extended his arms, and threw his head back, rejoicing in the hydration. I got up too, spun around, and laughed, letting it drench me as it quickly turned into a downpour.

It was glorious and refreshing, and I looked out onto the horizon, watching the dark clouds still descending. This wasn't going to be a small shower. This was real, healing rain, and I welcomed it with open arms of my own.

As I closed my eyes and let it soak my face, Liam surprised me from behind, snaking his arms around my waist. He spun me around, grasped my face, and kissed me firmly. I wrapped my arms around his neck and stepped up onto my toes, sinking into him as the rain fell in sheets around us.

"Come on, let's get you out of this weather." He laughed, taking my hand and pulling me toward our cave. We ran past the logs of our fire, which were now completely extinguished by the downpour. But we didn't even care. Starting a fire was a simple, amateur task for us now, and it was the least of our worries.

He pulled me into the protection of our shelter and wrapped his wet arms around me again. Damp strands of his hair hung onto his face, and I pushed them from his eyes.

"I love you," I breathed, taking his hand in mine.

"I love you too." He grinned.

Neither of us could say it enough.

I pulled him down to sit on the floor with me as I wrung my soaking hair out onto the ground. "I'm completely drenched." I giggled.

When Liam didn't respond, I looked up to see that he was staring at me with those eyes again—the ones that told me his mind was in a fiery place.

I bit my lip and blushed. "I should get out of these wet clothes."

"Let me help you," he responded gruffly.

I exhaled a deep, shaking breath as he moved forward to kneel in front of me. He slowly pushed the hair from my neck and began a trail of warm kisses down the sensitive skin there. His hands found my waist, pushing my wet shirt up further and further until he pulled it over my head. When he tossed it aside, it hit the ground with a resounding splat. I giggled, and the corners of his lips turned up too, but only for a second before he became serious again.

He kissed me firmly, pushing me gently down onto my back, and then his lips found my collarbone and trailed down my chest, leaving a hot path against my chilled skin. I watched the crown of his head and his dark, wet hair as he made his way lower and lower until his mouth was just below my navel.

He hooked his fingers around the waistband of my shorts and gently tugged them down, following the descent with his lips as I inhaled a sharp breath. I gripped the palm leaves tightly beneath me as his warm mouth closed over me.

If this was what it meant to take a step back and be more careful, I was completely on board. I sighed as I surrendered to his touch, wishing it would last forever, as the downpour of rain outside mimicked the downpour of emotions in my full and content heart.

TWENTY-SIX

"It's so hot…it's burrrrning…"

My eyes flew open and I looked around, trying to see what had woken me up.

Liam was shifting vigorously next to me. His face was contorted into a grimace as he tossed his head back and forth.

"I can't…it's too hot," he moaned.

I sat up quickly and touched his shoulder. "Liam, wake up, you're having a nightmare…"

"Too hot…I'm sorry, I can't…I'm sorry…" His voice became a whimper, and I rubbed his shoulder harder, trying to pull him out of his dream. But he continued to toss his head back and forth. Sweat beaded on his forehead as he sucked in shattered breaths.

"Liam…" I said louder this time. "Liam, hey, wake up."

"I'm sorry, I just…I tried…but it's too hot…" His voice was even louder, and I thought I'd have to take more drastic measures to wake him, but then his eyes suddenly opened and briefly met mine before he squeezed them shut again.

He flopped his arms down to his sides in defeat, breathing hard.

"Hey…it's ok…" I cooed, pushing the sweaty strands of hair from his forehead. "It was just a dream."

When he didn't respond, I rubbed my palm gently up and down his arm. He'd never had a nightmare since I'd known him. And during the last two weeks since we'd confessed our love for each other, we'd been nothing but purely happy. I had no idea what was causing this.

He brought his hand to his face and rubbed his temples with a deep sigh.

I stroked his shoulder slowly. "Are you alright? Do you want to talk about it?"

His tortured eyes met mine, and I saw the hesitancy flicker across them. But he inhaled slowly. "I was on the plane again…"

Oh no. I regarded him with sympathy.

"It was so vivid. It was exactly like it happened. I couldn't get to everyone. It was so hot…" He grimaced. "Fire all around…It was awful. I could almost feel my skin burning…but I couldn't get to them…"

I watched as Liam's eyes began to well up as he re-lived his torment. But he swiftly looked away, hiding his pain. I couldn't imagine what he'd been through, and how horrific it must have been to see the dead and the dying when he couldn't help them.

"I wish I could have done more…" He laid his arm over his eyes with a troubled exhale.

I placed my hand on his cheek and touched the scar that remained there, reminding us of the ordeal. "Liam…" I whispered. "You did absolutely everything you could. You did a wonderful thing that day, checking on so many of us—giving us a chance to live. You could have saved yourself first, but you chose to stay and search for life."

"I can't help but think if I would have tried a bit harder..." he said quietly.

I gently lifted his arm from his eyes and looked at him squarely. "Don't do that to yourself. You went above and beyond. No one faults you for that. It's the exact opposite. You saved a life that day. You saved *my* life."

He closed his pained eyes and pressed his lips together.

"I didn't realize you were still struggling so hard with this. I'm sorry," I spoke gently. "Do you know what brought this dream on?"

He slowly pulled himself up to sit, resting his elbow on his knee. "It's always been in the back of my mind. I'm not sure what triggered it to come out tonight though."

I scooted closer. "Do you want to talk about it some more?" It was still the middle of the night, but I wanted him to find some resolve if he needed it.

"I don't know..." he sighed.

I rested my chin on my palm, wishing there was something I could say to make him feel better, but knowing that there probably wasn't. "It sounds to me like, if you would have gone back, you probably would have hurt yourself even more, or died in the process." I gulped. "...and then maybe no one would have survived."

He stared blankly at the cave wall and nodded slowly.

I rubbed his back. "You can't let this eat you up inside. I can see now that you're still dealing with it. And I know you won't be able to let it go so easily. I'm sorry that I didn't notice before. But please talk to me about it when you need to. I was unconscious the whole time, so it doesn't affect me the same way. But you have another scar, like the one on your face." I touched it gently again, and then I moved my hand to his chest, right over his heart. "You have to let this one heal too."

Liam took my hand in his and gave me an unconvincing smile. "Thank you."

"Of course. I'm always here, whenever you need to talk… about anything." I replied warmly.

He leaned in and kissed me. "You get some more rest. I'm going to tend to the fire while I'm up. I don't think I can fall back asleep quite yet."

"Are you sure? You'll be alright alone?" I asked.

"Yes, love." He smiled, placing his hand on my cheek. "You go back to sleep."

I touched his arm affectionately as he stood up and left the shelter, and then I laid back down and ran my hand through my hair. I wish I'd known that he was still struggling. I *should* have known. It broke my heart to see him so shattered. Just like his body struggled when he'd been injured, his heart and his mind wrestled with this. I wanted to make it all go away for him. And I think I probably had done exactly that for just a bit—at least for these last few weeks as we explored our newfound love.

The days had been filled with dancing, laughing, and kissing…and many other wonderful moments that made my heart skip a beat when I thought about them. We'd stopped short of having sex again, but just barely, and only because we found an overwhelming enjoyment in what we *could* do. And oh, we could do plenty. I had quickly discovered how easily Liam's hands would wander if I let them.

And *oh yes,* I let them wander often.

I had a feeling that there would come a day when we'd start to lose our minds and our control again. I knew I daydreamed about it frequently. But for now, we were content.

Liam's leg was virtually healed over at this point, and he'd begun to spearfish again as well as hunt the birds that had returned to the island after the drought. We were regaining our strength and eating much better. I worried about him even more now every time he went out in the water, but he assured me that he'd learned from his accident and knew how to be more careful. Still, I tended to sit and watch him from the beach each time he went, just to calm my anxious heart.

My worries were not only for Liam's safety though. It had been thirty-two days since I'd gotten my last period, and its absence brought on a lot of anxiety. With the drought and the fact that I'd probably been dehydrated for a week or so, my cycle was likely out of sorts. I wasn't sure when to expect it, but the waiting was torture, and I could hardly bear it. My mind was starting to play tricks on me. Occasionally, I'd think I felt nauseous, or extra tired, but I figured I was probably being a hypochondriac, so I tried to ignore it. I noticed Liam eyeing me every morning, waiting to see if I felt sick or presented any other signs of pregnancy. He didn't verbalize his worries, but I could see them behind his gaze.

I stared at the ceiling of the cave, unable to fall back asleep. What if I *was* pregnant? What would we do? How would I give birth on this island? With no access to any medical supplies or knowledge, we'd have to do it all alone.

I rubbed my fingers across the bridge of my nose. We *had* really been careless, hadn't we? Had I really risked so much for a few moments of passion? Yes, I had. But I remembered the feel of him and the look in his eyes as he'd moved above me. In those moments, it had seemed like there was no other way.

Having a baby on an island couldn't be that bad, right? People used to do it all the time on their own. A baby with Liam. That could be sweet…someday. My heart skipped a beat. But what if we were rescued and I'd have to return *home* pregnant? How would we explain to everyone that we'd been so irresponsible and careless? What kind of reaction would there be?

Oh no. What would Kate think?

Shoot, I'd be the other woman *and* I'd be pregnant.

I shook my head, wiping her from my mind. Because more importantly, how would Liam feel? What if once we returned, he wanted to end our relationship? Would he feel trapped, like he had no choice but to stay with me for the sake of our hypothetical child? I squeezed my eyes shut. I did *not* want that.

I groaned and rolled over. The chances were so small, I needed to stop worrying. We'd been careful, after all.

I gazed at the empty spot on the ground next to me. I knew Liam was just outside, but I missed him when he wasn't here. It was too hard now to sleep alone without him next to me. There was a comfort in his presence that I couldn't ignore. It had been just the two of us for so long that his absence felt unnatural.

I heard a rustling of palm leaves, and then Liam stepped into the shelter and quietly sat down next to me. His eyes met mine in the dark. "You're still awake?"

"Mhmm…" I nodded, stretching my arms above my head.

"Can't sleep?" He laid down.

"Not when you're not here," I murmured, rolling toward him.

"Aww…" he replied, pulling me back into his chest. He kissed the top of my head and wrapped his arms tightly around me. "I'm here now."

I breathed him in and let out a long, contented sigh. "Are you feeling better?"

"Yes, I think so."

His chest was rising and falling calmly, so I trusted him and didn't push further. Instead, I let his protective arms lull me into a deep and peaceful sleep.

***

The next morning, I rested by the fire, peeling the husk from a coconut. Liam was away washing up, and I sat alone, thinking about how irresponsible I'd been when I drank from that rotten coconut over a month ago. I still couldn't believe I'd been so careless.

Liam came around one of the boulders, hair slicked back and wet from the ocean water. He held a small bottle of shampoo in his hand. "Water's warm this morning."

I cut a hole into the top of my coconut and smelled it. It was habit now. But I pulled it back quickly, thinking it might be rotten. I handed it to Liam. "Does this smell ok to you?"

He took it from me and brought it to his nose, but he had no reaction. Slowly, he handed it back. "It smells fine to me." He studied me closely. "Does it smell foul to you?"

I raised it to my nose again. This time, it smelled fresh. I tugged my eyebrows together. "I don't know, I thought maybe it did, but…I don't know." I looked back up into his uneasy eyes.

I knew exactly why he had that look. A heightened sense of smell was a common symptom of pregnancy. But I shook my head. "I'm probably just being too cautious after I got sick before. It's probably nothing." I waved him off as I took a drink. But when I peered up at him again, he was watching me with anxiety. "I'm alright. It's fine," I said quickly, and then I took a longer swig.

The water went down easily, and I set the shell down and looked back at Liam. He was still watching me.

"Do you feel ok?" he asked, eyes still slightly widened.

"Yeah, I'm fine," I repeated, standing up. I didn't want to freak him out, but I already knew that I was far past preventing that. I held out my hand. "Can I have that shampoo? I'm going to go wash up."

He extended it to me slowly, and we maintained wary eye contact for a moment. I quickly grabbed the bottle from him before gathering a new set of clothes and heading toward the beach, leaving him by the fire.

My heart thumped as I walked nervously toward the sea. The odd reaction to the coconut was nothing, for sure, it was *nothing,* I told myself over and over again as I went. I shook my head, trying to deny it.

But could it be?

I stopped at the water's edge and inhaled slowly. I placed my hands on my hips and closed my eyes, trying to accept whatever reality I would be faced with. I didn't feel nauseous exactly, I'd just experienced a moment of distaste for that smell. Maybe it was just a delayed traumatic reaction, like

Liam's nightmare had been?

I pulled my shirt over my head and tossed it aside, clasping my hand to my tight chest. It would all be ok. No matter the outcome. It would all be ok.

I began to pull my shorts off, and when I looked down, I stopped and let out a deep, relieved breath. I'd gotten my period. I *wasn't* pregnant.

I'd never been happier to greet Mother Nature in my life.

I let my head fall back and I started to laugh. I couldn't believe I'd been so worried. It *was* all going to be ok. I wouldn't be dangerously delivering a baby on a deserted island after all.

I picked up the bottle of shampoo and waded into the water, continuing my washing with a bright smile on my face. As much as I'd love to have a child someday, and maybe even with Liam, now was not the time. I began to feel a resurgence of hope. We could do this. We could survive, just the two of us.

When I was finished and had put on a new set of clothes, I wrung out my hair and walked eagerly back up the beach to tell Liam. It would be one less thing he'd need to worry about too.

When I rounded the last boulder and he came into view, I grinned widely at him. He was sitting against a rock, picking at a coconut when his eyes met mine.

"NOT pregnant." I beamed.

His eyes drifted shut and he let out the biggest, most relieved sigh I'd ever heard, letting his head fall back onto the rock. "Thank God…wow…"

"I know, right…?" I replied, leaning against another boulder, and setting the shampoo down.

"That's the best news I've ever heard." His chest was rising and falling as if he'd just run a marathon as he shoved his hand through his hair. "That would have been…awful."

"Yeah, it would have been bad," I agreed, scratching my head.

"I mean, can you even imagine?" He looked at me with big eyes. "Trying to raise a baby? What an ordeal that would be… No, thank you."

My smile started to fade. Was he talking about the idea of having a baby on this island, or just babies in general?

"Whew, Cora, that is such good news." He looked up at me, clearly exhausted from all his worrying. "I've been so distressed over this. I can't even imagine how we would have handled that. I'm so glad we don't have to find out."

I pursed my lips and looked down at the rock next to me, brushing some sand from its surface. From the way he was talking, it sure sounded like he had absolutely no desire to have a child with me; maybe not ever. Of course, I wasn't ready either, but he could have at least expressed a bit of affection at the idea.

I grimaced at my last thought, realizing I was being completely ridiculous. We'd known each other for just two and a half months. *Of course* he was happy I wasn't pregnant.

"So relieved…" he repeated quietly.

I nodded slowly. It was silly for me to be bothered by his response—we were not in a place to have a child—but a small part of me worried that maybe he was completely put off by the idea of having one with me even in the future. I'd definitely pondered it, imagining a short little bobbing mane of dark brown curls, running around the house—our house—in my dreams.

But I couldn't fault him for being so thrilled that I wasn't pregnant. I was beyond relieved too. I didn't know what kind of response I was expecting, but somewhere, deep down in the instinctual part of me, the part of me that craved a child in my arms someday, I wished he could have at least expressed a desire for that too. And with his residual feelings for Kate still placing doubts in my mind, his reaction had me even more concerned.

I took a deep breath and walked to the fire to adjust the logs.

"I think this calls for a celebration," Liam exclaimed. He stood up and grabbed me by the waist, spinning me around and looking into my eyes. I blinked up at him, attempting to plaster a smile on my face.

"I'm going to go get us a big, delicious bird, and we're going to cook it up with some of that seaweed. I saw some growing again just over there." He pointed toward the water and then his eyes met mine again as he smiled brightly. "I love you so much."

I pulled my lips into a small grin. "I love you too."

He gave me an affectionate squeeze before grabbing his bow and walking confidently from our campsite with a new pep in his step.

I stood alone; overcome by the barrage of emotions I'd just cycled through. It had all happened so fast I think I had whiplash. I was beyond happy that I wasn't pregnant, and I knew Liam should be too. But part of me—a part that maybe was not rational, but a part nonetheless—wondered if maybe he was relieved because he now knew he wouldn't have any permanent ties to me if we ever left this island…

TWENTY-SEVEN

The next afternoon, Liam was at the top of one of the taller palms while I stood a few yards away with his leather duffle bag, ready to collect the coconuts he tossed down.

"Is it almost full down there?" he called to me.

I looked inside. There was room for maybe one or two more. I sighed. "Yeah, pretty much."

Liam pulled one more and then began his descent down the tree. "We should gather some more firewood today too. Our stock is low."

"Sounds good," I replied, placing the last coconut in the bag and zipping it up.

Liam took it from my hands and slung it over his shoulder as we began to walk back to our campsite. "I'd also like to replace some of the leaves in the S.O.S. on the beach. They're getting a little worn out."

"Sure," I answered.

After a pause, he glanced at me. "Anything on your mind?"

I looked out at the horizon as it came into view. I wasn't hiding my emotions well, but I didn't feel much like discussing my irrational baby-making frustrations with him.

"No, I'm fine."

"Fine, as in, actually fine? Or fine, as in, I don't want to talk about it fine?" Liam raised an eyebrow.

I turned my attention away from him. I didn't want to try to explain how I was feeling when I didn't even understand myself completely, so I responded with something else that had been on my mind.

"Do you think they've...gotten rid of all of our belongings, at home?" I swallowed. "Have they moved on as if we've died?"

Liam walked slowly next to me, taking intentional steps around the tropical grasses. "I don't know about your parents, but my Mum is too sentimental to have done that so quickly. I do worry about my home and my flats though. Those ongoing rents are going to build up."

I blinked in mild shock at his nonchalant description of his multiple homes. But I shouldn't have been surprised that he was wealthy enough to afford several of them. "So, you have a permanent place in L.A? London? Where else?"

"I have three. My house is in Canterbury, and then I have a flat in London and another in L.A."

I raised my eyebrows. "Well...*I* have a tiny apartment I share with Tess. She's probably still living there. But you're right, I don't think my parents would have been able to part with my things just yet." I imagined my mother and father sitting at the kitchen table, sorting through memories of me.

"I'd like to see your *apartment* someday." He smiled, mimicking my use of the standard American term.

"It's not much." I waved him off. "Small and simple. It's all I need."

"But to see it would be a little glimpse into who you are; by the way you decorated it or how you keep things organized," he replied.

I smiled, thinking about what it would have been like to invite him into my home, to my *bed.* I took a controlled breath. "How do you keep up with three of them?"

Liam released the bag of coconuts from his shoulder and threw them down near our shelter. "Well, my Mum keeps an eye on my home in Canterbury when I'm not there, I have someone hired in London, and in L.A..." He paused. "Well... Kate took care of that."

"Ah," I replied quickly. "Well, maybe they've transferred that lease to her."

"I suppose that's possible," Liam answered quietly.

I imagined Kate helping his parents go through his belongings, reminiscing and bonding, all while he was here, alive and in love with someone else.

"I'd love a chance to see London for myself someday...if we get back, and things go well..." I tentatively mused.

Liam peered at me with his head tilted. "Well, of course. I'll be eager to get you over there and show you around—take you to some of my favorite places."

I smiled, glad to be reminded that he still seemed to imagine me as part of his life if we were ever rescued.

He leaned down and kissed me gently. "What a shock to everyone it'll be when we return."

"It'll be a shock to *me,*" I replied. "I'm honestly so used to this life now. I half expect us to be here forever."

Liam assessed me closely. "Would you prefer to be here forever?"

I looked at my feet. The longer we were here, the more I valued the bond that we'd created. I never wanted to lose that. I didn't want to stay here forever, but I wanted to continue to grow with him, and I had no idea what that would look like back in civilization.

I gazed up into his eyes, which were examining mine intently. "If it were the only way I could be with you, then yes."

There was compassion in his expression as he ran one of his hands softly through my hair, pushing it back from my face. "But you know that my love for you doesn't exist only on this island, right?"

His ability to read me so well was surprising, but it was also comforting, knowing he cared so much. I bit my lip. "I...think so..."

Liam took my hand and pulled me to sit down next to him. He took a preparatory breath. "Alright, I can tell you're worried. You think that if we are rescued, I'm just going to walk away and forget you ever existed. I obviously haven't done enough to show you otherwise, so let's talk about this."

I looked down at our hands, which were clasped together, and I rubbed my thumb over his knuckles. "No, no, you've been great. It's not that."

"Well, something's got you questioning it," he replied. "Is it because of who I am?"

I studied the shape of my fingers against his, wishing I could find the answers there. "I suppose, maybe. But it's more about who *I* am. I think you'd find me and my life incredibly boring and simple. I fear I'd lose you to something or someone flashier and more exciting."

"Cora..." he whispered. "Look at me."

I lifted my eyes slowly to his. They were kind and genuine, almost proving my doubts unnecessary. He continued carefully. "Do you remember the conversation we had in our first week when I told you I was exhausted from that extravagant lifestyle?"

I nodded.

"Did you not believe me?"

I inhaled deeply. "I don't think you've lied to me. I believe you. But I also know that this island is a bit of a trap, and you have no distractions or temptations to lead you away from me. I don't know what you're going to think if we're rescued and an endless array of options and opportunities are laid in front of you again."

I was surprised that I'd been able to put my doubts into words that made sense. I'd somehow described them perfectly. Except I'd been sure to leave out the part about being worried he'd feel forced to stay with me if a baby had come into the picture. That was something I was afraid to admit. At least that didn't matter now.

Liam angled his body toward mine. "Cora...the way I feel when I'm with you—I've never felt that with anyone else. Deserted island aside, I love growing with you, talking with you, laughing with you... Those things won't change if we're doing them in a sitting room under the light of a lamp, versus on a sandy beach by the light of a fire." His warm hands grasped mine tightly. "I love you. Not just the you on this island, but any and every version of you I'm lucky enough to know."

My cheeks grew warm at his words. I knew he was being truthful, but I wondered if that truth would still be valid once Kate came calling again.

He rearranged my hands in his. "When we return to civilization, some things will be different. We'll have our own obligations, we won't spend twenty-four hours a day together, and we'll have new obstacles to overcome. But I want to experience it all with you, and I want to see what that life may have to offer us…together." He took a deep breath again. "Nothing is flawless. There will be bits of our lives that won't fit together perfectly, but I'm eager to bend and adjust so that they will eventually."

I held his gaze for a few seconds, and then I closed my eyes, leaning in and resting my forehead against his. "There is one more thing…"

He pulled back and studied me closely. "What is it?"

I scratched my head and squinted at the ground. "How would you have reacted if I'd been pregnant?"

Liam tensed. "You're not, though…right?"

I shook my head quickly. "No, very much not pregnant."

He inhaled and shifted on his seat. "Well, I would have been terrified, honestly. I can't imagine trying to take care of a baby out here. Think of all the things that could go wrong."

"I know, and you're right." I nodded, realizing again how ridiculous my own emotions were.

"We would have figured it out, but I'm glad you're not," he said softly. "Now's not the time for that."

"But you do want kids someday?" I dropped my hand quickly from his. "I mean, not like…with me…I just mean… do you want kids someday *in general?*" I peered up at him, afraid I'd made him uncomfortable, but he was smiling at me.

"Someday, sure." He ran his fingers gently through my hair. "But what's important to me right now is *you.* I want you safe, and healthy, and happy. And I want to eventually take you home with me and show everyone what an amazing woman I've found."

I pursed my lips and looked at the ground.

"Sometimes I feel like you don't believe me," Liam whispered, taking my hand again. "I love you, Cora. I'm not letting you go. I want nothing more than for you to trust me."

"I'm trying," I whispered back. And I was. I believed that he truly did love me and that he wanted to continue to love me if we were ever rescued. I believed him when he said that he'd work to keep our relationship strong. I was ready to put in the work too, even though I didn't know exactly what that meant. All I needed now was the proof. His words were there, but actions would speak louder.

***

A few days later, I was away from our campsite, washing some of our clothes on the far side of the island. I went there often because the current wasn't as strong, and the water felt warmer. It was the part of the beach where we'd landed in our lifeboat, and I tended to reminisce about the moment I had woken up to see Liam's face looking back at me. I'd been so out of it, unsure of who he was, but as soon as the realization sank in, it had been like a dream to me; impossible and absurd. But I knew so well now that this was not a dream. This adventure was very real, and quite the opposite of absurd. It felt like the stars had aligned and brought us together because this is where we were meant to be.

When I'd been with Jacob, my feelings had been shallow. They were so dwarfed compared to the love I felt for Liam. Loving Liam was like seeing the sun for the first time after months of clouds. You had still seen some of the light before, but the warmth and the comfort that came unfiltered from the source and hit you straight in the face was unmatched by anything else.

I wanted to make sure that Liam was just as happy as I was. My heart was bursting with joy, and I wanted nothing more than to know that his always was too. It was my responsibility to keep being the person that he needed in his life: his greatest supporter and his greatest fan.

I laughed at the irony. I guess I'd had the greatest fan part down plenty prematurely.

I wrung out the last t-shirt. It was Liam's, and I smiled, feeling a bit like a housewife doing his laundry. Even though we'd been placed in this exotic and unforgiving landscape, there were so many parallels to life in the real world.

I placed the wet clothes into a woven basket and began to walk back across the island. It would be time for us to eat dinner soon, and I'd need to gather some seaweed. It was usually my contribution to the meal. I'd cook it like spinach with the bird or the fish that Liam provided. I hoped there would be an abundance tonight so that I wouldn't have to search for too long.

When I rounded the last boulder near our beach, Liam came into view. He was leaning over a waist-high rock just a few yards from the fire, adjusting something he'd placed there.

He turned around and stepped quickly in front of it when

he saw me. "Oh, you're back. Perfect." He grinned, looking mischievous.

I set the basket down slowly, suspiciously. "What's going on?"

He was holding something behind his back as he walked toward me, continuing to block the rock from my view. When he stopped in front of me, eyes sparkling, he took my hand in his.

I smirked as I studied his face, trying to figure out what he was up to.

He pulled his hand from behind his back and presented a large, pink, tropical flower to me.

"This is for you." His grin grew even more. "And I'd like to ask you on a date."

A surge of butterflies erupted in my stomach, which was silly, because we were so far past the stage of a first date, yet something about his innocent question made my heart flutter.

I beamed as I took the flower. "Thank you, and I'd love to."

"Perfect, I was hoping you'd say yes because I already have dinner ready." He turned and gestured to the rock, which was set up like a dinner table with the food and coconuts already arranged.

I laughed. "Wow, this is…you did it all?"

He placed his hand on my back and guided me toward the boulder. "I figured you deserved a night off from cooking, and I haven't taken you on a proper date yet."

There were two servings of cooked bird meat on beds of green seaweed, placed inside hollowed coconuts. On either side of the rock were large pieces of driftwood, placed as chairs. Liam led me to mine and held my hand as I sat down before taking his own seat.

"I hope you like island bird and mysterious seaweed. They didn't have much on the menu." He grinned.

I laughed and shook my head. "I love you."

"Wow, so soon, and on the first date," Liam teased.

I looked up at his crinkled, amused eyes. He was absolutely adorable.

"I love you too," he replied warmly.

"This was so thoughtful of you," I said, looking down at the meal and taking a small bite. "I had no idea."

"Well, that was kind of the point," Liam chuckled. "I knew you'd be away for a while this afternoon.

I set the flower down on the rock gently. "This is beautiful. Where did you find it?"

"The corner flower shop."

"Well, you are in quite the cheeky mood tonight," I laughed.

He shrugged. "I figured we needed a taste of home to keep us sane, and to catch a glimpse of what life might be like once we're there."

When I looked up, he was smiling genuinely at me. He was trying so hard to show me how much he cared and how much he'd be there for me if we were ever rescued. It was beyond sweet, and I felt my doubts slip away a little more.

"Thank you," I whispered.

He smiled and popped a bite of meat into his mouth.

We talked for a while as the flicker of the flames illuminated our dinner, and by the time we'd finished, I couldn't take my eyes off him. If we were ever rescued, I'd miss the way he looked in the light of a fire. It somehow softened and sharpened his features equally. I wanted to always see him the way I saw him now.

"That was wonderful," I thanked him, picking up my flower and holding it to my nose, inhaling its sweet fragrance.

He leaned forward on his elbows as his molasses eyes stared into mine. "I'm glad you enjoyed it."

I gazed yearningly at him, trying to burn his image into my memory.

"Would you like to take a walk?" he asked.

I set the flower down and stood up, stepping around to him. I held out my hand, and when he took it, I pulled him up to stand in front of me. "Maybe in a bit," I replied quietly, feeling more like showing him my gratitude instead.

He smiled and kissed my forehead. "That was undoubtedly the best first date I've ever been on."

My own eyes darkened. "I think it's about to get even better for you."

His expression was inquisitive, as if he didn't know what I meant, but I leaned in to kiss his neck and ran my hands down his chiseled chest. His blood ran hot under my lips as I trailed them toward the bits of hair that escaped above the neckline of his shirt.

He sucked in a breath as his hands found my hair, running his fingers through it, and I lifted my head to look at him and saw that his eyes were watching me with a fire that I knew I'd put there. I bit my lip and grinned before dropping to my knees and lifting his shirt, placing soft kisses on his navel, right at the edge of the waistband.

"I should take you on dates more often…" Liam breathed unevenly, closing his eyes.

I chuckled into his warm skin as I began to undo the button of his shorts. I couldn't have agreed more. I was almost as eager as he was.

TWENTY-EIGHT

I let out a long sigh as I finished etching the ninety-second mark into the hard stone of our cave wall.

Three months.

My eyes traveled to the first few ticks we'd made in our initial days. If we'd known how long we'd be here back then, would we have done anything differently? I'd been so sure that we'd be rescued quickly. It had been a waiting game in those early days, and we'd looked at our situation as though it were temporary. Now, we had no idea what the future held. After three months, for all we knew, we could be here for another three, or even longer. The crazy thing was, I think we were both ok with that possibility. We'd found routine and comfort in our lives here. There was still fear in the unknown, but the unknown was now an old friend to us. We lived with it every day, and we welcomed it as such.

Outside the shelter, Liam was tending to the fire. I stepped into the sun and began to walk past him toward our basket of coconuts, but he grabbed me by the waist before I made it there, pulling me into him. He held me firmly as he leaned in to kiss me passionately, and I smiled into his lips. I loved these spontaneous bursts of affection. They were a big part of his personality, and I adored him for it.

"You're irresistible, you know that?" he grunted against my mouth as he trailed his hands down the small of my back.

"Too bad you have to resist me." I teased, sliding my fingers along his neck, and grinding my hips against his.

His eyes darkened when they stared back into mine, and I could feel him against me, aroused by my words. I smirked and touched my nose to his. "I'm not sure I can resist you much longer…"

He let out a low groan and drew me even closer to him, closing his eyes and breathing deeply.

I shut mine too, tracing my hands up and down the familiar topography of his muscular arms. My mind flashed back to that night, now over a month ago, when we'd been together in our cave. As I imagined the sensation of him again, goosebumps rose on my skin. It was becoming harder and harder for us to stop before going that far once more. We were just one ounce of impulsivity away from giving in.

As much as I hated the idea of worrying about accidental pregnancy again, Liam did something to me that I couldn't resist. At what point did our fears become less important than the ultimate expression of our love? He had a greedy appetite, and needless to say, so did I. We took every chance we had to enjoy each other, and on a deserted island with nothing else to do, our chances were aplenty.

We tended to take turns being the stronger partner in our quest for caution. One of us always seemed to have a clearer mind when it came to restraint, but I was starting to anticipate the moment when our passion would mutually boil over once more.

I waited for him to open his eyes, and when he did, I grinned. "I need to go gather some more coconuts. Are you fishing or hunting today?"

He blinked seductively at me. "Whichever gets me back to you faster."

I smirked and kissed him quickly before turning and picking up his leather bag and heading toward the woods. "Don't let your mind wander and delay you too long," I called back over my shoulder. He wiggled his brows at me when I caught his eye.

***

Later that evening as the sun was hanging low on the horizon, Liam and I sat on a large piece of driftwood near the edge of the shore. He held my hand in his lap and was running his thumb across my fingers absentmindedly. I'd put on my yellow dress—the one he loved so much.

"I'll miss these sunsets if we leave here someday," Liam said quietly, observing the waves, sparkling with pinks and purples.

I watched his profile as he spoke, admiring the rugged beard that replaced the stubble I'd once loved. Turns out, the beard was growing on me.

"I'll miss a lot about this place," I replied, casting my gaze back out to the sea.

Liam scratched his cheek. "Sometimes, I feel like I'd rather just stay. Is that crazy?"

I shook my head slowly. I knew the feeling too well. "No…"

"I'm not sure how well I'll handle the fast pace of my life again."

I leaned into him. "You know, you don't have to jump back to full speed if you don't want to. You can slow down."

"Oh, yeah, I know. I don't intend to take on as many projects as I had before. But I know there will be pressure, and I'm sure I'll get used to it again."

"It's all about balance," I replied. "Don't give up doing what you love, but don't burn yourself out either."

Liam smiled and wrapped his arm around me. "Cora: my personal voice of reason."

I grinned and kissed his cheek. "Someone's gotta do it."

He rubbed my shoulder and nodded.

"Could you show me another dance?" I asked, wanting to feel him pressed against me again.

He smiled. "Another dance? Hmmm…sure. Let's see, how about my favorite?"

"What is your favorite?"

The corners of his mouth pulled up. "The Tango."

I laughed nervously, picturing the vibrant dance in my head. "I don't know if I have enough rhythm for that one."

"Ah, no I think you do," he assured me, standing and pulling me to my feet. "It's not so hard."

I reluctantly followed him and placed my hand on his shoulder, dragging my eyes up to his eager ones. He loved to take the lead and share his skills. Lucky for him, I'd gladly learn anything he wanted to teach me.

He took his time as he showed me the dance. But I could barely concentrate on what he said because I was too busy watching the way his lips moved as he spoke. I loved to listen to him, especially when he shared something he was so passionate about. His deep voice, laced with that endearing British accent, was so soothing. His voice was like home to me now, and home was where I always wanted to be.

He pulled me around the beach, teaching me the slow steps and the quick steps, and piecing them together in a way I could understand. My skills were sub-par, but he didn't care, and neither did I. We laughed, but not because I was so bad at it. We laughed because we were together, and nothing else mattered.

I caught a glimpse of my yellow skirt a few times, billowing out around me as he guided us effortlessly across the sand. It felt like a real dance even without the music when I wore a dress that fit the part.

As I began to pick up the routine, Liam started to relax into me. His muscled arms, which were once tense, began to ease as he closed the distance between us. His cheek found mine and the soft curls of his beard brushed against my jaw as we swayed to an imaginary melody. The intentional steps of the Tango faded into a slow and loving embrace.

"I miss music…" I said quietly, resting my chin on his shoulder.

"I do too…" Liam agreed. "You don't realize how much you could miss something until it's gone." He sighed and moved his hand to the small of my back. "Music…oh, and movies…I miss getting to just sit and enjoy a good film."

"Do you actually watch movies for enjoyment or just to study the acting techniques?" I smirked into his cheek.

Liam chuckled. "No, I can enjoy a good movie for what it is." He rubbed his hand gently up and down my back. "Hey, I don't think I've ever asked you what your favorite is."

I dropped my forehead to his shoulder and grinned, knowing my answer would make him roll his eyes. "It's a silly one."

"Try me. I bet I've seen it."

"Oh, I'm *sure* you have," I laughed.

"Well, then how could it be silly?"

"It's Dirty Dancing." I sighed, knowing that I must sound like a sixteen-year-old girl.

"Ahh, Swayze was brilliant in that one," Liam replied with a chuckle.

"Yeah, it's a bit of a guilty pleasure...but that epic ending though..." I mused, picturing Johnny and Baby swaying to the music, much like Liam and I were now.

Liam leaned his head back as his eyes met mine with a twinkle of recognition. "The lift?"

I blushed, remembering how she ran into his arms as he lifted her into the air. After all they'd been through, it was such a magical culmination of their love. "Yeah, I think every woman in the world was jealous of Jennifer Grey in that moment."

He grinned and opened his mouth like he was going to speak, but then closed it quickly.

I tilted my head, wondering what he was holding back.

He pulled his lips to the side, assessing me curiously. "Do you want to try it?"

I blinked widely. "What?"

His eyes crinkled as his smile grew. "Do you want to *try* it?"

My mouth hung open. "What? No. You can't lift me like that."

Liam rolled his eyes. "Pfft, sure I can. You're a small little thing."

I continued to gape at him. There was no way he was serious.

"Come on." He stepped back and grabbed my hand. "We'll try it first in the water, just like they did in the film."

I tugged back on his grasp. "Liam…I don't think I can."

He gripped my hand tighter and looked me square in the eye. "Cora, have you, or have you *not* dreamed of trying that lift someday?"

I knew I couldn't lie to him. Not about this. So, I responded in a small voice, "Yeah, I have."

"Well then, this is your chance. We'll be in the water. It won't matter if you fall." He tugged my hand again.

I held my ground for a moment, and he let me, standing patiently in place as I pondered his offer. I wanted to crawl back into my nervous, protective shell, but I took a breath and stepped slowly toward him.

"Oh, *alright,*" I sighed, trying to hide the fact that despite being uneasy, deep down I was actually giddy.

"Well, you don't have to sound so distraught about it…" he teased as he led me toward the shallow lagoon.

He waded into the water, pulling off his shirt and exposing his wide shoulders and muscular back. I was never *not* impressed by his physique. Maybe he *could* lift me…

I tugged off my dress and threw it to the side before following in my swimsuit.

"Have you ever done this before?" I asked when I stopped in front of him, waist-deep in the water.

"Nope." He grinned.

"That's comforting," I laughed tensely. "So, do you have any idea what you're doing?"

"I've done other lifts, I understand the basics behind it, and I've seen the film of course."

I eyed him cautiously, resting my hands on my hips. "Are you sure about this?"

Liam chuckled. "Yes, do you trust me?"

I gulped, still not certain. But he didn't wait for my response, stepping forward instead and touching his palms to my hips. "Ok, so I'm going to support you right here. The most difficult part for you will be keeping your balance once you're up there."

I nodded anxiously. *Once I'm up there.* I felt like this was going to be a major fail.

"Ok…" He looked at me directly. "On the count of three, you'll jump, alright?"

I laughed, shaking my head. "I can't believe we're really doing this…"

"We're really doing this." Liam smiled warmly, but he braced himself and positioned his palms on my hips. "Ready?"

I wrung my hands together. "No…wait…" I took a deep, shaking breath. "So, like, how high do I jump?"

He laughed and dropped his hands with a sigh. "As high as you can. I'll take care of the rest."

"But what if I don't jump high enough and I just crash into you? Will I hurt you?"

He shook his head. "No, we'll just go falling into this horribly choppy, dangerously vile lagoon."

I slid my gaze to the calm, glass-smooth surface of the water around us. *Well, ok, so maybe this won't be so bad.*

When I looked at him again, his eyebrows were raised, but there was patience in his expression too.

"Ok, alright." I took a deep breath and bounced on my toes a few times. His eyes told me to trust him, and I knew I owed him that after everything we'd been through.

"Ready?" he asked again.

I nodded and prepared myself in a small squat while he placed his hands on my hips.

"One…two…three."

I pushed off from the sandy floor of the lagoon, propelling myself up and toward him. His hands grasped me tightly as he lifted me into the air, sending a splash of water out around us.

I felt his arms shake slightly under my hips as he hoisted me upward, and my abs tensed, trying to keep my arms and legs extended. I caught a brief glimpse of my surroundings, realizing I'd made it above the water and above Liam. He'd actually done it. He'd lifted me completely over his head.

But just as fast as I realized we'd succeeded, I lost my balance and faltered, diving sloppily into the water behind him. I went completely under, and he fell with me, but he quickly grabbed my hand and pulled me back to the surface.

"You had it for a second there." He was breathing a bit harder, but grinning widely. "Try it again?"

I wiped the wet hair from my eyes and laughed. "Yeah, wow, you really did it."

"I told ya I could, didn't I?" He smirked.

I waded in front of him, ready to try again as we both caught our breath. Liam counted, and then I jumped, and he hoisted me out of the water just like he'd done before. The muscles in my torso burned as I held myself as steady as possible. This time, we lasted a few seconds longer, and the only reason I lost my balance was because I started to laugh out of pure shock that we'd actually done it.

We crashed down into the water again, and Liam pulled me into his arms, laughing too. He kissed me affectionately as his wet hair dripped down his face. "I think you're a natural."

I rolled my eyes.

"Want to try it up on the beach?" he asked.

I licked my lips and looked toward the sand. "Uhhh…"

"You've proven that you can hold yourself up there…that is, if you don't start giggling." He pressed his thumb into my hip where he knew I was ticklish, and I squirmed in his grip.

I focused back on the beach. "I don't want to hurt you."

"I'll be fine." Liam waved me off. "Let's try it?" He started to tug me in the direction of the shore but paused to wait for me to come on my own.

I took a deep breath and studied him closely. For so long, he'd been asking me to trust him, and I'd been holding back over and over again. If I wanted to believe him, I had to give his actions a chance to speak louder than his words.

"Ok, let's give it a try."

We stepped up onto the beach and I wrung out my hair as Liam took my waist and positioned me to face him. His warm hands on my cool, bare skin sent my heart rate skyrocketing as I looked up into his enthusiastic eyes. He probably didn't care one bit about Dirty Dancing, but he was making this fantasy come true for me. It was incredibly sweet, and it was certainly a dream of mine, but he had to know that he'd made a thousand of my greater fantasies come true already, just by being here with me.

"Ok, stand right here," he said, watching me carefully. He placed one hand on my shoulder. "I promise, I won't drop you."

"That's a big promise," I gulped, brushing my foot through the sand to assess its softness.

"Yes, and I keep my promises."

I blinked nervously, feeling a strong inclination to doubt him again, but I nodded.

He backed up about twenty paces and staggered one foot in front of the other, prepared to catch me.

"Ok, ready?"

"No," I gulped, shaking my hands anxiously at my sides.

"Do you want me to sing the song?"

"NO, no, no." I laughed, bouncing my weight from one foot to the other.

Liam smirked, still in position. "Because I'll sing the song—"

"NO. I'm going." I wiped my hand down my face and breathed deeply. It was one thing to jump into his arms in the water, but to run toward him and throw myself into the air above the sandy ground was an entirely different beast.

He stood with his hands extended in front of him while his eyes held mine steadily. They were reassuring and confident, and he nodded his head in encouragement. He'd told me that I could trust him, and I had to make the conscious decision to do just that.

I bit my lip and took one last breath before thrusting myself into the moment, digging my toes into the sand, and beginning to run toward him. In the few seconds before I reached him, I thought I might chicken out, but I gained a surge of confidence and jumped just in time as his hands met my hips and he lifted me easily into the air.

I outstretched my arms and legs, briefly feeling free like a bird, high above him with the calm island around me and the soft breeze in my hair. I could almost hear the magical song that had played in the film, even though Liam never had a chance to sing it.

His hands were steady on my hips as he held me. My heart swelled as I realized that trusting him had paid off. Trusting him was easy once I finally let myself do it. But, succumbing to my giddy tendencies, I started to laugh again, and my balance wavered. Liam sensed my fault and quickly lowered me down to him as I fell. His arms wrapped around my back as we went tumbling gently to the ground, both bursting with laughter.

His low chuckle resounded below me as I grinned, pushing myself up onto my elbows and looking down into his entertained eyes.

"You did it." He grinned, running his hands gently up and down the curves of my waist.

"I think you did most of the work there," I laughed. His almost bare body was firm and warm beneath me, and I swallowed, feeling myself succumb to that nagging hunger that I'd been trying to suppress.

"Thank you for trusting me." His gaze searched deeply into mine.

I smiled and closed my eyes, lowering my head to touch my nose to his. I wanted to trust him with everything—not just this. He was starting to convince me that maybe I finally could.

He reached up to tuck a strand of hair behind my ear. "So, is your fantasy fulfilled? Did you have *the time of your life?*"

I smirked at him. "Yes…" I paused. "But the lift wasn't my fantasy…*you* were."

His fingers lingered in my hair as his eyes met mine, resting there for a moment. They darkened as he recognized the intention in my words. A low sound reverberated from deep in his throat as his hand found the back of my neck and he pulled me down into him, kissing me fervently. I collapsed onto him, letting my full weight rest on his hips. And then he was hooking his palms around my upper thighs urgently, pressing me into him, tracing between them, and causing my breath to catch against his lips.

"I don't think I can resist you anymore," he grunted.

I was already reaching for the button on his shorts. "I don't want you to resist," I whispered against his mouth, tracing my tongue over his lower lip.

"Shit, Cora…" He pressed his head back into the sand, putting a short distance between us. He looked up at me with hesitation. "Are you sure?"

He was holding me tightly, but I managed to grind my hips against his, bursting with an unrestrained hunger and a need to feel all of him again, connected with all of me.

"I need you…" I sighed into his jaw, brushing my lips across his beard.

He was still for a moment, so I lifted my head to gauge his reaction. When he met my gaze, his eyes were just as burning and deprived as mine probably were. They lingered for a long moment before he closed them and sucked in a deep breath.

With a groan, he released me, and his fingers feverishly found the ties of my swimsuit top and then the edge of my bottoms, stripping them both off quickly. He wrapped his arms around me and turned me onto my back as he rolled on top, sliding his shorts off as he went.

I ran my hands down his chest and then back up to his arms, memorizing every angle of his form. He dropped his head to my breasts, dragging the tip of his nose across the dip between them and then settling his lips over my nipple and sucking it into his warm mouth. I parted my legs, hooking my heels around his calves and trying to pull him closer.

He chuckled into my chest and peered up at me with sparkling eyes. "Eager, are we?"

I gave him an incredulous sigh as I gripped his shoulders tightly. "You're about to make me lose my mind."

He smirked, kissing his way back up my neck, across my jaw, and to my mouth, darting his tongue between my lips. He positioned himself against me and paused.

"Liam…" I pleaded, breathlessly. I couldn't wait any longer.

He rested his forehead against mine as he finally pushed into me in one fluid movement. I couldn't hold back the sigh that fell from my lips.

This. This was what I needed.

He showed less hesitation than our first time as he met my hips firmly with his. He interlaced his fingers tightly with mine as he drove into me, and when I opened my eyes, his gaze was unwavering. The connection between us was so much more than just physical. And after a moment, he squeezed his eyes shut and settled his face into my neck.

He was like a wave, crashing into me, over and over again, like standing in the ocean, feeling the power of the sea against my flesh. This was like that, but it was also something else entirely. Because of everything we'd been through together, it was so much more.

Liam's breathing grew erratic as he lost himself completely. My fingers dug into his back, holding him to me, kissing his shoulder, and sighing his name.

When the waves met their final surge, I crashed over the edge, arching my back off the sand and crying out into the twilight. He let out a low and unrestrained growl as he pulled out and finished himself, panting and trembling above me.

He collapsed into the sand, and I stared up at the stars that had appeared in the softly lit sky, letting the warmth of afterglow ripple through me. I rolled into him and ran my fingers through his hair, clearing it from his damp forehead. His eyes were closed as he sucked in deep breaths through parted lips. I smiled and kissed his cheek.

He opened his eyes to mine as I perched myself on my elbow next to him. He didn't speak, but a warm smile formed on his face as he wrapped his arms around me and pulled me into him.

I stared at the same spot on his chest for a long time, trying not to feel guilty for taking a risk again. It was funny how quickly common sense came back after the heat of the moment wore off.

"I love you," Liam whispered, kissing my forehead.

I touched a bit of hair near his collarbone. It took me a moment to respond. "Thank you…"

"For loving you?"

I peered up at him and mirrored his grin. "For being patient with me. I know I haven't given you the trust that you deserve. But I'm getting there."

His gaze softened and he ran his thumb across my lower lip. "I never expected you to trust me implicitly from the start. I know I have to earn that. And I don't mind being patient. We have all the time in the world."

I let my eyes drift shut as I kissed his spent lips gently, and then I lowered my head to his shoulder again. Love wasn't always built in the big, monumental moments like this one, it came on gradually in the small joys and sorrows peppered throughout our days. Yet, in the connections like this, when we could give flight to the desires and the cravings of our hearts, I felt it more profoundly than ever before. Liam was my north star, guiding me home, straight to his heart.

As we laid in each other's arms on our deserted island, I knew I'd finally made it home. Home wasn't a place. It was a person.

TWENTY-NINE

A calm breeze blew across the soft waves that billowed up along the shore. The peaceful sound of the ocean was all that filled my ears as I stared sleepily at Liam's hand in mine. As we laid quietly on the beach next to our fire, he raised them both above us and traced his outstretched fingers across my own as the light of the rising sun flickered in the spots between them.

It had been just over two weeks since he'd lifted me into the air like Johnny had done with Baby after they'd danced their final dance. I'd felt completely free as I soared high above him—free to love him, free to trust him, free to be content.

And as soon as he'd brought me back down to Earth, I'd allowed myself to be free to show him those things. Maybe we should have held back. Maybe that would have been the smart choice. But the longer we were here alone on this island with no idea when or if we'd be rescued, the more painful it was becoming to deny ourselves to each other.

Since that night, we'd pulled in the reigns again, finding our restraint once more. I'd woken each morning during these last few weeks, concerned to feel a wave of nausea or some other terrifying symptom, but none of them came. I felt perfectly normal, and even though I was still waiting for my period, I was more confident this time that it would come soon.

We frequently came out to the beach in the mornings to watch the ever-unique colors of the sunrise. Usually, we sat and watched by the edge of the water, but this morning we were so tired that we laid down on the softer sand upshore.

It was moments like this one that I wished would never end. We had food and water, we had our health, and most importantly, we had each other. I loved Liam for all that he was; for his playful, cheeky spontaneity, for his motivated and protective nature, for his compassion, and for his unyielding affection and care for me. I hardly thought I'd done enough to afford such a wonderful man in my life.

I let out a small sigh of happiness.

"What's on your mind, love?" Liam whispered softly, touching his lips to my hair.

I grinned and tilted my head to look into his eyes. "You."

The corners of his mouth turned up. "What about me has got you sighing like that?"

"I'm just happy to be here with you in this moment. I never want it to end," I replied quietly, admiring his joy-filled expression.

He wrapped his arms around me and hugged me close. "Well, we've got plenty of coconuts from yesterday, and the lifeboat is full of water. We have all day to lay just like this."

I kissed the edge of his beard, yawned, and buried my head in his warm neck. "I'm so exhausted, I *could* stay like this all day."

His fingers traced up and down my spine gently. "It's like time passes more slowly here, but not in a bad way. I love how slow it feels."

I peered at him, understanding his feelings completely because they perfectly mirrored mine. "I wonder where I'd be if our plane had never gone down…"

Liam's eyes crinkled. "You'd probably be re-watching *Until Dawn.*" He smirked as the words left his mouth. He was proud of his little joke.

I grinned and rolled my eyes, kissing his shoulder gently. "You're probably right."

"I can tell you this about *me,*" he began. "I'd be a lot less happy than I am now. I was heading for exhaustion, completely wearing myself thin. This life is much better suited for me, I'm finding."

I studied his weary face. "When I think about where I'd be…if I weren't here, it scares me."

His finger traced my cheek as he watched me.

"I don't want to think about it. I don't want to imagine not having you in my life." I frowned. "I love you…" I leaned in and kissed his lips. "And I love us…" I laced my fingers through his. "And I love this place." I looked around at the peaceful beach that surrounded us.

He watched me absorbedly, eyes glistening in the morning light. "I love you very much, Cora."

I laid my head on his chest and closed my eyes. I could hear his heart beating under my ear, and I relaxed into its rhythm and the comfort that it represented in my life. The fact that I felt so at peace in such an unpredictable place said everything about our relationship and how close we'd grown. He was mine, and I was his, and nothing here on this tiny island was going to change that.

I felt Liam turn his head to look out at the ocean, and I opened my eyes to admire it as well. The sky was a deep purple, but a small, rich-orange sliver of sun was beginning to crest. Liam's chest rose and fell evenly under my head as we took in the view together.

I scanned the line where the sea met the sky and watched the brilliant colors contrast where they touched. But as I began to close my eyes again, I caught sight of something on the horizon that wasn't usually there. Liam's chest suddenly stopped moving and I knew he'd seen it too.

In the far distance, barely lit by the rising sun, a small white sailboat moved smoothly across the calm waters.

Neither of us made a sound for what felt like an eternity. I watched the tiny boat leave a wake in its path as it made for its destination to the west. I hardly understood what I was seeing, and I was almost afraid to.

"Oh my God," Liam finally whispered, grabbing my arms and pulling me up with him to sit. Neither of us took our eyes off the boat. We were perfectly still, gaping in shock.

"The fire…" I whispered breathlessly.

All at once, Liam jumped to his feet and spun in a circle, shooting glances around our campsite. His face held a panic as he pointed toward a stack of old dried-out palm fronds. "Quick, help me light these. I think it's still dark enough that we can signal to them."

My heart was beating out of my chest and adrenaline coursed through my veins as I watched him spring to action. And for just a split second, and almost too quick for me to even register the emotion, I wondered what would happen if we just ignored the boat and laid back down in the sand together. Would I be happier that way? But the fleeting thought was gone before I knew it, and I scrambled to my feet and picked up a large bunch of branches, holding the ends to the fire. They caught quickly, as did the bunch that Liam grasped, and we both ran out to the water's edge and waved them wildly in the air.

"They've got to see us," Liam breathed heavily, squinting out at the boat.

In the dim light of the early morning, the flames that we raised into the air shined brightly, and I realized that he might be right.

"Come on…come on…" Liam growled.

I watched breathlessly, holding my branch in the air. My chest was tight with indecision, and I glanced up at him, wondering if he felt it as well. But his eyes were trained solely on the boat, so I put my focus there too.

Soon, the tiny sail caught the wind as it slid across the water, and then it began to turn. Someone was adjusting the ropes, and the boat began to bank toward us.

My heart stopped.

"They've seen us…" Liam whispered.

I sucked in a shallow breath as I held the leaves steady over my head and forced the lump down my throat.

"They've seen us, Cora…."

I looked up at him. He was still watching the boat at first, but then his eyes met mine. And in that moment, we exchanged an unspoken realization that *this was it.* This was the turning point. From this moment on, everything would change. Everything we knew about our life together and our relationship with each other was now subject to a new set of challenges and a new reality.

I swallowed nervously as Liam took a step toward me. He extended his hand and interlocked his fingers with mine. It was a small act on his part, but it was his way of telling me that we were still in this together, no matter what happened next.

I looked back out at the water to see the boat still approaching, growing closer and closer. I could just barely make out two figures standing on its deck now. Liam and I waited, hand in hand, silently watching it advance.

My throat was starting to constrict. The air was hot and thick, threatening to close in around me. *This was it.* Our journey here was complete. So many times, it had seemed as though we'd be here forever. I'd begun to lose hope of a rescue. And I was content with that. But now, I was forced to shift my mind to a new reality—one where Liam and I went home.

To my family. To my friends. Back to everyone I loved.

As the boat drew nearer, I recognized that it was much larger than it had seemed on the horizon. It looked to have full living quarters below deck and a large seating area above. Two men stood at the bow with their hands on the railing, staring at us intently.

Liam continued to wave his branch until one of the men lowered a smaller boat from the side and climbed down into it. He started the motor and made his way through the choppy waves toward shore.

We tossed our branches into the water and the fires sizzled

out, sending smoke and steam spiraling into the air. Liam wrapped his arm firmly around my waist as the man approached, and my fingers found the back of his shirt, gripping it tightly as if I were anchored to it.

It was only then that I realized we had no idea who this man was. Who's to say he wasn't here to hurt us instead of help us? But looking closely, he appeared clean-cut in a white t-shirt and slacks with shiny sunglasses and well-combed, greying hair.

When he was within earshot, he called out to us. "You look like you might need some help?" His voice was filled with a thick Australian accent.

I hadn't heard a voice other than Liam's in months, and the lump returned to my throat as I understood that this was all very real.

Liam held me tightly to him, and his voice was deep and loud as he called back to the man. "Yes. We're survivors of a plane crash. We've been stranded here for three and a half months."

The man squinted at us as if he didn't comprehend what Liam had said. Behind him on the sailboat, the other man was still at the railing watching us closely.

As the first man powered his boat up to the shore, Liam spoke up again. "We were on a flight from L.A. to Auckland. The engines failed. It went down and we drifted here."

The man slowly stood up as realization crossed his face. "Flight NZ19?"

Liam blinked and looked at me to see if I had a response, but I shrugged my shoulders. I couldn't remember what our flight number had been.

The man stepped onto the shore, studying us closely, probably eyeing the sad state of clothing we were wearing and the deep tans that graced our skin from so much sun exposure.

"Flight NZ19 that went down back in October?" he repeated as his eyes started to widen.

Liam answered, and I was glad he did because my throat was so dry that I couldn't manage it. "Yes, October. We were the only survivors as far as we could tell."

The man brought his hand to his mouth. "My God…" He looked around the island, studying our shelter and the fire in the distance. "You've been here all alone this whole time?"

Liam nodded.

The man continued to stare at us in awe, clearly amazed that we'd made it this long, and then he shook his head. "Well, it was a good thing you had the fire to flag me down. Barely anyone comes near this island anymore. There's not much here…"

Liam and I knew that all too well.

"Where is 'here,' exactly?" Liam asked.

"French Polynesia, Tuamotu Archipelago. You're on Rekareka atoll. You're about 100 kilometers from the nearest inhabited island."

I gasped internally. We really *were* in the middle of nowhere.

"We're headed toward Makemo." He gestured to the man back on the sailboat. "My brother and I. We'd be glad to take you there. Trip's about fifteen hours with a strong wind. They have an airstrip. Should be able to get you on a puddle-jumper flight over to Tahiti." His eyes traveled from Liam's face to mine. "We have lots of food and water back on board. I'm sure you could use it."

Liam extended his hand to the man. "Thank you, sir."

The man took it in a strong handshake. "Absolutely. I'm glad we came out this way. Might have been another few months had we not." He continued to grip Liam's hand. "Name's Harrison Lee."

"Liam Montgomery," Liam responded confidently.

Harrison turned and extended his hand to me. I smiled anxiously as I took it. "Cora Parker."

"Pleased to meet you both," Harrison replied, and then he turned his focus back to Liam and furrowed his brow. "I remember hearing about an actor that had been on board. You look familiar. Wasn't that you?"

Liam nodded.

Harrison blinked rapidly and shook his head. "Wow, this is going to be huge. The whole world's been pretty torn up about this. Your plane just disappeared into thin air. They still haven't found it. They figured there were no survivors." He gestured to the boat. "Come on, let's get you two home."

I looked out into the vast waters and grasped Liam's shirt even tighter.

Home. What did that even mean anymore?

Liam sensed my tension and turned toward Harrison. "Would you mind…giving us a few minutes…to collect our belongings?"

Harrison nodded and took a step back. "Of course, take your time."

Liam slid his hand into mine and turned us toward our shelter, looking over his shoulder at Harrison. "We'll just be a moment. Thank you."

Harrison shoved his hands into his pockets and nodded as he waited next to his boat.

My body was numb as I walked with Liam toward our

campsite. His hand was warm, and it gripped mine encouragingly, but I gazed blankly at our surroundings as the memories flooded back; the basket of coconuts we'd eaten from every morning, the large rock where Liam had taken me on our first "date," the spears we'd used to catch so many of our meals, the cave where we'd made love…

He was silent as he dropped my hand and leaned down to pull the lifeboat full of water toward the fire. He lifted the edge and flipped it over, sending its contents onto the flames and extinguishing them completely.

The wet wood smoked and steamed immensely as we both stood silently in our spots, staring at it for a few long seconds. It felt so odd to be dumping our water supply and dousing our vital cooking source. But suddenly, we didn't need them anymore. There was a boat full of fresh drinking water and food just a hundred yards away, and we'd been welcomed upon it.

Liam tore his eyes away and stepped into our shelter. I followed him quietly, my legs carrying me forward blindly. He bent down and began picking up his clothes and his belongings and placing them into his duffle bag. I didn't move. I just stood and watched him pack.

When he sensed my stillness, he glanced up at me. I stared down at him with a remorse I couldn't hide from my face. His expression softened and he rose, taking my hands in his and looking carefully into my eyes.

He didn't speak. We understood together the enormity of the situation we were now presented with. He simply pulled me into his chest and wrapped his arms tightly around me.

I squeezed my eyes shut and buried my face in this shirt, breathing in the familiar, comforting scent of him. Would he still smell this way when we got home? Would he still be my Liam?

He leaned back and placed his hands on my shoulders, a warm smile touching his lips. "We did it, Cora. We're going home now, to see our families and our friends. We're not in danger anymore. We were strong, and we made it through this. We're going home *together.*" He put an emphasis on the last word.

I thought about my parents and Tess, and how they would all feel when they found out I was alive. I missed them all so much. I imagined the joy on their faces and their warm arms enveloping me when we'd finally be reunited. That would be a truly beautiful thing to know they didn't have to grieve anymore. I looked up into Liam's eyes and returned a tiny smile, feeling a small surge of joy at the realization.

He slid his hands back down to mine and grasped them tightly. And then he let go and turned around to continue with his bag. I knelt down next to mine, placing my clothes and remaining toiletries inside in a methodical manner. It was strange, packing items to bring home that really didn't matter. We were going back to a place where we'd have an unlimited supply of all these things. They wouldn't hold the same value there as they did here.

But I looked to my left and saw the wooden heart that Liam had carved for me so many weeks ago. I picked it up and ran my fingers over its smooth edges. This small piece of our island held more meaning than anything else I would take with me. I wrapped it in my yellow dress and placed it carefully in my bag before zipping it and standing up.

Liam slung his own bag over his shoulder and took my suitcase in his hand. "Ready?"

I inhaled a deep breath and nodded. "Let's go home."

He leaned in and placed a soft kiss on my lips, and then pushed the door open. As we strode out onto the beach, I reviewed our campsite one last time, burning the image into my memory. I didn't want to forget even one single detail. I'd truly *lived* here. We'd built a *love* here.

Liam squeezed my hand gently, and I squeezed his back in return. When I met his tender gaze, I saw my home. I had him by my side, and that was the saving grace that would allow me to leave our perfect island behind.

And with one final deep breath, we stepped forward into the unknown, toward our rescuer and his boat, ready to face our next adventure, *together.*

The story will continue...

FOUND *with* YOU

Part two of the *Lost and Found* series

COMING IN 2022

www.annalenore.com

ACKNOWLEDGEMENTS

Three years ago, I discovered a dream hidden within me to write a novel. It was something I hadn't particularly considered before, but once I recognized the ambition, it gripped me like a vice. I had no idea how difficult it would be, but I also wasn't prepared for how incredibly rewarding it would be. Over the last few years, I've been on an amazing journey, realizing how much joy I find in writing love stories and developing my own author voice, thanks to an amazing support system.

First, I'd like to thank my group of original readers who have been with this story since the very beginning. There are way too many of you to name, but you know who you are. You were around for the story's inception, giving me the drive and the motivation to chase my dream and eventually make this published novel a reality. You will all always have a special place in my heart.

I'd also like to thank my best friend, Emily. You've known me since we were thirteen, and when I told you that I wanted to write a romance novel, you jumped on board and cheered me on immediately. Thank you for being a fantastic beta reader and helping me see the story from a new set of eyes. Your confidence in me means the world.

And last, but certainly not least, I want to thank my husband. When I told you I wanted to write romance, I wasn't sure how you'd respond, but you've absolutely blown me away with your support and encouragement. Thank you for letting me bounce ideas off you at all hours of the day (and night), and for believing in me, even when I didn't believe in myself. Ours is my favorite love story.

ABOUT THE AUTHOR

Anna has always adored sappy, happy endings, easily finding her home in the romance genre. She thrives on diving deep into the hearts of her characters, taking them on journeys of self-growth as their lives intertwine together.

She lives on the East Coast with her handsome husband, who has been her biggest supporter since the very beginning, and her spirited cat, who helps with the writing process and frequently vocalizes her critiques.

Lost with You is Anna's debut novel.

Find Anna on Instagram and Facebook:
@AnnaLenoreAuthor

Subscribe to the newsletter for updates,
new releases, and cover reveals:
www.annalenore.com

Manufactured by Amazon.ca
Bolton, ON

21044541R00217